SAINT CITY SINNERS

Japhrimel was taken, I was on my own. Things did not look good.

That was how they found me, crouched in the alley and sobbing. But my hand was still closed around the hilt of my sword, and I felt them coming bare seconds before they arrived—enough time for me to make it halfway up the fire escape. Plasbolts raked past me, splashing against standard-magshielded walls. Plasglass shattered.

Even the toughest bounty hunter around will run when faced with four police cruisers and a cadre of what appeared to be augmented Mob shocktroops. And all for one tired almost-demon.

By Lilith Saintcrow

Working for the Devil
Dead Man Rising
The Devil's Right Hand
Saint City Sinners

LILITH SAINTCROW

SAINT CITY SINNERS

orbit

www.orbitbooks.net

ORBIT

First published in Great Britain in 2008 by Orbit

A CIP catalogue record for this book
is available from the British Library.

ISBN 978-1-84149-670-2

Papers used by Orbit are natural, recyclable products made from
wood grown in sustainable forests and certified in accordance with
the rules of the Forest Stewardship Council.

Typeset in Garamond by Palimpsest Book Production Limited,
Grangemouth, Stirlingshire
Printed and bound in Great Britain by
Mackays of Chatham plc, Chatham, Kent
Paper supplied by Hellefoss AS, Norway

Orbit
An imprint of
Little, Brown Book Group
100 Victoria Embankment
London EC4Y 0DY

An Hachette Livre Group UK Company

www.orbitbooks.net

For Maddalena Marie.
Never forget who loves you, baby.

A woman always has her revenge ready.
—Molière

In revenge and in love woman is more barbarous than man.
—Nietzsche

The rate of success for female bounty hunters, once one takes into account the statistical weighting of the X chromosome carrying psionic markers more often than the Y, is still two and a half times that of their male compatriots. More male psions go into bounty hunting, but female psions are better at it, bringing in their bounties quicker and with less destruction of lives and property.

This is balanced by the fact that male psions are embarrassingly better than their female counterparts at assassination. There are very few female psions operating in the assassination trade. Morley's quip that perhaps they are better at keeping their identities from authorities need not be mentioned more than once.

However, when comparing female assassins to male, one fact stands out with crystal clarity: the psionic females who do deal in assassination are by far the most thorough, tending to engage far less in messy "personal" kills (Datridenton, On Criminal Justice, pp. 1184–1206) in favor of getting the job done efficiently with whatever tool is best. This very thoroughness necessarily means they are higher-priced and far less likely to be indicted.

What conclusion can we draw from this? Morley, tongue-in-cheek as usual, concludes, "It may be well for men, especially men married to psions, to speak softly to their wives and girlfriends." This researcher would submit differently: that we are indeed lucky, given how good psionic women tend to be at coldly planned bloodshed, that most appear uninterested in it . . .

—from Ethics and Gender
Differences in the Psionic World,
by Caitlin Sommers, Amadeus
Hegemony Academy of Psionic
Arts

Overture

Japhrimel stood in the middle of the wrack and ruin of the Haunt Tais-toi, his long wet-dark coat lying on his shoulders like night itself. Lucifer faced him, the Prince of Hell's lovely face twisted with fury, suffused with a darkness more than physical. Japhrimel's hand closed around Lucifer's right wrist, muscle standing out under Lucifer's shirt and Japhrimel's coat as the Devil surged forward—and Japhrimel pushed him back.

If I hadn't seen it, I would never have believed it possible. But Japh's entire body tensed, and he forced Lucifer back on his heels.

The Devil stepped mincingly away, twisting his wrist free. Retreated, only two steps. But it was enough.

Lucifer's aura flamed with blackness, a warping in the fabric of the world. They looked at each other, twin green gazes locked as if the words they exchanged were only window dressing for the real combat, fought by the glowing spears of their eyes. The two hellhounds wove around them, low fluid shapes. Lucifer's indigo silk shirt was torn, gaping, across his midriff, showing a slice of golden skin—and as I watched, a single drop of black blood dripped from one torn edge. More spots of dark blood smoked on the silken pants he wore.

I'd cut the Devil.

One dazed thought sparked inside my aching head. Jado must've given me a hell of a good blade.

Then another thought, ridiculous in its intensity. Here. He's here. Everything will be all right now.

Childish faith, maybe, but I'd take it. If it was a choice between my Fallen and getting killed right this moment, I'd settle for Japh, no matter how much of a bastard he'd been recently. Funny how almost getting killed radically changed my notions of just how much I could forgive.

Japhrimel's eyes didn't flick over to check me, but the mark on my shoulder came to agonized life again, Power flooding me, exploding in my belly. White-hot pokers jerked in my viscera. My scalp twinged, I tasted blood and burning. My sword rang softly, the core of the blade burning white, blue runic patterns slipping through its keen edge and painting the air. I managed to lift it, the blade a bar between me and the Devil facing his eldest son.

The red lights were still flickering, sweeping over the entire building in their complicated patterns, eerie because there were no dancers. "You would have me believe—" *Lucifer started. Stone and plaster shattered at the sound of his voice, dust pattering to the wracked floor.*

Japhrimel interrupted him again. I felt only a weary wonder that he was still standing there, apparently untouched, his long black coat moving gently on the hot firebreeze. "We were told by the Master of this city—your *ally and Hellesvront agent—that you wished to meet Dante here alone. Did you lure your Right Hand here to kill her, Prince? Breaking your word, given on your ineffable Name? Such would conclude our alliance in a most . . . unsatisfactory fashion."*

I could swear Lucifer's face went through surprise, disgust, and finally settled on wariness. He studied Japhrimel for a long, tense thirty seconds, during which my throat burned and tickled but I didn't dare to cough.

Japh clasped his hands behind his back. He looked relaxed, almost bored. Except for the burning murderous light of his eyes, matching Lucifer's shade for shade.

I stayed very still, my left arm cramping as my belly ran with pain and my right trembling as I held my sword. A small part of me wondered where Lucas was. The rest of me stared at Japhrimel with open wonderment.

If I survive this, I'm going to kiss him. Right after I punch the shit out of him for lying to me. If he lets me. *The nastiness of the thought made me suddenly, deeply ashamed of myself.* He was here, and he was facing Lucifer. For me.

He had given up Hell. He had also taken me to Toscano and let me heal from the psychic rape of Mirovitch's ka, protecting me from dangers I hadn't had the faintest idea existed. He was loyal to me after all.

In his own fashion.

Lucifer finally seemed to decide. The flames among the shattered wreckage twisted into angular shapes as some essential tension leached out of him. "I rue the day I set you to watch over her, Eldest." The darkness in his face didn't fade, however—it intensified, a psychic miasma.

The tickling in my throat reached a feverish pitch. I had to cough, shoved the urge down, prayed for strength. Anubis, please don't let me attract their attention. Both of them look too dangerous right now.

Japhrimel shrugged. "What is done, is done." His voice pitched a little higher, as if he imitated Lucifer. Or was quoting him.

The Prince of Hell set his jaw. I saw one elegant hand curl into a fist, and perhaps the other one was a fist too, but I couldn't see it. I think it was the first time I saw the Devil speechless, and my jaw would have dropped if I hadn't clenched it, trying not to cough. I took a fresh grip on my belly, trying not to hunch over. I wanted to see, needed to see. My sword held steady even though my hand was shaking, the blade singing a thin comforting song as its heart glowed white.

He finally seemed to regain himself. "You deserve each other," he hissed. "May you have joy of it. Bring me back my possession and eliminate those who would keep it from me, Tierce Japhrimel, or I will kill you both. I swear it."

Japhrimel's eyes flared. "That was not our bargain, my lord."

Lucifer twitched. Japhrimel didn't move, but the mark twisted white-hot fire into my shoulder, a final burst of Power. The urge to cough mercifully retreated a little. I blinked drying demon blood out of my eyes. I wanted to look for Lucas.

I couldn't look away from my Fallen. He stood tense and ready, in front of the Devil.

"I am the Prince of Hell," Lucifer said coldly.

"And I was your Eldest." Japhrimel held Lucifer's eyes as the air itself cried out, a long gasping howl of a breeze coming from them, blowing my hair back. I felt the stiffness—blood and dust matted in my hair. I was filthy, and I ached. I stayed where I was. "I was the Kinslayer. Thus you made me, and you cast me away. I am yours no longer."

"I made you." The air itself screamed as the Prince of Hell's voice tore at it. *"Your allegiance is* mine.*"*

"My allegiance," Japhrimel returned, inexorably quiet, *"is my own. I Fell, I am Fallen. I am not your son."*

One last burst of soft killing silence. I struggled to stay still.

Lucifer turned on his heel. The world snapped back into normalcy. He strode for the gaping hole torn in the front of the nightclub. Red neon reflected wetly off the street outside. A flick of his golden fingers, and the hellhounds loped gracefully after him, one stopping to snarl back over its shoulder at me.

Well, now I can guess who sent the hellhounds. You bastard. You filthy bastard. *I sagged. My sword dipped, and the urge to cough rose again. It felt like a plasgun core had been dropped into my gut.*

The Prince stopped, turned his head so I could see his profile. "Japhrimel." His voice was back to silk and honey, terrible in its beauty. "I give you a promise, my Eldest. One day, I will kill her."

Lucifer vanished. The air tried to heal itself, closing over the space where he had been, and failed. He left a scorch on the very fabric of existence.

Japhrimel was silent for a moment, his eyes fixed forward. He didn't look at me. I was glad, because his face was full of something terrible, irrevocable, and devouring.

"Not while I watch over her," he said softly.

1

*C*airo Giza has endured almost forever, but it was only after the Awakening that the pyramids began to acquire distinctive etheric smears again. Colored balls of light bob and weave around them even during daytime, playing with streams of hover traffic that carefully don't pass over the pyramids themselves, like a river separating around islands. Hover circuitry is buffered like every critical component nowadays, but enough Power can blow anything electric just like a focused EMP pulse. There's a college of Ceremonials responsible for using and draining the pyramids' charge, responsible also for the Temple built equidistant from the stone triangles and the Sphinx, whose ruined face still gazes from her recumbent body with more long-forgotten wisdom than the human race could ever lay claim to accumulating.

Power hummed in the air as I stepped from glaring desert sun into the shadowed gloom of the Temple's portico. Static crackled, sand falling out of my clothes whisked away by the containment field. I grimaced. We'd been on the ground less than half an hour and already I was tired of the dust.

One worn-out, busted-down part-demon Necromance, sore from Lucifer's last kick even though Japhrimel had repaired the damage and flushed me with enough Power to make my skin tingle. And one Fallen given back the power of a demon pacing behind me, his step oddly silent on the stone floor. The mark on my left shoulder—*his* mark— pulsed again, a warm velvet flush coating my body. My rings swirled with steady light.

My bag bumped against my hip and my bootheels clicked on stone, echoing in the vast shadowed chamber. The great inner doors rose up before us, massive slabs of granite lasecarved with hieroglyph pictures of a way of life vanished thousands of years ago. I inhaled the deep familiar spice of *kyphii* deeply as my nape prickled. My sword, thrust through a loop in my weapons rig, thrummed slightly in its indigo-lacquered scabbard.

A blade that can bite the Devil. A cool finger of dread traced up my spine.

I stopped, half-turning on my heel to look up at Japhrimel. He paused, his hands clasped behind his back as usual, regarding me with bright green-glowing eyes. His ink-dark hair lay against his forehead in a soft wave, melding with the Temple's dusky quiet; Japhrimel's lean golden saturnine face was closed and distant. He had been very quiet for the last hour.

I didn't blame him. We had precious little to say now. In any case, I didn't want to break the fragile truce between us.

One dark eyebrow quirked slightly, a question I found I could read. It was a relief to see something about him I still understood.

Had he changed, or had I?

"Will you wait for me here?" My voice bounced back from stone, husky and half-ruined, still freighted with the promise of demon seduction. The hoarseness didn't help, turning my tone to granular honey. "Please?"

His expression changed from distance to wariness. The corner of his mouth lifted slightly. "Of course. It would be a pleasure."

The words ran along stone, mouthing the air softly.

I bit my lower lip. The idea that I'd misjudged him was uncomfortable, to say the least. "Japhrimel?"

His eyes rested on my face. All attention, focused on me. He didn't touch me, but he might as well have, his aura closing around mine, black-diamond flames proclaiming him as *demon* to anyone with otherSight. It was a caress no less intimate for being nonphysical—something he was doing more and more lately. I wondered if it was because he wanted to keep track of me, or because he wanted to touch me.

I shook my head, deciding the question was useless. He probably wouldn't tell me, anyway.

Was it wrong, not to hold it against him?

I heard Lucas Villalobos's voice again. *Take what you can get.* Good advice? Honorable? Or just practical?

Tiens, the Nichtvren who was yet another Hellesvront agent, would meet us after dark. Lucas was with Vann and McKinley; Leander had rented space in a boarding house and was waiting for us. The Necromance bounty hunter seemed very easy with the idea of two nonhuman Hellesvront agents, but I'd caught him going pale whenever Lucas got too close.

It was a relief to see he had some sense.

Then again, even I was frightened of Lucas, never mind

that I was his client and he'd taken on Lucifer and two hellhounds for me. The man Death had turned his back on was a professional, and a good asset . . . but still. He was unpredictable, impossible to kill, magick just seemed to shunt itself away from him—and there were stories of just what he'd done to psions who played rough with him, or hired him and tried to welsh. It doesn't take long to figure out so many stories must have a grain of truth.

"Yes?" Japhrimel prompted me. I looked up from the stone floor with a start. I'd been wandering.

I never used to do that.

"Nothing." I turned away, my boots making precise little sounds against the floor as I headed for the doors. "I'll be out in a little while."

"Take your time." He stood straight and tall, his hands clasped behind his back, his eyes burning green holes in smoky cool darkness. I felt the weight of his gaze on my back. "I'll wait."

I shook my head, reached up to touch the doors. The mark on my shoulder flared again, heat sliding down my skin like warm oil.

He was Fallen-no-more. I would have wondered what that made me now, but he hadn't even told me what I was in the first place. *Hedaira,* a human woman given a share of a demon's strength. Japhrimel just kept saying I would find out in time.

With Eve to save and Lucifer looking to kill me, I just might die before I found out. Wouldn't that be a bitch and a half.

I spread my hands—narrow, golden, the black molecule-drip polish slightly chipped on my left fingernails—against rough granite, pushed. The doors, balanced on oiled mag-

hinges, whooshed open easily. More *kyphii* smoke billowed out, fighting briefly with the burning-cinnamon musk of demon cloaking me.

The hall was large, all architectural space focused on throned Horus at the end, Isis's tall form behind him, Her hand lifted in blessing over Her son. The doors slid to a stop. I bowed, my right hand touching heart and forehead in the classic salute.

I paced forward into the house of the gods. The doors slid together behind me, closing Japhrimel out. Here was perhaps the only place I could truly be alone, the only place he would not intrude.

Unfortunately, leaving him outside meant leaving my protection too. I didn't think any demon would try to attack me inside a temple, but I was just nervous enough to take a deep breath and welcome the next flush of Power spreading from the scar.

Another deep breath. Panic beat under my breastbone. I told myself it was silly. Japh was right outside the door, and my god had always answered me before.

Still, ever since the night Anubis had called me out of slumber and laid on me a geas I couldn't remember, He had been silent. Losing that compass left me adrift in a way I'd never been before. If I'd ever needed direction and comfort, it was now.

Cairo Giza had been Islum territory in the Merican era, but Islum had choked on its own blood during the Seventy Days War, along with the Protestor Christers and the Judics, not to mention the Evangelicals of Gilead. In a world controlled by the Hegemony and Putchkin Alliance, with psions in every corner, the conditions that gave rise to the Religions of Submission have fallen away. After a brief re-flowering of fundamentalist Islum during the collapse of petroleo use, it became just another small sect—like the Novo Christers—and the old gods and state religions had risen again.

The single biggest blow to the Religions of Submission had been the Awakening and the rise of the science of Power. When anyone can contract a Shaman or Ceremonial to talk to the god of their choice, and spiritual experiences becoming commonplace—not to mention Necromances proving an afterlife exists and Magi definitively proving the existence of demons—most organized religions had died a quick hard death, replaced by personal worship of patron gods and spirits. It was, in all reality, the only logical response on humanity's part.

Here in Egypt those old gods have returned with a vengeance, and the pyramid Ceremonials are slowly taking on the tenor of a priesthood. Most psions are religious only to the extent that the science of belief makes Power behave itself. Necromances are generally more dedicated than most; after all, our psychopomps take the faces of ancient gods and act a little differently from the average man's deities.

Part of that probably has to do with the Trial every accredited Necromance has to face. It's hard not to feel a little bit attached to a god who resurrects you from the psychic death of initiation and stays with you afterward, receiving you into Death's arms when it is finally time to go into What Comes Next.

The debate remains—could a Ceremonial be a priest or priestess, and what exactly did the gods *want* anyway? Only nowadays, people aren't likely to murder each other over the questions. Not often, anyway. There's a running feud between the priestesses of Aslan and the Hegemony

Albion Literary College, who say the Prophet Lewis was a Novo Christer, but only ink is spilled in that battle, not blood.

I turned to my right. Sekhmet sat on Her throne, lion-headed and strangely serene, heat blurring up from the eternal fire in a black bowl on Her altar. The heady smell of wine rose; someone had been making offerings. Past Her, there was Set, His jackal-head painted the deep red of dried blood. The powers of destruction, given their place at the left hand of creation. Necessary, and worshipped—but not safe.

Not at all safe.

Japhrimel's last gift before breaking the news that Lucifer had summoned me again had been a glossy obsidian statue of the Fierce One. That same statue, repaired and burnished to a fine gloss, was set by the side of the bed in the boarding house even now. *Please tell me She isn't about to start messing around with me. I have all the trouble I can handle right now.*

I shivered, turned to the left. There, behind Thoth's beaky head, was the slim black dog's face of my own god, in his own important niche.

I drew *kyphii* deep into my lungs. A last respectful bow to Isis and Her son, and I moved to the left.

Thoth's statue seemed to make a quick movement as I passed. I stopped, made my obeisance. Glanced up the ceiling, lasepainted with Nuit's starry naked form.

Plenty of psions worship the Hellene gods. There are colleges of Asatru and Teutonica as well as the Faery tradition in Hegemony Europa. The Shamans have their *loa,* and there are some who follow the path of the Left Hand and worship the Unspeakable. The Tantrics have their *devas* and the Hindu their huge intricate assemblages, Native Mericans and Islanders their own branches of magick and Shamanic training passed down through blood and ritual; the Buddhists and Zenmos their own not-quite-religious traditions. *There are as many religions as there are people on the earth*, the Magi say. Even the demons were worshipped one long-ago time, mistaken for gods.

For me, there had never really been any choice. I'd dreamed of a dog-headed man all through my childhood, and had taken the requisite Religious Studies classes at Rigger Hall. One of the first religions studied was Egyptianica, since it was such a popular sect—and I'd felt at home from the very beginning. Everything about the gods of the Nile was not so much learned for me as deeply *remembered,* as if I'd always known but just needed the reminding.

The first time I'd gone into Death, Anubis had been there; He had never left me since. Where else would I turn for solace, but to Him?

I reached His niche. Tears welled up, my throat full of something hard and hot. I sank down to one knee, rose. Stepped forward. Approached His statue, the altar before it lit by novenas and crowded with offerings. Food, drink, scattered New Credit notes, sticks of fuming incense. Even the normals propitiated Him, hoping for some false mercy when their time came, hoping to live past whatever appointed date and hour Death chose.

My rings sparked, golden points of light popping in the dark. From the obsidian ring on my right third finger to the amber on my right and left middle, the moonstone on my left index, the bloodstone on my left third; the Suni-figured thumbring sparked too, reacting with the charge of Power in the air. The Power I carried, tied to a demon and no longer strictly human myself, quivered uneasily.

My Lord, my god, please hear me. I need You.

I sank down to my knees, my katana blurring out of its sheath. Laid the bright steel length on the stone floor in front of me, rested my hands on my thighs. Closed my eyes and prayed.

Please. I am weary, and I hunger for Your touch, my Lord. Speak to me. You have comforted me, but I want to hear You.

My breathing deepened. The blue glow began, rising at the very corners of my mental sight. I began the prayer I'd learned long ago, studying from Novo Egyptos books in the Library at Rigger Hall. *"Anubis et'her ka,"* I whispered. *"Se ta'uk'fhet sa te vapu kuraph. Anubis et'her ka.* Anubis, Lord of the Dead, Faithful Companion, protect me, for I am Your child. Protect me, Anubis, weigh my heart upon the scale; watch over me, Lord, for I am Your child. Do not let evil distress me, but turn Your fierceness upon my enemies. Cover me with Your gaze, let Your hand be upon me, now and all the days of my life, until You take me into Your embrace."

Another deep breath, my pulse slowing, the silent place in me where the god lived opening like a flower. *"Anubis et'her ka,"* I repeated, as blue light rose in one sharp flare. The god of Death took me, swallowed me whole—and I was simply, utterly glad.

The blue crystal walls of Death rose up, but I was not on the bridge over the well of souls. Instead, the crystal shaped itself into a Temple, a psychic echo of the place my body knelt in. Before me the god appeared in the cipher of a slim black dog, sitting back on His haunches and regarding me with His infinitely-starred black eyes.

I had not come here of my own accord since Jace's death.

I had wept. I had raged against Him, set my will against His, blamed Him, sobbed in Japhrimel's arms about the utter unfairness of it. Yet I know Death does not play favorites. He loves all equally, and when it is time, not all the grief of the living will dissuade His purpose.

This, then, my agony—how do I love my god and still rage against His will? How do I grieve and yet love Him?

Here I wore the white robe of the god's chosen, belted with silver dripping like fishscales. My knees pressed chill against blue crystal floor, the emerald burning against my cheek like a live brand. It was His mark, set in my skin by humans but still with His will, the gem that marked me as Death's chosen. I blessed whatever accident of genetics gifted me with the Power to walk in His realm and feel His touch.

I met His eyes. I was not bringing a soul back from Death, so I did not need the protection of cold steel—but my hand ached to close reflexively around a swordhilt. His gaze was blackness from lid to lid, starred with cold blue jewels of constellations none of the living would ever see and glazed with blue sheen. Galaxies died in Death's eyes as the god's attention rested on me, a huge burden for such a small being—though I was infinite enough in my own right, being His child. That in itself was a mystery, how I could contain the infinity of the god, and how He could contain my own endless soul.

He took the weight from me, certainty replacing the burden. I was His, I had always been His. From before my birth the god had set His hand upon me. He could no more abandon me than I could abandon Him. Though I had set my will against His, even cursed Him in the pain of my grief—and still, sometimes, did—He did not mind. He was my god, and would not desert me.

But there was Lucas, wasn't there? The man Death had turned His back on.

Thought became action instantly in this space; my question leapt, a thread of meaning laid in the receptive space between us, a cord stretched taut. The sound brushed through me, an immense church-bell gong of the god's laughter. The Deathless's path was not mine, Anubis reminded me. My path was my own, and my covenant with Death was always unbroken, no matter if I cursed him in my human grief.

I am clay—and if the clay cuts the hand of the potter who created it, who is to blame?

He spoke.

The meanings of His word burned through me, each stripping away a layer. So many layers, so many different things to fight through; each opening like a flower to the god. There was no other being, human, god, or demon, that I would bow my head in submission to. And so, my promise to Him. I accepted.

The geas burned at me, the fire of His touch and some other fire that moved through him combining. I had something to do—something the god would not show me yet.

Would I do what the god asked? When the time came, would I submit to His will and do what He asked of me?

Bitterness rose inside me. Death does not bargain, does not play favorites, and had already taken people I loved.

Doreen, Jace, Lewis, Roanna . . . each name was a star

in the constellations filling His eyes. I could have raged against Him, but what would be the point? His promise to me was utter certainty. The people I loved went into Death and He held them; when my own time came I would see them again. No matter what else What Comes Next contained, I could be certain it held the souls of those who mattered to me in life, whose love and duty still lay upon me, a welcome weight of obligation.

That weight was the measure of my honor. What is honor without promises kept?

As for myself, going into Death's embrace would be like welcoming a lover, a celebration I feared even as I ached for it. Every living creature fears the unknown. To have even a small measure of certainty in the midst of that fear is a treasure. Unlike the poor blind souls who have to take my word for it, I know who will clasp my hand when I die and help me through the door into What Comes Next. Knowing helps the fear, even if it does not lessen it.

I bowed, my palms together; a deep obeisance reaching into my very heart. My long stubborn life unreeled under His touch.

I am Your child, I whispered. Tell me what I must do.

The slim black dog regarded me with awful, infinitely merciful eyes. Shook His head, gravely. Even the geas was only to tell me what choice was required when the time approached. I was free. He only asked, and in the asking, did not promise to love me less if I denied Him.

Such perfect love is not for humans.

There was no other answer I could give, for all the freedom He granted me.

I would not deny Him, it would be denying myself. His

approval warmed me, all the way down to my bones. How could I have doubted Him?

There was one more question I had, and meaning stretched between us again, a cord strained to its limits.

I could not help myself. I lifted my head, and I spoke his name to the god. Japhrimel.

The emerald on my cheek flared, sparks cascading down. The god's face changed, a canine smile. His eyes flashed green for the barest moment.

My god released me, unanswered—and yet, with a curious sense of having been told what was important, holding the knowledge for one glorious heart-stopping moment before the shock of slamming—

—back into my body drove the understanding away. I gasped, bent double, my cold, numb hand curling reflexively around my swordhilt. I leapt to my feet, my boots slamming against stone floor. My heart pounded inside its flexible cage of ribs. I swallowed several times, blinked.

The entire Temple was full of shadows, soft nasty laughter chittering against its high roof. Demon-acute sight pierced the gloom, showed me every corner and crack, down to the flow and flux of Power wedded to the walls. There were no other worshippers, and that was strange, wasn't it? It wasn't like a temple—especially this one—to be empty, especially in the middle of the day.

Copper-tasting demon adrenaline jolted me. The chill of Death flushed itself out of fingers and toes. Other Necromances use sex or sparring to shake the cold of Death and flush the bitter taste of it away. I used to go slicboarding, using speed and antigrav danger to bring myself back to the land of the breathing. This time, I was brought back by the sense of being *watched*.

No. The *knowledge* I was being watched.

But I saw nobody. My heartbeat finally returned to something like normal, and I let out a soft sigh. I was in a temple, under the gaze of my god and with Japhrimel right outside the door. What could harm me here?

My sword sang, sliding back into the sheath. *Fudoshin*, Jado had named it, and it had served me well. Very well, considering it had bit the Devil's flesh without shattering. There was some Power locked in the steel's heart my *sensei* hadn't told me about.

You're not thinking what I think you're thinking, are you Danny? You can't kill the Devil. It can't be done. That's why he's the Prince of Hell, he's the oldest of demons, the one they're all descended from. It's impossible.

I couldn't. But maybe Japhrimel could—he had, after all, pushed Lucifer *back*. Away from me.

Or, if Japh couldn't *kill* him, he might at least *persuade* the Devil to leave Eve alone. It was the least I could do for Doreen's daughter.

My daughter, too. If she could be believed.

I looked up again, at the god of Death's face. He deserved an offering, though I had precious little to give Him right at the moment. Everything I owned had gone up in flames, one way or another.

Including my relationship with Japhrimel. I love him, but how am I going to convince him to leave Eve alone? And how the hell am I going to get him to stop simply using his strength to force me to do anything he wants me to? He's apologized, but the precedent's been set.

I slid one of my main knives free, steel glittering in the light from the forest of novenas. Set the blade against my palm, worked it back and forth to penetrate tough golden skin. This earned me a handful of black demon blood I tipped carefully into a shallow bone dish full of strong red wine, someone else's offering. I used the knife to saw off a handful of my hair—longer now, since Japhrimel had brought me back after the hover incident. Shoulder-length instead of hacked around my ears—but it was still odd to walk around without a braid bumping my back whenever I turned my head.

I bowed again, the cut on my palm closing, black blood sealing away the hurt. "I wish I had more for You," I said quietly to the statue, knowing He would hear and understand. "My thanks, my Lord."

Did the shadows move to cloak Him? I blinked, the sense of being watched strong and inarguable. It wasn't like my sight to be clouded—I'd had excellent vision even before being gifted with demon-acute senses. I stared up at the dog's head above the narrow black chest, the crook and flail held in his long black hands, the kilt of gems running with reflected candlelight. *Strong One,* we who followed Anubis called him; *Protector.* And also, the most loving name—*the Gentle One.* The one who eased all hurts, the god who never left us, even at life's end.

"Anubis et'her ka," I repeated. "Thank you."

As I paced away, the statues didn't move. I wondered if I should offer to Sekhmet, discarded the notion. It was dangerous to attract Her attention—I had all the destruction I could handle in my life right now. I bowed one last time to Isis and Horus, made my way to the granite doors. They opened inward for me, Power sparking and spiraling through their cores, and when I stepped out into the entry hall Japhrimel still stood in the same spot, his hands clasped behind his back, examining the walls.

The doors swung closed behind me. Finally, his eyes returned to mine. "Did you find what you needed?"

The air between us was brittle and clear as thin crystal. He was trying so hard to be careful with me.

I'm trying too, Japhrimel. I love you, and I'm trying. I shrugged. "Gods." I gave him a smile that tried to be natural. "I'm hungry. Did you mention food?"

2

The boarding house was a large sloping mudbrick building, stasis and containment fields glimmering over every window and door. The heat was almost as tremendous as the blowing sand. I spent a few moments on the sidewalk outside the building, basking in sunlight. Japhrimel, a blot on the tawny day with his long black coat, waited silently.

There were spots of green, of course. Water pumped up from the brown ribbon of the Nile and local areas of climate control made for gardens, plenty of date palms, an oasis tucked in every courtyard. The technology of water-makers was in its infancy, but here it was being used to its fullest extent—which wasn't very far, but it was nice. There would at least be enough water to bathe with, a far cry from the recent thirty-year drought that had gripped the entire northern half of Hegemony Afrike. They were still hashing out the environmental consequences of the technology, but life was beginning to spread away from the river and into the desert. There was even talk of making the desert green again, but the environmental scientists were up in arms about *that*.

I'd run a few bounties down in Hegemony Afrike. There was the Magi-gone-bad I'd tracked through the back alleys of Novo Carthago and the Shaman I'd caught in Tanzania—thank the gods for antivenom and tazapram, that's the only time I've ever been poisoned so bad I thought I'd die. I had almost gone into Death's arms after being bitten six times by a collection of boomslangs the Shaman had tickled into regarding me as an enemy. I hadn't known he was secondarily talented as an Animone.

Then there was the gang of four normals, combat-augmented and hyped on thyoline-laced Clormen-13, who'd thought the Serengeti Historical Preserve would hide them. I'd had to dock my fee 50 percent for bringing in two of them dead and the other two in critical condition, but they shouldn't have shot me and beat me up. And they additionally shouldn't have left me tied up and gone to slam hypos of Chill cocktail.

They should have killed me when they had the chance.

My memories of Hegemony Afrike are all of heat, dust, danger, and heart-thumping adrenaline. Not to mention pain. If I got in a transport when we were finished here without getting into a fight, it would be the first damn time I ever lifted off from Hegemony Afrike soil without bleeding.

Well, a girl could hope, couldn't she?

One thing I'll say for being almost-demon, I don't mind hot weather the way I used to. I used to hate sweating, but nowadays I like heat—the more the better, like a cat in a square of sun.

When I followed Japhrimel in through the containment field, shuddering as it tickled and nipped at my skin, we found square brown Vann waiting for us in the cool, shaded lobby. The Hellesvront agent's face looked better; he was healing much faster than a human but not as quickly as with a healcharm. The bruises Lucas had given him were going down and the bandage had come off his right eye, revealing a wicked slash down his forehead through his eyebrow. He was lucky he hadn't lost that eye, and I felt a little guilty. After all, I'd hired Lucas—but he'd been squeezing Vann for information on my whereabouts so he could show up just in time to save my life.

I was fairly sure Lucifer would have killed me if he could. Just one more time I'd tangled with the Prince of Hell and come away with my miserable life. I was beginning to feel lucky.

Not really.

Vann nodded at me, his brown eyes turning dark. I nodded back cautiously. The desk in the lobby was deserted, a holovid player glowing pink in the office behind it. I caught the sound of a human heartbeat, a cough, shuffling feet. The floor here was an intricate mosaic pattern in tiles of blue and yellow; a dracaena grew in a brass pot near the door, next to a rack of newspapers and cheap holomags.

"News." Vann's tone held uneasy respect, as if I was a poisonous animal he wanted to avoid offending. I looked longingly at the little café tucked into the boarding house's first floor. I was *hungry*.

"Go find a table, Dante," Japhrimel said quietly. "I will join you in a moment."

I weighed hanging around to hear what Vann would say, and decided I probably didn't want to know. I'd find out eventually, and if there was something Japhrimel didn't want me to be told Vann wouldn't say it anyway. I

might as well get something to eat for my trouble. "Fine."
I couldn't resist a bad-tempered little goose. "I suppose
if there was something you didn't want me to know he
would wait to mention it to you later anyway, right?"

With that, I turned on my heel and would have stalked
away, but Japh caught my arm. I knew better than to struggle—he was far stronger than me. It would do no good.

"Stay, then. Hear everything." His eyebrows drew together as he examined Vann. "Well?"

"It left Sarajevo, we don't know where for. McKinley
says there's something going on in Kalif that sounds suspicious, but I don't think anyone would be stupid enough
to look *there*. We're collating the reports right now. I'd
bet it's following the route with no problems." His tone,
as usual when he spoke to Japh, was utterly respectful and
curiously unafraid.

Japhrimel nodded thoughtfully. His thumb moved on
my arm, a gentle absent caress, and I cast back through
memory to piece this together.

Something had been in DMZ Sarajevo, something
Japhrimel had wanted to collect. The Anhelikos—a feathered thing living in an old abandoned temple—had told
him it had been taken to the Roof of the World, whatever
that was.

Thinking about Sarajevo made a shiver go through me,
suddenly cold in the climate-controlled interior. A town
full of paranormals and Lucifer's fingers closing around
my windpipe—my belly was still a little tender from the
Devil's last kick. A parting gift.

Japh's thumb moved again, soothing. "The treasure is
moving," he said meditatively. "Such a thing has not happened for millennia."

"Millennia?" Vann didn't sound surprised. He scratched at his bruised face with blunt fingertips, grimacing slightly. "You're sure about the route?" It was rhetorical instead of doubting.

Japh shrugged, a fluid lovely movement. "I was the one to leave it with Kos Rafelos, and it had just left his care when I arrived. The game has begun. Now it is the Key they will seek."

Key? What key? And who's they? I didn't say it out loud, but Japhrimel glanced at me, as if gauging how much he should say. I swallowed sudden impatience. He'd earned a little bit of slack, though I still wasn't happy about being shaken like a naughty puppy and held up against the wall in a Sarajevo subway station. The thought of him using his superior strength to force me to do something still filled me with a combination of unsteady rage and sick anticipation, as if bracing myself for a gutshot.

But he had kept Lucifer away long enough to give me a chance to heal my shattered psyche. He had hidden me so well other rebellious demons couldn't find me and even lied to the Prince of Hell to protect me.

Not only that, but he'd given up all chance of returning to his home. For me.

He had, indeed, earned a little slack.

I bit back impatience and simply listened, my eyes moving over the graceful curve of balustrade going upstairs. *Go figure. Danny Valentine, holding her tongue for once. Let's mark it on the calendar and call the holovid reporters; it's a frocking miracle.*

Vann made a sudden movement, as if he couldn't contain himself. The leather fringe on his jacket swayed, whispering. "You're just going to let her walk around?

You know what they're after. If they take her, it could mean the end of everything."

That brought my eyes around in a hurry, but he stared at Japhrimel, whose gaze had gone distant, focused on the far wall of the foyer, an intricately-carved screen showing the fresh green coolness of the garden beyond. His thumb moved again, caressing my upper arm.

"My lord." Vann gave me a nervous glance, forged ahead. "It might be better to act first and apologize later. This is dangerous. *Truly* dangerous."

"Act first, apologize later." Japh sounded thoughtful. "What do you think of that, Dante?"

He's actually asking what I *think? Another banner occasion. Call the holovid reporters again.* "Sounds risky," I answered, carefully. "If *who* takes her? And what's the Key?" *And what the bloody blue fuck are we talking about here? Me?*

Vann's cheeks actually flushed. "My lord." He was beginning to sound desperate. Was he sweating? "I've served you for years and never questioned your orders or methods. But this is *dangerous*. If *he* finds out, *he'll* kill her, and possibly the rest of your vassals too."

Japhrimel shrugged. "At present I am too valuable for him to risk anything of the sort."

"Vassals?" My voice cut across his. "He who? Lucifer? Kill me? He's already tried. If he finds out *what?*" *Served Japhrimel for years? That's news, too.*

Vann winced when I spoke the Devil's name. I didn't blame him, but I was too busy staring up at Japh's profile to worry about his tender feelings. "Japhrimel?" I heard the quiet, deadly tone in my voice. "Care to shed some light on this? I'm a little lost."

I thought he wouldn't answer, but he blinked, as if returning from a long and unpleasant chain of thought. "This is not the place for such a discussion," he said, finally, slowly. Choosing his words with great care, a tone I'd rarely heard from him before. "I would prefer to see to your comfort first, and explain privately. For now, will it satisfy you if I say you have suddenly become far more important to the Prince than even *he* realizes, and Vann is worried because your life is so very precious?" His eyes flashed green as he turned his head slightly, looking down at me with a very faint, iron-clad smile touching his lips. "If you are taken or killed, I will be unable to protect those whose allegiance lies with me, and they may find it . . . worrisome."

I don't think I've ever been struck so speechless, and that's saying something. I am normally not the type of girl to be at a loss for words. I turned this around in my head once or twice, the mark on my shoulder pulsing softly again with velvet heat. Then I realized he hadn't answered either of my questions.

Still, that's more than he's given me since this whole mess began. I suppose it's a step up. I thought it over, and Vann visibly braced himself.

What does he think I'm going to do? "Okay." I nodded, sharply, once. My hair fell over my shoulders, tumbled in my face. "I'm going to go get something to eat. Come along when you're finished, and you can explain to me over breakfast."

Japhrimel shook his head. "I would prefer to explain in private, Dante." He paused. "If it would please you to accede."

Well, I can't very well argue with that, can I? We were

being so very careful with each other, I might have burst out laughing if it hadn't been so deadly serious. "Sure. After breakfast, then. We'll head up to our room and you can explain everything."

Vann was crimson under his bruises. He also looked shocked. I got the idea he wasn't used to hearing Japhrimel express a preference instead of just telling someone what to do. I was pretty surprised myself. And pleased. He was trying, at least.

Japh nodded. "As you like." He let go of me slowly, reluctantly, and I found myself smiling as I backed up two steps, then turned and headed for the small café, an unaccustomed light feeling under my breastbone.

To my surprise, Lucas Villalobos sat at one of the tables, his almost-yellow eyes wide open as he looked over a menu. He'd cleaned up, gotten out of his blood-stiff rags and into a fresh microfiber shirt and jeans, bandoliers crossing his narrow chest and his lank hair lying clean and damp against his shoulders. He had his two 60-watt plasguns, and the river of scarring down the left side of his face looked pink and rough-scrubbed.

He looked none the worse for wear despite being almost eviscerated by the Prince of Hell.

Just how fast did the Deathless heal, anyway?

I scuffed the floor deliberately as I threaded between tables and finally dropped into the chair opposite him, my sword resting in its scabbard across my lap. He was working for me, but still . . . he was Lucas. It doesn't pay to be lazy even around people you employ. "Hey." *Gods, I'm grinning like an idiot. Japhrimel asked me, he asked me, he's treating me like an equal. Thank the gods.*

Lucas's eyes flicked over me once, descended back to

the menu. "Valentine." His whispering, ruined voice almost hurt my own throat. "Where's your pet demon?"

I suppose for him that passed as a polite greeting. "Getting news from one of his stooges." *Proving he's one of the good guys, as far as I'm concerned.*

The café was windowless, but one whole pillared wall of graceful arched doorways gave out onto the courtyard garden, where green flowered lush under a shimmer of climate control. Linen napkins, heavy silverware, the glasses real silica instead of plasglass, a tiled floor and smooth adobe walls—if the outside of this place looked shabby, the inside at least was very nice. There was a breath of warm breeze from the garden, heavily spiced with jasmine that would fairly drench the place once night fell. "So what's good here?"

"Don't know. The Necromance recommended *huevos Benedictos.*" Wonder of wonders, Lucas shuddered. "No matter how old I get, I ain't gonna eat that shit."

I was startled into a laugh. If I'd still been human I would have been too terrified to enjoy any of his jokes. "I don't blame you. How are you feeling?"

It was a stupid question, and his yellowing eyes simply came up and dropped back down to the menu. He didn't respond, and my good mood soured only a little. Lucas wasn't a small-talk type of guy.

The waitress came, a sloe-eyed Egyptiano in jeans and a blousy cassock of a shirt, traditional lasetattoos on her dark hands. The shirt, fine cotton, was embroidered with red around the cuffs and collar; her hair, long and black, pulled back in a simple ponytail. She still looked exotic, helped along by the gold nose-ring and the thin gold rings on each finger as well as the slim chiming bangles on her slender wrists, startling against dusky skin. "Would you like today sirs?" she chirped in passable Merican, taking no notice of my tat or Lucas's scarred face—or the fact that both of us were armed.

Most normals blanch or flinch on seeing my cheek. They think psions have nothing better to do than rummage through their messy, stinking minds. It never occurs to them that going through a normal's psyche is like wading neck-deep in festering shit. Even corporate and legal telepaths don't like dealing with normals and always use a filter between their own sensitive, well-ordered minds and the untrained sludge in most people's heads.

Besides, I was a Necromance, not a Reader or a legal telepath. The emerald on my cheek shouted what I was; there was no reason for normals to be afraid of me unless they were running from the law or attacked me first. I've been feared by normals most of my life, but it never gets any easier. Not even when you're part-demon.

I picked up a flat plascoated menu. One side was in Erabic, the other in Merican and Franje. I scanned the offerings while Lucas ordered curry, a small mountain of rice, and coffee.

She looked at me, smiling. Her teeth were very white. I asked for the same thing—Lucas probably knew what he was about, despite his show of ignorance. I did ask for a synthprotein shake too, but just because I felt peckish.

She accepted the menus with a smile. It was comforting to sit in a café as if I was on vacation—even though Lucas had his back to the safe spot and I had to put mine to the archway leading from the lobby. That made me nervous.

Then again, he'd taken on the Devil for me. Like Japhrimel.

Besides, Lucas's reputation would suffer if one of his clients got hashed at the breakfast table with him. I was pretty sure he cared about his reputation, if nothing else. There was a story that he'd once taken on a whole corporation's security division when a stray shot had accidentally killed his target before he could get to it.

The rumor further was, he'd won—*after* being knifed, shot, blown up, knifed again, shot five more times, and blown up the last time with a full half-ounce of C19. No, you didn't mess with Lucas Villalobos *or* his reputation.

I watched the waitress sway away. There was only one other occupied table—a normal male in a hoverpilot's uniform buried in a huge broadsheet newspaper covered with squiggles of Erabic. It looked a little like Magi code and I narrowed my eyes, staring intently at the inked lines. My left hand was solid around my katana's sheath.

I finally felt as if I'd survived Sarajevo. *And* my last meeting with the Prince of Hell. Getting kicked around and half-strangled by the Devil was getting to be almost routine, by now.

Not really. That sort of thing *never* gets routine.

I let out a long breath, my shoulders dropping. It was going to be a long time before I could smell baking bread again without being reminded of the Anhelikos in the empty temple, its wings mantling and cloying perfume brushing through my hair as my legs turned to butter.

It was going to be a long time before I could begin to forget Lucifer's hand circling my neck, little things creaking and crackling in my throat. My husky broken voice bore no relation to what it had been while human. What was it with demons and strangling me?

"What you gonna do?" Lucas asked finally.

I found him studying me, his dark eyebrows drawn together and his thin mouth twisted down at one corner. "About what?" *Dammit, I never used to wander off in the middle of conversations. Got to keep focused.*

He gave me a look that could have cut plasteel. "The Devil. And Ol' Blue Eyes."

Eve. Lucifer had contracted me to kill or capture four demons, without mentioning Doreen's genetically-altered daughter was the fourth. The more I thought about it, the more it seemed like he'd been using me to draw Eve out.

But if he wanted her dead or captured, the other hunters he'd sent after her—and her cohorts—would be more than enough, wouldn't they? To christen me his new Right Hand, wind me up, and send me after her fellow rebels while simultaneously throwing noisy obstacles in my way and showing up to capture or kill her himself . . . what game was that part of? It wasn't like the Devil to crawl out of his hole personally before everything was all neatly wrapped up.

Bait. And some other game is being played here. Lucky me.

Japhrimel had to know I wouldn't agree to take Eve down or return her to Lucifer. And last but *definitely* not least, what the hell did it have to do with this treasure, the Key, and me?

"I don't know," I lied. "I can't hunt down Doreen's daughter, Lucas. Santino killed Doreen, and I killed Santino." *Boy, is that ever an understatement.* For a moment my right hand cramped, but I spread my fingers under the table and it passed. My good mood was fading even more. "Lucifer took Eve. She . . . ."

She said I was her mother too, that the sample Vardimal took from Doreen was contaminated with my genetic material. I hadn't told Japhrimel, it was too private. Too *personal.* It was different from the omissions he'd made to me, I told myself.

Wasn't it?

"You contracted me for four demons," Lucas reminded me.

And she's one of them. The remainder of the funny, light feeling under my breastbone disappeared, returning me to sour anticipation and a faint headache. I looked away from the table, out toward the garden, steaming sweet green under the glaring hammerblow of desert sun. "I know."

Maybe I would have said more, but the datband flashed on my left wrist. I looked down, my eyes snagging on the silvery wristcuff above my dat, carved with its fluid lines. The Gauntlet, Lucifer's little calling-card, marking me as his extra-special deputy. My skin crawled at the thought of wearing it, but there hadn't been a chance to take it off. Getting chased around by hellhounds and half-strangled by demons will cut into any girl's accessorizing schedule.

My datband flashed again. I had a message. I dug in my bag for my datpilot, wrinkling my nose a little. The heavy black canvas bag had gone through hell with me— literally. Both to the home of demons when Japhrimel had been sent to fetch me the first time and the other hell of my return to Rigger Hall.

My skin prickled with phantom gooseflesh. I took a

deep breath, dispelling the feeling. The bag was singed and smelled of hard use and gun oil, its strap frayed but still tough. I fished my 'pilot out, flipped it open, and tapped at the screen while it genescanned me and decided I was, after all, Dante Valentine.

I was glad the electronics recognized me. Some days I didn't even recognize myself anymore. Ever since that rainy Monday when my front door resounded with shattering knocks, my life had taken a definite turn into "gigantic mess."

The screen flashed, cleared. Then the message came up, priority-marked urgent, I knew who it was from. There was only one person it could be from, only one person whose messages would go straight to my datband.

Gabe. Gabriele Spocarelli.

I blew out between my teeth. The icon flashed, waiting for me to tap it to bring the message up. The waitress came with thick aromatic coffee you can get in Hegemony Afrike or Putchkin Near Asiano, syrupy-sweet and fragrant. She also set down my synthprotein shake and gave me a bright smile, her dark eyes passing over my tat with nary a hitch. I looked up at Lucas, who studied his shotglass with apparent interest before lifting it slowly to his mouth with the air of a man embarking on a sensual experience.

I tapped the icon. I'd spoken to Gabe a couple months ago, one of our semi-regular calls. Like most psions, I wasn't good with a regular schedule unless I had a datpilot and a messenger service to keep my life straight; I would sometimes think only a few days had gone by before my 'pilot would beep and tell me it had been a month or three and Gabe was due for another call. Time had taken on a funny elasticity, maybe because I was hanging out with a creature older than even *I* had any idea of.

Usually I dialed, she picked up, and we both did our best to sound like the things we couldn't say to each other weren't crowding the telephone line like apparitions pulled from fresh bodies, shimmering and seeming-solid. We talked about old cases and bounties, told a few jokes, and generally said nothing of any real importance whatsoever.

She didn't mention Jace Monroe. I didn't mention Japhrimel, who observed a strict silence during the phone calls when he didn't withdraw to another room, granting me privacy. Nor did Gabe and I engage in anything even remotely resembling real conversation. Still, I called regularly, and each time I called she picked up. It was good enough for me.

Better than I deserved.

The screen flashed, and a chill touched my nape. The message was simple. Too simple.

> *Danny,*
> *Mainuthsz.*
> *I need you. Now.*
> *Gabe.*

"Who is it?" Lucas's eyes flicked over my shoulder. I looked, seeing Japhrimel. He skirted the tables, obviously intending to join us. My heart began to pound, and if I hadn't been so hungry I might have bolted from the table. Not to avoid him, but because the need to *move* suddenly all but throttled me.

I sat very still, searching for control. It came slowly,

tied to the deep breathing I began. All the way down into the belly, blow the breath out softly through the lips. *Anubis grant me strength. All right, Gabe. I'm on my way.*

"A friend." I flipped my datpilot shut with a practiced flip of my wrist. "Let's have breakfast. Then I've got a transport to catch."

3

I waited until after breakfast—the curry was fantastic, searing hot over fluffy rice, washed down with more of the fragrant coffee and plenty of ice water. The shake also took the edge of hunger away, leaving me feeling a bit more solid. I had the standard doses of tazapram in my bag, but my stomach had seemed to get even stronger as a *hedaira*. If it was edible, it mostly looked good to me; I wondered if there was anything I *couldn't* eat. Most Necromances had cast-iron guts anyway, funny for a bunch of twitchy, neurotic prima donnas.

Oddly enough, it reminded me of Emilio, the round Novo Taliano cook at our house in Toscano. He used to beg me to eat, considering it an insult if I didn't consume as many k-cals as he deemed appropriate on a daily basis. When I thought of our house, I thought of Emilio, his pudgy hands waving; he was one of the few normals who didn't seem to fear me at all. He seemed to view me as a pretty and pampered but not-too-bright daughter of a rich family, who had to be bullied and petted into eating properly. It should have irritated me, but *damn* the man could cook.

The meal was quiet. Japhrimel drank a glass of silty

red wine, probably more out of politeness than anything else. Lucas didn't ask any more questions about my little message, and I spent the time thinking of how to break the news to Japhrimel.

I didn't think he'd take it calmly. Besides, there were a couple of things we still had to sort out. Like what the hell the Key was, and what the bloody blue hell was going on *now*.

After breakfast—which Japhrimel paid for, as usual— Lucas excused himself to go upstairs and catch some sleep. And probably to give me a chance to talk to Japh, since I'd been monosyllabic all through the meal. I stared at my coffee glass and tried to think of the right words.

Japhrimel waited, his eyes scorching green. Normals didn't seem to notice he wasn't human. Other psions could see the black-diamond flames twisting through his aura, and could call him what he was. Demon.

Only not quite demon. *A'nankhimel,* Fallen.

His fingers played with the wineglass, the long dark Chinese-collared coat as wetly black as the lacquer urn I'd once kept his ashes in. I drew in a deep breath, gathered my courage, and opened my mouth.

"Japh, I have to go to Saint City. I just got a message from Gabe. She needs me."

Japhrimel absorbed this, staring into his wineglass. Said nothing.

I took another gulp of coffee. I really wasn't doing service to it, swilling it like cheap freeze-dried. But I was nervous. "Japhrimel?"

"The Necromance." Faintly dismissive, as if reminding himself. "With the dirtwitch mate."

I swallowed roughly. "She's my friend. And she

says she needs me, it's an emergency. Everything else is going to have to wait." *Including Lucifer. Especially Lucifer.*

His eyes half-lidded. The look was deceptively languid, but the mark on my shoulder turned hot and aching under his attention. His hair fell over his forehead, softly, my fingers itched to brush the inky strands. Trace down his cheek like I'd done before, maybe run my fingertip across the border of his lips while he submitted to my touch, his eyes darkening for just a moment.

Stop it. You've still got a few questions to answer, Japh. Like what the hell's going on. Explanations, remember?

But still . . . *One day,* Lucifer had said as I crouched, my throat on fire and my belly running with pain, *I will kill her.*

Not while I watch over her, Japhrimel had replied.

The more I thought about it, the more it seemed like a declaration of war. I wasn't sure how I felt about that, except gratefulness that I was still alive.

"I'm catching the first transport I can," I told him. "I'm going back to Saint City. You can come with me if you want, but not before you explain everything to me. In detail. Leaving nothing out. Clear?"

He took another sip of wine. His eyes burned. A soft weight of Power folded around me, eased against my skin as if he had wrapped me in Putchkin synthfur. "You swore allegiance to the Prince as his Right Hand. You have four demons to hunt, *hedaira.*"

I winced. *Well, it's now or never, I suppose.* "I won't hunt Eve, Japhrimel."

A single shrug. I was beginning to hate the way demons

shrug all the goddamn time. I suppose most of what humans do deserves no more than a shrug—but still.

I struggled with a sharp bite of irritation, took another swallow of coffee. "I mean it. I promised Doreen I'd *save* Eve; I won't hunt her. And I was bamboozled into this Right Hand thing, fine—but my promise to Doreen predates my promise to Lucifer. He can . . . ." *He can go to hell,* I meant to say, realized how absurd it was and swallowed the rest of the sentence. "It's not like it matters," I continued, bitterly, forgetting to pitch my voice low and soft. The cups rattled on the table. "He's sent others to hunt her down. I'm just another game piece."

Not to mention the fact that Eve asked me not to look too hard for her. Simply asked. No manipulation, no lying, no trying to twist me into a game I'm bound to lose. I had to admit she was the demon I was most likely to feel good about helping.

He set his wineglass down and laid his hand over my left wrist. Incredibly gentle, his warm skin against mine; he could have crushed the small bones if he'd wanted to. Instead, his thumb stroked the soft underside of my wrist. Fire spilled up my arm, through my shoulder, made the mark burn again. I had to catch my breath, biting the inside of my cheek savagely. The pain reminded me again I was a Necromance, that I didn't respond sexually to Power.

Though I'd responded to Eve, hadn't I? And Japhrimel knew me, we'd shared a bed for a long time. It's hard to fight someone who knows your body that intimately.

"You are not simply a game piece, Dante. You are my *hedaira,* and you must trust me to do what you cannot."

What the hell does that mean? "What does that mean?" I cast a quick glance around—the garden was empty, the waitress leaning in an arched doorway and exchanging soft laughter with an invisible someone I guessed was the cook. The pilot folded his newspaper, tucked it under his arm, and tapped at his datband to pay his bill.

Japhrimel smiled. It was a sad smile, his eyes flaring with laser-green intensity; another human expression. There was a time I would have been glad to see any feeling on his face, especially his rare smiles. But this expression made cold prickles ripple down my back. I don't get goosebumps, but it felt awfully close. The breeze from the garden filled my nose with green sweetness, overlaid with demon musk. "What you cannot do, I will. Don't trouble yourself. It is, after all, what I am meant for."

After facing down the Devil, I never thought I'd be frightened of anything else again. I was wrong. I stared at him, my pulse beating thinly in my throat. When I could speak, it was no more than a strangled whisper. "You leave her alone. I swear, Japhrimel, if you—"

"Do not." His voice cut through mine, he shook his head. "You know better than to swear such an oath. You must live to your word, Necromance."

I tore my wrist out from under his hand. He let me. I rocketed to my feet, the chair scraping along tiled floor, my sword in my left hand. My fingers tightened on the scabbard. Our waitress stiffened, looking back over her shoulder, the dark sheaf of her ponytail contrasting with the cotton of her shirt.

I leaned forward, my hair falling over my shoulders, inkblack as his. "Don't push me on this, Japh. That's Doreen's daughter." My tone, flat and cold, rattled the entire table. It might be an empty threat—he was, after all, so much stronger and faster than me, and had proved it too many times.

But by my god and my sword, I didn't care. She was Doreen's daughter, most of all. But maybe she was mine too. If she was, it was my job to protect her. My *duty* to protect her.

He had nothing to say to that. I straightened. My bag lay heavy against my hip, I still had my guns and my knives. And my sword, the blade that bit the Devil.

I wasn't able to hurt Japhrimel, not in a fair fight—but if he killed Doreen's daughter or tried to return her to the Prince of Hell we were going to see just how sneaky and inventive I could get when facing down a demon.

A Fallen demon. A man I happened to love, even if he wasn't strictly a man. Wasn't it less than an hour ago I'd promised myself I would give him the benefit of the doubt?

"I swear it, Japh." My right hand closed around my sword hilt. He was too damnably quick—I knew from sparring with him. Even though he sat at the table, looking down at his wineglass, I still felt the nervous urge to back up, get some distance in case he decided to move on me. "By all I hold holy, I *will*."

A fluid shrug. He rose slowly to his feet, his chair scraping more quietly than mine had. "What is it you want me to say?"

I don't know. "I'm going. With or without you, I'm *going.*" *Goddammit, Danny, he dangled you up against a wall once before. You keep pushing him, he's going to do it again. Or worse.*

"You will not leave my side until this matter is finished. I thought I explained as much in words even you could understand." How could he sound so calm? As if it didn't matter what I said or did, he had spoken and that was that. A breeze drifted through the garden outside, filled the café suddenly with the scent of growing things and the cinnamon-musk of demons; it was the psychic equivalent of static, dyeing the air around us both. I was radiating again. If I wasn't careful I would start affecting the sloe-eyed waitress and any other human in the place, flooding them with pheromones I couldn't fully control.

I tensed, my left thumb ready to click the blade free of the scabbard. Eyed Japhrimel. *Don't push me. We were just doing so well; don't push me on this.*

His gaze moved over me, from the top of my tangled black hair down to my scuffed boots, the loose easy stance I dropped into, though I didn't draw just yet. "Ever a battle, *hedaira*," he said quietly. "I will go with you, to see what has befallen your fellow Necromance."

Thank you, gods. Thank you. My breath came harsh and hot. I stared at him. "You mean it?"

Did I imagine the shadow of pain that slid over his face? Probably. "I prefer you where I may see the mischief you intend. I see no reason why we may not stop in Santiago City."

I couldn't help myself. "Really?"

He moved, a single step. Another. Closer, but he didn't look at me. Instead, he looked over my shoulder. His fingers closed around my right hand, the sword kept home in the sheath. "Save your blade for your enemies, *hedaira*."

I do. Oh, I do. Closed my lips over the words. "Japhrimel?"

"What?" He still looked over my shoulder, a muscle flicked in his golden cheek. As if he expected me to yell at him, maybe. His fingers slid up my arm, cupped my shoulder, tightened but didn't hurt me. I swallowed dryly. He was so close the heat of him blurred through my clothes, less intense than the sun outside but scorching nonetheless.

"Explanations. Remember?" *This is going too well. We're going to hit a hitch soon.*

He still didn't look at me. "When we are finished with your business in Santiago City, I will give you all the explanations you are ready to hear."

Goddammit, Japh. I knew you were being too reasonable. "You promised." I heard the hurt in my voice, couldn't help myself.

"You accepted a bargain with the Prince. That is a promise too."

"It's not the same thing." *It's not. Goddammit, you know it's not.*

He switched tactics. "What did the Androgyne tell you, Dante? She is *in rebellion,* she has no hope of winning. I will not allow you to be dragged down with her." He waited for me to speak. When I didn't, he tried again. "What did she say to make you so stubborn?"

I set my jaw. *I knew you'd ask sooner or later.* Said nothing.

His fingers tensed, hard iron against my skin. "Dante? Tell me what she said to you."

Silly me. I should have known. "Does it fucking matter? You aren't going to explain anything to me. *You* make promises you never intend to keep." The words were flat, final, and terribly sad. *Am I really standing here in the middle of a Cairo Giza café, trying to persuade a demon to explain something to me? How do I get myself into these things?*

"Tell me what the created Androgyne said to you, Dante." Did he sound *pleading?* It couldn't be. Japhrimel had never begged *me* for anything. "What did she tell you? What did you *believe* of what she told you?"

I believed enough. My arm ached, his fingers tense and hard, digging into my flesh. I looked down, the tiles on the floor melting together as my eyes unfocused. It was an old trick, learned back in primary school—if I unfocused my eyes and let the roaring fill my ears, whatever happened to the rest of me wouldn't matter. It didn't work if the physical pain reached a certain level, but short of that. . . .

Japhrimel's fingers loosened. I still felt his hand—if I was still human I might have been bruised. It was so unlike him. He was normally so exquisitely careful not to hurt me. *What does it matter what she told me, Japh?*

"Dante." His tone was quiet, dark with something too angry to be hurt. "You *will* speak of it, sooner or later. You cannot hide from me."

I took a sharp shuddering breath. The café was utterly still. I wondered if the waitress was staring at us or if she had decided to retreat to the kitchen. "I need a transport out of here as soon as possible." It took work to keep my voice level, not weak but quiet. *I'm not backing down on this one, Japh. Do your worst.*

"As you like." He stepped away, dismissing me. "Leave it to me. I suggest you rest."

The scar in the hollow of my left shoulder throbbed. *I don't care. He can do whatever he likes, what happened between me and Eve is private. It's none of his business.*

What I did next surprised me. I caught his arm, the sleeve of his long dark coat—I knew what it was made of, and it hadn't bothered me for a long time. I tensed my fingers, clawtips sliding free to prick the lacquered material. I squeezed as hard as I could, in turn. It probably didn't

matter, I wasn't able to hurt *him*. "You hurt me. Again."
Gods, I sound like a whining little girl. But it's true. "You
promised you wouldn't."

I was looking at his boots, so I missed whatever expression that produced.

"Do you truly think I would harm you?" He tore his
arm out of my fingers, the material of his coat slick against
my fingers. It was wings masquerading as clothing; he was
literally of the Greater Flight of demons. He could have
killed me without even trying.

*How do we define "harm," Japhrimel? I'm not bleeding
or dead, so I'm fine? Is that it?* "Fine." I turned on my heel,
headed for the stairs up to the rooms Leander had rented.

I barely saw the stairs through the welling water in my
eyes. But I blinked it away. Crying wouldn't do any good.

4

"You're what?" The emerald on Leander Beaudry's cheek sparked, the thorny yin-yang accreditation tat on his left cheek twisting under the skin. My own cheek burned, my gem answering his in greeting.

"I've got some business in Saint City." I dropped down in a lyre-backed, overstuffed maroon chair and stared at the room. Japhrimel was downstairs with Vann, making arrangements for us to blow this town. "Getting on the next transport. I'm putting the hunt on hold for a while." *For as long as I possibly can. Thank you, Gabe.*

Lying cheek-by-jowl with the throbbing ache in my scarred shoulder was a new, unsteady panic. Gabe wouldn't call me like this unless it was dire. She wouldn't have sent that particular message unless it was a personal matter instead of another job for the Saint City PD. *That* added up to only a few possible scenarios: revenge, a bloody personal bounty, or *bad* trouble.

Add yet another layer of welling mistrust about Japhrimel's motives, and I was bound to be a nervous wreck before long. He'd given in too easily. *Far* too easily. I'd expected a full-out fight instead of just an aching shoulder and verbal fencing over whether or not I was "hurt."

"What's the business in Saint City?" Leander pushed his hand back through his dark hair.

I squashed a flare of irritation. It wasn't an unreasonable question—after all, he'd signed on to the hunt after spending a lot of Power after that hover incident in Freetown New Prague. Then he'd come to Giza and started making arrangements for further hunting. He was a good Necromance if what I'd read about him was true, and he seemed honorable. Plus he was a bounty hunter, which meant he could probably handle himself in any normal situation.

Too bad nothing about this was normal.

And he's human. I squashed that thought too, sent it packing.

It refused to go quietly.

I sank into the chair. Gravity suddenly weighed down every inch of my skin. "A debt to an old friend. She's called for my help."

He studied me for a few moments, leaning back in his chair with his long legs stretched out, his katana laid across his lap. For a moment he reminded me of someone, though I couldn't think of quite who.

The room was large and airy, containment fields humming over tall windows. Red tile decorated the plaster walls, heavy low furniture sat obediently in prearranged places; through a half-open door I saw the edge of a bed swathed in mosquito netting. Another bedroom door was closed—Lucas, getting some shut-eye. McKinley was nowhere in sight, and I was grateful for that. The black-clad

Hellesvront agent with his oddly metallic left hand made me uneasy.

"And?" Leander's eyebrows raised.

I've got to go. Not only that, but I've got to figure out a way to keep Japhrimel occupied so Eve can . . . what? What is she doing? I hope she has some kind of plan. "I don't know the specifics." I strangled another hot welling of irritation. "She's called, she'll tell me what she needs when I get there. It's that simple."

He absorbed this. "Your friends are lucky. Not many people would fly halfway around the world just on the strength of a phone call."

"It was a datpilot message." I leaned my head back into the chair's embrace, closing my eyes. "I made a promise. That's a magickal law, isn't it? *Thy word is thy bond.*"

I could tell by his faint exhaled laugh he recognized the quotation—attributed to Saint Crowley the Magi, no less, though it didn't sound much like the treatises I'd read. I wish someone would tell my bounties that." The wryness of the comment matched the dry humor in his tone. "Well, it's Saint City then. All right."

And that, apparently, was that. I let one eye drift open just a crack. "You're not required to come along."

He shrugged. A human shrug—it didn't irritate me the way it did when Japhrimel gave one of his evocative noncommittal movements. "Call it my curiosity. I've got some time."

"Might not be too healthy to hang around. People have a distressing habit of dying around me." *You're human. Fragile. Or at least, more fragile than I am, and I'm not doing too well when it comes to facing down demons and the like. When did my life get so freaking dangerous?*

I'd never considered forgoing combat training and hunting bounties. Freelance law enforcement had always seemed the only possible route for me; Jace had taught me about mercenary work and corporate espionage when I'd been desperate for cash after my Academy training and a few years in the field. It had only been a small step—I was, after all, familiar with the idea of fighting.

What you cannot escape, you must fight; what you cannot fight, you must endure. Life was dangerous in and of itself, I was privileged to know the fact from a young age.

It meant I wasn't as nastily surprised as I got older.

"I'm a Necromance." His tone managed to convey disdain and excessive neutrality in one pretty package. In other words, *Death's my trade too, kid.*

Yeah, but I'm tougher than you and I'm having trouble keeping myself together here. Do I really want to be looking out for you? "Me too." An unfamiliar smile spread over my face. It's rare to find a Necromance I enjoy talking to; we're such a bunch of neurotics. Using Power and psionic talent means most of us have distinctly odd personalities as well as a fair helping of *Schadenfreude,* and dealing with Death like we're trained to will make even the most courageous human paranoid on one hand and adrenaline-addicted on the other.

Case in point? John Fairlane, the other Necromance left in Saint City besides Gabe. I couldn't stand Fairlane; his white linen suits and pretentious lisp drove me up the wall. The feeling was most emphatically mutual. Two Necromances in the same room usually ended up with either a catfight or a pissing match. "You know what? You're all right."

"Thanks. That means something, coming from you." Dry, ironic, and amused. He had a nice voice.

That won a tired giggle from me. His own laugh was warm caramel, the air suddenly relaxing between us. On the ebb of that laughter, Japhrimel entered the room and I heard the door close softly. The silent static of anger—*his* anger—touched me, made the mark on my shoulder turn hot and soft.

I wasn't ready for that. I'd expect the mark to hurt when he was mad at me. It had certainly hurt plenty before, usually when I was already in dire trouble and sinking fast.

My eyes flew open. I turned my head to see him standing by the door, his hands clasped behind his back as usual. "The next transport for a hub leaves past midnight," he said. "We can be in Paradisse by late morning, North New York by the following nightfall, and Santiago City by the next afternoon. Slow, but more efficient than layovers."

Too slow, Gabe needs me now. "What about the hover Lucas had? That would be faster."

He shrugged. The crackle of anger around him hadn't abated. What did *he* have to be upset about? "Vann has already taken it."

The faint, precious good humor I'd been feeling drained away. "Why?"

"To convince the Prince we are hunting in good faith instead of following your whim." His voice was a little harsher than its usual even irony. "I suggest you rest, Dante. We will not leave until tonight."

I would have liked to settle down in a bed and do some heavy brooding, but being ordered to do it took all the fun away. Instead, my eyes swung over to Leander, whose hand was just a little too tight on his katana. He was muscle-ropy and probably deadly with his blade, but I wasn't quite human anymore. My strength and speed were closer to a demon's—though not close enough.

Not *nearly* close enough for what I had to do.

"Well, I'm here in Cairo Giza and there's a couple hours to kill before we can catch transport. It'd be a shame to miss the Great Souk. I can probably even pick up a little something for Gabe." I stretched, yawned, and made it to my feet. "Hey, boy, this is your town. You want to show me around?"

"Happy to." Leander turned his own leaning-forward into a graceful movement bringing him up to his feet. "You've never seen the Souk? You're in for a treat."

"Good. Guess the day's not going to be a total loss, then." Was it just me or did my cheerfulness sound forced?

Then again, *cheerful* didn't seem to be on the menu lately. Here I was about to go running back to Saint City, to a disaster in progress. Lucifer would be breathing down my neck soon. I was under contract to the Devil himself to hunt the escaped demons down, which meant I had to think of some way to keep Japhrimel away from Eve for the length of that contract—a cool seven years of fun and games.

And Japhrimel was hiding some new nasty surprise from me, not to mention making it eloquently clear I was by far the weaker half of our partnership. There was a time I'd thought I'd learned to know him, when I'd thought nothing could break the bond between us—but all that crashed down when Lucifer started poking his nose in my life again.

I glanced down at the metal cuff on my left wrist. The space for my arm to slip free *had* narrowed, or maybe my wrist had gotten bigger. The Gauntlet's fluidly-etched lines weren't glowing green, but the feel of the warm metal against my skin suddenly turned my stomach. The feeling of being watched returned, my nape prickling.

You don't survive as a bounty hunter by ignoring that feeling.

Well, we can start fixing what's wrong right here. I shoved my sword into the handy loop on my rig and dug my fingers in, curling them around the metal, twisting. It didn't want to let go of my skin but I pried it loose, finding that I *could* just squeeze my wrist through the slim opening.

I stuffed the heavy barbaric silver in my bag, and looked up to find a demon and a Necromance both staring at me.

"Let's go." I almost hoped Japhrimel would stay behind, the faint line between his eyebrows and slight downward tilt to the corners of his mouth told me he wasn't pleased at all. My pulse pounded thinly in my throat, fear and sharp defiance mixing.

You can't control me, Japh. I love you, and you're stronger than me—but I won't let you win.

When I followed Leander out the door, Japh was right behind me, the weight of his disapproval a stone in my throat.

The Great Souk of Cairo Giza seethes under fierce sun, dust and sand drifting on a vast rectangular stone plaza glowered over by plasteel-reinforced mudbrick buildings. Climate control and the floating shadows of hovers in parking patterns overhead provide some relief from the heat, but not much. Plenty of the Souk hasn't changed in hundreds of years. Vast baskets of dates, figs, and other delicacies; whole hanging sides of slaughtered animals—I shuddered to see those, but even in Saint City they still have fresh meat—with stasis fields humming to keep the flies away, children laughing and playing among the shifting crowds, professional pickpockets and thieves scamming through the tide of humanity, every conceivable merchandise on display.

You can get just about anything in the Souk, from vat-grown diamonds to legitimate indentured servants to not-so-legitimate slaves—though that trade is relegated to back alleys and in perennial danger of Hegemony police coming through and cleaning them out. You can buy drugs, augments, or enzyme treatments; the *sedayeen* communes have open-air clinics and biolabs, and Skinlin sell herbal remedies. A Ceremonial or Magi can do a quickshield or tell a fortune. There are even paranormals who have their own booths—swanhilds run messages, werecain sell bright woven rugs or rent out as protection duty. And plenty more.

There's an advantage to being sandwiched between a demon and a Necromance in a crowd, you do get a certain amount of space. The Egyptianos seemed less likely than other normals to look askance at my tat and Leander's; they didn't seem to have much of the fear of psions I'd seen in other parts of the world. Japhrimel looked normal, but the breath of *alienness* he carried seemed to communicate itself to them more readily and he was given more strange looks than either of us psions. Maybe it was the long black Chinese-collared coat in the heat, or his straight face, or maybe it was the way he loomed behind me.

I won't admit to uncritical delight, but I will admit to feeling a lot better than I had in a long time. Haggling was the rule here. It took only a few times of watching Leander artfully bargain in pidgin Merican before I got an idea of the going prices, and soon I was munching on the dates he'd bought while fiercely arguing down the price of a pair of beautiful Erabic daggers. They were the finest in the stall, perfectly balanced for throwing—and metal that doesn't need to be filed down for throwing is a rarity indeed. Their hilts were dark wood, plain and serviceable, but the shape of the blades and their balance made them works of art.

We finished bargaining, I paid the man with New Credit notes and stuffed my thinning bankroll back into my bag. The keepcharm on my bag bristled—not many quick fingers would try a Necromance's bag, but you never know. I accepted the knives from the hawk-faced stall proprietor, who bowed, touching his forehead with his right hand and crying out his praise. I must have been smiling, because Leander gave me a curious look. "You do that like you've lived here for years." He handed me another date.

If you only knew how much time I've spent haggling around the world. "I'm a quick study. Is there statuary here?"

"Down on the west side; take us a while to get there." We pushed back out into the milling mass of people come to buy or sell. An iceseller's traditional plaintive cry split through the noise, a bright thread drawn through the dark surfroar. "Want to go through Jeweler's Alley, and then the rugs?" Leander shouted over the crowd noise, dark eyes dancing. I wrapped the two sheathed knives together and put them in my bag as well.

"Lead the way!" I shouted back. I normally don't like crowds—the messy overspill of emotion from each normal presses against a psion's shields, takes energy to push away. But I was enjoying this. For the first time since hearing that Lucifer wanted to see me again, I was almost content.

Except for the nagging worry about what trouble Gabe had landed in. And the nervous sense of being watched, of disaster hanging just around the corner.

Japhrimel followed as we made our way through the dappled shadows of hovertraffic. I checked the sky more than usual—getting hit with a few hovers will make a girl nervous—and took in the kaleidoscope of sound, color, and throbbing Power that was the Souk.

If I'd still been human I would have been acclimatizing to the different flow of organic energy here. But being almost-demon meant my body had taken to this new sea of Power within seconds. Here in Cairo Giza the pyramids were sonorous bass notes at the very edge of psychic "hearing," throbbing against bones and viscera like a subsonic beat. The well of Power tasted like sand and spice with the faint heavy odor of animals from the pens on the outskirts, goats and camels mostly. Add the heavy spiced langorousness from the coffee, and it was a heady brew indeed.

Maybe that was why I let Leander buy the bag of candied almonds. We shared them out under the overhang of a rugseller's tent, and even Japhrimel took a handful when I pressed them on him, his skin warm and dry and his face still and set.

A thin trickle of sweat kissed Leander's pale temple,

and I sipped from one of the bottles of *limonada* I'd bought while Leander cracked his open with a practiced twist. The jewelryseller's alley glittered under the sun, gold and silver and gems, both vat-grown and natural, flashed.

I was suddenly fiercely glad I was a Necromance. Most normals never get the chance to see more than a little slice of the world; I'd been all over and was even now standing in the Great Souk, something I'd seen in holovids and mags but never thought I'd get around to experiencing for myself. It must have shown in my face.

Must have? Well, I was grinning like a fool. Any minute all hell might break loose, between Lucifer, Japhrimel, and whatever was going down in Saint City; but for right now I was actually—was I happy?

I guess so. Gabe must be right about credit therapy. "Shopping is the perfect antidote, Danny. Just remember that."

Thinking of Gabe, I sobered. But I still felt my cheeks swell with the smile.

"Like it?" Leander asked.

"It's something." Was I being idiotic? The mark on my left shoulder burned, sending waves of Power through me like heatshimmer above pavement. I tried not to feel it, tried to forget the way my shoulder still twinged every now and again with Japhrimel's attention. "It's really something."

"Nothing like it on earth," was his easy reply.

"Ever been to Moscow?" I tried again to banish the smile from my face, failed.

"Yep. Did some work there for the Putchkin Politburov, and some less-legal stuff for the Tzarchov Family.

You been to Freetown Emsterdamme?" He swiped at his forehead with the *limonada* bottle, condensation gleaming on his skin.

"Took down a bounty there once. Great light, they still have the tulip fields instead of clonetanks. What about Free Territorie Suisse?"

"Oh, yeah. On vacation though, no work. The Islands?"

"Which ones?" A cool breeze brushed my naked wrist without the weight of the bracelet, I wondered why I felt so vulnerable without it. The sense of being watched had faded, but still prickled at the corners of my awareness.

"Let's say Freetown Domenihaiti. I spent a year at the Shaman college out there, they've got this amazing vaudun festival."

"Been there. What about the Great Wall? I had a bounty run all that way." The memory didn't hurt that much now, oddly enough. That job had almost killed me.

"You hunted down Siddie Gregors out that way. Even the steppe couldn't hide that motherfucker." He sounded complacent and awed at once.

I laughed. So he knew about the Gregors bounty. "I used to have a scar." I lifted up my left wrist. "From here—" Touched my inner elbow. "To here." Indicated my wrist. "A plasilica knife. Had to get patched up by an Asiano Yangtze doctor. Foulest-smelling herb paste I ever had smeared on me, but it healed up like a dream and even the scar went away after a couple of years. Gregors was a real bastard, I didn't sleep the whole time I was bringing her in."

"I did this bounty in Shanghai once—"

The conversation went on like this for a while, swapping

stories as we moved down Jeweler's Alley. We stopped for quite some time at a booth with rings, I looked over their glitter spread over scruffy black velvet. I'd bought my rings one at a time from ethnic shops in Saint City's Tank District, but I'd dearly love to have a memento of this. Something for Gabe would be nice too.

I took my time, sipping at *limonada* and exchanging yet more stories with Leander. Finally, I selected a dainty cascading silver fire-opal bracelet for Gabe, but didn't see anything for myself. I paid for the bracelet with no haggling—it was a gift—and spotted something else.

I hadn't seen it before, which was odd in and of itself. The piece was even odder, a short delicate spun-platinum chain holding a star sapphire the size of my thumb from distal joint to tip, glittering mellowly in the afternoon light. It was plain, restrained, and cried out to me with its own tongueless voice.

I pointed. "There. That one."

Again, I paid without haggling, explaining to the woman running the stall that it was a gift and I couldn't bargain for gifts. She dropped the price by twenty credits when I told her that, and I paid with my datband—she had an old-fashioned creditswipe. The necklace and bracelet went carefully wrapped into my bag as well, and I looked up to find Leander examining me again. "I'm done," I said. "Thanks."

"It's a pleasure," he replied, and we plunged into the crowd again. I had almost forgotten Japhrimel, he was so silent behind me. I looked over my shoulder a few times to find him thoughtfully looking at something else each time. Was he bored as well as angry? What the hell did *he* have to be angry about? I was the one he manhandled.

I wondered if he was enjoying himself. It didn't seem likely.

That's a real shame, I thought, but then Leander started telling me about the Souk's history, and I listened, fascinated, as we drifted with the crowd until dusk started to paint the sky.

5

I dropped down to sit on the bed, laying my sword aside and wriggling my toes with relief. It was nice to be out of my boots; I wasn't footsore from wandering through the stone-floored bazaar, but it was close. Japhrimel closed the door, his golden hand spread against it for a moment and his head bowed.

"Japh?" I dug in my bag. "Hey."

He didn't move. Stood with his head down, his eyes closed, leaning his entire weight against his hand on the door. His shoulders slumped, as if he was tired.

"Japhrimel?" I saw no complex twisting of Power that would tell me he was performing a work of magick. Saw nothing but the same black-diamond glitter of his aura, hard and impenetrable, shouting his essential difference. He was demon, he wasn't human.

I'd almost forgotten that, before. *Never again,* I promised myself. Still . . . I couldn't help trying to get through to him. I was an idiot.

For him, I seemed to be nothing but.

He looked back over his shoulder, his face arranged in

its usual ironic mask and his shoulders coming back up to their accustomed straight line. "You should rest, Dante."

"Come on over." I patted the bed next to me. Plasilica whispered as I lowered the bag with my most important purchase in it to the floor. I'd bought another small statue of Anubis to replace the one I'd lost, this one easily able to fit in my palm and carved out of a single chunk of black marble veined with gold. The other thing that mattered— the statue of Sekhmet, repaired with infinite care—sat on the bedstand, glassy obsidian glowing mellow. "Please?"

He crossed the room slowly, lowered himself down. The bed creaked. I finished digging in my messenger bag, easing the strap over my head and settling the bag itself on my other side with a sigh. Carrying the damn thing never got any easier.

"Close your eyes." The remains of my good mood and the excitement of the Souk made me smile. *I'll just try this one more time.*

He studied my face for a long few moments before complying.

I undid the clasp and leaned close, my bag clinking as it slid against the bed. Then I settled the sapphire against his coat and fiddled with the clasp, my fingers suddenly clumsy. It took a little while, and when I retreated I found he'd opened his eyes. He looked at me like I'd just done something extraordinary.

"There." I felt very pleased with myself. "I think it suits you."

He said nothing.

A little bit of the good mood slipped away. Then a little more. He examined my face, his eyes moving from my forehead to my mouth to my cheeks to my chin to my eyes and then repeating the process again.

Great. He doesn't like it. He probably doesn't like me very much either right now. If he'd just listen *to me.*

Shame rose inside me. Rebuffed by a demon, a new low even in my dating life. "If you don't like it, I—"

"No." He set his jaw. "It's beautiful, Dante. Thank you."

He didn't sound thankful. He sounded flat, and a little amused, and terribly furious. I wondered if he was going to hurt me again, and kept my hands in view. He could move with eerie blurring demon speed, but I might still have a little warning if he decided to get nasty with me again.

It didn't take much sometimes to tell what he was feeling—you only had to look closely enough to see the tiny changes, a millimeter's quirk to the eyebrow, a fractional lift of a corner of his mouth, a slight flaring of one elegant nostril. The ever-so-tiny lift of one shoulder. I used to think he wasn't as beautiful as Lucifer, used to think he just looked blandly normal.

Well, Dante, you were wrong on that one.

My chest was on fire, a pain that wasn't from any physical wound lying against my heart. *Why does this hurt so much?* "You don't sound happy." I was too tired to keep the hurt out of my voice. "Did I just violate some arcane demon protocol by giving you a present?"

He shook his head. I waited, got nothing else.

"Fine." I turned away, grabbed my bag's strap and my sword, and slid off the bed. Padded around to the other side, then dropped down and stretched out, wiggling my bare toes and almost groaning as comfort closed around me. My bag settled against my stomach, I clasped my sword in my hands. "Take it off and burn it if you don't like it. I don't care." *After all, you held me up against a wall and lied to me. You're a bastard.*

Why can't I hate you?

Long pause. Silence ticked through the room, only slightly marred by hovertraffic and desert wind outside, the call of a candyseller on the corner, the humming of the containment field over the window. Mosquito netting on the bed, pulled aside, swayed on the breeze. I saw a corner of a chair and a slice of plaster wall before tears blurred my vision and I closed my eyes.

"What would you have me do?" Japhrimel's voice, surprisingly, was raw and hoarse. Probably with fury.

It took a few swallows before I could reply through the stone in my throat. "Give a little," I managed. "Tell me what's going on. Don't lie to me. Quit manhandling me when I don't do what you want. And for the sake of every god that ever was, quit being so . . . so—"

"Inhuman? Is that the word?" Terrible sadness weighted his tone. "How many times must I tell you that I will act to protect you; I will not bother you with trifles? You need only obey my requests, Dante, and this will be easier."

Obey? Are you going to start beating me like a pimp beats his favorite hooker? "Don't hunt Eve." My voice was muffled, I pressed my left hand against my mouth. "Please. If you ever cared about me at all, *don't* do it." *I'll do anything you want, Japh, just leave Doreen's little girl alone. Hurt me if you have to, but leave her alone.*

"I will not risk you in a rebellion doomed to failure. The Androgyne is young, untested. She *cannot win,* Dante. I will not lose you to her foolishness. Why will you not understand?"

The injustice rose to choke me. I swallowed it, tried

again. "You don't have to declare yourself on her side. We can look anywhere in the world for her, Japh. We just don't look too *hard*. In seven years the contract's over, we're free, and you—"

His voice drained all the warmth from the room, made the air stir uneasily. "How *free* do you think the Prince will leave us if these four are not caught and brought to his justice? It is a choice between them and us. They will die, or we will. And if *she* has clouded your head with some appeal or treachery, it becomes my task to save you from yourself."

Silence. Soughing of the wind as it rose at dusk, the sun sinking below the arc of the horizon and night reaching up to fold ageless desert and ancient city in its embrace.

"You want to save me from myself, and you'll hurt me if I don't do what you want. Is that it?" I swallowed dryly. Tensed myself, waited for him to explode.

"I am sorry. I am a fool." Well, chalk it up to a miracle, he *sounded* sorry for once. "I do not mean to hurt you. You do not understand, and it frustrates me past all reason when you will not listen—will not *see*. When the escaped are brought to Lucifer's justice, you may extract whatever penance you desire from me. Until then, we are at *war*. It is *us* or it is *them*, and I will not have it be us."

"It's not a choice between them and us, Tierce Japhrimel." It was my turn to sound sad. "It's your choice between me and Lucifer." A bitter laugh rose up in me, was savagely repressed, escaped anyway. "Guess I know where your real loyalty lies."

"If it pleases you, continue to think so." He rose, the bed creaking slightly as his weight moved. "When this is finished, I will ask an apology for that accusation."

You might get one, if we can hash this out between now and then. If we have time, between whatever's going down with Gabe and whatever Lucifer's cooking up next. I would have cursed, but he closed the door to the bedroom before I could. I clamped my left hand around my katana's scabbard, the right around the hilt, and settled down to brood before we had to catch the transport. The tears dried up, leaving my eyes dry and hot, scoured by a whole desert's worth of sand.

6

I hate traveling transport, and my recent experiences with hovers falling on me hadn't cured me of it. It was with profound relief that I stepped onto the concrete dock under a familiar plasilica dome and filled my lungs with soupy chemical-laden tang, the familiar cold radioactive glow of Saint City's power well rising to greet me.

Goddamn, it's good to be home. The thought surprised me; I'd never considered the place *home* before. Never thought about what *home* would feel like.

Lucas jostled me from behind, Leander sighing as he worked the kinks out of his neck. "Damn transports," the Necromance said, and I felt sneakingly glad my own claustrophobia was shared by at least one member of our little troupe.

I looked over my shoulder. To the side, Japhrimel murmured to McKinley, who had showed up on the transport dock at midnight in Cairo, along with Tiens. The Nichtvren left to help Vann with whatever errand Japhrimel had sent him on, and the black-clad Hellesvront agent had boarded the transport with us. I didn't like that. The man—if you could call either Vann or McKinley a "man"—made me nervous. The oddly silver metallic coating on his left hand puzzled me too. I still didn't have the faintest idea what the Hellesvront agents were, precisely, but they were part of the net of financial and other assets the demons had in place on earth. Vann had said something about "vassals." Maybe they were organized into a feudal system, like some federated Freetowns.

Which meant that Vann and McKinley were loyal to Japhrimel—if they weren't exclusively loyal to Lucifer. Either way, neither of them was likely to be any help to me, or to give me any information. The Nichtvren didn't seem very likely to help me either.

Which left me with Lucas, Leander, and my own wits. Put that way, I seemed damn near rich. The Deathless and another Necromance were far from the worst backup I could have.

Don't say that, Danny. You're dealing with demons. All the backup in the world might not be enough.

As I watched, McKinley nodded and set off for the other end of the dock, apparently given his marching orders. Japhrimel watched him for a moment, but the mark on my shoulder was alive with heat. No matter that he was looking the other way, Japh's attention was all on me.

I wasn't quite sure how I felt about that. "Lucas?"

"Huh?" His whispering, painful voice barely reached through the sound of people disembarking. The North New York–Saint City transport run was a full one since both cities were hubs. That hadn't stopped us from having a whole first-class compartment to ourselves all the way from Cairo. Maybe Japhrimel had arranged for that, I didn't know.

Didn't care, either.

"Two things," I said out of the corner of my mouth.

"Find out what Japhrimel's business in Saint City is, and tell Abra I'll be coming by to see her. Good?"

"You got it." He detached himself from us and melted into the crowd. It was a relief to have a professional in my corner. Whatever Japh was up to, Lucas was my best bet of finding out sooner rather than later.

Leander raised an eyebrow as Japhrimel approached us, threading through a string of disembarking normals who didn't even look at him twice but cut a wide swath around the human Necromance and me.

I thought I'd grown past being hurt by that sort of thing. My mouth tipped up into the same faint half-smile I'd worn as a shield through so many bounties and apparitions as a Necromance. My cheek burned, the tat shifting under golden flesh, I wondered suddenly why my tat hadn't vanished like my other scars when I'd become *hedaira*. "I'll have a job for you too," I told Leander. "Just wait."

"Take your time." Amused and confident, his smile widened.

I grimaced, good-naturedly. He sounded like Jace.

The thought of Jace pinched hard deep in my chest, in a place I'd thought was numb.

Guess it isn't so numb, after all. If I took a slicboard and rose up into the traffic patterns, I would eventually see the huge soaring plasteel-and-stone pile that was St. Ignatius Hospital, where Gabriele had done what I could not and freed the empty clockwork mechanism of Jace's body from the illusion of life.

Leander's low laugh combined with the surfroar of crowd noise—different from the Souk's genial roar and tainted with fatigue from the long transport haul. I'd slept between Paradisse and North New York, my head propped on Japhrimel's shoulder; the black dreamless nothingness I needed every two or three days. How odd was it that I could only sleep when he lulled me into it, when he was close?

I brought myself back into the present with a jolt. *Stop wandering, Danny. Why are you getting so distracted? It's not like you.* "First things first, though. Can you get us a cab?"

"All things should be so easy."

"You are truly a master," I called after him as he loped away to find and reserve us a hovercab in the queue that would be waiting outside along Beaumartin Street.

It was regular bounty-hunter banter meant to ease our nerves. When Japhrimel reached me, his fingers braceleted my left wrist. I controlled the nervous twitch—that was the hand holding my katana, as usual.

Did he think I was going to run now? Especially when he knew I would only go to Gabe's, a place he'd been before? "McKinley will search for information and find us accommodation." His voice cut through the crowd noise like a golden knife. "I thought that would please you."

There was no sign of the necklace I'd given him, and I had too much pride to ask what he'd done with it. Instead, I tried to pull my wrist out of his hand and got exactly nowhere, though his fingers were gentle. "There's no need for this. We should get going."

"I feel a need." His thumb stroked once across the underside of my wrist. Fire spilled up my arm again, I tugged harder. Achieved nothing. He might not be hurting me, but he wanted me to stay put. "This is unwise, Dante. I am not to be trifled with at this moment."

What the hell? Sekhmet sa'es, *what the fuck are you*

talking about? "I'm not the one who's *trifling,*" I hissed back. "You're the one who won't tell me a damn—"

"I will tell you something now," he said in my ear as if we weren't surrounded by a crowd of normals who shuffled toward a transport or away from one. Above us rose the vast dome of the transport well and the different levels of huge hovers docking like blunt whales at each level, the spine of the AI's relays bristling around each floor, failsafes and double-synaptics glowing and humming with electrical force and reactive-painted buffers.

I went still, closed my eyes. My shields shivered. "Fine." *I would never have thought a demon could throw a tantrum.* My rings popped, sparking, I wondered what the normals around us made of this. His aura covered mine, pulled close and comforting, but I felt the echo of his attention. He was doing it again, listening to a sound I couldn't hear, set at a harsh watchful awareness I couldn't imagine anyone keeping up for very long.

Why? I'm only here for Gabe, but Japh seems to think I'm in danger. Of course I'm in bloody danger, there are demons after me. Still—

"I never knew dissatisfaction before I met you, *hedaira.* The only time I feel any peace is when you are safe and I am near you. Be careful who you spend your smiles on, and be careful of what you make of me." Japhrimel paused. "I am seeking to be gentle, but frustration may make me savage."

In all the time I'd known him, he had never said anything even remotely like this. My throat went dry, my heart banging at my ribs and in my neck, the darkness behind my eyelids suddenly blood-warm. "You mean more savage than you already are?" I pulled against his hand again. I might as well have been chained to the dock.

"You have no idea of the depth of my possible savagery." It wasn't so much the content of his words as the way they were delivered, with a chill even tone I could have thought was indifference except for the well of sharp rage behind it. Japhrimel for the first time in my memory was *furious,* holding himself to control with an effort of will. "I tell you again, be careful. And again, I do not expect your forgiveness or understanding. I require only your cooperation, which I will get by any means I deem necessary. We are here to see what is so urgent with your Necromance friend, well and good. But do not taunt me."

Taunt you? "Taunt *you?* I'm not the one who keeps playing manipulative little games here, Japh. It's you and Lucifer who have the corner on that one. Let go of me."

Much to my surprise, he did. I almost stumbled, the release of tension against my arm was so quick. I opened my eyes, the world rushing back in to meet me, and lifted my left hand slightly. The katana's weight was reassuring. "We've got a cab to catch," I said over my shoulder. "Unless you're going somewhere else."

He didn't dignify that with a reply. It was probably just as well.

Gabe's house crouched on Trivisidiro Street, behind high walls her great-great something-or-other had built. Her family had been cops and Necromances for a long time, passing along Talent and training in a haphazard way before the Awakening and the Parapsychic Act. They had survived because they were rich, and because they did everything possible to blend in before the Act made it possible for psions to come out of the shadows.

I deliberately did not look when we passed over the block that held a huge pile of stone with high holly hedges and walls. Aran Helm's house, where I'd begun to figure out just what nightmare had risen from the depths of Rigger Hall.

I didn't want to see if Helm's house still stood.

The first shock was that the neighborhood had changed. The winds of urban renewal had swept through what had once been a bad part of town, I saw several little boutiques and chic eateries as well as other restored homes.

The second shock, when we got out of the hovercab and Japhrimel paid the driver, was that the shields over Gabe's walls had changed. The hovercab lifted away with a whine, and my skin chilled again. I was really getting to hate hovers.

I caught Japhrimel's arm. He stilled, looking down at me. Leander stood on the corner, his eyes moving over the street and probably marking it in his memory; it was the same thing I did in an unfamiliar city. "Her shields are different," I said quietly, knowing I had Japh's full attention. "Look, can you and Leander wait for me?" He moved slightly, and I interrupted him before he began. "I give my word I won't go anywhere but into Gabe's house, I promise I'll come back out to you. I *swear.* But please, Japhrimel, this is private."

"You continually try to push the limits of—" he began and I squeezed his arm, sinking my fingers in. I couldn't hurt him, but just this once, I *wanted* to. I wished I could. My claws slid free, pricking into his coatsleeve, my entire hand cramping with the effort to stop them.

"*Please,* Japh." My voice gentled, it took an effort that

would have made me sweat in my human days. Something suspiciously like tears pressed against the inside of my throat, so it came out muffled and choked instead of only soft. "Don't make me beg you over something like this." *I can't stand begging you over something so simple. I can't stand begging you at all.*

"You do not have to." He nodded, once, sharply. "An hour. No more. Or I will come in for you, Dante, and I will demolish her precious shields. If I even *think* you may be in danger—or seeking to escape me—I will do the same. Is that clear?"

"Crystal." I let go of his arm, finger by finger. *When did you get so arrogant? You were so gentle in Toscano, Japh.* Drew in a sharp deep breath flavored with the smell of dusk in Santiago City—the taint of chemicals, damp, and mold rising from the ground, the tang of the sea and the further iron-rich smell of the lake to the east, the throbbing whine of hover traffic. "Thank you." I didn't sound grateful, but I suppose I might have been.

"There is no need to thank me, either. Go." A muscle flicked in his golden cheek again.

I moved away, across the sidewalk, and stepped up to Gabe's gate. Brushed against her shields, a familiar touch, and realized what was wrong. The shields Eddie had put up, the spiky earth-flavored magick of a Skinlin, were fading rapidly, as if they'd been mostly dismantled and left to shred away from the other defenses.

A curious flutter began under my pulse. Eddie and Gabe had been together so long they seemed eternal.

She was home, and awake. One of the things about visiting psions, when we have a minor in precog we're usually home when you need us. Her shields flushed red as I laid my hand against the gate; the lock clicked open as Gabe's work recognized me. I pushed at the gate before it could close again and stepped through.

The gardens were another shock, full of weeds. Eddie had always kept them pristine—of course, a dirtwitch's trade is in his garden. Skinlin are mostly concerned with growing things, like hedgewitches, but hedgewitches are more interested in using plant material to accessorize spellwork. Skinlin are the modern equivalent of kitchen witches; most of them work for biotech firms, getting plants to give up cures for mutating diseases and splicing together plant DNA with sonic magick or complicated procedures. Their only real drawback is that they're berserkers in a fight. A Skinlin in a rage is like a Chillfreak—they don't stop even when wounded. Eddie was fast, mean, and good; I never wanted to fight him.

I trudged up to the front door as night began to breathe in the garden, more disturbed than I could have ever admitted. The mark on my shoulder pulsed steadily like a heartbeat. Japhrimel, keeping contact with me the only way he could.

Is it the only way he can? I've heard his voice inside my head before, been able to call him without words. The thought froze me on the step, my hand raised to knock on Gabe's red-painted door. The house simmered above me, three stories of brownstone with even more shielding wedded to its physical structure. Would I know it if Japhrimel was inside my mind right now, a thin shadow under my thoughts?

The idea called up a nervous flare of something close to panicked loathing. Communication was one thing, but thinking the cubic centimeters inside my skull might not be wholly my own was . . .

You learn early that your body betrays you—it's your mind *that has to stay impregnable.* Polyamour's voice echoed in my memory, husky and beautiful. I shivered, pushed the thought away.

The door opened. Gabe regarded me with her dark eyes. The final shock was the worst one, I think, the one that made the world go gray and the mark on my shoulder smash with pain that shocked me, brought me up and made me gasp. My emerald burned on my cheek, answering hers.

Gabriele Spocarelli, Necromance and my friend, had aged.

7

Gabe made tea, moving around her kitchen; the house smelled of dust and I saw . . . well, there were toys scattered through the hall, toddler's toys, blocks and small hovercars made of primary-colored nontoxic plasilica. Other things. A small shoe in one corner of the kitchen, the heavy spice of *kyphii* in the air mixed with other smells no longer familiar.

She hadn't said anything about a kid during the phone calls. Not a single word. Not even a hint.

Gabe's long dark hair was threaded with gray since she'd stopped dyeing it, and the wrinkles fanning from the corners of her eyes spoke of frequent smiling. She was still slim and strong, shorter than me and with an air of serenity and precision I had envied so many times. I wondered if she still carried her longsword, a piece of sharp metal far too big for her. When I'd been human, I often thought I never wanted to face her for real over that steel—she was capable of cool clinical viciousness not many other fighters possessed. She'd been a cop all her life, going from the Academy into the Saint City PD, fighting the good fight.

She wasn't *old*, not by any stretch—but being a cop

had marked her, turned her hair prematurely gray. That gray alone told me volumes. For Gabe to go against Codes and not dye her hair black was either exceeding vanity or a sign she wasn't working professionally anymore. She still moved with the ease of combat practice and flexibility; she hadn't gotten sloppy like some old bounty hunters or cops do. But there was a slight stiffness, a shadow of slowness, that hadn't been there before. She had graduated from the Academy a full five years ahead of me; one of the few psions to have taken a break between primary training at Stryker and entering for her accreditation. She'd spent those years in Paradisse becoming a cosmopolitan, then come dutifully home and done what her family had always done—gone through advanced schooling, taken her Trial, and settled into being a cop.

We'd been friends a long, long time.

I sat at the old breakfast bar, looking at the fall of fading sunlight through the kitchen window, and felt the full consciousness of time settle in on me.

She had aged, and I hadn't. I still looked the same as I had when I opened my eyes in a Nuevo Rio mansion to find a demon had Fallen and shared his power with me. My hair was shorter, true; but otherwise I was the same. On the outside.

They were only tiny changes, the lines on her face and the threads of gray in her hair. If I'd stayed in Saint City I probably wouldn't have even noticed.

"How long has it been?" *I should know. I should know how long it's been.*

She cast me a shuttered, dark look. "You've lost track? Of course, you disappeared. And time's not your strong suit."

I opened my mouth to defend myself, shut it. I *had* disappeared. With Japhrimel, and she didn't know. We'd settled in Toscano, and I'd buried myself in decoding Magi shadowjournals, searching for the clues that would tell me what I was because he would not. I thought it was a matter of embarrassment—most demons are very touchy about the whole subject of the Fallen, and I thought perhaps Japh didn't want to speak of something painful and degrading.

Now I wondered.

Her bitter laugh brought me back to the present. "Only a couple years. Don't worry, Danny. I understand, as much as I can. I saw you after the Lourdes case, remember? You were dead on your feet, sunshine. I'm just glad to see you now."

"You called." I couldn't produce more than a croak. "*Mainuthsz.* Of course I came."

Her back stiffened as she faced the kettle on the stove. "I wasn't sure you would."

"You know me better than that." *Or at least you should.* Was I hurt?

"You and your damn sense of honor." She cleared her throat. "There's two things I want from you, Valentine. I'll make you tea and we'll talk."

I nodded, though she was facing the other way. Her aura, bright with the trademark sparkles of a Necromance, swirled steadily. Where was Eddie? I couldn't imagine him leaving her.

Memory swallowed me again.

"I'll catch him, Eddie. Or her. Whoever's doing this."

He snatched his fingertips away, his dark eyes scarred holes above hollow unshaven cheeks. "Yeah. You do that.

Word of advice? When you do catch 'em, don't bring 'em back alive. Anything to do wit' Rigger Hall is better off dead."

"Including us?"

Eddie moved, sliding his legs out of the booth and standing up. He tapped at his datband and looked down at me, his shaggy blond hair tangling in his eyes. "Sometimes I think so," he said, quietly, and his eyes were haunted wells. "Then I look at Gabe, and I ain't so sure."

I found nothing to say to that. Eddie stumped away toward the door, and I let him go.

No, I could not imagine Eddie leaving her.

I surfaced. This was proving to be harder than I'd thought, past swallowing present as it so often did these days. Was it because I was older too inside this slim golden body? I had been no spring chicken when Japh changed me. Most bounty-hunting psions have a short shelf life, despite genesplicing repair bodies under constant hard use.

Gabe poured the tea. I stayed silent. She'd tell me what she wanted, she would either solve the mystery or not. If not, it would be obvious she didn't want to talk about it, and the least I owed Gabe was a measure of tact. If anything happened to her, the last person who remembered my human self—*truly* remembered my human self—would be gone.

How would I go on then? Getting more and more distracted, shackled to Japhrimel, maybe forced into ever more complex games with Lucifer when he had some further use for me, trying to preserve some shred of my humanity . . .

Stop it, Danny. You'll go nuts if you keep thinking like that. Just stop it.

Chamomile tea for me, in a long black sinuous mug familiar enough to make a funny melting sensation begin under my breastbone. Chai for her, in a new mug—a sunshine-yellow one. That was a change. She usually wasn't a sunshiny-yellow type of person.

I wonder if it's having a kid that does it. Where is the little person who plays with the toys, Gabe, and why didn't you tell me? That qualifies as major life news. I would have liked to have been here for that.

She hadn't told me, hadn't even hinted. Why? Of course, I hadn't ever hinted I was living with a demon who had resurrected himself from ash, either. One secret balancing out the other?

She leaned against the breakfast bar, her fingers clasped around the tea mug. I saw the beginnings of a papery dryness on the fragile skin on the back of her hands, and felt that melting sensation again. Swallowed hard against it.

"No questions?" Gabe smiled. "No, you wouldn't ask me a damn thing, would you. You'd wait for me to tell you, or never mention it if I didn't. Hades, I forgot what it's like to talk to you." She turned away, stalked across the kitchen, and scooped something up from the cluttered counter. The clutter was something new too, her house had always been neat before. Dishes were stacked in the sink, a few holo-mags scattered across the far end of the breakfast bar, and dust lay on the counter next to me.

"I hope it's pleasant." It was just the thing Japhrimel might have said.

"Sometimes." She tossed it on the counter in front of me. It was a file folder. "I want you to help me kill whoever did this," she said tonelessly, and I realized she was holding onto her serenity by the thinnest of threads.

"Okay," I said promptly, opening the folder. *Consider 'em dead, Gabe.*

I would have agreed to it because I trusted her. I *also* would have agreed to it because looking at the first sheet in the folder—a nice glossy laserprint—showed a body lying on a white floor, a wrack and ruin of shattered glass winking up and dusting the blood that had dried sticky, spreading out in an impossibly large stain. But what drove the breath from my lungs was the face at the top of the ruined mass of flesh.

The mark on my shoulder crunched again, dragging me out of shock. I swallowed something that tasted like human bile. "Eddie," I whispered.

It was his body, indisputably dead. The experience of many other murder scenes rose under my skin, I noted the bullet holes clinically. Projectile weapons, a good way to take out a raging Skinlin. His shaggy head, the arc of his cheekbone as his chin was tipped back, the dark-blond whiskers telling me he hadn't shaved for a day or so before his death. Mercifully, if age had ravaged him, it wasn't visible in the picture.

"When?" The sinuous black mug chattered against the countertop, I reined myself in with an effort.

"Ten days ago." Her hands tightened again around her mug. I could almost taste the gunpowder anger roiling off her, used like a shield against the shock of loss.

I knew that territory. I'd seen it as a Necromance in the families of the departed, and been through it myself when Doreen, and later Jace, died. Two events, seeming as if they happened to different people, completely different Danny Valentines. Then there was the terrible almost-year I'd spent mourning Japhrimel as he lay dormant, ash in an urn. I remembered the abyss of loneliness and black despair, the mind bumping against the single word *gone* because the word *dead* was too final, no matter that Death was my trade.

We all think we're immortal, even Necromances. Necromances, really, should know better. And yet we never do.

"There's one more thing," Gabe said. "Before you agree."

"Too late. I've already agreed." My throat was dry and raw as a scraped-clean coremelt. *"Mainuthsz."*

She made a low hurt sound, but when I looked up her eyes were dry. She reached down under the counter, as if she was digging in her pocket, and brought out another small piece of paper. I took it, and found myself looking down at a laserprint of a beautiful little toddler with Gabe's dark eyes and Eddie's wild blond hair, wearing a pair of denim overalls and grinning up without a care in the world. Behind her, the green of a laurel hedge writhed.

So this was who had been using the toys. The world had indeed changed while I'd been in Toscano, burying myself in books. Had she been pregnant during the hunt for Kellerman Lourdes? Either then or right after, it was a distinct possibility.

Why didn't you tell me, Gabe?

"My daughter," Gabe said tonelessly. "When I die, Danny, I want you to look after her. Swear to me you'll protect her, and if I . . . I want you to raise her."

I choked. *What the hell? I can't—a kid? But—* My fingers tightened, almost crumpling the laserprint, she tore it out of my hand. *"Gabe?"*

"Swear it, Dante. *Swear.*" Her lips peeled back from her

teeth, her face dead-pale and her eyes flashing with something I'd never seen in her before.

I had to tell her. "Japhrimel's alive, Gabe."

She froze. Her pupils dilated. The perfume of fear and rage poured out from her in waves, a coppery chemical smell. "I know," she said, and my heart almost exploded inside my chest. "The fire at your house. The shadow inside. With wings."

I nodded. Black guilt rose, choked me, I pushed it fiercely away. I couldn't afford to stop now.

"I lied. I'm sorry. I *couldn't* tell you, Gabe." *I was . . . I was afraid of what you'd think of me. I'm afraid of what you think of me now.*

"You stupid bitch." Cold as the creeping chill of Death. "Of course I knew. It doesn't matter. *I* need you now." Tears stood out in her eyes. One fattened, slid down her cheek, leaving a shiny trail behind.

If she'd slapped me, I would have been less surprised. I would have deserved it.

"I'm here." I held her eyes across the air suddenly gone hot and straining between us. My rings crackled, spat, her emerald shifted with light. "As Anubis is my witness, Gabriele, I'll do it. I'll do anything you ask." My voice made a few holomags flutter off the end of the counter, their soft smacks hitting the hardwood floor.

She gazed into my eyes for a good thirty seconds, neither of us blinking. Then she held up the laseprint. "Swear," she said, and I saw the hardness in her. Gabe would not stop until Eddie's killers were dead. "Swear to me. On your name and the name of your god."

I didn't hesitate. "I swear to you, Gabriele Spocarelli, on my name and on the name of my god Anubis lord of Death,

I will help you hunt Eddie's killers. I will kill them myself if you're unable to. And for the rest of my life I will look after your child and her children." *Since I don't know how long I'll be around.* "I *give my word.*"

The world rocked slightly underfoot. There. It was done.

I owed her this much, and so much more. She'd been my friend, my only friend, since the Academy. She had tried to help me protect Doreen. She had gone into the icy hell of Santino's lair with me to hunt down Doreen's killer, and nearly died herself. It never occurred to her to bow out of that hunt, any more than it occurred to me I might bow out of this one.

Not only that, but she had done what I couldn't, and let Jason Monroe go. Performed the duty of a Necromance at his bedside, for me. It had been an act of mercy, one I didn't deserve and would never be able to repay.

Japhrimel's not going to be happy with this.

On the heels of that thought came a second, colder and harder. *I don't fucking care. Let him try to stop me. This is more important than the fucking Devil.*

Gabe slapped the laseprint down. "Good fucking deal." Tears trickled down her cheeks. "Now go away. Take the file with you. Come back tomorrow, ready."

You better believe it. "Where's your daughter?"

"In a safe place." Gabe's fingers curled around the counter, bloodless white with clenching rage. Her aura trembled. She was very close to losing control. Going nova, her aura exploding with pain, loss, fury, abandonment. If that happened, she'd come at me, and while I was fairly sure I could fend her off without hurting her I wasn't at *all* sure how Japhrimel would react if even a breath of what was happening got out to him. "Now get *out*. I'm not safe right now, Danny."

I know. Hadn't I once burned my house to the ground after I'd lost someone?

Someone once tried to tell me grief is passive. Whoever says that doesn't know women, and doesn't know Necromances either.

I left my mug there, but I took the file. I backed away from the counter. My left hand clenched around my sword's scabbard, her anger echoing in my own shields. The air spat, sparks showering from my rings. When I backed down the hall, out of sight of the kitchen, I turned around and left her house, walking as quickly as I could with eyes blinded by tears.

I owed her that, too.

I didn't want to think about the hot salt spilling down my own cheeks and dropping onto my shirt. I especially didn't want to think about the low hoarse sobbing sound I made as I flung myself out of her gates and straight into Japhrimel's arms.

8

Leander didn't ask any questions. I chalked it up to tact and was grateful, at least.

The "accommodations" were the Brewster Hotel on Ninth Street, cozy, expensive, and vulnerable enough to attack that I should have protested. I, however, did nothing of the sort. I merely banged through the hall and into the room Japhrimel indicated, dropped my bag containing its horrid new cargo, and fell onto the bed with my sword clutched in my hands, staring at the awful pale blue wallpaper with its tasteful pattern worked in gold spongy paint. Night had fallen over Saint City, a night I would have felt comfortable in years ago.

Now the night here had knives, all of them pointed at me.

Japhrimel exchanged some words with a mystified Leander; I heard McKinley, too. "I'll get him settled," the agent said, and the door to the suite closed softly.

Japhrimel's soundless step reverberated as the humming intensity of demon magick rose around the walls of the room, wards and layers of shielding that would make this space psychically almost-invisible.

He stood for a little while in the doorway. Then he paced quietly over the plush carpet and the bed sighed as he lowered himself down on the side my back was presented to.

Don't touch me. Don't fucking touch me, and for the sake of every god that ever was, if you try to manipulate or hurt me now I swear I will try to kill you, I don't care what it takes. Please, Anubis, don't let him push me now.

Another long pause. He moved, stretching out and lying down. Power smoothed down my body, a soft velvet caress.

His fingers touched my hair, stroking evenly. Soothing. He found a knot in the silky strands, worked patiently at it until it was gone, untangled with infinite care. He continued, pulling his fingers expertly through, massaging my scalp. Little rills of pleasure slid down my spine, fighting with the trembling that had me locked in its teeth.

Tears leaked out between my squeezed-shut eyelids. Just when I thought he was going to act like a bastard, he turned around and did something like this. I needed his quiet, even touch; I *needed* the feel of his fingers in my hair, of his arms around me. For just one goddamn minute I wanted to let down my defenses and let go of some of the awful, crushing, terrible burden of being myself.

But that would leave me vulnerable, wouldn't it.

Gods, please. Please. I know how to suffer through a beating, but I can't take this. Don't let him be gentle. Please.

The mark on my shoulder went hot, sustained heat like a candleflame held close to the skin. Power poured into me, stroking along my flesh, sparkling like impulses between the gaps of dendrites and axons, an electricity that would have been painful and prickling if not for the fact that my body cried out for it. Craved it.

My fingers, tipped with chipped black molecule-drip polish, shook. The sword, inside its indigo lacquer sheath, hummed.

Bit by bit, Japhrimel slid one arm under me. His other hand worked down to my neck, slid over my shoulder, skimmed down my tense, shaking arm. His fingers, blunter than mine but with unerring delicacy, slid between mine, loosened the grip on my sword. After a short struggle, he pushed the blade over the side of the bed and I made a small moaning sound like a rabbit in a trap.

I *needed* my sword. It was the only thing that made me feel safe.

His arms tensed, drew me back into him. Still he said nothing, his breath warm against my hair, his arms closed around me like chains. Like a support.

He simply held me.

The sobs came. Not slow ceaseless trickling from my eyes, not the smothered sounds I'd tried to keep to myself all the way to the hotel while Japhrimel's silence grew more and more obdurate and Leander's puzzlement and curiosity more obvious and restrained. No, there was no secrecy left in these. They tore out of me in deep hurtful gasps, each one worse than the one before. Shaking all the way up from the deepest blackest pit inside me, I convulsed with agonized guilt and grief.

It took a long time for the sobs to judder into little hitching broken gasps, my eyes streaming and my nose full, the mark on my shoulder hot through the ice creeping up my veins from my fingertips and toes. The heat fought for me, pushed back the ice of numbness,

Japhrimel's arms tightening until I could barely breathe. It made little difference—I could not breathe through the gasps anyway.

He murmured something I didn't catch. Probably in his damnable demon language, the one he wouldn't teach me because he said it wasn't fit for my mouth.

The one he'd used to bargain with Lucifer, without my understanding, getting me involved in this whole damn clusterfuck in the first place.

His left hand, fingers threaded through mine of both hands, squeezed. Reassuring, not hurtful.

I don't know how long it took. Finally, I lay hot-eyed and limp in his arms, staring at the wallpaper and the edge of a chunky antique table that held plasticine-wrapped information sheets about how to call for room service and what to do in case of a fire or general catastrophe.

I wished one of them had a guide to deal with being a part-demon whose loved ones were going to die; or maybe a few words about how to live with the utter shame of knowing you'd failed your few friends when they needed you most. I wished one of the plasticine sheets could have told me what to do about the sudden feeling of empty loneliness, so intense my entire body felt like a stranger's.

And why not? It wasn't *my* body; it was the body Japhrimel had given me, altered, made into a *hedaira*'s. He wouldn't even tell me what that was. He was hiding things from me even now. I was a fool if I thought otherwise.

Japhrimel pressed his lips against my hair. Said something else, too low for even my demon-acute senses to hear. The drilling heat from his mark on my shoulder finally flushed the last of the ice out of my fingers and toes. I closed my eyes, squeezing out hot tears. Opened them again. His arm curled under me, wrapped around me, his flattened hand pressing into my belly.

"I'm all right," I whispered finally, raw and uncertain.

Did I feel his mouth move with a smile? "I do not think so, beloved." Soft, the tone he used in the dead regions of night or the laziness of a hot Toscano afternoon.

It made me giggle, a forlorn broken sound. "You never used to call me that." I heard the note of tired hurt in my voice, wished I hadn't said it. Exhaustion pulled at my arms and legs, as if I was human again.

I wish I was. Oh, gods, how I wish I was human again.

"What do you think *hedaira* means?" He hugged me again, the soft pulsing of the mark on my left shoulder turning into a golden spike for a moment.

"You won't teach me anything." My eyes drifted closed. The weariness swamped me, made my arms and legs turn to lead.

"Have you ever considered that perhaps I cherish you as you are?" He sighed, a very human sound. "Were I to teach you too quickly, my curious one, you might well decide to fear me unreasonably. I prefer your anger. You will learn soon enough, in your own time. And I will wait, as long as I must, and with more patience than I have shown so far." Another kiss, pressed onto the top of my head. "What does your friend want of you?"

I swallowed several times, dryly, and told him. The darkness behind my eyelids was comforting again. I couldn't fight him when he was like this. Gods, all he had to do was be *gentle* with me, and I wouldn't be able to stop him from doing anything he wanted. I would even *help* him.

If he was gentle. If he could just remember to tell me the truth.

For a long few moments he was silent. Could I feel the thoughts moving through his alien brain? He'd been alive far longer than me, far longer than *anyone,* even Lucas or the Nichtvren I infrequently met. How could I possibly deal with something that old, that essentially different?

Never mind that I had thought it possible, never mind that I'd trusted him with my life, slept with him, told him things I'd never told anyone else. I'd treated him as if he was human, and he'd responded by becoming *A'nankhimel.* Fallen.

Whatever that was. I doubted I knew even a quarter of it. If I ever thought I did, in the future, all I would have to do is touch my shoulder, feeling the scar twist on the surface of my skin. Or remember being held up against the tiled wall of a New Prague subway stop, shaken like a disobedient puppy while his knuckles dug into the thin skin over my breastbone.

"She's my friend," I went on, barely pausing to take a breath. "Fuck Lucifer, I owe Gabe, I owe her *everything.* I don't care what you think, I'm—"

"Your debts are mine," he interrupted. "Rest, Dante. Shock is still a danger for you."

"You'll help me?" I sounded amazed even to myself. *Ask him about the treasure, Danny. He seems to be in a talkative mood, ask him what the Key is and why all of a sudden everything's so different. Use this.*

Another hot helping of shame boiled up under my breastbone. Even in the middle of a crisis I was still trying to figure out how to manipulate him back, trying to play his game.

He made a small sound, as if annoyed. "The sooner this is over, the sooner I may return to the task of seeing you alive through the demands the Prince has placed on us. I worry it may be too much of a task even for my skill." There was a curious inflection to the words, as if he had chosen them with finicky care. I was too tired to think about it, too warm, and too grateful for him.

Even if he was a lying demon. "I can't imagine a job *that* big." I yawned and settled further into his warmth.

"Hm." His arms tightened, just a little. "Besides, you obey your honor, Dante. I can do no less. I am your Fallen."

My sudden question surprised me as much as it might have surprised him. "What does *A'nankhimel* mean, Japhrimel?" My voice was slurred, heavy, the sound of a woman in a nightmare that didn't stop when she opened her eyes.

He kissed the top of my head again. "It means *shield*. It also means *chained*. Go to sleep, my curious. You are safe."

I shouldn't have rested. But I was still tired, aching from Lucifer's last kick, and craving grateful oblivion. There wasn't enough sleep in the world to make me feel better.

But I'd take what I could. Just for that moment, there in Japh's arms.

9

Despite waking up warm under the covers—with Japhrimel sitting across from me in a chair situated so the thin rainy light of a Saint City afternoon fell over him, turning him into an icon of dark coat and golden skin with jeweled eyes—the day started out unsatisfactorily. For one thing, it was still strange to be up during daylight hours. I've been a night creature all my human life—most psions are, something about our metabolisms and a gene marker for nocturnalism. During the day I felt sluggish, not slow enough to handicap me in a fight but as if a veil of misty fatigue was drawn over the world. It was when night fell that I truly felt alive.

I finished tugging my boots on and pushed my damp hair back. One thing I haven't grown out of is my love of hot water; even though I rarely sweat I like to have a daily shower. I've gone without on too many bounties not to appreciate being clean.

The other unsatisfactory thing? Leander was gone.

"What do you mean, *gone?*" I fixed McKinley with a steely glare the Hellesvront agent bore all too easily. He glanced at Japhrimel, who said nothing.

Apparently deciding that meant I could know, the agent went on. He still wore unrelieved black to match his hair and eyes, and only two knives. McKinley didn't appear to need much in the way of weapons. I'd seen him with a gun once, on a rooftop in New Prague, never again. "Not in his room this morning. No luggage, not that he had much to begin with. I can comb the city. . . ." He didn't sound too concerned, I realized.

"Not necessary." Japhrimel stood slim and dark, his hands clasped behind his back. "Perhaps he had an attack of good sense."

There it was again, that faint note of disdain. Why didn't Japhrimel like him? "*Anubis et'her ka.* So what if he's human? I am too, remember?" *Still human where it counts, Japh.* I rose to my feet, stamped to settle my boots, and slid the strap of my bag over my head, settling its weight properly against my hip. Rotated my shoulders to make sure my rig was all right. Closed my left hand over my sword. "I swear, you're as bad as a normal. Always thinking that a human can't be good enough for anything, just like normals think all psis are mindstealers." I stalked between them, toward the door of the suite, wishing the room wasn't done in pale blue with old Merican Era fustibudgets for decoration. Even in Sarajevo the rooms had been better decorated.

Japhrimel fell into step behind me, McKinley said nothing. He was going to stay behind, thank the gods.

I made it out the door and down the hall, pushing the door to the stairwell open. I would be damned if I'd take an elevator. My nerves were raw enough.

My footsteps echoed on the stairs; his were soundless. I could have moved quietly, but what good would it have done me? Besides, I was in a mood.

I felt Japhrimel's eyes on me as I stalked through the lobby and out through the climate control, into the familiar cold chembath of a rainy Saint City early afternoon.

Immediately, habitually, I checked hovertraffic and reached out with all my senses to take in the mood of the city. The flux and glow of Power here was so familiar another lump rose in my throat.

Stop it. You've barely ever cried before in your life; stop being an idiot and use those brains you're so famous for.

The feeling—which I had to examine thoroughly before admitting it was relief and a sense of being home again—filled my entire body with an odd combination of lightness and a completely uncharacteristic desire to weep-angst like a holovid soap star. I swallowed the blockage in my throat, glancing down Ninth to see the familiar bulk of the skyline lifting its scallops and needles around the bay. I wanted to get to Gabe's quickly, of course; but still I walked. Japhrimel, saying nothing, walked behind me.

Three steps behind and to my left, soundless as Death Himself, his presence felt like sunshine on my back. His mark on my shoulder was warm, comforting. The streets were familiar, resounding under my boots. One moment I wanted to dance with crazy joy.

The next I felt the weight of my bag, with the folder inside it. Then my eye would fall across a slight change—a new building, an old building remodeled, something *different*—and the change would hit me hard in the solar plexus.

It was small consolation that with a war shaping up between Lucifer and Eve, and something else in the offing Japh couldn't be prodded to tell me about, I might not live long enough to see other changes.

I finally hailed a hovercab at the corner of Fifteenth and Pole, right at the edge of the Tank District. The driver—an Asiano man—didn't look happy to find out his fare was a psion, but he'd descended and flipped the meter before seeing my tat. Japhrimel gave the driver Gabe's address in flawless unaccented Merican. His control of the language—indeed, of most languages—was phenomenal.

Then again, demons like languages just as they like technology, or genetics, or meddling with humans.

Meddling with humans—but not feeling any affection for them. Or Falling, for them.

The unsteady flutter of my stomach as the hovercab rose into the sky intensified as I studied Japhrimel's profile. He stared straight ahead, laser-green eyes burning intently as if they intended to slice through the plasilica barrier between us and the driver, out through the front bubble, and cut the sky with a sword of light. "Japh?"

"Hm?" As if startled out of his own uncomfortable thoughts. His eyes turned to me, and I found it slightly easier to meet them.

"Can I ask you something?" My left hand eased on my katana, I even drummed my fingers a little bit against the scabbard.

"Gods protect me from your questions, my curious. Ask." Did he smile? If he did it was a fleeting expression, moving over his face so quickly even my demon-sharp eyes barely caught it.

No time like the present. Since you won't explain anything else, I might as well ask for the moon. I plunged ahead. "Why did you Fall?"

I expected him to turn the question aside, refuse to answer it. He would always make some ironic reply before, or simply, gently, refuse to tell me anything of *A'nankhimel*. Would tell me myths about demons, old stories, tales to make me laugh or listen wide-eyed with a sweet sharp nostalgic terror like a child's—but never anything I could use to find out what I was, what the limits of my new body were. Nothing about himself, or what his life had been like. He would only talk about things that had happened since I'd met him, and even some of those he wouldn't speak about.

As if he'd been born the day he showed up at my door.

I never knew dissatisfaction before I met you, hedaira.

Today, he cocked his head. Considered the question. I felt his awareness again, closing around me. His aura stretched to cover mine, the mark on my shoulder staining through the trademark sparkles of a Necromance's energetic field with black diamond flames.

When he spoke, it was soft, reflective. "I lived for countless ages as the Prince's Right Hand and felt no guilt or shame at what I did. I still do not."

No philosophy for me, he'd said, during the hunt for Santino. *I don't take sides. The Prince points and says that he wants a death, I kill.*

He was silent for so long, his eyes burning green against mine, that I finally found my lungs starving for breath and remembered to inhale. He'd refused to kill me to gain back his place in Hell. I had it on good authority; better authority than if he'd tried to tell me himself. So what did that *mean?*

"Then, the Prince set me to fetch a human woman and use her in a game that would end with the created Androgyne under his hand. I found myself in the presence of a creature I could not predict, for the first time in my life."

He shrugged, a simple evocative movement. "I did not understand her—but knew her in a way that seemed deeper than even my kinship with my own kind. And thus, my dissatisfaction."

"Dissatisfaction?" I sounded breathless. What a surprise—I *was* breathless. Damn hard to breathe when he was staring into my eyes like this.

"I Fell through love of you, *hedaira*. It's simple enough, even with your gift for complicating matters. I don't want your fear of me; I have never wanted you to fear me." He looked as if he would say more, but ended up shutting his mouth and shaking his head slightly, as if mocking himself for what he couldn't say.

I don't want to fear you either. "I don't want to be afraid of you. But you make it so goddamn hard, Japh. All you have to do is *talk* to me."

"I can think of nothing else I would rather do." He even looked like he meant it, his eyebrows drawn together as he studied me, his eyes holding mine in a cage of emerald light. "I cherish my time with you."

That made my heart flip and start to pound like a gymnasa doing a floor routine. *All right, Japh. One more try. One more chance.* "What aren't you telling me?" My fingers tightened on the scabbard.

A long pause. The hovercab began to descend, the driver humming a tune I didn't recognize. There was a time in Saint City when I would have known all the songs.

"Like calls to like," he repeated, softly. "I am a killer, Dante. It is what I *am*."

So, by extension, that's what I am. That wasn't what I meant, I wanted you to talk to me about Eve. I thought about this, turned it over inside my head. "I don't kill without cause." My eyes dropped away from his, to the slender shape of the katana. *Fudoshin.* A blade hungry for battle, Jado had said.

Jado lived in Saint City. I wanted to ask him about this sword. *Yeah, sure. Like I have so much free time.*

"Anyway," I continued, "a killer's not *all* you are. If it was I'd be dead too, right?" *You've never let me down when it counted, Japh. You even stood up to Lucifer—and pushed him* back. *You made the Prince of Hell back off. He's scared of you.*

He had no pat reply for that. The hovercab landed with a sigh of leaf springs. He paid the cabdriver. I wondered—not for the first time—where all the money came from.

Then again, Lucifer had paid me too. Cash was no problem to demons. Some Magi even said they'd invented the stuff. It certainly made sense, given money's seductive nature and the chaos it could create.

I decided to push a little more, since he was so willing to talk. "So what's this Key, and what's going on that's changed everything?"

He didn't reply for a few moments, watching the cab lift off and dart back into the stream of hover traffic. "Later, my curious. When we are finished with your Necromance friend."

Disappointment bit sharp under my breastbone. I folded my arms, my sword a heavy weight in my left hand. "Japh?"

"Hm?" His eyes returned to me. "More questions?"

If I didn't know better, I'd think he was baiting me. "Just a request. Quit being a bully. Stop keeping me in the dark."

His mouth pulled down at both corners. But I'd already

turned on my heel and dropped my arms, heading down Trivisidiro just like I always used to do, the click of my bootheels marking off each step. *How about that? I think I finally got the last word in.*

I didn't feel happy. What I felt was uneasy, and growing uneasier by the moment.

I blinked at Trivisidiro Street and cast around, vaguely troubled. If I hadn't been so bloody distracted, I would have noticed it right away. As it was, it took me a few seconds before I realized why I was disoriented.

Gabe's front gate was slightly open. Not only that, but the shields on her property line were torn, bleeding trickles of energy into the early afternoon.

10

I would have gone first, being accustomed to taking point on any job; it was a habit thirty-odd years in the making and difficult to shake. Japhrimel, however, grabbed my arm in an iron grip that stopped just short of pain and gave me to understand with a single vehement emerald look that *he* was going first, and if I didn't want an argument I would be well advised to just let him.

I was so badly shaken I did. I followed him, my thumb pressing against the katana's guard, right hand clamped around the hilt. I suppose I should have drawn a plasgun, but I was operating on instinct. A blade is the weapon I find most comforting. Give me a sword and some open ground, a clear enemy in front of me, and I know what to do.

It's just everything else in my life that confuses me now. The thought was full of bleak humor. Gallows humor, meant to take the edge off my nervousness but failing miserably.

My mind turned curiously blank as I followed Japhrimel's black coat and inky head. As he stepped through Gabe's gate, soundless, the static of his attention stretching to take in the smallest of details, the bleeding shields on her property line flushed red and began to fizz.

I calmed the restive layers of energy with a mental touch, deftly binding together holes ripped in the shielding. It was strange, but there was no sense of *personality* behind the rips and holes.

If another psion had cracked the shields, there would be a distinct stamp, a flavor to the rents. Something I could track, no matter how good the other psion was. That was part of the trouble with the use of Power, it was so unutterably *personal*. A bounty hunter, like me, developed a set of psychic muscles and sensitivities perfectly suited to tracking. We had to; it was how we did our jobs. I still thought like a bounty hunter, never sitting with my back to a door if I could help it and seeing the world as a tangle of connections, some chance some not, that if pursued systematically with a healthy dose of instinct would lead me to the person or piece of information I wanted. Nobody—especially anybody who has done something to make someone like me hunt them—manages to get through life without randomly bumping into something or spilling some energy into the ether. Everybody fucks up, sooner or later—and fuckups are mostly what a bounty hunter snags on.

But there was no flavor to the rips and tears in Gabe's exquisitely careful, beautiful shielding.

Japhrimel ghosted over the gravel walkways of the garden. The house shields were still intact, vibrating with distress of a peculiarly remote kind. I would have thinned my shields to try and reach for Gabe—after all, we shared magick and deeper bonds—but the mark on my shoulder clamped down with fearful pressure and I realized Japhrimel's aura had hardened into a demon-tough shield around me, on top of my regular shielding.

That was something I hadn't expected he could do,

and I looked around the weedy garden with my heart in my mouth. Tension brushed my skin with thousands of delicately-scraping pins, and copper filled my mouth.

I felt alive.

We found her around the back of the house, in the garden near the back wall Eddie had used for his more useful but less happy plants—aconite, horehound, belladonna, poison sumac (for repellant spells and treating slagfever), fireweed 12, wormwood, castor, meadow saffron, foxglove, hellebore, you name it. All the datura had been grubbed up, leaving a rain-softened hole in the dirt, and that was puzzling. If Eddie had died ten days ago, why was his garden weedy? And where had the datura gone?

Then Japhrimel turned to me. "Go to the front of the house," he said, but I pushed past him. He caught my left arm, gently. "Dante. You do not wish to see this. *Please.*"

I looked, and I saw. It was no use, all the good-intentioned wanting to protect me in the world couldn't have stopped me from looking.

Gabe lay tangled in a young hemlock. She bent back as if doing an enthusiastic full-wheel pose for a gymnasia illustration, except for the bloody holes in her dark shirt and jeans. *Dead for at least six hours if not more,* the Necromance in me thought, tasting the fading tang of what we call foxfire—the false glow of nerves slowly dying. The ground around her was chewed with bullets, white underbark and broken green things glaring through the rainy day. Mist had collected on her face, the angle of her jaw upflung, her hair a hanging skein of gray and black silk.

Her feet were bare and very white.

Her sword, blackened and twisted with her death,

spilled out of her right hand. Her eyes were closed, and except for the bloody hole in her left cheek where a bullet had ripped through the flesh and shattered teeth she looked peaceful.

My pulse beat a padded drum in my ears.

The *click* sounded in my brain. I looked at her feet, down at the gravel path. Glanced back toward the house. She had to have come over the lawn, barefoot and in a hell of a hurry. Why?

The part of me that had seen so many murder scenes jolted into operation, like an old-fashioned gearwheel. It slid into place evenly, and I thought quite clearly, *I'm going to feel this soon. Before I do, I need to think. Think, Danny. Think.*

I examined the angle of the bullets, where they had torn through plants and dug furrows in the wet earth. The smell of death rose with the perfume of fresh green garden, newly-churned dirt. The computer deck inside my head took over, calculated angles and wounds, came up with an answer. I looked over my right shoulder, up over the wall at a point some twenty feet above. There was a rooftop there, just right for a projectile assault rifle.

Why was she still lying here? That much hot lead whizzing through the air—someone should have called the cops. Heard something. *Done* something, especially in this neighborhood.

Why had Gabe come out here? Her property-line shields were torn and her house shields vibrating, probably with the psychic shock of her death. I was a Necromance, here with a fresh body—but if I went into Death now, I might not come out. I was too tired, too distracted, and too goddamn upset. To top it all off, Japhrimel would have to question

Gabe; he might not know the right questions to ask to elicit the underlying logic of what had happened. There were *rules* to questioning the dead, rules he might not know any more than I knew the arcane rules of demon etiquette.

More than that, something deep and colored a smoking red in me rose in revolt at the thought of using Gabe's body as a focus. She had gone into Death, into the halls she'd walked so often before, and into the clear rational light of What Comes Next. If there was any justice in the world, she was with Eddie now. I wouldn't pull her away from that.

Admit it, Danny. You're afraid of facing her after you've failed her again.

A litany of my life's failures rose before me, all the dead I'd loved. *Roanna. Lewis. Doreen. Jace. Eddie.* And now a new name to add to that long string. *Gabe.*

A long, despairing scream rose inside my chest, was locked away by an iron hand descending on my heart and *squeezing,* its bony fingers sinking into warm flesh and spreading the cold of stone. Cold. Like the gray fuzzy chill of shock, only deeper. This was a killing cold, ice to be polished, sharp as my katana and deadly as the demon standing beside me.

Gabriele. The final echo of the promise I'd made her yesterday sounded a brass gong inside my head.

Whoever did this I won't just kill. I'm going to erase them. I swear to every god that ever was, I am going to make them pay.

"Dante." Japhrimel's voice, quiet. "I am sorry."

My mouth worked silently for a moment. I considered screaming. Then my jaw shut with a click of teeth snapping together. Harsh dragged-in breath tore at my throat with the smell of fresh dirt. My right hand cramped once, viciously, around the hilt of my katana. Released. I shoved the sword into the loop on my rig. Looked at the statue of Gabe's body.

Gone. The word echoed in my head. *Gone.*

Failed again.

The knife whispered out of its sheath. Japhrimel cast me a measuring look, as if weighing whether I would use it on him. I set it against the flesh of my palm and ripped down in one unsteady movement, dropping the blade now smoking with black demon blood.

I lifted my hand, made a fist. Black blood dripped between my fingers, squeezed so hard I heard my own bones creak. My throat locked around a black well of screaming.

This I swear on my blood. I will find who is responsible for this, Gabe. And I won't just kill them. I will make them pay.

"*Dante!*" Japhrimel grabbed my hand, a hot pulse of Power sealing the wound even more quickly than welling black demon blood.

I blinked at him. *Gods, does he sound frightened? Never heard that before.* I finally found my voice. "Don't worry," I rasped. "That was just a promise." *Am I in shock? I don't feel like it. I feel like I'm thinking clearly for the first fucking time in a long time.*

He studied me. "I am sorry." His eyes measured me. As if he wanted to express more than sorrow, as if there was something else he wanted to say.

I doubted there was anything in all the languages he knew that would suffice.

I pulled my hand away from his. Bent to scoop up my knife, approached her body. The air steamed around me, heat bleeding out from a demon metabolism struggling to cope with the killing cold creeping into my chest.

He said nothing, but the shield of Power around me moved uneasily.

I bent carefully, dug in her right-hand jeans pocket. Almost choked as I leaned over a pool of her blood, diluted by the fine misting rain. Her datband was blinking. Why hadn't aid hovers been dispatched from the central AI well as soon as her datband's pulse monitor figured out her heart wasn't working? A *sedayeen* with an aid unit might have been able to help her.

No, with that much lead in her—especially in her chest—she'd probably bled out in seconds.

Still, why wasn't there a cadre of cops here with a Reader, examining the scene?

A rectangle of laseprint paper crinkled under my fingers as I drew it out. Gabe's daughter grinned up at me, the edges of the glossy paper wrinkled with blood. I tucked the picture securely in my bag, reached up to push a strand of wet heavy hair out of her face. My fingertip slid over her emerald, dead and lifeless now; the tat that would never shift to answer mine again. My cheek burned, though her emerald was dark.

A slight crackling buzz sparked between the gem and my fingertip. *An EMP. Of course. They trigger an electromagnetic pulse, and everyone's so busy trying to get their holovids reprogrammed they don't notice a Necromance's murder. But what about the AI well? Her pulse monitor would have sent distress signals every half-second! Unless . . . unless it was a focused EMP pulse, that would reset the hardcode.*

I touched the datband with one finger. It flushed red.

Hardcode wiped. It was about as useless as plain plasilica now. A focused EMP pulse, cop or Hegemony hardware.

Which meant I was dealing with someone very serious about killing her for some reason. Someone who had the funding and hardware to get away with triggering an EMP pulse within the borders of the city's hoverzones.

"I have to go inside." I straightened, my fingers leaving Gabe's cold motionless wrist reluctantly.

"We must be quick." Japhrimel cocked his head. "I hear sirens."

In a city this size, of course you hear sirens. It was useless, he had some way of knowing the cops were finally coming. Hours too late.

Why? Why were they coming *now?*

I took one last long, lingering look at Gabe's body. Fixed every line, every curve, every drop of blood in my Magi-trained memory.

Roanna. Lewis. Doreen. Jace. Eddie. And now, Gabe. My throat swelled again, I swallowed the scream. Some of those deaths I had avenged, never enough to assuage the deep sleeping sense of guilt; there is only so much satisfaction to be had from spilling blood for vengeance.

But I owe it to her. To both of them, to Eddie and Gabe.

I turned on my heel and stalked away. Japhrimel fell into step behind me, silent again. The pressure of his attention wrapping around me helped to keep the scream inside—I couldn't let it out while the velvet fingers of his aura stroked my skin, the mark on my left shoulder burning deeper and deeper into my flesh.

Gabe's house shields quivered. They would eventually lose Power and become no more than shadows, holding the psychic impressions of her family, generation upon generation of Necromances and cops. But since her family had been shielding this house for a very long time, it might well take hundreds of years for the Power to fade.

The back door was unlocked and open, and I peered in. Let out a sharp breath. This door gave into the kitchen, and I could see smashed plates and appliances. Someone had tossed the hell out of Gabe's beautiful, expensive, comfortable kitchen.

My boots ground on broken ceramic and plasglass as I picked my way inside. Japhrimel laid a hand on my shoulder. "I do not like this," he said quietly.

I inhaled. Sage, and salt. Someone had been cleaning up in here, erasing psychic traces. "Her shields aren't torn here. Someone she knew, then. Someone who didn't have to break in."

Which pretty much ruled out demon involvement. I was fairly sure this had nothing to do with Lucifer, which was a huge bloody relief. Finally, something the Prince of Hell *didn't* control.

The thought of Lucifer turned my stomach over hard, splashing its contents against the sides of my ribs.

I slid through the hall—even the pictures had been torn down, some yanked out of their frames. The first-floor living room, where Gabe and Eddie had done their meditating and had their altars, was a shambles. Gabe's exquisitely painted ceramic statue of Graeca Persephonia lay smashed on the floor, Persephonia's sad flat eyes gazing up thoughtfully at the ceiling. The tang of sage was very thick here, nose-stinging, overpowering Gabe's *kyphii*.

I made my way to the stairs, counted up to the seventh one, and knelt below it. My fingers ran along the bottom of the wooden lip of the seventh step.

"Dante? They are drawing closer. Do you wish to be seen here?"

I ignored him. My fingers found the slight groove, pressed with a small tingle of Power along my nails, and the nonmagickal lock yielded. The top of the step came away in my hands. I let out a low sigh.

There, in the hidey-hole, were four sheets of heavy-duty paper with Skinlin notations—snatches of musical notes, ancient Judic symbols, and complicated chemistry equations. There were also four vials of a white, grainy substance. Otherwise, the hole was empty and suspiciously clean. Gabe must have hoped I'd find this—or hoped nobody *else* would.

Her house exhaled around me, shaking free of sage-reek, the frowsty smell of old construction and uneven, sloping, renovated floors mixing with the heady spice of *kyphii* and the comfortable soft scent of a well-lived-in home. Faint tang of synth-hash smoke—she'd been smoking, probably not around the kid.

Where exactly was Gabe's daughter? Had she been kidnapped? *In a safe place,* Gabe had said. I wondered where, and hoped the place was safe enough.

What the hell is going on?

I scooped everything up. Paper crackled in my hands. "Let's go."

11

$\mathcal{L}$eander still wasn't back at the hotel, and Lucas was nowhere in sight. I stalked past McKinley without a glance, into the suite I'd slept in. Dropped down on the bed, laid my sword down carefully, and dug in my bag, retrieving Eddie's murder file. Pearly sunlight fell through the window, making a thin square on the blue carpet. I swallowed a scorching curse, my rings sizzling and sparking. Tasted bile.

Japhrimel closed the bedroom door and leaned back against it, his arms folded and his eyes alight. I looked at the file, set it aside with the sheets of paper covered in Skinlin scribbles, and held up one of the vials.

The grainy substance inside glowed faintly in rainy afternoon light. Silence stretched inside the room. The curtains fluttered uneasily, once, and were still. Between Japh's taut alertness and my own furious, tightly-controlled pain, the walls groaned a little and subsided.

My chest ached. My eyes burned, dry and determined to stay that way. Nevertheless, my hand shook a little, making the fine grains inside the glass vial tremble and spill from one side to the other.

The mark on my shoulder lay quiescent against my skin now, no longer burning or spurring me away from shock. But the deep prickling sense of Japhrimel's attention remained, sliding around me the way a cat might, rubbing its head against its owner. Offering comfort, maybe.

Was it so bad of me to want to accept it? Things were as hopeless as ever between us.

I looked over at the door. His eyes were half-lidded, the green glow muted; perhaps for my sake. Still, they were the most vivid thing in the room, so bright they cast shadows under his high cheekbones.

We paused like that for twenty long seconds, each ticked off with a single deadly squeeze of my heart. My traitorous pulse still beat, reminding me I was alive.

"She's dead," I said finally, dully. *Who is that, using my voice? She sounds defeated. Hopeless.*

"I am sorry." It was the first time I heard his voice shake with sadness, ever so slightly. "If I could make it otherwise for you, I would."

I almost believed him. No, that's a lie. I *did* believe him. How was that for ironic? If he could have torn Death away and brought her back, he would have. Simply another present for his *hedaira,* a token of his strength given because he did not know what else to give me. How else to make me *happy.*

It was a shame he couldn't do it. I would have begged him for it, if he could have.

But Death will not be denied. I knew that, even as something old and screaming inside me rose up in rebellion that was quelled by what had to be done now.

I held up the vial again, shook it gently. The grains inside rattled softly, mocking me. "What do you suppose is in this?" The words hitched, caught. I closed my eyes, dropping my hand. It was getting harder to breathe. The air had turned to clear mud.

I heard him cross the room, his booted feet making noise for my benefit. He stopped by the bed, and his fingers slid through my hair again. The touch was gentle and intimate, a gesture he habitually performed in Toscano to request my attention away from my feverish research. He trailed his fingertips down my temple, over my cheek, infinitely gentle.

"I would almost prefer your weeping." His voice stroked the air, turning it to golden velvet. Soothing, a tone so far divorced from his usual flat dry irony he hardly sounded like the same person. "What would you have of me? Tell me what to do, Dante."

My bag clinked as it shifted against my hip. "How savage can you be?" The words turned to ash in my throat. "Because when I find whoever did this, I want them to *suffer*."

Another long pause as he stroked my cheek again, his sensitive fingertips skimming my skin, sending comforting tingles and ripples of fire down my back. My breath caught, the spiked mass of pain inside my chest turning over.

"Demons understand vengeance." He touched my upper lip, tracing the curves.

Gods. "What *don't* demons understand?"

"Humans." He said it so promptly and ironically I laughed, a forlorn little chuckle that didn't sound like me at all. I scooped up three of the four vials and handed them to him.

"Keep these. They're safer with you." *If I can trust you*

to give them back, that is. But this is nothing you'd be interested in, I'm betting.

His fingers flicked, and the small plasglass containers disappeared just like the tiny origami animals he'd made out of my notes. He said nothing else, simply stood and watched me, waiting.

Thinking of how fast his hands were made me wonder where all the little folded-paper animals had ended up. Now that I thought about it, I really couldn't remember seeing creases in any of my notes; I couldn't remember seeing any piece of paper he'd selected to fold and amuse me with ever again.

Dammit, Danny, don't lose your focus. Your problem isn't Japhrimel. Not right now, anyway.

You know, if it wasn't so grim, that'd be a relief. Guilt scored me even as the black humor of the thought helped.

I let out a long shuddering sigh. Held up the small vial again, shook it. I opened the file, scooting back and pulling my legs up onto the bed, retreating from him. "Come take a look at this, if you want. It's Eddie's homicide file." *Hooray for me. I sound almost normal, except for the way my voice cracks.* I sounded like a vidsex operator, my ruined throat giving each word a rough husky pleasantness. Except for the unsteady fury smoking under the soft surface.

"The dirtwitch." Japhrimel settled on the bed next to me. Did he sound uncertain? "He was . . . he was a good man."

What, for a human? But that was unfair. Japh was trying to be kind. I swallowed around the hard lump in my throat, tasting bile. "He was." I steeled myself. Looked down to find the laseprint of Eddie's mangled body glaring accusingly up at me. "Gods above." A shocked whisper, as if I'd been punched.

"Perhaps you should be still for a moment." Japhrimel leaned back until he half-reclined on the bed, propped on his elbows. It was a curious pose for someone so controlled, especially with his hair slightly ruffled. A vulnerable stance, exposing his stomach.

Are you crazy? I just got up late and found my best friend—my only friend—dead. I'm not resting. Not for a long, long time. I shook my head. "No." The lamp rattled on the bedside table, pushed by the plascharge of Power in my voice. My rings sparked again, golden crackles in the charged, swirling air.

The temptation to draw my sword and start hacking at the graceless, ugly furniture was overwhelming.

I looked back down at the file. Hot bile whipped the back of my mouth, and my blade rang softly inside its sheath.

Japhrimel reached over, his golden fingers closing on the file. He pulled it away from my unresisting hands. I heard the rattling whine of a hover outside the hotel's windows, human footsteps in the hall. I heard the walls groaning their long slow songs of stress and windshift, heard the faint sound my hair made as it slid against my shoulders.

He closed the file, set it aside. Then, deliberately, he lay back on the bed, his fingers laced behind his dark head. I felt the weight of his eyes on my back, looked down at my hands.

Chipped black molecule-drip polish on my nails, the graceful architecture of demon bones, the fragility of my wrists. "I should look at it. I have to start . . . finding out what I can. I *have* to."

"I know," was the quiet answer. "But not yet, Dante. Not just yet."

"Why not?" *Goddamn you, why not?*

"There is nothing you can do at just this moment. Be still. A hunter does not rush blindly after prey." A thread of gold in the room, his voice brushed the paint, ruffled my hair, touched my cheek. The soundless static of his attention filled empty space; I wouldn't have been surprised to find he was aware of every dust mote, every fiber of the carpet, every stitch in the curtains. Japhrimel was tense, edgy.

Ready for anything.

It didn't help that he was right. I was so keyed-up I would maybe miss something important—or crucial—by forcing myself to look through the file now. I had to think clearly. I had to be cold, chill, logical; I *had* to be.

So what could I do?

Think about it. Just sit still. Study.

But sitting still only made me more aware of the weight behind my eyes, the clawing in my chest. Wine-red, wine-dark, sharp as my sword and chill as the ocean I'd been dumped into after I'd killed Santino—

I shuddered. *Don't, Danny. Don't think about that.*

I jerked, moving as if to lever myself off the bed, but Japhrimel caught my wrist and pulled, catching me by surprise. My balance tipped, I landed hard enough to drive a small sound out between my teeth, ending up trapped in his arms with my sword between us, my rig creaking, the holster of a plasgun digging into my hip and a projectile gun higher up, shoved painfully against a floating rib. Knife-hilts dug against my ribs and pressed into my back.

"Be *still*," Japhrimel hissed in my ear, his breath touching my skin and sending a hot spill of sensation through my flesh. "Please, Dante."

I kicked him, twisting to get free, the plasgun digging even deeper into my hip. "Let me *go!*"

"No."

I wriggled, tried to knee him, but his arms turned to iron bands. It was a novel kind of sparring match. He was demon; I was only a lousy human infected with demonic Power. No contest. I started to struggle in earnest, earning myself a starry jolt of pain when I cracked my head against his shoulder and finally collapsed, breathing heavily, his leg over both of mine, his arms almost crushing me.

"Let go," I said into the hollow between his throat and shoulder. I contemplated biting him. "What are you fucking *doing?* Let *go* of me!"

"You are in a mood to harm yourself." His breath was warm in my hair. "When you are calm I will let you go, not before."

Goddamn him, he's right. I was in a fey space between agony and revenge, I could easily see flinging myself out the window, running, smashing my fist through the wall just to break something, hurt something, *kill* something. "I am not going to harm *myself,*" I whispered. "I'm going to kill whoever did this to her."

"Very well. This is only a hunt like any other. You are starting ill and will finish badly if you do not calm yourself." He was breathless too; the spice and musk smell of demon drenched the bed, filled my nose, coated the back of my throat.

Damn demon pheromones. He smells safe, dammit. Oh, gods. Gods help me. I choked back a panicked giggle. After a long pause, he rested his chin atop my head. I shut my eyes tightly, willing the stone egg inside my chest to stay hard and smooth. Impenetrable.

It didn't help that I could see the cool logic of what he

was saying. If I started out half-cocked and crazy, I'd get nowhere—and Gabe might be unavenged.

Like Doreen had been unavenged for so long.

If I'd been smarter or faster—or a Magi—I might have recognized Santino for what he was, and Doreen might still be alive. If I'd been stronger and not half-crippled from killing Santino, I could have kept my promise and saved Eve. If I'd been faster, able to use all the preternatural speed Japh had given me, Jace might still be alive. If I'd been home instead of hiding out with a demon in Toscano, Eddie and Gabe might still be alive.

If, if, if. I *hated* that dried-up, prissy, disapproving little word.

I'd even blamed myself for Japhrimel's first death, though he had indisputably come back. Had it been death at all, or a kind of sleep? The word he used—*dormancy*—conveyed only a type of rest. A sleep of a body ground to cinnamon-smelling ash, with only a will to survive left in its crystalline matrices, calling out to me.

Japhrimel drew in a long, soft breath. "Calm," he whispered into my hair. "Calm, my curious one." He said more, but I didn't listen. It wasn't the words, it was the rumble in his chest telling me I was safe, that he was with me, that I had to calm down.

A small *click* echoed inside my head, the same sound a work of magick makes sliding whole and complete into place. It was the sound of a hunt starting, of the right moment to begin. I inhaled deeply, drawing musk-spice smell all the way down to the bottom of my lungs. Here was a demon who had lied to me, misled me, hurt me, dragged me into working for the Prince of Hell again—but he still comforted me. He'd *protected* me when it mattered most.

He had even matched his strength against Lucifer's and come away the winner.

I was still soothed, listening to the strong slow beat of his pulse echoing mine.

How was that for crazy?

"I'm all right," I managed. "Really."

"I doubt it." He kissed my hair, a slight intimate movement. I was glad I don't blush easy. "If you continue in this manner, you may well drive me mad."

Drive you mad? What the hell does that mean? When he didn't continue, I wriggled impatiently and he eased up a little. His arms were still tense; if I tried to escape he'd just clamp down again. "What?"

"I do not like to see you in such pain. What will you do first?"

I contemplated the question, trying to find a comfortable way to lie with my rig on. It didn't happen. I took in another deep breath of his smell, male and spice and demon musk, felt my heartbeat slow just a little. "Japh, let me up. I've got a plasgun trying to burrow into my hip and a projectile gun looking for my spleen the hard way. Okay?"

"Perhaps I like holding you. We have had little closeness, of late."

We may not have a whole lot in the foreseeable future, either. "If you'd quit hiding things from me and pushing me around, maybe we'd have more." I didn't have time to get into a spat with him. I really didn't.

"I am not your enemy." He stroked my hair, his fingers slipping between the silky strands.

My reply startled me. "Oh, yeah? Prove it." Then I felt like an idiot; I sounded like a spoiled brat.

"If you like." He laughed, as if genuinely amused. That

only irritated me more. The fresh frustration was tonic, pushing aside the numb blackness of shock and grieving horror.

I bit his shoulder, sinking my teeth in, and he sucked in a breath. But his arms didn't loosen, and his body tensed in a way I was all too familiar with.

Well, now. Don't I feel silly. The taste of musk and night and demon filled my mouth, as intimate as a kiss, the material of his coat slick and pulsing with Power against my lips. It reminded me of just how long it had been since I'd had him, felt the blessed relief of not having to think, trusting him with my body. I tried to pull away from him again, achieved nothing.

Dammit, quit treating me like a kid! "Japhrimel—"

His voice cut across mine, soft and inflexible. "Not just yet, Dante. I am not yet convinced you are quite in control of your temper."

It was too much. One thing after another, from Sarajevo to Saint City, so much death and destruction piled on top of an already-strained mind. How much more could I stand without breaking?

I'll show you temper, you supercilious son of a bitch. I pulled back, inhaled, and held my breath, my eyes squeezed shut. Fifteen seconds. Thirty.

The blackness behind my eyelids exploded with pinwheels and bursts of color, far more vivid than real life. The blue glow of Death rose too, the place inside me where the god lived opening like a flower. For the first time, I didn't want to escape into that glow, kept myself away by a sheer effort of will, lungs crying out, pulse throbbing in my ears and throat and the rising tide of desire along my skin swamped by the sudden urgent need for oxygen.

Even demons need to breathe, don't they? A second thought, *I'm acting like a kid. Well, he treats me like one, I might as well. I've reverted to a spoiled three-year-old.*

The fact that I understood I was acting like an idiot couldn't stop me, for once.

Japhrimel's arms loosened. He shook me, hard but just short of hurting, my hair rasping against the pillow. Pent-up air rushed out, I breathed again. Opened my eyes to find him watching me.

The arc of his cheekbone took me by surprise, as it always did. The sculpture of his lips, now pulled tight and thin into a straight line, his eyebrows drawn together, a faint line between them. His eyes were incandescent, silken green. For a moment, he looked like Lucifer. The resemblance was so sudden and striking my heart slammed into my throat and demon adrenaline jolted my entire body, leaving me gratefully alive and thinking clearly for the first time since passing through Gabe's front gate that day.

"Do not," he said quietly, in a voice like the Prince of Hell's, "*ever* do that again."

Bingo, Danny. We've found something that works to irritate him. I felt equally childish and vindicated, as if I'd suddenly gained some kind of control over the situation. "Or what?" I finally worked my way free of his arm. If my voice hadn't been shaking so badly, I might have almost sounded tough.

"Or I will *teach* you not to do so." The bed creaked as he flowed away and to his feet, without a single hitch in the movement. "Think what you like of me. I begin to believe you will anyway."

Gods above and below, does he actually sound hurt? I could barely believe my ears. He stalked away, and I was too badly shaken to say a word. Lucifer called Japhrimel his Eldest, and I wondered how on earth I could live with a being that old, that powerful—and that *alien*. He wasn't human, for all he'd successfully mimicked it for me.

Not human. *Inhuman.*

But then I was no longer fully human either, was I? Maybe only human inside my head. Or my aching, pounding heart.

Wherever I'm still human, it will have to be enough.

The bedroom door closed behind him. I hunched on the edge of the bed, buried my face in my hands, and shoved down the tears. After a long, shaking moment or two, I sighed and dropped my fists into my lap. Looked over at the file, lying innocent against the now-rumpled bedspread. Japhrimel was right, I hadn't been thinking straight. Even if he'd irritated me past human endurance, he had still helped me clear my head.

First thing I've got to do is wait for nightfall. It was a relief to have a single, clear, definable thing to do in the complex mess my life had become.

Then I've got to go see Abracadabra.

12

I lay curled on my side, my sword clasped in my hands, my rig at the end of the bed near my booted feet. I puzzled over the idea of the Key and the Roof of the World, I thought of what I would do when I saw Abra, and I thought of what I would do to whoever had hurt Gabe.

I brooded most on that, and on how I would find Gabe's daughter. I chewed over the problem in my head, not coming up with anything new.

I tried not to think about acting like a spoiled little brat. I was beginning to deconstruct under the stress. I needed a good clean-out meditation session to keep my head straight. The faster and harder I ran, the more I'd need a clear head and a sure hold on my temper.

First, though, I had to rest.

A twilight doze fell over me near dinnertime, just as I heard Japh and McKinley speaking in the other room. It was hard to ignore, my hearing was so acute, and I strained for the sound of Japhrimel's voice despite myself.

"Tiens is right. You should—" McKinley, getting braver by the moment.

"I did not ask for your opinion on this matter, McKinley." Japhrimel didn't let him finish the sentence, which was irritating in the extreme. "I asked for your loyalty as my vassal. There is a difference."

A long pause. "I've served you faithfully. I'd be remiss in my duty if I didn't warn you it is *dangerous* to allow her to treat you like this."

"What do you suggest? I should chain her in a sanctum like a Nichtvren's plaything? Or that I should allow her to commit a foolhardy suicide and fall with her into darkness?" Each word was underlit with savage anger. I snuggled deeper into the softness of the bed, drowsily glad Japh never spoke to *me* like that. And fuzzily alarmed at what I was hearing.

Foolhardy suicide? Just what does he think I'm going to do? Of course, he can't have too high an opinion of my maturity right now. I actually winced at the thought.

It was time to get a few things straight with him. I lay utterly still, pieces of both puzzles revolving inside my head. Waiting for dark, when I could uncoil like a snake under a rock. And begin hunting.

"You put it that way, it gets a lot clearer." McKinley sounded like he was smiling, for once.

I was tired. My eyes were heavy, and the mark pulsed and rang with soft Power, sliding down my skin, easing me into relaxing. I couldn't cry anymore, could barely dredge up the energy to keep listening.

I listened anyway.

"It is no small choice." Japhrimel sounded heavy, and sadder than I'd ever heard him. "Her hatred or her pain, I do not know which is harder to bear."

If you'd just talk to me, Japh. Precognition tingled along my skin, prickling with tiny diamond feet. It isn't my strongest talent, not by a long shot, but sometimes when the quicksand is getting deeper and deeper I can get a flash of something useful.

Sometimes. But not when my heart was aching this badly. Not when I all but vibrated with the blood-deep hunger for *revenge*. I wanted to start killing, and I wasn't too choosy about who I started with.

Anyone would be fine. And that alarmed me a little.

The precog refused to come. Just the sense of danger, and a creeping sensation against the flesh of my wrist, above my datband. I'd taken the Gauntlet off, but my skin still tingled with the feel of it. Loathing touched the back of my throat, I forced it away.

Relax, Dante. Nothing you can do right now. Just breathe, and wait. Hold yourself still. Don't even think. Just breathe.

I did.

I tipped over the edge into gray nothingness. It wasn't the dead unconsciousness Japhrimel could lull me into, the sleep that was a restorative for my human mind. No, this sleep was more like the restless tossing I'd had all my mortal life, my conscious mind paralyzed by too much stress and sliding out of commission like a disengaged gear, spinning fruitlessly while the deeper parts of me worked, intuition and insight grinding finer and finer until they would present me with the wrench jamming the works.

Inducing a precognitive vision is hard goddamn work, and I failed miserably. But something else happened, something I hadn't done since I'd been human.

I *dreamed*.

* * *

This was not the hall of Death.

I gathered up my skirts as I negotiated a wide, sweeping staircase; the vast parquet floor of the ballroom below shimmered mellow under many layers of wax and care.

I recognized this place.

It was the Hotel Arméniere in Old Kebec. I'd stayed here once on a bounty hunt ending with a clean collar in the teeming sink of the Core in Manhattan. The Arméniere was expensive, but a Hegemony per diem had covered it and right after Doreen's death I hadn't cared if it was pricey; it was magshielded, had a sparring hall, and the staff were mostly psi-friendly. That was worth a little credit. Besides, I'd just been knifed, shot at, and hit on the left arm with a ringbar while engaging in a slicboard duel with the bounty I was tracking. I figured I deserved a little relaxation while I waited for him to screw up and give me something to work with to bring him down.

The ballroom had been one of my favorite places, mostly deserted during the day; quiet and full of space where I could run through katas without being gawked at or challenged to a sparring match I wasn't in the mood for. Long narrow windows looked out on a night pulsing with neon and citylife, I heard distant traffic and the thump of a nightclub on the other side of the wall by the stairs. That told me it was a dream—the Arméniere was on a busy street, but the walls were thick and you would no more hear a nightclub than you would hear the staff whistling the Putchkin anthem.

The other clue that I was in a dream was the fantastic pre-Merican-era illustration of a dress. Red silk, long whispering skirt, a bodice just short of indecent, and long sleeves that belled over my hands.

My human *hands, not gold-skinned demon hands. I saw the well-healed scar on my right thumb, the different texture of pale human skin, the crimson molecule-drip polish I used to use. A fading bruise was turning yellow on the back of my right hand.*

With the fuzzy logic of dreams, it all made perfect sense. Even the dream-copy of the necklace Jace made for me, silver-dipped raccoon bacula and blood-charged bloodstones, was there. The real necklace was on my sleeping self, but this copy hummed with Power, throbbing against my collarbones.

I reached the bottom of the stairs, my pulse pounding like the thump of bass coming through the wall. I felt naked—I had no sword, none of the familiar weight of a rig against my shoulders. Crimson silk mouthed the floor as I moved, cold waxed wood and the grit of dust against my bare tender human feet.

You look beautiful.

The necklace's throb settled into a sustained heat. I whirled.

He leaned against the wall between two windows, his face in shadow except for the bright points of light in his blue eyes. A stray breeze touched a sheaf of wheat-gold hair, and my mouth turned dry and slick as desert glass.

Jace Monroe hooked his thumbs in his belt. He wasn't armed either. Hey, Danny. Spare a kiss for an old boyfriend?

I'm dreaming, I thought. Dreaming. Have to be.

Of course you're not dreaming. *His lips shaped the words, but the air didn't move. Instead, the meaning resounded inside my head. Like the tone of psychic music that was a god's communication, fraught with layers on layers of complexity. A wash of amusement, bitter spice of regret, a thin thread of desire blooming through and sparkling like an iron wire to hold it all together. Under it, the smell of peppered honey that was Jace's magick, the smell of a Shaman, the smell I'd missed without knowing.*

He moved forward into the dim light. Don't think much of the choice of venues, sunshine. Never did have you pegged as a romantic.

Another shock. He was the young Jace of the days of our first affair, moving smoothly and without the telltale hitch from his injured knee, his face smoother without age and the bitterness that had crept up and glazed over him like varnish. Even his haircut shouted it—shaggy, but obviously expensively trimmed. I'd forgotten that about him, forgotten the antique Bolgari chronograph he used to wear glittering over his datband. Forgotten the lopsided, charming smile he used to use on me, the one I'd fallen for.

He folded his arms. This has got to be the first time I've ever seen you speechless. Don't talk too soon, I'm enjoying it.

You're dead. *My lips shaped the whisper. The pulse in my temples and throat was made of glass.* Mirovitch killed you. Gabe set you free in the hospital. You're dead.

Of course I'm dead. *He shrugged.* But am I gone? Not on your life, Danny girl. I don't have much time right now, you're heading into dangerous waters. I'll help all I can.

A shuddering impact hit next door, the wall behind the stairs creaking. Dust pattered down from the ceiling. I flinched, my right hand searching for a weapon that wasn't there. I didn't just feel naked without my sword. I

*felt lost, and panicked, and uncomfortably like I was hav-
ing a nightmare.*

Jace's hand closed around my wrist. I damn near levi-
tated—anyone getting that close without my knowledge
spooks me. Listen to me, *he said, his skin warm and dry
and blessedly human against mine.* You have to wake up
now, Danny. No time for fun and games. Wake up and get
moving. You got a lot of trouble on your tail.

*I opened my mouth to say something, anything, but he
shook his head again. I drank in his face, the angle of his
jaw, each small detail lovingly polished. It was lifelike,
incredibly vivid, right down to the individual grains of
grit under my bare feet. Jace's fingers burned, clamping
down hard on my left wrist, clasping like chill heavy metal
quickly warming to my skin.*

Wake up, Danny. Wake up.

I don't want to! *I wailed. My hair slid forward—my
old human dyed-black, dead dark lifeless hair. I never
thought I'd be so glad to see split ends again.* I don't want
to wake—

*Another shuddering boom. A visegrip clamped around
my right shoulder and ripped my body free of its moor-
ings. I felt the snap as whatever space holding me was
torn away and I fell, arching my back, screaming and—*

—landing on the floor beside the bed, an undignified squeak cut short as my teeth clicked together *hard.* I
blinked up, a pair of familiar yellow eyes meeting mine;
the tip of my blade caressed Lucas Villalobos's throat.
Blue flame ran through my sword, its heart showing a thin
thread of white fire; I had also lifted my left arm instinctively into a guard position when I'd landed on my ass.
My eyes snagged on my raised wrist—clasped against

my golden skin, the cuff of silvery demon-wrought metal glowed.

I didn't put that back on. I choked. I wasn't sure what surprised me more—a human dream, or finding out I was still *hedaira*. The thin hitching sound of a sob rose in my throat; I denied it.

"Time to go," Lucas wheezed. Darkness broken only by the glow of a small nightlight fastened into a wall plug filled the room like deep water, shadows lying over the top of unfamiliar furniture. "Get up, Valentine."

My sword whispered back into its sheath. It was small consolation that I'd been ready to kill him, he could have slid a knife between my ribs while I was lost in whatever trance had taken me. My eyes were grainy, and my entire body felt torpid, like I'd been shaken out of a dead sleep in the middle of the afternoon. It was a very human feeling.

It was also profoundly unsettling. *Where's Japhrimel? What's going on?*

Of all the things I could have said, I settled for the most predictable. "What the *hell?*"

"Had to wait until your boyfriend left, *chica*. Come on." Lucas's sleeve was torn and floppy, soaked with blood. His yellow eyes were dead and dark, his lank hair fell in his face, and he wore the widest, most feral smile I had ever seen on him; either post-coital or post-combat, it was wholly scary. His teeth gleamed white in the dim bedroom. "Abra wants to see you tomorrow. I found out some o' what the demon's up to."

"Great." I ducked into my rig. *Where's Japhrimel? I thought he wasn't going to let me out of his sight.* I didn't smell him, and the mark on my shoulder pulsed softly, absently, coating my skin with now-familiar Power. A few seconds worth of buckling had all my weapons riding in their accustomed places, I passed the strap of my bag over my head, shrugged into my coat, and was ready to go. My katana weighted my left hand as I followed Lucas out into the rest of the suite.

Which was, to put it kindly, a shambles. The furniture was destroyed, chairs and tables smashed, the holovid player shattered, and a large imprint rammed into the wall between the suite and the bedroom. Japhrimel was still nowhere in evidence; I wondered where he'd gone. *"Sekhmet sa'es,* I slept through *this?"*

"You been sleepin' a lot, *chica.* Even on your feet. It ain't like you." Lucas jerked his chin at a shape lying on the floor by the nivron fireplace. It was McKinley, bleeding from the nose and ears and gagged with an anonymous bit of cloth held down with magtape, trussed with a thin golden chain that shivered and smoked in the light from the upended lamp. The carpeted floor groaned under him as he caught sight of me and started to struggle.

Leander, now shaven-cheeked, his accreditation tat twisting under his skin, nodded from the windowsill. He stood with one hip hitched up against the sill, his sword shoved into his belt and a plasgun in his right hand, peering down into the street below. His dark hair was wildly mussed. "Hi, Danny." His tone was excessively even. "Sorry I had to bail, I thought it best I didn't stick around after the demon warned me off." His emerald sparked, and one corner of his mouth pulled down.

Warned you off? What the hell? I contented myself with a noncommittal noise. "Mh. What the hell's that?" I pointed at McKinley, whose black eyes narrowed. He was either furious or terrified, I couldn't tell. A whiff of burning cinnamon and dry naptha scented the air, as if his glands had opened to pour out chemical reek.

"The demon left him here, probably to watch out for Sleeping Beauty." Leander sighed, shrugging, but his dark eyes flicked nervously over the room as if expecting company any moment. "Let's go, the back of my neck's itching."

So was mine. *Left him here? What the hell?* It wasn't like Japhrimel to leave me alone. Where the hell was he?

The last time Japh had left while I was unconscious, it was to go into Hell and start the process of dragging me back into a huge mess full of demons. One happy little home in the Toscano hills burned to smoking rubble in a reaction fire and my life crashing down around my ears again.

What was he doing *now?*

"What's Japh been doing, Lucas?" My hand dropped to a knifehilt as I contemplated McKinley, who went absolutely still. He was bruised all over his face and I was sure one shoulder was dislocated by the way it rotated too far back. This was twice Lucas had faced down a Hellesvront agent and come away the winner.

I am so glad I hired him. Well, technically, Eve started out hiring him, but I'm glad he's working for me. With a clear-cut emergency in front of me, I felt better than I had since I'd received Gabe's message.

Gabe.

I pushed away the thought of her broken body, the emerald dark and lifeless in her pale cheek. *Focus, Danny. Goddammit, focus!* Broken plasilica ground into the carpet under my boots. The dangling almost-chandelier light fixture had been yanked out of the ceiling. The wet bar was a chaos of broken glass and the simmering stink of alcohol, reminding me of DMZ Sarajevo. A shiver bolted up my spine, was ruthlessly quelled.

"There's another demon in town, and word is your green-eyed boy is tracking it down, as well as some other interestin' shit. I got you an interview with a Magi who might know what the fuck's goin' on." Lucas shrugged. "Let's get the hell out of here. The whole fuckin' city's seething. Something about a dead Necromance and your name tangled up together. I can't leave you alone for a fuckin' minute, can I?"

Gabe. So someone knows. Chill fury boiled up behind my breastbone again, was suppressed. "Guess not." I drew a knife with my right hand. McKinley's black eyes met mine, and he strained against the gag, making a low muffled anonymous noise.

One problem at a time. Japhrimel was hunting Eve's rebellion here in Santiago City. Why hadn't he *told* me?

You must trust me to do what you cannot, then. Japhrimel's voice, even and chill. He rarely said *anything* he didn't mean.

And here I thought he came along because I needed him. Silly me. Yellow bitterness coated the back of my throat. *Stupid and blind, Danny. He's doing the same thing he did before, going behind my back.*

Of course. Why expect him not to? It was what he *did*. Too bad I was only finding out now.

The knife flicked from my right hand, burying itself in the carpeted floor with a *chuk,* less than an inch from McKinley's nose. He flinched, barely but perceptibly, and I tried not to feel the hot, nasty wave of satisfaction curling through me. *You told Japh it was better to tie me up and do whatever he wanted, didn't you? And he left you here alone with me. You son of a bitch. No wonder you work for demons.*

"Tell Japhrimel," I said quietly. "Tell him *exactly* what I am about to say, McKinley. If he comes after Eve, he's going to have to get through me first."

That spurred the agent to frantic motion, twisting like a landed fish inside the thin golden chain. I didn't even *want* to know what it was made of. Another desperate smothered noise pressed against the gag as his eyes rolled.

My thumb caressed the katana's guard as I stared down at him. The blade thrummed, hungry inside its sheath.

Lucas pushed me. "That won't hold him forever. Come on."

You're right. I don't have time for this, I have other hovers to fly. There was a time when the thought of Lucas Villalobos touching me would have made my skin crawl with frantic loathing and send me scrabbling for a weapon to protect myself. He was *dangerous,* as dangerous as a big venomous snake or a Mob Family Head. Just because he hadn't bitten me yet didn't mean he wasn't going to.

But along with being dangerous, Lucas was professional. He was indisputably working for me—and in any case I was no longer human. I was fairly sure I could outrun him. Besides, he'd taken on the Devil for me. Something like that will make a girl feel mighty charitable even when it comes to Villalobos.

Leander ducked out the window onto the fire escape, I did too. At least the window wasn't shattered. Someone was going to owe the hotel a bundle for that room—the noise had probably already been remarked.

Outside, the night was cool and cloudy, orange glowing on the clouds and hovers moving in silent formation overhead. The cuff was heavy on my left wrist above my datband; I wondered if Japhrimel had put it on me before he'd left. While I'd been dead to the world, unconscious or tranced into a high-alpha state.

Dreaming of Jace. Or not-dreaming.

The Gauntlet shimmered, my skin crawling underneath it. It bothered me more than I wanted to admit. I wanted to stop and peel the damn thing off again, but we had precious little time and I didn't want to have my hands full of jewelry if the other shoe dropped.

"So where are we going?" I asked Lucas, who had taken a position just behind my left shoulder, watching my back and scanning the street in front of us at the same time. "Where's this Magi?"

"In the Tank District," Lucas said easily. "Just follow Leander, *chica*. We'll get you there."

13

Anwen Carlyle lived in a rickety, filthy apartment building in the Tank District; and not a nice part of the Tank either. This close to the Bowery, the worst festering sore in the middle of the Tank, the air was full of pain. Bloodlust, desperation, Chillfreaks, pimps, hookers, Mob runners, and other human flotsam congregated there. The Tank is where you go if you're a rich technoyuppie slumming, or a bounty hunter looking to connect with the shadow side. It's also where you *don't* go if you want to get through the evening without a fight. It isn't as bad as the Core in Manhattan or the Darkside in Paradisse, but it's bad enough. The urban renewal that had gone through Trivisidiro hadn't visited this part of the Tank, it was likely none ever would. This close to the Rathole where the sk8 tribes congregated, renewal wasn't a priority. Survival was.

The smell inside the sloping tenement was incredible: dirty diapers, piss, desperation, food cooked on little personal plasfires. "What the hell's a Magi doing here?" I asked, quietly enough, as I followed Lucas up the stairs. There was an elevator, but it didn't work. I didn't mind, even through the titanic stink of human despair and dying cells. I'd rather smell stink than be caught in an elevator, unable to breathe as claustrophobe terror crawls down my throat. "She can't make rent?"

Leander, behind me, made a low snickering sound. "Taken in by appearances?" His tone was light, a welcome distraction from the close dank quarters that almost triggered latent claustrophobia. My sword was heavy in my hand, and the cuff was chill against my skin.

I ignored the itching, nagging desire to take the thing *off* again. "Lucas?"

His bloody sleeve flopped as he climbed the stairs with shambling grace. "Anwen don't like company, *chica*. But she owes me."

I shivered at the thought of what a Magi might owe Lucas. I wondered if he liked to keep a few debts in reserve, for just such an emergency. My skin chilled at the thought of the price he usually demanded from a psion, anyone with Talent would have to be *really* desperate to hire him.

Japhrimel had paid him. What would a demon pay the Deathless?

I decided I could live without knowing. "Great. So she owes you." I looked at the intaglio of graffiti rioting over the walls in permaspray. Most of the lights were broken or burned out. The ones that remained gave enough of a glow I could see every crack and splinter, every patched and unpatched hole in the wall, every small bit of trash and scuttling cockroach. Demon eyes need a few photons to work with, not like Nichtvren and their uncanny ability to see in total dark.

The thought of Nichtvren sent another shiver up my back. For some reason they scare me more than demons.

It's an atavistic fear; a human fear of something higher up the food chain. It's also completely unrealistic, a demon will kill you quicker. But I was more scared of suckheads. Go figure.

Let's just get this over with so I can go talk to Abra and start untangling this mess. Impatience rose; I pushed it down. I didn't want to be here in the Tank, I wanted to be somewhere else, anywhere else, tracking down a killer.

Gabe's killer, Eddie's killer. I had revenge to get started with. But if I could also find out exactly what Japh was up to, I had to at least *try*.

What wasn't he telling me, and where the hell *was* he? I didn't like my protection—the only protection I was certain of—vanishing while the inside of my head turned into a bad holovid show. I was sinking fast, as usual, without any clue what the hell was going on now.

Well, we're here to figure some of it out, aren't we? A Magi who owes Lucas. Let's hope she has something useful to tell me.

We reached the sixth floor, Lucas and Leander both breathing a little more raggedly than usual. My own breath came deep and slow, the mark on my shoulder pulsing softly with Power, I wasn't winded in the least.

"One thing," Lucas wheezed. He smelled like copper, dried blood, and the dry throat-stinging tang of a stasis cabinet, under a screen of male effort and stale sweat. "Try not to scare her, Valentine."

"I'll do my best." My left hand tightened on my sword. "Why anyone's scared of me when *you're* around. . ." *Good gods above, I'm actually bantering with Lucas Villalobos. Christer Hell must be frozen over by now.*

Amazingly, he gave a whistling, wheezing laugh as he

pushed the heavy fire door open. I saw a glimmer down at the end of the hall—shields, powerful subtle shields. "I'm a reasonable man, Valentine. You ain't."

Not reasonable, or not a man? I feel pretty damn reasonable, considering my best friend was just murdered and the man I love won't give me a straight answer when it comes to the Prince of Hell and why I'm suddenly such a high-priced chip in this goddamn game. "I'm reasonable," I muttered darkly. "Considering everything that's going on, I'm pretty *damn* reasonable." My throat was dry, my voice soft and seductive in the dark despite or maybe because of my damaged trachea.

"Hear, hear." Leander bumped into me, maybe his human eyes couldn't pierce the dark like mine could. He still smelled like sand and the thick langorously-spiced coffee of Cairo Giza under the cloak of dying cells that meant *human*.

I wondered why the smell sent such a frisson of distaste up my back. I liked him, didn't I? And Lucas's dry stasis-cabinet scent was no better.

"Shut up, deadhead," Lucas snarled. He seemed to have no trouble navigating over the debris in the hall—soymalt bottles, empty takeout cartons, rancid clothing, other shapeless bits of stuff. "I do the talkin' here."

"Leave him alone." My own tone was flat and bored. "He knows enough to keep his mouth shut when dealing with an edgy Magi." *Although how dangerous a Magi who chooses to live in a dump like this is, I won't venture to guess.*

Villalobos didn't dignify that with an answer. We reached the end of the hall, apartment 6A; he knocked once, twisted the knob, and pushed the door wide.

Well, that's interesting. I watched the shimmering layers of Power shunt aside from his aura, magickal energy refusing to touch him. It was something I'd noticed about Lucas, he didn't use Power himself, but it couldn't be used against him either. An impasse, and food for thought . . . if I could figure out what to think about it.

A breath of *kyphii*-scented air puffed out, caressed the hall. I followed Lucas, stepping nervously through a cascading sheet of energy that parted to let me through before flushing a deep beautiful rose-spangled gold as whoever inhabited this place felt the Power flux change around me. *Female. Magi. Not too young, but not old.* I took a deep breath, all the way down to the bottom of my lungs, tasting the air as if I was on a bounty. Leander followed, sweeping the door shut behind him, and we found ourselves in a hardwood-floored entryway, smelling mellowly of beeswax, *kyphii,* and Power.

Anubis et'her ka, she's powerful, whoever she is. The shields were carefully done, a subtle taint of demon spice threading through them telling me she was an active, demon-dealing Magi.

Like "Shaman", "Magi" is a catch-all term for a wide range of variously-talented psions. A Magi might or might not know what to do with a demon when it pops up, depending on their study—and depending on the demon. Magi have been trafficking with Hell since before the Awakening, but before that great collective human leap forward in psionic and magickal Power, their methods had been spotty and uneven at best. Still, when the Awakening happened, the Magi were the only ones who had an idea of how to train psionic talent, or a framework for making Power behave. Nowadays all psions are Magi-trained in memory, Power-handling, and theory of magick, but that doesn't make us all Magi.

I knew how to call up an imp and constrain it in a circle now; I knew how to consecrate tools to be used in closing an etheric portal into Hell and send a Low Flight demon *back*, I even knew a few more things about demon anatomy than I had before. But demon-dealing Magi are secretive in the extreme, committing information about their successful experiments in breaking the walls between our world and Hell to only one apprentice at a time and writing their shadowjournals—the equivalent of a Skinlin's mastersheets or a Ceremonial's grimoire—in codes that could take months to break. Even if they work with circles, they don't share many of their private secrets, and I couldn't lay my hands on the great books of magick the accepted circles had access to. Another impasse, this one frustrating in the extreme because I *needed* to know more about what I was.

What Japhrimel had made me.

The inside of the apartment was a surprise. It held no trace of clutter or poverty; the floor was polished hardwood and the walls painted varying shades of rose, pale pink, and white. Lucas led us into a living room decorated with an altar draped in silver cloth and sporting a three-foot-tall statue of Ganej the Magnificent, the elephant god. There was a restrained fainting-couch done in rose velvet and a Vircelia print on the wall, an original if my eyes didn't fool me, and the windows were cloaked with heavy silken drapes.

Ganej. The Remover of Obstacles. Odd, but an effective choice now that I think about it. What better way to break the barriers between here and Hell than with the help of a god who surmounts barricades? The statue was an antique, creamy marble veined with gold, and thrumming with Power. So this Magi took her god seriously, as seriously as I took mine.

I cautiously decided to reserve judgment.

There was a click from the doorway opposite the one we'd come in through, and my sword left the sheath in a singing blur as I stepped instinctively in front of Leander.

After all, I knew I could take more damage.

The Magi, a slim caramel-skinned woman with long dark-brown hair and a pair of wide gray eyes, stared at us. She held a very nice 9 mm Glockstryke projectile gun in her right hand, her stance braced and professional. She was pretty in an unremarkable way that wasn't helped along by the design of her tat, which wasn't flowing or graceful; she'd chosen an angular Varjas design, like a Ceremonial. It didn't do a thing for her face, being too thick-lined and sharp. But her aura flamed with Power; she was strong for a human.

Gods, did I just think that? I'm human too. I am. "Drop the gun, girl. Or I'll make you eat it." My voice stroked the drapes, made the walls groan.

"Fuck me with a hover," she breathed, her gray eyes flicking from Lucas to me, settling on me, and widening. The gun dipped slightly, ended up pointing at the floor. She wore jeans and a pretty blue wide-sleeved, square-necked shirt embroidered with Canon runes around the collar and cuffs. "*This* is your client, Villalobos?" The high edge of fear colored her voice, and a rill of excitement slid down my back. Her aura jittered slightly, her dread coloring the air like wine.

It wasn't quite as drunkening as Polyamour the sex-witch's fear, but it was still pleasant. Because Carlyle's terror was tinted with the edge of attraction, a promise that filled the air like the smell of anything fragrant and good, and comprehension flowered in those wide-spaced, rainy-gray eyes.

She knew something. A Magi that knew something, and owed Lucas a favor.

My sword slid back into the sheath, clicked home. "That's right." My pulse pounded in my throat. "I'm his latest employer. And I think we have some things to talk about, Magi."

She didn't offer us anything to drink. Instead, she pointed us toward a pile of cushions on one side of the living room, then stood with her back to her altar and her gun trained on Lucas. I didn't blame her, if I'd been human it's what I would have done.

Her eyes kept flickering over to me, no matter how steady the gun was. "So it's true," she said finally, her voice low and pleasant and reeking of terror. Her tat shifted and strained uneasily under the skin of her left cheek.

"What's true?" I didn't sit on a cushion but I did try to keep my aura close and contained, not wanting to scare her more than was absolutely necessary. After all, she'd just let a part-demon, a Necromance, and Lucas in her front door. The Necromance she was probably sure she could handle—Leander was human, just like her. But still.

Lucas gave me a slanting yellow-eyed look, pushing his lank hair back from his forehead. His breathing had evened out, and he was back to looking like every psion's worst nightmare. "Just tell her what you told me, Carlyle."

She licked her lips, examined me. The gun shook just a little, her sleeve trembled, and her aura shivered right on the edge of going hard and crystalline, locking down. Her pulse throbbed under the damp mortal skin of her throat. *Was that what I looked like when I met Lucas in Rio? Was that what I looked like to Japhrimel? So fragile, and so scared?*

And the even more uncomfortable thought, *Do I still look that way to him? Does he smell my fear, and does it taunt him like hers taunts me?*

"This cancels the debt?" Her voice shook. There wasn't a psion in the building, but the psychically-dense atmosphere kept her shields from being seen. She was almost perfectly hidden, like a scorpion under a rock. Not many people would brave both the Tank and the filth of the building outside to intrude on her privacy. Even if she did have to live with the psychic noise and stench of so many angry scrabbling people, it was a fair trade-off.

I wondered what type of work she did, and I also wondered how she'd managed to turn this apartment into such a clean, luxurious nest. She was combat-trained, the way she held the gun—the way she *moved*—told me as much. It struck me that I was looking at someone very much like the person I had been.

Before Rio. Before Japhrimel.

"Mostly," Lucas rasped. "I did you a *big* favor, Carlyle."

That made her aura turn sharp and pale. "I paid you," she insisted. "I may not be able to kill you, but I can hurt you plenty."

Irritation and impatience rose under my skin, spiked and deadly. *Will you two just get on with it so I can do what I have to do?* I took a deep, sharp breath, kept a firm hold on my temper. The vision of Gabe's body retreated just a little.

Just a very little. I wasn't going to be able to see Abra before the next sunset, so I might as well spend my time getting some information on demons and *A'nankhimel.*

I was hoping like hell she knew something about *hedaira* too. It would be a regular Putchkin Yule down here in the Bowery if she did.

I was suddenly aware of three pairs of eyes on me. Gray Magi eyes, Lucas's almost-yellow, and Leander's dark worried gaze a weight I could feel even though he was behind me. I must have been radiating, despite trying to keep my aura close and contained. "I don't have time for petty bargaining," I finally said, softly. "So if you two could finish up sometime this week I'd appreciate it. I've got a lot of business to handle."

Lucas raised an eyebrow. "Tell her what you told me, Carlyle. I promise I won't make any sudden moves. Unless you get jumpy again." His smile, stretched over his pallid thin face, was enough to send a faint shiver down even *my* back.

She cleared her throat. The perfume of her fear made the mark on my shoulder throb, pleasantly. Was it because she was a Magi? I'd damn near drowned in Polyamour's pheromones before; this was a sharper feeling, like synth-hash spiked with thyoline.

A stimulant, like Chill.

She cleared her throat. "There's talk going around. There are demons boiling through the Veil to our world. Imps have been sighted in ever-growing numbers, and there've been some . . . disturbing signs, at the collegia meetings."

Her eyes flicked over me again. "Gods. It's true," she whispered. "It has to be. You're . . . you were *chosen*."

My eyebrows threatened to nest in my hairline. *Imps coming through, and she's mentioned collegia. I thought they were a myth, secret societies of Magi getting together to work collective magicks across Circle affiliations. Wow.* My pulse abruptly slowed to its usual regularity. *At last we're getting somewhere.* "Chosen for what?" I kept my tone absolutely dead level, reined in. Controlled. Still, the husky honey of my voice turned the air dark. Not like it needed any help—the only light was from the novenas ranked under Ganej, his eyes twinkling merrily in the flickering gloom.

"To be a . . . human bride. A fleshwife." Her pupils dilated, and the salt tang of her fear filled my mouth.

Goddammit, none of the bounties I hunted made me feel like this, psion or normal. What's wrong with me?

"I believe the proper term is *hedaira*," I corrected, dryly, as if I knew what the hell I was talking about. My emerald spat a single green spark, and she flinched. "Why don't you tell me everything you know about it, and everything you know about what's going on with the imps and these 'disturbing signs'? I'm sure Lucas will be very satisfied with that."

She eyed Lucas, eyed me, her cheeks were cheesy-pale under the even caramel. Then, far braver than I would have been in her shoes, she eased the hammer of the gun back down with a small click. "I don't know much. But what I do, I'll tell you. And this cancels the debt, Villalobos." Her sharp chin lifted defiantly. "If anyone, Magi or demon, knew I was talking to you like this, my life wouldn't be worth a bag of Tank trash."

"You got it," Lucas rasped. "I'll even let you talk to her alone." His grin was wide and chilling in its good-natured satisfaction. "Your kitchen still in the same place?"

Her hands were shaking, but she glared at him. I was beginning to like her. "Don't drink all the wine, you greedy bastard. Go. And don't touch anything else. You, too, Necromance." Her lip didn't curl when she said it, but she still sounded disdainful. I wondered why, it wasn't like a psion to be so dismissive of another.

Then again, precious little about this woman was normal even for a Magi.

Lucas shuffled out of the room, deliberately noisy with his worn-down bootheels. Leander touched my shoulder before he left, an awkward gesture that oddly enough didn't irritate me.

Immediately, Carlyle became a lot calmer. She holstered the gun at her hip and took a few steps away from the altar. "When did it happen? The change. You're not Magi, how did you convince the demon to do that? Which demon was it? Can you call him anytime you want, or—"

What the hell? "I came here for answers, not to be interrogated," I said frostily. The smell of *kyphii* made me think of Gabe, and the sharp well of pain behind my breastbone made water start in my eyes. "Keep it up, and you'll owe Lucas more."

She actually flinched, again. Her hair fell down over her forehead in a soft wave. Then she collected herself. "May I see it?"

See what? "See what?"

Was she blushing? She appeared to be *blushing.* "The . . . ah, the mark. If it's not in a sensitive . . . place."

Huh? I reached up with my right hand, pulled the neckline of my shirt out of alignment, popping a button so she could see a slice of the twisting fluid scars that made Japhrimel's mark in the hollow of my left shoulder. "It hurts sometimes." I let go of my shirt. *So having the mark is something that's supposed to happen. But I got it from Lucifer when he made Japh my familiar. On the other hand, it's the only scar that stayed after Japh changed me. And it seems to be a link between us. I wonder, does the link go both ways? He said he could use it to track me, to find me, and I can see through his eyes if I touch it. That qualifies as both ways.* "What can you tell me about *hedaira*? And *A'nankhimel*?"

Another flinch, as if I'd pinched her. "I only have one book that mentions this," she said. "I got it out when Villalobos asked me. Shaunley's *Habits of the Circles of Hell*, Morrigwen's translation. The relevant passages are on pages 156–160." She sounded like she was reciting for an Academy thesis defense, her gray eyes suddenly soft and inward-looking. A Magi-trained memory is a well-trained memory; she could probably see the page in front of her right now. "I remember it because it's so utterly unlike anything else I've ever read."

I nodded and folded my arms, the sword in my left hand bumping against my ribs. *Any time now, lady. I don't have all fucking night.*

But if I hurried her along, I might miss a critical piece of information. I couldn't see Abra until tomorrow now, so I supposed I *did* have all fucking night. Impatience rose hot as bile in my throat, I swallowed it. My hair brushed my shoulders, I could almost feel the tangles breeding. Since the hover incident I hadn't bothered fastening it back.

"Shaunley says he came across old texts that assert the

relationship between demons and human women goes back to pre-Sumerian days, back in the times when demons were seriously worshipped as gods. Of course, they were worshipped as late as the Age of Enlightenment, off and on, but that's neither here nor there. The point is, priestesses in the temples—and other women—were sometimes *chosen.* The term Shaunley used is *fleshwife,* but he also used a very old Graeco term for *courtesan;* it's close to a word that means more like *companion* or *beloved* in the demon tongue. Apparently there were quite a few of the Greater Flight who bound themselves to mortal women, granting a piece of their power and receiving something in return—nobody knows quite what." She leaned back against her altar, probably taking solace in the nearness of her god. Her hand rested on the butt of the 9 mm, the cuff of her sleeve falling gracefully down; I wondered where her other weapons were. She wasn't carrying steel.

I made a restless movement, stilled myself. *What did Japh get from this? He said my world is his in exchange for Hell, but . . .* I waited. This was confirming several guesses I'd made, but I needed more.

"They were wiped out in a catastrophe that took plenty of humans with them," she finished heavily. "There haven't been any more."

Except me. Wonderful. I took a firm hold my temper. The silk drapes fluttered as Power pulsed out from the mark again. "So the *hedaira* is what, half-demon? A quarter?" *Give me something I don't know, anything, come on!*

"It's not that simple." She inhaled. "As close as I can figure, the demon and the fleshwife are literally *one* being. Whenever they're written about, it's in the singular, as if each pair is one person. The demon survives in our physical world through the fleshwife."

While you live, I live. Japh's voice echoed in the bottom of my head, smooth and fiery like old dark whiskey. "So what happens if the fleshwife dies?" It was the one question I never expected to be able to answer.

Carlyle brightened. She was into the explanation now, like a yuppie bursting to tell someone about a new techtoy. Her eyes actually sparkled. "If the fleshwife dies, the Fallen demon is sentenced to a slow fall into a mortal death, since she's his link to *our* world. That's straight from an inscription, Shaunley actually made a rubbing of the original. The demon seems to be a lot harder to kill, you hear of them almost dying and they're fine again on the next page."

Comprehension swirled through me. I knew I could resurrect Japh, I'd done it once before, hadn't I?

What if he couldn't resurrect *me?* It had never occurred to me to put things in that light. Even a Necromance doesn't like to contemplate her own messy, imminent demise, especially when trying to stay one hop ahead of the Devil. I'd never thought of what might happen to Japh without me.

It certainly put a different complexion on things. "Oh, boy." My mouth went dry and I dropped my arms to my sides. The candleflames flickered, drenching Ganej's supple curves in light. "Whoa."

She shrugged. "That's all I know. I'm sorry."

It confirmed a few pleasant and unpleasant guesses, and with my grounding in magickal theory I could make a few more assumptions. Good enough, and not a bad bargain for her or for me. "What about these disturbing rumors? And the imps?" I braced myself for the worst.

She didn't disappoint me. "There's a war going on in

Hell, Necromance. Someone's rebelled against the hierarchy of demons, and there's chaos. Four Magi in the last two weeks—dead when they summoned an imp and got *something else* entirely. There are things riding the air, and demonic activity we haven't seen on earth since the Awakening. They're looking for something, I don't know what."

Chills crawled up my spine. I stared at her, hoping I didn't look like an idiot, my mouth gaped open like a fish's.

Looking for a treasure and a Key. Japh took me to visit the Anhelikos, who had the treasure, but who had sent it, probably along a prearranged route. So there's something demonic bouncing around in the world, and a key to it, and all Hell will probably break loose when someone gets their hands on it. Lucifer? Or the rebellion?

The logical extension to that line of thinking unreeled inside my skull. *Or me?*

A thin finger of ice traced up my spine, remembering the Anhelikos and its wide white wings, the smell of clotted sweetness and feathers, and a predatory face once its beautiful mask slipped. If Japhrimel hadn't been there . . . but he had, and he'd treated the thing like it was no big deal.

Quit it. Be logical, Danny. Eve is the rebellion, isn't she? But maybe she's not all *the rebellion. They're testing Lucifer because Santino got away, and nobody knows Japhrimel was acting under orders and setting Santino free.*

My head began to hurt with complex plot and counterplot. No wonder Japhrimel hadn't told me any of this. I'd visited the Anhelikos with him and seen Eve afterward; if Japh thought Eve was after this treasure he probably wasn't sure what I'd told her—or what I was *likely* to tell her.

I had to admit, if she'd caused a war in Hell and was

making this amount of trouble for Lucifer, I was feeling more fucking charitable toward her all the time.

I didn't give a good goddamn about most of it. The only thing I was worried about right now was getting to Abra's and starting to track down Gabe's killer. "Okay. Anything else you can tell me before I get Lucas out of your hair?"

Carlyle sagged against the altar. "You mean it?" Her dark eyes were wide and haunted. "This cancels my debt?"

I don't know what he did for you, sunshine, but if I was you I'd be happy to still be alive. I forced myself to shrug, my rig creaking slightly as good supple leather sometimes did. "That's between you and Lucas. He's reasonable."

"Far more reasonable than the alternative." She tipped her head back. The perfume of her fear was stronger, taunting me, she was giving out pheromones like a sexwitch. "You . . . are you staying in Saint City?"

I nodded. "I have some business to sort out." *Someone to kill. And Gabe's daughter to find, wherever she is.* "In a safe place." *I wonder.* "Why?"

"If you want to come back." She swallowed, and I wasn't sure I liked the gleam in her rainy eyes. "I'll trade, for information. About demons."

I had a sudden, nasty mental image of bringing Japhrimel here, quickly shoved it away. "I don't think you'd like that," I hedged. "They're worse than Lucas, Carlyle. Much worse." *You should know that.* A chill, unhappy thought surfaced. *What if she smells like that because she's a demon-dealing Magi? Polyamour smelled good because she's a sexwitch, what if this Magi smells good because she's been dealing with demons and I'm somehow picking up on it?*

"I've called imps." Her eyes were definitely bright and moist. Her mouth pulled down in a grimace, the smell of *kyphii* tanged with the deeper brunette scent of adrenaline-laced fear. "Properly constrained in a circle, they—"

Sekhmet sa'es, *you have no goddamn idea, woman.* "No." My right hand curled around my swordhilt. I'd taken on an imp once and gotten poisoned claws through my chest; the only reason I was still alive was because, of all things, reactive paint had turned the Low Flight demon into a bubbling greasy streak. The memory of a soft maggot-white babyface snarling as the imp came for me in the rocketing flexible tube of a hovertrain made the sensation of gooseflesh rise under my golden skin, hot and prickling. "Forget it, Magi. Just forget it."

Curtains moved slightly at the closed window, and I stilled, glancing at them. I hadn't done that. The Gauntlet turned cold on my wrist, a tugging sliding against the surface of my skin.

What the hell? What was the damn demon-thing doing now? It had warned me of attacks before, but it had never done *this*.

I shook the sensation away and eyed the Magi, whose cheeks had gone back to that alarming pale shade. Her hands shook. *Wait a second.*

"*Lucas!*" My tone was sharp, and my hand curled around my swordhilt. Three inches of steel leaped free, and I had to clamp down on my control not to draw the rest of the way.

"You bellowed?" he said from the door, and the look he gave the trembling Magi could only be described as *predatory.*

I squeezed down the temptation to voice my sudden certainty that Carlyle might be having other visitors soon, visitors who would be very interested in us. It was a faint mercy, at best.

But no matter what side of the demon's field she was playing, she was scared to death of Villalobos, and I remembered that feeling so well I had no desire to put her through any more of it. I wondered bleakly if she was a Hellesvront agent, or if Japhrimel was looking for me and it was just easier to find me when I hung around a demon-dealing Magi.

The Gauntlet chilled again, a hard frost clamped to my wrist. The feeling was like icy water closing over my head. I surfaced, blinking, and the premonition passed me by again.

Dammit. I hate it when a precog just won't land.

The other possibility, of course, was that it was another demon looking for me, or this Magi was working for someone other than Japhrimel. Since Japh was off doing gods-only-knew-what.

Still, when she looked at Lucas I was reminded of being human, of feeling that gutclenching fear I couldn't even admit to myself now.

Be human, Danny. Prove you're still capable of it.

"Time to go," I said shortly. "Her debt's canceled. Come on."

14

I spent the daylight hours pacing the inside of a cheap Cherry Street hotel room, wishing I could get *out* and do something productive, shoving away the mental image of Gabe's body, the bite of frustration sharp and smelling of gun oil as I ground my teeth. Leander slept, Lucas settled in a chair by the window and contented himself with oiling and cleaning his projectile guns before falling into a healthy doze. Night was the time to go see Abra; she didn't truly open up until dusk. Darkness would also give us some cover.

There was another component to my unease: we were near the same patch of sidewalk where the man who had raised me since infancy, had been knifed dead by a Chillfreak because his old chronograph looked pawnable. I used to visit the site every year, hadn't since the hunt for Mirovitch. I wondered about going back, maybe buying some flowers. Wondered if I would be alive for the anniversary of his death, wondered if I could make up for the recent time spent with Japhrimel, when I hadn't brought myself to the site because of distance or just plain cowardice.

Time had become fluid while I lived with Japh. I wasn't

even sure what month it was. Only that the trees had lost their leaves but the streets weren't cold enough for dead winter yet.

Finally, after dark, Leander led us up Ninth Street and cut over on Downs, probably meaning to work down on Fiske to Klondel. I could have told him to take Avery instead—after all, Fiske would take us right through a really ugly part of the Tank District—but I was too occupied taking note of all the other changes that had happened to my city.

I kicked at a Plasmalt Forty bottle; it clanked against the sidewalk. Downs was deserted this time of night, since all the reputable frowning businesses patronized by normals closed about seven. At Fiske and Twentieth we would start to see some nightlife, it was the edge of the hooker-patrolled part of the District. Even though Downs was deserted I could see changes—graffiti scrawled in permaspray, magbars on some windows—that warned of the Tank spreading this way. Trivisidiro was getting better; Downs was getting worse.

Lucas and I also had other things to talk about. "A dead Necromance and my name. Lovely." Someone had linked Gabe and me. It wasn't surprising, given how often we'd worked together.

"Yeah, you managed to stay incognito a whole twelve hours. Now everyone knows you're back, and plenty know you look like a serious genetic remodel. Abra's is getting hot, what with people coming and asking about you." Lucas scanned the rooftops, blinked like a lizard, and massaged his left shoulder. It bothered me to see his clothes stiff with dried blood, though I couldn't have said why.

"Who's asking about me?" *When did I get so fucking*

popular? And do any of these people want to know about me so they could figure out if Gabe had time to talk? It felt good to consign all my problems with demons to the back of my brain. Even if the image of Gabe flung over the hemlock wouldn't go away, making a strange choking sensation rise in my throat. I pushed it down.

"Courier messages from the Tanner Family, four or five bounty hunters. A werecain—some shaggy bastard with striped fur. A Nichtvren girl; she left you an envelope. Couple slic couriers, a Shaman who works on a clinic out on Fortieth—"

"*Sekhmet sa'es,*" I breathed. "Fuck."

He gave a small, whistling laugh. *There he goes again, finding me funny. When did I become so amusing?*

"That's not all. A corpclone from Pico-PhizePharm, too. *Everyone's* lookin' for you; lucky me findin' you first." Lucas's steps matched mine on the sidewalk. Ahead of us, Leander turned on Fiske Avenue. His shoulders were level under his rig. He hadn't flinched once. The streetlamps painted his hair with soft darkness, and he moved with the caution all bounty hunters acquired after a few successful but hard-fought collars.

I like him, I decided. *I'm glad he didn't skip out on me.*

Lucas's eyes followed mine. "Good kid," he said grudgingly. "Came and found me at Abra's. Told me the demon was slipping out while you were asleep."

I don't know what's he's doing or where he's gone. Par for the course, just when I could have used him. "Well." My fingers ached around the katana's scabbard.

Trust me, Japhrimel kept telling me. *Do not doubt me.* He'd faced down Lucifer to protect me, and now he was gone hunting Eve and leaving me behind like a piece of luggage. Just when I thought I had Japh pegged as a good guy or a bad guy, he did something to confuse me all over again.

"Beaudry also told me Boy Black warned him to stay away from you. Seems your demon's jealous." Lucas sounded far too interested and amused for my comfort.

I shivered. Did Japhrimel think I belonged to him? Demons were possessive, everyone knew that. *Way* possessive. Had I put Leander in danger just by smiling at him? Enjoying his company?

Well, let's be honest here, Danny. You like the man; he's a bounty hunter, and he's human. Human, something Japh isn't. You like hanging around him, and Japhrimel reacted the way any jealous lover would.

I decided a subject change would be a fantastic idea. "How are we going to get in Abra's front door without anyone noticing? If so many people are looking for me, at least one of them will figure out just to stay near Abra's until I show up." It was a dumbass question, and the sidelong look Lucas gave me showed he didn't think much of it.

"Abra's spread a quiet rumor that there's bad blood; you gypped her on the payment on that hush-hush Rio bounty. Said she's going to take it out of your hide if you come near. Figured that was enough to keep most of 'em away. I'm gonna take you in the back door, Leander will waltz in the front and see if we have any eyes." Lucas coughed, spat to one side. He sounded horrible, like a man dying of slaglung.

"Good." *I didn't even know Abra had a back door.* "So any more word on the demon Japh's after? Other than your Magi's, I mean." *Eve. Is she here? If she is, where is she hiding? Why would she come here?*

Why would so many people—and other species—be looking for me? And bounty hunters too. Goddammit, Gabe, what's going on?

Gabe couldn't answer, but it felt good to think of her as if she was still alive.

I swallowed the lump in my throat, felt the rage rise again. Corralled it, again, with an almost-physical effort that made my rings ring with light.

I couldn't *afford* to get too angry, too soon. The trouble was, my control was wearing thin. The Gauntlet was so cold against my wrist, the metal heavy and dissatisfied. I shivered again, the feeling of a precog rising, pressing maddeningly out of reach.

"Hope you got something worthwhile out of that bitch, that was an expensive favor I did her. All I've heard is there's a demon in town and it's dug in deep, gonna take a lot to blow its bolthole. But if anyone can, it's your sweetheart." Lucas let out another wheeze of amusement. I wondered why he always sounded so choked.

"Don't call him that." I scanned the street again, the back of my neck prickling. "Lucas, we're being watched." Or had the sensation of being examined just stayed with me all the way from Cairo Giza?

"Probably. You gonna give the demon a niner, Valentine? Or maybe send him a datflash breakup?"

Maybe he thought he was being funny, but irritation rasped against my skin, along with the maddening feeling of something I'd forgotten to think about. "I'll deal with Japhrimel."

He had the great tact not to laugh. *A bloody great success you've been at that so far, Danny.* My bootheels clocked against the pavement. The sense of being watched faded a little. Maybe my nerves were just raw . . . but just to be sure, my rings swirled and sparked again, anger turned to good use, bled off so I could think clearly. Saint City was big enough that the flux of Power would confuse my trail, but a half-decent Magi might be able to find me. After all, I was linked to a demon. "Lucas, do you know any other Magi that could be induced to talk?"

"Depends on what you want to talk about." He looked around again, a quick reptilian movement that made his lank hair swing. "Thought you said her debt was canceled."

"She gave me enough, Lucas. I just want to find out more. Another Magi might have a piece of the puzzle, might be able to tell me more about what I . . . am." *And tell me more about this little rebellion in Hell. I've thought all along that there were more players in this game than just Lucifer and Eve; it doesn't make sense otherwise.*

"You don't *know?*"

Imagine that. Lucas the Deathless, sounding shocked. "I don't know *all* of it. I've got some good guesses, I'm figuring everything out." I checked the hovertraffic again, rolled my shoulders back under the rig. Why was I so uneasy? It felt familiar, a half-remembered sensation of my skin crawling with little prickling teeth.

It's not a premonition. Then what is it?

"You're an idiot." Lucas wheezed out another laugh. His lank hair ruffled with the night breeze, and I was struck by the fact that the unscarred side of his face was actually not bad-looking. I'd been too terrified to see it before, but he was almost handsome in a pale, yellow, wolfish sort of way.

Well, except for the scars. And the slightly reptilian cast to his eyes. And his thin colorless lips.

If you only knew how much of an idiot I really am, Lucas.
I kicked another Plasmalt Forty bottle. Someone had a
taste for something a little more expensive than soymalt. It
must be bad around here, for the streetdrones not to come
through and collect the bottles. Paper trash rustled wetly in
the uneasy wind. The graceful arcs of plasteel streetlamps
cast sickly orange circles on the street. No streetside hovertraffic, and the sudden sense of a storm approaching. "*You*
try shacking up with a demon and killing Santino. Then try
hunting down a rabid Feeder and having your brains turned
into a barrel of reactive mush. I'm *figuring it out,* Lucas.
Don't fucking ride me, I'm not in the mood."

"What's got you in a twist, *chica?*" True to form; my
snarl didn't even make a dent.

Leander's footsteps slowed. We caught up to him, but
before Lucas could open his mouth I dropped my news. I
had to tell him sooner or later.

"Gabe Spocarelli's dead. So's Eddie—Eddie Thornton.
Something got them both hit—but before she was hit, Gabe
got my promise to hunt down Eddie's killers. It's personal."
*You may decide it has nothing to do with you, Lucas. If you
do, we're going to part ways.*

I got a full five seconds of deathly silence before Lucas
sighed. "Don't suppose it would have anything to do with
the bounty hunters or the Mob, would it?"

"Or the Nichtvren or the werecain? Could be Lucifer
playing with the mix again." For a moment chills danced
along my skin, the Gauntlet heavy on my left wrist. I wondered if somewhere in Hell, the Devil heard me when I
spoke his name.

The anger simmering in my belly rose to a fresh pitch.
I should have never answered my door that rainy Monday

morning. I should have never followed Japhrimel out of my house and into the subway.

You must trust me to do what you cannot, then. The thought of Japh somewhere out in my city, hunting Doreen's daughter despite anything he felt for me, made me glance over my shoulder and check the street. The whine of hover antigrav overhead made me want to look up. The silent street itself made me itch to get under cover. *I told him not to hunt Eve. I told him I couldn't let him hurt her. I warned him.*

"I hate to interrupt," Leander said quietly, "but I think we're being followed."

My thumb caressed the katana's guard. "This is personal, and it looks *big*. It's not what you two contracted for. You can take a vacation until I finish looking into—"

I didn't even get a chance to finish the sentence before a low sleek shape melded out of an alley on the west side of Fiske and loped down the street toward us. Lucas cursed, stepping away from me, a 60-watt plasgun appearing in his hand. Leander's jaw dropped, and my sword clicked free of the sheath, my right hand closing on the hilt as the shape shook itself. A pleased little squeal sliced the bleeding air, ending with a rib-shaking growl as the hellhound hunched its massive corded shoulders and looked straight at me.

Its eyes were glowing red coins. Heat smoked off its lithe, lethal body of living obsidian. It raised its head, sniffing like a dog scenting fresh meat. The cuff of metal on my left wrist suddenly ran with cold fire, blazing with lines and whorls of green flame over its smooth silver surface. And to top off the fun and games, Japhrimel's mark on my left shoulder crunched into painful life as I tasted copper.

"Leander," I said quietly, "get behind me. And for the sake of every god that ever was, when I tell you to, *run.*"

Lucas faded left, moving out into the street in a gentle arc to put himself between me and the thing. My right arm tensed, three inches of burning-blue steel leaping free of the scabbard. *Gonna have to drop the scabbard and go for a plasgun, Lucas shot the other hellhounds, and it stunned them.*

The thing seemed indisposed to attack, just crouched there watching us. Watching *me.* I finished drawing my sword, and the steel's heart turned white again, flaring with sharp pavement-drenching light. Runes of blue fire curled along the edges of the blade—a blessed weapon, but one that had its own strange ideas.

Yet another thing to add to my rapidly growing to-do list: go visit Jado and ask him about this sword.

Right after I visited Abra and started unraveling whatever had happened to Gabe. And hopefully before Japhrimel got back to find his agent tied up and me gone. I was getting very good at running away from him.

He was getting very good at finding me. Now *there* was an uncomfortable thought. Of course he was good at finding me; I carried his mark and was referred to in the singular.

Maybe he wouldn't find me too quickly this time, though. After all, I was on home ground. Even a few years away shouldn't have changed the boltholes and fluxpoints of the city *too* much. If there was one place on earth I felt capable of hiding in, it was Santiago City.

Hiding sounds like a good idea. Just as soon as we figure out what to do about this thing.

The hellhound paced forward a step. Two. Its eyes were still fixed on me, crimson coins in the shifting seaweed shadows. It hugged the opposite side of the street, and I began to feel a little . . . well, nervous. *Fine time to wish Japh was here, at least now I'm absolutely sure he has a vested interest in keeping me alive, not just something as fragile as caring about me. Always assuming, of course, that Shaunley's right and a Fallen demon suffers a mortal death if his* hedaira's *killed.*

The hellhound's slow, gelid growl rattled the air. Cool wind kissed my face, rich with the promise of rain.

Okay, I was a *lot* nervous. My sword dipped, instinctively taking the guard against attacks from below. What was the thing *doing?* A hellhound had never hesitated before. No, they'd just come straight for me.

A very nasty assumption began to surface under my conscious mind. I stepped forward, my sword ringing softly. Leander had turned to a stone, his aura flushed deep purple-red like a bruise. "Kel?" I whispered. "Velokel?"

The hellhound growled again, and launched itself at me.

Lucas shot four times, streaks of red plasbolt sheeting the air. I held my ground, dropping my scabbard and clasping the hilt in both hands, an instinctive decision that might cost me my life. But Lucas already had a plasgun, and he'd missed.

Four times.

"Run!" I barked, not looking to see if Leander did because the thing—dense heavy hot demon animal—crashed into me. It was appallingly quick, blurring with spooky demon speed, my sword chimed off claws as I spun aside, the mark on my shoulder lighting up with a fierce spike of pain. The cuff blazed green, a thin crackling whip of fire

snaking out to lick at the hellhound, which let out a basso yowl of rage.

What the hell was that?

The swordhilt floated up, blade blurring, I made a low sound of effort as shining metal streaked down, sinking into the hellhound's haunch with a deadly low whistle. It coiled on itself, I gave ground, shuffling back. My entire world narrowed to the threat in front of me; streaks of blue fire painted the air as my sword wove a complicated pattern.

I had the oddest sensation—as if a rope attached to the cuff on my left wrist was jerking my arm around, quicker than I was meant to move. Didn't matter—I set my teeth as the hellhound came for me again, another pass that drove me back. It was trying to pin me against the buildings on either side of the street, a death sentence. I remembered how eerily fast the hellhounds were in Freetown New Prague and was vaguely surprised to still be alive. The world narrowed to one thing—the hellhound, its scraping scrabbling nails on pavement and my own harsh breathing, its low plasglass-rattling growl and my boots stamping as I smashed down with my blade and leapt like a cat, narrowly missing getting three glassy obsidian claws as long as my hand slicing into my midriff. I'd been eviscerated twice, had no desire to ever go there again.

It was too quick. I could barely hurl aside its claws and had to fade to the side as it looped impossibly, turning with a much smaller radius than something so big should be able to. Its spine crackled as it jerked fluidly, turning. Black smoking blood striped the beast, and it favored its left forepaw as it hunched and snarled at me, apparently chiding me for my lack of ability to die respectfully when it attacked me.

I snarled back, lips peeling from my teeth. Frustrated fury rose under my breastbone. I was happy to have the outlet—too happy, adrenaline overtaking good sense. I'd make a mistake, this thing was too quick for me to have a chance of winning the fight. Heart pounding, sweat sliding down my back and soaking into the waistband of my jeans—it took a lot of effort to make me sweat, nowadays.

It backed up, one slow fluid uncoordinated step at a time, growling all the while. I considered advancing, my ribs flaring with deep harsh breaths. My left leg burned, high on the thigh—had it gotten me? I honestly couldn't remember.

Darkness breathed between streetlights. Fiske Avenue was utterly still. My aura pulled close, demon shields pulsing, my rings spitting golden sparks. The mark on my shoulder had settled into a slow steady burn, as if flesh had been partly torn away but not yet started to bleed. The wristcuff squeezed mercilessly, I almost heard small bones in my wrist splintering. A ragged *huff* of breath left my lungs; I tried frantically to think of something *else* to do. Throwing a runespell or two at it, or a tracker, would probably not work—I'd tried a tracker on an imp once, and gotten a head-ringing case of backlash for my trouble. Japhrimel had made the other hellhound rot with a word in the demon language, but he had also refused to teach me any of his native tongue.

A plasbolt raked in from the side, splashing on the creature's hide. It shook its head, stunned, and I threw myself back as Leander and Lucas, both firing, yelled something shapeless.

The hellhound thudded to the ground, its hide smoking.

I looked up. Leander was white-faced, staring at me like

I'd grown a new set of kobolding arms. Lucas's upper lip curled. He looked grimly pleased, yellow eyes blazing.

I tried not to gasp, failed miserably. My heart raced, thudding as if it intended to fling itself out through my ribs and dance a few nightclub kicks on the pavement of Fiske Avenue. Sweat dripped, stinging, in my eyes. "We'd better . . . get out . . . of here."

"You think it's dead?" Lucas kept his gun trained on the loose lump of hide and shadow. I saw no flicker of movement, was unconvinced.

"No. Probably just stunned. Come *on,* let's *go!*" I regained my breath with an effort, Lucas tossed me my scabbard. My hand flashed, caught it, the cuff was back to dull silver on my wrist. I flipped my hand palm-up, palm-down; there was no space in the Gauntlet anymore. *Dammit, how did that happen?* It was a solid band of metal welded to my wrist above my datband, and its sudden chill was enough to cause a swift flash of pain through my temples. *Not going to think about that right now. It just helped save my life, good enough, let's go!* "Anubis et'her ka, let's not stand around!"

We left the stunned hellhound lying slumped in the middle of the street, and I had the uncharacteristic urge to glance over my shoulder all the way to Abra's. I even *did* glance back once or twice, unsure of what I expected to see—another low fluid hellhound shape, or a pair of green eyes and a long black coat.

It's anyone's guess which would have scared me more.

15

This part of the Tank District had grown even more forlorn. Half the streetlamps on Klondel were dead and dark, either broken or fallen out of service. From the rooftop of the row of buildings Abra's pawnshop was in, the darkened streetlights looked like spaces left by broken teeth. A flock of unregistered hookers milled in dark doorways, and hovers with privacytint and magcoding crawled streetside, cruising the strip. I smelled sour human sweat, decay, synth-hash and the salt-sweet odor of Clormen-13.

Chill.

Chill always raises my hackles. Chillfreaks in Saint City seem to smell worse than anywhere in the world. Maybe it's the radioactive cold of the city's Power well. Maybe it's just the rain giving everything a musty smell. I hate Chill anyway; the drug is instantly addictive and a blight upon the urban landscape. I've lost good friends to Chill and Chill junkies, starting with my foster-father Lewis and continuing down the years in successive waves. Each time a new flood of Chill hits the street someone—or several someones—dies.

Leander came through the shadows, flitting down the

street as if trying to stay unremarked. He did a good job, showing just enough of a flicker of movement to make an onlooker believe he wanted to stay unseen.

"Let's go in," Lucas wheeze-whispered in my ear. He stood by the hatch, I melted away from the low wall sheltering Abra's roof. "After you, *chica*."

I jammed my sword into the loop on my belt and dropped into the dark hole, negotiating the slick iron ladder with little trouble. It took my weight easily, something I was glad of. Denser muscle and bone gave me more strength, but also made me a little too heavy to trust sometimes-rickety human construction. My left leg throbbed, my jeans flopping loosely. Black demon blood had coated the slice from the hellhound's claws and healed it, but I still moved gingerly.

Lucas followed. I heard the whine of an unholstered plasrifle as my feet touched dusty wood floor.

"Dammit, woman," Lucas rasped. "Put that thing away!"

"Sorry." Abra didn't sound sorry at all. She rarely did.

I turned slowly, keeping my hands away from weapons. The attic was low and dusty, the roofhatch sealed and magshielded now, and I felt the crackle of magickal shields springing back into place. Abra had been expecting us.

My nostrils flared, demon-acute eyes piercing the dimness with little trouble.

She looked just the same.

Abracadabra had long, dark, curly hair and liquid dark eyes, a nondescript triangular face with a pointed chin. A blue and silver caftan fell to her slim ankles, sandaled brown feet met the floor but rested only lightly. Large golden hoops dangled in her ears, peeking out from under her hair.

The shop's smell—beef stew with chilies, dust, human pain—was the same. But Abra, of course, didn't smell human. She smelled like sticky dry silk and short bristly hairs, a smell that rubbed me the wrong way. Japhrimel hadn't liked her, and if his instinctive response was anything like mine I could see why. But I'd never had any trouble dealing with her while I was human. Even afterward, running infrequent messages between her and Jado, I never had cause to complain. She was always the same, mind-numbingly cautious and looking to drive a hard bargain. She never left her pawnshop, and I had amused myself several times by trying to deduce exactly which paranormal species she was.

The Spider of Saint City blinked her long lashes at me. "Valentine. Might have known. You're trouble all over."

Oh, if you only knew. "It's not my fault I'm a popular girl, Abra. How are you?"

Her lip curled. "Be a lot better if Nichtvren and 'cain weren't showing up at my door. Where's the demon?"

So she knew Japhrimel was in town, and connected to me. Sometimes I wondered how much she knew that she didn't tell. "I left him at home tatting lace. And you *like* being in the thick of things; you get all your information that way."

Abra tilted her head. "The Necromance is here. Your idea?"

"Lucas's." I moved aside as Lucas leapt down, landing cat-silent. "Are you sure you trust him unattended?"

"What, like he'll steal from me?" A mirthless little-girl giggle, she made a complicated parade-drill movement, ending up with the plasrifle slung over her shoulder like an old-time bandido. "Come on down, I'll make tea. This is a *complex* situation."

"You better believe it. Abra, Gabe Spocarelli's dead. So's Eddie Thornton. And I'm hunting their killers." Dust stirred in the air.

Silence. Finally, Abra sighed. "Come on down." Was it my imagination, or did she sound weary? "You're not going to like this."

Abracadabra Pawnshop We Make Miracles Happen was stenciled on the front window with tired gold paint, and the windows were dark with privacy-tint. That was a new trick, Abra had never been the tinted type before. Racks of merchandise stood neatly on the wood floor, slicboards and guitars hung up behind the glassed-in counter that sparkled dustily with jewelry. Her stock did seem to rotate fairly frequently, but I'd never seen anyone come into Abra's to buy anything physical.

No, we come to the Spider of Saint City for *information.*

There was a rack of the new, hot Amberjion pleather jackets, with shoulderpads up to the ear; a display of antique chronographs stood in a plasilica cube on one counter. Otherwise, it looked just the same as it always had.

Nice to have a friend that doesn't age.

Leander leaned hipshot against the counter, studying a display of necklaces. His eyes flicked every so often to the door, and his hand rested on his swordhilt. "Any eyes?" I asked.

"Two. A 'cain two alleys up, and someone right across

the street." He shrugged. "I made sure both of them saw me." His dark eyes were alive; he was enjoying himself.

Not too much, I hope. I sighed, rubbing at my eyes with one shaking hand. I'd just fought off a hellhound.

A *hellhound.* Japhrimel had told me to run if I ever saw one; they had been used to hunt *hedaira* in the time of the first *A'nankhimel,* the Fallen Lucifer had destroyed because one of them might possibly breed and spawn an Androgyne, a demon capable of reproducing.

Like Lucifer himself. Like Eve.

Now I had more of the story verified. Temples and priestesses, and the demons who traded a piece of their power and got something in return.

Japh bargained to get a demon's Power back—he's different now. And so am I, if I share some measure of that Power.

I shivered, and Abra handed me a screaming-orange pottery mug. She looked a lot more comfortable perched behind the counter in her habitual space. "Here. Tea." By far the most civil she'd ever been. "You and Spocarelli were tight, weren't you." It wasn't a question.

Lucas took up a position on the far side of the room, settling between a rack of slicboards and a wooden box holding different-sized pairs of combat boots. His yellow eyes slitted but I wasn't fooled, he didn't look tired at all. Despite the floppy blood-crusty rip in his shirt, he looked very alert indeed. We matched, both of us bloody and air-dried.

I was beginning to believe I was still alive. The mark on my shoulder remained curiously numb. Was Japhrimel tracking me?

I hope so. This is getting ridiculous. I nodded, blew across the top of the mug to cool the liquid. "Way tight.

Someone pumped Eddie full of enough projectile lead to trade him in at the metalyard, they did the same to Gabe in her own backyard." I didn't mention Gabe's daughter. One thing at a time. My tone was flat, terribly ironic through the lump in my throat. "I promised Gabe I'd take out Eddie's killers. He was working on something, I guess."

"I know. I got a visit from a Shaman—Annette Cameron. Works at that clinic on Fortieth, a *sedayeen* commune attached to a Chill rehab." Abra's lip curled.

"There's no rehab for Clorman-13," I muttered habitually. "Okay."

Abra didn't respond. Everyone knows how I feel about Chill. "Seems Eddie was working with the *sedayeen* out there. You might want to try it. Anyway, Annette was anxious to find you."

"Just like everyone else." *I'm just the most popular girl around nowadays. Even demons want a piece of me.*

"Yeah." Abra reached slowly beneath the counter and drew out a white envelope with a heavy, old-fashioned blob of wax sealing it. "And a Nichtvren came, with this. Said to give it to you."

I broke the seal without looking and tore out a piece of heavy hand-made linen paper that felt rich and perfumed against my fingertips. The dusty, deliciously wicked smell of Nichtvren clung to the paper.

It was a very brief note.

Miss Valentine, I have information for you. Come to the nest at your convenience; I'm not hard to find.

It was signed **Selene**. The consort of the Nichtvren Master of Saint City, the prime paranormal Power. Nikolai.

One scary son of a bitch.

"Wonderful," I muttered. "The suckheads love me."

"If they love you, the 'cain must hate you. There's a contract going around, two hundred thou for your delivery, alive even if messed up, to a buyer on the East Side. Bounty hunters, werecain, and mercs are all jumping at the bait." Abra's jaw set, her caramel skin tight over her bones. "I don't have to tell you what it's costing me to keep quiet."

I tucked the note in a pocket, picked up my mug, and took a cautious sip. Vanilla-spiked tea, very sweet, oddly calming. "And here I thought we were friends." *Bounty hunters?* "If bounty hunters are after me, there must be a claim registered with the Hegemony 'net."

Abra shrugged. "Not necessarily, if they want to keep it quiet. There was also some spliced son of a bitch from Pico-PhizePharm, name of Massadie." Her gold earrings quivered as she shook her head. "Threw money at me and acted like he was going to pay me more if I dug up anything on you. Stupid. But what you should be worried about is the Mob. They've got some serious hard-on for you. If I didn't have such a good working relationship with the Tanner Family they might have tried to torch my shop."

Tanner Family? They must be new. "What about the Chery Family?" There was no love lost between me and the Mob, but if I could play one Family off against another I might be able to continue on my way unmolested.

Abra made a short snorting noise of disapproval. "Chery's been eradicated, along with every other major player. Tanner's the only game in town."

When did that happen? Gods, I'm out of touch. "Great."

"For their profit margins, yeah. Not so good for the rest of us."

I nodded. "Thank you, Abra. Now give me the real dirt."

The ensuing silence was so long I set the mug down and let my eyes meet hers. Her long dusky finger lay alongside her long, slim nose. Her hair was glossy and her cheeks slightly pink. Abra looked plump, well-fed. Business must have been good lately.

"I hate to say it, Danny, but what are you going to pay me?" Her eyes were dark and velvety, fixed on mine, and I saw a sparkle deep inside them. The sparkle off bloody bits of metal as a survivor picked through the battlefield, dispatching the wounded and picking pockets.

Picking pockets? Like Gabe's pockets, soaked with blood and holding a holostill of a toddler with merry eyes?

I don't even remember moving. The next thing I knew, I had Abra against the wall behind her counter, my left hand around her throat and her feet dangling as she tore at my fingers with her slim brown hands. She gagged, my aura turned hard and hot, and I heard Leander swear. Lucas blurted something shapeless that ended with, *"—get it, she's fuckin' crazy, back off!"*

I *squeezed*. Abra's dark eyes bugged, she made a thick strangled noise. The cuff on my left wrist rang softly, and so did my sword.

I was past caring.

"You listen to me," I said, very softly. *I sound like Japhrimel.* A horrible nasty laugh rose inside of me, was squashed, and died away. "I like you, Abra. Any other hunt I'd pay you anything your little heart desired. But not now." My tone didn't reach above an even whisper, a Necromance's usual voice. The wall shivered behind her, plasglass display cases and windows creaking and groaning as the mark on my shoulder lit with a fierce, pleasant pain. I felt as if I stood in the center of a humming vortex of magick, as if a Major Work had been triggered and was gathering itself to leap through time and space to work my Will, undeniable and absolute. "I don't care who's after me. I don't care who would pay you how much for jackshit. *This is personal.* Whoever killed Gabe and Eddie is going *down.* You get in my way and I will go right *over* you. Clear?"

I eased up a little, and she hissed, her eyes lighting with inhuman fire.

"Clear?" I didn't shake her, but it was close. So close. I trembled with the urge, fire spilling through me from the mark on my shoulder. I'd actually *drawn on it,* pulled magickal force from the scar.

How the hell—I didn't know I could do that! But it made sense. I was Japhrimel's link to the human world, and the scar was the link between us. There was Power there for the taking—and I wasn't as wary as I should be about using it.

Any tool to get the job done, Danny.

"Clear," she rasped. Her eyelids flickered, and she'd gone chalky under her dusky skin. I dropped her. I'd never been behind the counter before, and was vaguely surprised to see that the floor here was just like the rest of the store— mellow dusty hardwood. Nothing special except a few weapons and shelves of paper-wrapped oddments waiting for different people. It was a little disappointing.

Abra rubbed her throat and darted me a venomous glance. "That wasn't necessary," she rasped.

I felt suddenly sick under the bald edge of rage. I'd been held against a wall and throttled, I knew what it felt like. Why had I done it to Abra, of all people?

The vision of Gabe, lying broken and dead, rose in front of me again. *That's why. Because you were too late to save her, you slept in. Maybe because of Japhrimel, maybe not. It doesn't matter. Now the only thing left is revenge.*

If I was going to go for revenge, I might as well go all the way. Which brought up an interesting question: would I be able to stop when I killed whoever had slaughtered Eddie and Gabe? I might as well declare open war on Japhrimel for going after Eve—and pursue revenge on Lucifer himself for the mess he'd made of my life.

I realized with a kind of horror that I had no real problem with that. It was only a question of *how.* Access to whatever Power I could draw through the scar was in the asset column, but my own chill rational consideration of ways and means frightened me. *When did I get so cold? Something's very wrong with me.*

"Let's take it from the top." My voice sounded just the same—flat, whispering, and sharp as a razor drawn over numb skin. The Gauntlet chilled, sending a wave of cold up my arm, pushed back by the heat of the scar. "In great detail, Abra."

Oh, gods above. I don't sound like Japhrimel.

I sound like Lucas.

16

The tea had turned to cold swill, but I finished it anyway and dropped the last of my bankroll on Abra's counter. She could tell me precious little—just that a biotech company was somehow tied up in Eddie's work, perhaps bankrolling it; someone wanted me dead; the Mob wanted me brought in; the Nichtvren wanted to see me, and the werecain—who knew what they wanted? Revenge, maybe, I'd killed a couple 'cain awhile ago during the hunt for Mirovitch. They have long memories.

Or maybe it was something else.

In any case, I owed her, both for the information and for losing my temper.

She looked at me, rubbing her throat. "Put that away." She was still hoarse. "I don't work for you, Danny."

"I know you don't." The apology stuck in my throat. *I'm sorry, Abra. I shouldn't have done that.* I didn't touch the money, just left it there. Backed up two steps, my eyes not leaving hers.

She shrugged, the thin gold hoops shivering against her cheeks. "What are you going to do?"

I never thought I'd live to see Abracadabra ask me

that with her eyes wide like a frightened child's. I looked away, toward the privacy-tinted windows. Out there in the streets were Mob freelancers and assassins, corpclones and bounty hunters—not to mention werecain and Nichtvren— all waiting for a piece of me. Lucky me, dropping into the middle of a turf war and not even realizing it.

"First I'm going to go out your back door," I said tonelessly. "Then I'm going to start digging. I want you to put the word out, Abra. Tell everyone who comes to you that whoever hit Gabe and Eddie should put their estate in order. 'Cause when I get finished with them, even another Necromance isn't going to be able to bring them back." I paused. It wasn't for effect, but Abra's eyes widened.

"Danny . . . be careful." She folded her arms. "Although you're never careful, that's how you ended up smelling like a demon."

That reminded me. "You know of any Magi willing to let go of trade secrets for a price, Abra?"

"No." The gold hoops shivered as she shook her dark head, looking puzzled. "Closemouth bastards. Why?"

The mark on my left shoulder pulsed slightly, responding to the thought of Japhrimel. The almost-constant pulses of Power had settled into a rhythm, one I welcomed despite the way they made my skin crawl. *I drew on this mark, I could do it again. Will that tell Japhrimel where I am?* "I need to get some more answers about demons. And Fallen. And *hedaira*."

Her jaw dropped. "You mean you—"

If one more person said *You mean you don't know?* I was going to scream. I knew enough, I just had to figure out how to make it work for me.

I headed for the stairs behind the *Employees Only* door.

"I'm going out the back. Spread the word, Abra. Whoever hit Gabe and Eddie is dead, they just don't know it yet."

Lucas fell into step behind me.

"Valentine?" Leander sounded uncertain.

He's human, and he could have died back there facing down a hellhound. I'm too dangerous to hang out with, even for combat-trained psions. This is going to get real interesting really quickly. "Go home, Leander. Forget all about this." I ducked through the door, my boots moving soundlessly. "We're even."

"Valentine—*Valentine!* Dante!"

But I shut the door and threw the deadbolt, sure Abra would have a key and just as sure she wouldn't give it to him right away. She was never one to *give* anything, and Leander couldn't effectively threaten her. If he decided to go out the front door she'd delay him for a few minutes, long enough for Lucas and me to vanish.

Lucas matched me step for step. We made it up the stairs, he pushed in front of me and led me up the ladder to the attic in the top hall; we pulled it up after ourselves, hinges squeaking. "Which one we gonna do first?" he finally asked as I fitted the attic hatch back into its seating. He fiddled with the trapdoor leading to the roof.

"The werecain. He's the bigger mystery. We'll get him roped up and then you can chat with our other set of eyes. Meet me tomorrow at the corner of Trivisidiro and Fourth, at dusk. Have I thanked you lately, Lucas?"

"No need, your boyfriend fuckin' paid me." *Now* he sounded irritated. I shrugged, though he probably couldn't see it in the darkness of Abra's stuffy, dusty attic. Her house shields vibrated uneasily, then pulled back a little so we could slip out the back door. I wondered again just what she was, and felt shame rise behind my breastbone. Had I really half-strangled her against the wall?

Just like Lucifer. Just like a demon.

The thought spilled cold down my back. When you hunt monsters, you have to be a monster—but not too much of one.

Bounty hunting taught me as much.

How close to the edge of monster was I? "What did Japhrimel pay you, Lucas?"

"Enough that I'm going to see this through." Cold air sparkled through the trapdoor as he eased it open. "You comin', Valentine?"

I shoved my sword into the loop on my rig. "You better believe it."

We dropped on the werecain two alleys away. Literally dropped, I went over the edge of the roof soundlessly and landed cat-light, my main knives reversed along my forearms. Lucas actually landed *on* the 'cain, destroying the advantage of surprise, but the eight-foot-tall bundle of muscle and fur was so busy with him it gave me time to streak up through piles of stinking human refuse.

I willed myself to ignore the thunderous odor as I slashed at the 'cain's hamstrings. The alley was too narrow for swordwork and I didn't want to make the noise of plas or projectile guns. Flesh gave like water under my blade and my rings ran with golden sparks. The 'cain would have howled, but I leapt and dragged it back, my slim arm over its throat, strangling its protest. Hot copper stink of blood, the blade of my left-hand knife singing against my forearm, my right-hand blade pricking just under the 'cain's floating ribs on the left. I could work the knife in here and go for a kidney, if my knowledge of werecain anatomy was sound. It was in full huntform, and not *that* different from a human if you knew where to jab.

The amber rectangle on my right-hand second-finger ring sparked as I yanked on Power, deftly snapping invisible weights tight around the werecain's wrists and ankles. It would cost me—but better to be safe than sorry where an eight-foot bundle of lethal muscle and claw is concerned.

Besides, all the Power I would ever need sang through the demon mark on my shoulder. I didn't precisely *want* to use it—gods alone knew what the price would be—but if it came down to it, any tool at hand was all right by me. I'd deal with consequences later.

If there was a later.

In short order, Lucas had the 'cain trussed-up with a length of discarded plasilica fiberoptic grubbed up from the floor of the trash-strewn alley. *I'd almost suspect you've done this before, Lucas,* the lunatic voice of hilarity in the middle of an impossible situation caroled through my brain.

The Deathless vanished into the shadows at the alley's entrance, going to take care of the other pair of eyes. I promptly put both problems out of my mind.

I kept my arm across the cain's throat as it pitched and struggled, trying to throw me off. The advantage of almost-demon strength was a thin one—I was breathing hard by the time I got him wrestled to the ground, my knees braced against cold wet concrete that smelled like . . . well, garbage.

Mercifully, my nose shut off. Something about 'cain scent, it overloads nasal receptors in everyone other than swanhild and other werecain after a while.

Given how most of them reek, it's a goddamn blessing.

"Cooperate with me," I snarled in his ear, "or I'll use psi on you. I *mean* it."

The eight-foot hulk writhed one last time under me and went still. Harsh breathing echoed in my ears, I heard a low growl and choked up on its throat again.

Werecain don't like psions. As a species, they're generally vulnerable to psychic attack. Nichtvren and pre-Paranormal-Species-Act Magi used that vulnerability against them too many times. The big advantage werecain had was their longer lifespan—when human psions get old and weak 'cain can struggle free of psychic enslavement and make life difficult. They are also—mostly—pack animals. A pack of werecain can even take on solitary Master Nichtvren and give them a hard time. Enough 'cain in a pack spells bad luck even for a preternaturally powerful suckhead.

"Your choice." Fur rasped against my shirt and my chin. "Either you play nice or I'll clean the inside of your head out like a transport toilet flush. Just try me."

The 'cain snarled, struggled . . . and subsided.

I eased up a little on its throat. "Who you looking for, huh? Who you waiting for out here?"

"Necromance," he growled. Definitely male. I could have told by the genital ruff, but the light wasn't good enough to be staring at a werecain's crotch. Never mind that I could use demon sight, right now I was too busy making sure Wolf Boy didn't heave me off and snap his bonds, or shift shape and slither free. They tend to be pretty big as humans, six-four to six-eight; shifting to a smaller human form would let him get his hands out of the bonds. I was only an inch or so taller than I had been while human, topping out at five-six, I needed leverage to deal with him no matter which form he was in. A 'cain in human form can still shift a hand into claws and strike before you realize what's up. "Long dark hair, pretty tan. Smell like a goddamn bakery in heat. You."

"How sweet." My heart began to thud. I did probably smell like a bakery, thanks to the cinnamon sweetness of almost-demon. With the musk underneath it, it was probably extremely distinctive to a 'cain's sensitive nose. "Who were you going to deliver me to, furboy? Huh?"

"Agh—" He gurgled, I eased up a little. "You know I can't." His voice was choked not only by my arm across his trachea but also by a mouth not truly shaped for human speech. Too many sharp teeth and a wrong-sized tongue.

"Give it up, or I'll brainwipe you." To give the threat a little more credence, I extended the borders of my awareness and *pressed,* very gently, on the edges of his mind. Curiously unprotected, the cranial fire of his consciousness shivered under my touch like a dog begging to be stroked. It would be so *easy,* so very easy—and he was paranormal; his mind wasn't the open sewer of a normal human's.

I caught a breath of something—more musk, the smell of oranges, and heart-pumping fear. *Demon.*

This sparked a few more moments of furious struggling, ending up with me yanking back and choking until he went limp. Then I eased a little. *Wait a second, how did a demon get mixed up in this? Or is it just that anyone following my trail is going to come across demon stink?* "Names, furboy. I want *names.*"

"Mob!" he half-barked. "I think he's Mob, he *acts* like Mob, corner of Fifth and Chesko, East Side. Paying two hundred thou for you. Fifty thou for information; where you are, who you visiting."

"A bargain, all things considered."

The werecain didn't see the humor in it. I suddenly longed for Japhrimel. He'd get the joke, it was just the kind of thing *he* might have said. Another few seconds of furious struggle, and the 'cain began to whine a little, far back in his throat. The sharp stink flooded my nostrils again, my nasal receptors suddenly waking up. Garbage, wet fur, werecain—what a combo.

"Relax. I'm not going to brainwipe you, you've been a good boy. Spread the word: Dante Valentine's back in town, and she's on the warpath. Whoever knocked off Gabe Spocarelli is already dead. Got it?"

A growl was the only answer I received. I could have pistol-whipped him a few times to give myself enough room to get away, but that would have been too much. My arm loosened a little, he drew in a whooping breath, his flexible strong ribs heaving under me.

I was at the mouth of the alley before I realized it, my body moving too fast for me again. I still wasn't used to how damnably *quick* my demon reflexes were.

It was a good thing too, I heard scrabbling and a snarling roar behind me. *Time to move, time to move*—I almost wasted precious moments worrying about Lucas while I blurred through patches of streetlight shine, the wind making a soft sweet sound in my ears, combing my hair back. I was fairly sure I was fast enough to outrun a werecain—but it wasn't just the running I was worried about, it was breaking my trail. Werecain are *extremely* good trackers, and the only thing keeping them from putting psion bounty hunters out of business is the fact that criminal psions are generally unwilling to be brought in without exploiting a 'cain's psychic vulnerability. And normal criminals aren't averse to hiring out a little work from a psion to keep 'cain away. Not to mention the fact that the Hegemony only licenses 'cain to hunt down criminals among the other paranormal species.

Running. *He's not still behind me, he can't be, got to be sure.* . . . Breathing coming hard and harsh, muscles burning. Burst out into the confusion of Klondel and Thirty-Eighth, streaking through the crowd and probably bowling over a few of them; I went for the darkest alley I could find and crouched in the garbage, shuddering and hyperventilating, the mark on my shoulder numb as if I'd been shot up with varocain. As I crouched there, my back against the damp brick wall of the alley, I silently berated myself.

He's not following you, a 'cain knows better than to follow a wary combat-trained psion. He's going to head straight to the East Side to sell his information, and this possibly-Mob connection is either going to pull up the stakes and vanish in a hell of a hurry or hire a hell of a lot of security posthaste. Probably the latter if he has to stay put to receive information and possibly your own sweet self trussed up like a Putchkin Yule turkey. You can't fight off every mercenary and paranormal in the city, Dante. You just can't.

Besides, what was the breath of demon I'd caught in the 'cain's memory? What if the people watching Abra's shop weren't there because of my search for Gabe's killer? Or what if only some of them were, and the rest were the hunters looking for Eve, or looking to snatch me because I was suddenly so goddamn important?

More important to the Prince of Hell than even *he* realized, Japhrimel had said.

Great. I have such a choice of enemies it's not even funny. I leaned my head back against the weeping brick. The smell of a demon rose around me, a cinnamon-laden filter to keep out the reek of human filth.

"I've got to steal a slicboard," I whispered.

17

I massaged my numb shoulder while melding into the shadow of a large holly hedge, watching the intersection of Fifth and Chesko on the East Side of Saint City. My skin prickled with harsh hurtful awareness and my heart pounded a little too rapidly. The icy cuff of metal on my left wrist didn't help, taunting me with its dull dead surface.

This made only the second time I'd been on the east side of the river since boarding the transport to take me to the Academy. I suppressed a guilty start every time I realized where I was—and found, without any real surprise, that my hands were shaking a little. So I braced them with my sword in its scabbard, and settled down to watch. The slicboard I'd stolen—a nice sleek Chervoyg deck—leaned against the hedge next to me, hot-taped and magwired. I'd lifted it from a rack outside a yuppie club in the Tank District. More than likely some rich kid gone slumming would have to take a hovercab home, I wouldn't have stolen a slic courier's deck.

I waited, my knuckles almost white as I clutched the scabbarded blade. I hoped I wasn't too late.

I couldn't even enjoy the fact that I'd ridden a slicboard

again. It used to be after every Necromance job I'd take a slic up into the hoverlanes until the adrenaline hammered my heart and brain into believing I was *alive*. Now the rushing speed and sense of being balanced on a stair-rail, sliding down with knees loose and arms a little spread, was oddly diluted.

Maybe because I was on the East Side again. On the same side as Rigger Hall.

I looked back over my shoulder again, checking the empty street under its drench of streetlamp light. At any moment I might hear a soft sliding footstep, or catch a whiff of chalk, offal, and aftershave.

Stop it. Mirovitch is dead. You killed him. You scattered his ka and Japhrimel cremated Lourdes. He burned Rigger Hall to the ground, wiped that cursed place off the map. Just stop it. Stop.

A different set of memories rose. Japh touching my back gently, his fingers digging into cable-strung muscles as I sobbed and shook with the aftermath of Mirovitch's psychic rape tearing through my vulnerable head. My own hands clenched in fists, my wild thrashing when the flash-backs returned, Japhrimel catching my wrists in a gentle but inexorable grip, stopping me from beating my head against the wall or flinging myself into damage. The pulse beating in his throat as we lay in the darkness, his voice a thread of gold holding me to sanity.

I let out a soft breath. *I wish he was here.* It was a trai-torous thought—would I be in this position if he hadn't maneuvered me from square to square in Lucifer's game? He'd been sneaking out while I was asleep, maybe hunting Eve, and keeping important information from me.

What choice did he have, Danny? Lucifer trapped him,

just like he trapped you. Japh's doing what he has to do. You can't argue with his methods if they're keeping you alive. And who was it that just held Abra up against the wall and scared the hell out of her? You're losing your moral high ground here.

I could have done with a little backup at the moment. Where *was* he?

A flicker of movement caught my eye. There, a quick feral flash, leaping over the fence of the mansion on the northwest side of the intersection.

Well, what do you know. Idiocy strikes again.

I eased myself out of the shadows—or I would have, if the air pressure hadn't changed and a faint shimmer coated the air beside me. I pressed back into the spiny greenness of the hedge, my right hand closing around my sword-hilt—and the figure of a tall, slim, dirty-blond and blue-eyed holovid angel appeared, resolving out of bare air. One moment gone, the next *here,* Tiens closed his hand over mine, jamming the sword back into its scabbard. "*Tranquille, belle morte,*" he whispered, stretching his lips and showing his fangs. "Do not go in there. It is," and here he sniffed disdainfully, "a trap."

Nichtvren generally only Turn humans if they are either exceptionally pretty or exceptionally ruthless; I've never seen an ugly Nichtvren. Truth be told, I've barely seen *any* Nichtvren despite the mandatory Paranormal Anatomy and Interspecies Communication classes I'd taken. In the relatively short time I'd been an almost-demon, I'd met more Nichtvren than in my previous thirty-odd years combined.

Then again, Nichtvren don't like Necromances.

What species that prizes immortality would like Death's children?

Tiens was a tall male with a shock of dirty-blond hair and a beautifully expressive masculine face, his eyes curiously flat with the cat-sheen of his nighthunting species. Below the shine, they were a pale blue. He had a slight flush along his cheekbones—he'd fed somewhere. He wore dusty black, a V-neck sweater and loose workman's pants, his feet closed in scarred and cracked boots; he looked just the same as he had in Freetown New Prague.

Though I'd begun to feel a little easier around Lucas, I was still *very* wary of a suckhead Hellesvront agent. Suckheads scare me more than demons, and a suckhead working for demons is enough to make my hand itch for my swordhilt.

He was right, the house at Fifth and Chesko was a trap. It didn't take much more than a few moments for the werecain to come back out. When he did he circled the block and plunged back over the wall again. If I'd just arrived— or been chasing him all along—I might have been fooled. Maybe my own blind panic had actually served me.

Tiens's warm fingers eased off my hand as he looked back over his shoulder, noting the werecain's re-disappearance with a slight smile as if at the antics of a not-too-bright child. *"Cretín."* The word was softened by an accent as ancient as South Merican. "Come. Here is not the place for you, *belle morte.*"

"I'm not going anywhere with you," I told him quietly, and he cocked his head, smiling. For some reason that smile chilled me more than a snarl would have—especially since his fangs were slightly extended, dimpling his exquisite lower lip just a little. His eyes lit up with cheerful good humor, as if it was a foregone conclusion that I *would*, indeed, go with him, once he found the proper way to explain to me I had no choice.

"An old friend wishes a word with you." His eyes passed down my body and back up again. His smile widened a trifle, appreciative; I shuddered. *Appreciation* is not what I want to see on the face of any Nichtvren. "Selene, the Prime's Consort."

"Where's Japhrimel?" *And just what "errand" did he send you on, suckhead? A Nichtvren working for demons, there's no reason for me to trust you any farther than I can throw you.*

"*M'sieu* should be with you." Tiens shrugged. "Since he is not, I will remain. We shall go swiftly. You are expected, *le chien* there was obviously meant to lure you. There are soldiers hidden behind the walls, with tranquilizer guns."

I examined him in the difficult light, demon eyes piercing shadows to show me his faint, charming smile. His eyes all but sparkled. Nichtvren eyes, capable of seeing in total blackness. He was at the top of the night-hunting food chain. While I was fairly sure I could handle individual werecain, Nichtvren—especially Masters—were something else entirely. The few suckheads I'd met since I'd become almost-demon were scary if only for the amount of Power they carried.

Let's face it, they were also old enough to make me feel like an idiot child. Too old to be strictly human anymore. If I survived, how long would it be before I was like them?

That was the scariest thing of all.

"You go in front of me." I shoved my sword in the loop on my rig and bent to pick up the slicboard. "Where I can see you." A few quick flicks of my fingers stripped the magwiring off, a press against the controlpad activated the home-return function. Then I dropped it. It would be picked up by the next maintenance bot and returned to its owner, a little worse for wear, maybe. I wasn't strictly a thief.

Not of something so paltry as a slicboard, anyway. The next thing I would steal would be a life.

My left arm felt cold and clumsy. The scar throbbed, holding back the chill from the Gauntlet. I wished I had time to figure out how to take the damn thing *off*.

He made a slight, pretty moue with his sculpted mouth. "You do not trust me?"

"I'm getting to the point where I don't trust *myself*. If you really don't know where Japhrimel is—"

"He should have been with you, *belle morte,* guarding his prize. If he has left your side, it is something *extraordinaire.*" Tiens took one graceful backward step, making a fluid gesture with his hands, expressing surprise and resignation all at once. The flat sheen of an alleycat's eyes at night closed over his blue eyes as he contemplated me, folding his arms. "I think we shall go slowly, for your sake."

I took a deep breath, struggling with irritation and the fresh urge to draw my sword. "Just tell me where the Nest is, and I'll go. You can do what you like."

"If I am to do as I please I shall accompany you, pretty one. A pleasant job in a world full of unpleasantness, *non?*"

And while you're keeping an eye on me you'll be hoping for Japh to show up. I gave up, and followed him. It wasn't worth a fight. Besides, I wanted to see Selene and Nikolai anyway.

18

The Nest was downtown on Ninth, in a building that looked like a renovated block of apartments. It was incongruous in the middle of a parklike lawn, prime downtown realty treated like a suburban estate by a Nichtvren. Then again, Nikolai was the Prime of the City; he could afford it. For him to have a grandiose lair was expected.

Inside, the halls were dim and restful. I smelled lemon oil, beeswax, polish, and the delicious wicked perfume of Nichtvren. They smell so distinctly sweet, maybe it's the decaying blood. But there's also a hint of sinful dark chocolate, wine, and secret sex to them. My Paranormal Anatomy professor at the Academy had called them "the pimps of the night world" once, right before he was fired. I guess Doctor Tarridge had a bone to pick with Nichtvren.

Lots of people do.

The cloak of Power laid over the Nest was cold and prickling, full of defenses and the weight of a Master's will. My own shielding drew close, my numb shoulder prickling a warning.

I saw nobody but was sure we were watched. When Tiens swept open a pair of double mahogany doors and led

me into a firelit hall floored in parquet worthy of the Renascence, I had to suppress the urge to applaud sardonically.
My eyes were hot and grainy, my shoulders tight, and I was
hungry. I hadn't noticed it before, but when the adrenaline
faded I was reminded I hadn't eaten for a while. I needed
the physical fuel—not like Japhrimel.

*Will you stop thinking about him? He's fine, he can take
care of himself. Besides, he left you with McKinley. He
can't have been too worried about your well-being.*

A tall broad-shouldered shape stood in front of the fire,
his hands hanging loose and graceful at his sides. Selene,
the Consort, was thrown down in a huge red-velvet wing-
back chair, one leg hooked over the arm, her head resting
against the high back. She tensed and flowed to her feet as
we approached, pulling down the hem of her black sweater
with one graceful yank. "Valentine." She managed to sound
happy and disapproving at once. "Thank you, Tiens."

He swept a courteous bow. All he needed was a feathered hat, like in the old Dumas holovids starring Bel Percy.
"For you, *demoiselle,* anything."

Nikolai stirred. He was a tallish Nichtvren male, dark
eyes under a soft shelf of dark hair and a face an Old Master might have painted—wide, generous mouth now com-
pressed into a thin line, sculpted cheekbones, winged dark
eyebrows. An angel's face, carved in old Renascence stone.
Not as sexless or alien as a demon's face could be. "I suppose I have you to thank for this chaos, demonling." Cat-
shine folded over his dark eyes.

*One trashed hotel room qualifies as chaos? Does he
know about Gabe?* "Two of my friends have been murdered and there's a price on my head that shouldn't be

there," I replied shortly. "If there's chaos it's not my fault. You promised to look after Gabe."

It hadn't quite been a promise, but he'd sent a credit disc she could use to get into his office building downtown if she was in trouble. And I'd been secure in the knowledge that Nikolai and Selene were looking after Gabe, after the whole Mirovitch thing. Nikolai didn't take it kindly when sexwitches were attacked; Selene had been one before she'd Turned. Whatever story was behind that, I didn't want to know. I only wanted to know why the Nichtvren hadn't stepped in to protect Gabe.

Nikolai inclined his head, and the air went cold and still. Selene moved forward between us.

"Let's not start like this. I asked Tiens to look for her." Her dark-blue eyes were eloquently wide, and far more human than his. "Hello, Dante. I'm sorry for your loss. We *were* watching over Gabriele Spocarelli. Whoever killed her and her husband—"

I almost choked. "Husband?" *Gabe married him? Wow. She didn't invite me to the wedding* or *tell me about her kid. Gods. What, did she think I'd refuse to come?* "Oh." I shook my head. "Go on. I'm sorry."

"We have troubles of our own." Nikolai's voice was clawed silk. "A *sedayeen* clinic under our protection has been firebombed. And there are demons in my city, causing damage and killing Magi. What do you know of *that*, demonling?"

Tiens whistled, a long low sound that sliced the tension in the air. The fire popped and crackled. *What are Nichtvren doing around open flame? I've seen them burn.* I discarded the question, shivering at the memory. My right hand itched for my sword.

Tiens said something low and fast, in Old Franje. Nikolai blinked, his attention shifting from me to the other Nichtvren. He replied in the same language, and Selene shook her head slightly at me, as if I was supposed to listen.

I should have learned a couple of languages instead of slogging through Magi shadowjournals.

I'd been studying shadowjournals and breaking code for years now. All useless, because I knew next to nothing about the Fallen. Nothing about *hedaira* except for what I'd figured out on my own—and what Anwen Carlyle had just told me. I'd have been better off spending my time studying Old Franje and Czechi. Or trying to figure out the language of demons.

The conversation lasted just over eight minutes, but when it was done Nikolai's eyes returned to me. "Well. It appears you are an innocent. I never thought to say that of a demon."

"I'm not demon," I said. "I'm *hedaira*." *But I barely even know what that means. I only know enough to get myself in trouble.*

Selene folded her arms. Every time she spoke or moved Nikolai paid attention to nothing else, the rumor was she was the only thing in the city he cared about. The way he looked at her, I could believe it. "Why don't you come with me, Dante? I have a few things to tell you."

"Selene." Nikolai's voice was soft, warning.

She shook her dark-blonde hair back, the gold threaded through her mane reflecting the ruddy firelight. If Tiens was pretty and Nikolai severely angelic, she was exquisite, every line expressly designed for maximum beauty. She looked almost unreal, especially since she had lost a little of the nervous energy I'd seen in her last time. Besides, she was fragrant even for a Nichtvren—a smell that reminded me of sexwitch musk. If she'd once *been* a sexwitch, that would explain it. "Loosen up, Nikolai."

"Remember our bargain."

I shivered. I'd heard that kind of thing before, and could only guess what sort of agreement could be reached between two Nichtvren. Especially a Prime and his Consort.

"I thought we'd gone beyond bargains." Her attention fixed on a point above my right shoulder, her back presented to him as her shoulders stiffened.

"You make it necessary, *milaya*. Not me." From where I was standing, I saw his face change, softening. He seemed to have forgotten Tiens and me, his eyes focused on Selene's back.

It felt vaguely voyeuristic, to watch his face as he looked at her, his mouth softening and his eyes speaking in a language I didn't need to be Nichtvren to understand. Whatever else happened between the Prime and Selene, he was in it hoverwash-deep over her. It was a very human look, and it made a lump rise in my throat.

She managed to sound disdainful and amused at once. "I don't force you into bargains, Nik. You're the one always trying to *bargain*. You'd think after a few hundred years you would learn it doesn't work."

He shrugged, a fluid inhuman movement she probably felt, even if she couldn't see it. "You are still here, are you not? I keep my promises."

"Good." She moved forward, turning on her heel when she reached me and threading her arm through mine. I twitched—it was my right arm, and if I needed to draw I'd have to shake her off. "And I keep mine. I'm going to help her. You can just sit and rot if you want."

"Selene—"

"No, Nik." Her jaw set.

"Selene—" Was that *pleading* in his voice? It was a unique experience, to hear a Nichtvren Master pleading.

Selene was having none of it. *"No."* Her voice made the pictures rattle on the wall, furniture groaning just a little under the weight of her Power.

"Lena." His voice turned soft, private. I wanted to look down at the floor to give them some privacy, couldn't move.

She tensed. "You don't *own* me, Nikolai. I stay because I *want* to. Do we need to have this discussion again?"

His shoulders slumped, he ran one stiff-fingered hand back through his dark hair. I think it was the only time I ever saw a Nichtvren look defeated. Tiens studied his boot toes, not-paying-attention *very* loudly for such a silent pose.

"Do not leave the nest, *milaya*. Not without me. Please."

So he thought she was going to come out to play with me? Was that it? *Thanks but no thanks.* It was ridiculous of me to be more frightened of suckheads than demons, but there it was.

"I'll think about it." She tugged on my arm. I had no choice but to follow. "Have fun, boys."

Nikolai's eyes rested on me for a long moment. I wasn't sure if he was going to blame me for whatever lovers' spat was happening between him and his Consort. I didn't care—all I wanted to do was pump her for information about Gabe and the *sedayeen* clinic. Eddie was hanging out with *sedayeen* right before he died; and a Shaman from that same clinic had come to Abra's trying to find me. And now the place had been bombed? Was it the same clinic?

How many *sedayeen* clinics were at risk of being bombed in Saint City? It was vanishingly unlikely that it wasn't connected.

Well, great. At least I know where I'm going next.

Not to mention the deaths of a string of Magi and demons causing havoc. Nikolai assumed it had something to do with me, and I wasn't sure he was far wrong, no matter *what* Tiens had told him or how little I knew about it.

Selene all but dragged me out of the room and shut the door behind us, then let out a gusty sigh. "Come with me." She let go of my arm, indicating the hall with one graceful movement. "You don't know Franje."

I headed the way she pointed, she fell into step beside me. Our boots clicked against the flooring. "No."

"Tiens told Nik that the green-eyed Eldest is hunting a stray demon in this city, and you were being kept out of the fray for your own good. Nik asked if the Eldest was calling in the favor, and Teins replied there was no favor to be called in, but that the Eldest would be extremely displeased if you were not given some shelter, at least." She sounded grimly pleased with herself. "I don't think Nikolai realizes I've been using hypnotapes to teach myself languages. I *hate* it when he tries to talk to people around me."

I was surprised into a short bitter laugh. "You and me both. What demon is Japh hunting here?"

Her shrug was a marvel of fluidity. "I'm no Magi. Someone demon management wants captured alive, I'm told. That's all."

There was only one demon fitting that bill. Japhrimel *was* hunting Eve, here in Saint City.

And he expected to hide it from me. Even Tiens and Nikolai knew more about what was going on with the demons than I did. I was fairly sure the "green-eyed Eldest" didn't mean Lucifer. Anyway, Lucifer wouldn't want me sheltered. He would want me *dead;* especially if he figured out I'd met with Eve and was determined to help her.

I was beginning to wonder if he would get his wish—and beginning to wonder if there was anyplace on earth where someone didn't owe a demon a favor. "Which clinic?" I asked. Fortieth was a big street.

"Fortieth and Napier. Edge of the Tank District. I remember when that was empty lots, before the first transport well was excavated."

"How long have you been with Nikolai?" It was a rude question, but I was honestly curious—both about that and about why she seemed to have taken such a shine to me.

"Long enough to know he'll come looking for me soon to make sure I'm not doing anything 'rash.' I swear, he gets more paranoid every decade, it's a wonder he isn't suspicious of *breathing.*" She led me through dim, quiet halls, I saw a bust of a Roma emperor and a couple of other priceless artifacts. I was willing to bet she'd done the decorating, it didn't look overblown enough to be a really old Nichtvren nest. A couple of holovid-still mags were exclusively dedicated to paranormal homes; I'd glanced through one or two and come away with the idea that the older Nichtvren got, the more cluttered and tasteless their interiors became, crammed with valuables.

Selene paused in front of a double door made of oak and barred with iron. The shields on the room behind it were tough and spiky, no type of magick I'd ever seen before.

The mercenary in me was appalled—a totally new type of shielding? Gods, I was slipping. The trained Power-worker in me was fascinated. "Who did those?"

"Nikolai. And he hired a couple of Magi to do a few more layers. But don't worry, you're with me." She walked right up to the doors, the layers of energy shimmering and pulsing—then softening as they touched her. It was oddly intimate, even the Prime's defenses recognized her.

It reminded me of Japhrimel's aura closing around mine, and I swallowed as heat rose to my cheeks. The mark on my shoulder was *still* numb, my left arm cold. Not the cold prickling numbness of Japhrimel gone dormant—I remembered that feeling. This was something new. Was he closing me out? Maybe. I'd seen through his eyes before, when I touched the ropy scars with bare fingertips; was he doing something he didn't want me to see?

Or was the mark fading? No, the flushing pulses of Power still coiled along my skin at even intervals, and I'd drawn on the mark, pulling magickal energy through it. I'd given up wondering if flooding me with Power was something Japh was doing consciously. Maybe it was just the overspill from his renewed status as a full demon.

Fallen, with a demon's power. I shivered and followed Selene. "No offense, by why are you being so helpful?" The doors swung open. They looked heavy, even for her slim Nichtvren strength.

"Not many people visit Nikolai armed to the teeth. I was interested. You've got quite a reputation, you know." Her hair swung as she closed the doors behind us. "Then the Eldest visited us. Nice-looking man."

My jaw threatened to drop. "Japhrimel came here?"

"A few nights ago. He and Nikolai were talking in Putch-kin Russe, very old Russe. I *still* can't get the hang of that language, but at least it's better than Politzhain. Politzhain is like talking through razor blades. Anyway, Nik was very quiet for a long time after the Eldest left. Still won't say a word about it. But I've still got the books, so . . . ."

So Japh had come here our first night in town. Right after I'd visited Gabe, he'd left me with McKinley, and I'd been dead asleep. *Goddammit, Japh. How could you?*

I found myself in a long, high-ceilinged room full of dimness and a crawling breathless sense of evil. My right hand closed around my swordhilt; Selene held up both white hands, her sweater sleeves falling back and exposing delicate wrists, both scarred with old, white ridged tissue. *Nichtvren don't usually scar. Where are those from?*

"Easy there, Valentine. It's just the items." She pitched the words deliberately low, deliberately soothing. She did have a beautiful voice, beautiful as the rest of her.

"Items?" There were glass display cases, some of them holding full bookshelves. A cold exhaled breath of something cruelly evil behind all that glass touched my skin, and I felt it struggle to open one yellow eye before retreating, watching balefully.

"Nikolai collects cursed objects. Says it's better for them to be out of the way." She dropped her hands. "There's something here you should have."

"You're going to give me a cursed object?" I made my hand unclench from the swordhilt. My fingers almost creaked. The Gauntlet's weight grew colder, a shiver jolting up my arm and stopping at the scar in the hollow of my shoulder. The sense of being watched lessened, but still was enough to keep me on edge.

"No. This is where he keeps the demonology books too. I've been studying since we last met. Besides, this is the one place his thralls don't come. We won't be overheard." She glanced over my shoulder at the door. "This way."

I followed her. There, on a high shelf, a spider-shaped idol made of obsidian shifted restlessly as I glanced at it. A venomously glowing yellow orb pulsed on a shelf underneath it. Off to my left, a vaguely hover-shaped thing sat draped in a dustcloth. A rusted bucket perched in a glass case, exhaling desperate sadness.

"*Sekhmet sa'es,*" I breathed. "He collects these? Doesn't he care about the curses?"

"He says he's cursed enough, what does one more matter? Regrettable pessimist, that man. I keep trying to get him to loosen up and have a little fun. Here we are." She stopped, brushed a tendril of dark-blonde hair out of her face. "Dante, there's something else Tiens said, right before I sent him out to find you."

We faced a cube of glass. Inside sat a three-foot-high shelf of leatherbound books. I looked for a hinge or a door, any way into the glass. "What? How are you going to—"

Her slender fist struck with enviable grace. I wouldn't have been surprised to hear a *kia*. Instead, she brushed the glass—*real* glass, not plasglass—from her hand. The entire case crumpled, shivering with a lovely tinkling sound.

"Tiens said the Eldest prizes your happiness and wants you kept unharmed. That's a big thing when it comes to demons."

Prizes my happiness? He's certainly not making me happy with this run-off-and-leave-me-alone business. But my heart gave a funny, melting little skip. "Oh, wow." I couldn't dredge up anything spectacular to say.

She knelt, her knees crunching on glass. Ran her finger along the bottom edge of books. "I was curious after our last meeting. Did some quiet asking around. You wouldn't believe what I paid for this, Esmerelda drives a hard bargain . . . . Here it is." A slim volume almost fell into her hands. "*Hedaraie Occasus Demonae*. The only copy in the world. It's rumored to be written by one of the last of the Fallen demons, back before they all died in some catastrophe or another. I can't translate it, but maybe you can."

She reached her feet in one smooth movement. My shields thickened reflexively against the danger in the air. Some of the things in here probably weren't asleep.

Some of the curses in here probably never slept.

"Do you know anything else?" My heart beat thinly in my throat. *I don't like the picture I'm beginning to get.*

"Just that it's hard to get anyone to talk about the Fallen. Demons don't like to, the Magi can't force them into talking, and Magi won't let a Nichtvren in on their secrets. And *nobody* knows what's going on with Magi dying and imps running around causing damage. Nikolai's fit to be tied." Her dark-blue eyes were amused. "I do know a few things, though. You're stronger than human, faster than human, and capable of using your Fallen's Power. You're his link to this world, if something happens to you. . . ." She shook her head, the weight of her gold-streaked hair swinging.

"So I'm basically a hostage if any other demon gets hold of me." *And here I was thinking everyone was in love with my sweet disposition and charming smile.* "Great."

"I suppose so." Her eyes were shadowed, now. "I was a hostage once, Dante. It's not comfortable. If I could give you one piece of advice?"

Oh, go ahead. I can't stop you. "What?" I tried to sound gracious.

"Don't be too hard on your Fallen. He's . . . well, he was very worried about your safety, from what I heard before he and Nik switched to Russian." She held the book, swinging it gently, the edge of its cover bumping her hip. "Be kind to the Eldest. Do you know why demons Fall?"

If he was so damn worried, why did he leave me alone with McKinley? Be kind to him? He lies to me, manipulates me—and you're saying to be kind? "They don't talk about it." *He says it's love. If this is love, I'll take a sparring session.*

Her smile was wonderful, just a curve of her beautiful lips, her eyes turning inward. "They give up Hell for the love of a mortal. It makes them helpless, and if there's one thing a demon hates, it's helplessness."

"How did you—" *How long did it take you to find that out? Not as long as me, I'd bet. And demons aren't the only ones who hate being helpless.*

"I've twisted a few arms." Selene pressed the book into my hands. "Be careful with this. Now listen, you'd better get out of here. Go to the clinic on Fortieth and Napier. Ask for Mercy or Annette—they were working with your friend's husband. And for God's sake be careful, there's a price on your head. Nikolai and I will do all we can to keep the werecain and other paranormals off your back, but it's tricky. There's a lot of mercenaries in town, and we can't interfere too directly in a human affair *or* in anything involving demons. So don't trust *anyone*. If you need a safe place to sleep, go to the House of Love on—"

"Polyamour's?" I tried to keep the disbelief out of my voice. "She's mixed up in this?"

"No, she's not. Which is why she's safe. She also has something for you—but *after* you take care of your business." She paused. "I wish I could go with you. It's been ages since anything really exciting happened."

"Yeah, well." *I've been abandoned by my demon lover, hit with hovers and reaction fire, and strangled by the Devil—again. Not to mention chased by hellhounds and nearly duped by a dumbass werecain. You can have the excitement, I'll take being bored.* "It's not all it's cracked up to be."

Her elegant nose wrinkled. "I remember enough excitement to value boredom too. It's just wishful—" Selene cocked her head. "Oh, *lovely.* Here comes Nikolai. Hurry. Up the stairs there, go through the third door on the left. It's only a two-story drop, and that window has a malfunctioning security latch. I was saving it for the next time I go out dancing. One last thing, Dante: don't trust *anyone.* Including me. Demons are in town, and nobody's safe when they get involved."

Don't I know it. "Thank you," I managed. "You're honorable." *Polyamour has something for me? Of course.* Comprehension bloomed under my skin. I'd been stupid; not guessing it. *One less thing to worry about.*

She waved it away. "Go. I'll delay Nik and Tiens."

19

The night was old and turning gray by the time I got to Fortieth and Napier. The streets were curiously hushed, even the Tank District; thin predawn drizzle dewed my hair with heaviness and made me acutely conscious of heat from my metabolism sending up tracers of steam from my skin.

My left shoulder was heavy and numb, my entire left arm cold. I almost slid my hand under my shirt to touch Japhrimel's mark. That fleeting contact would be enough for him to possibly track me, and I . . . missed him.

If there's one thing a demon hates, it's helplessness. Well, that made us about even, I hate being helpless too. But it was a huge stretch to think of Japhrimel at anyone's mercy, including mine. After all, he had no compunction about using superior strength to force me into being a good little obedient *hedaira*. Helpless? *Him?* Not bloody likely.

But still.

The only time I feel any peace is when you are safe, and I am near you.

Maybe the helplessness wasn't a physical thing.

He had actually grabbed Lucifer's hand and pushed the Devil *back.*

The Gauntlet rang softly, like a block of ice touched by a sonic cutter. I didn't want to think too much about that. It made my hands want to shake and my knees go a little softer than usual. Lucifer had intended to kill me, quite probably painfully. I was still looking at a very short lifespan without Japhrimel around to keep my skin whole, even with a demon artifact clapped on my wrist.

I took advantage of the shadows across the street from the Danae Clinic. Their windows were boarded up, a smell of scorched plasteel and plurifreeze drifting across the street. I inhaled deeply, my nose sorting out the different tangs, and extended a tendril of *awareness* toward the clinic.

I retreated as soon as my receptive consciousness touched the shields. Careful, heavy *sedayeen* and Shaman-laid shields, layers of energy pulsing and spiking. They had probably deflected most of the explosion, I caught no flavor of Power in the lingering echoes of the bomb. Just explosives, probably C19 or vaston. Which meant Mob work, most likely.

The tang of *sedayeen*—violets and white mallow—slid a galvanic thrill through my bones. I hadn't sought the company of a healer since Doreen's murder.

That thought made me shiver again, hearing my own harsh breath and feeling the claws tear through my human flesh again. Memory rose, swallowed me whole.

"Get down, Doreen! Get down!"

Crash of thunder. Moving, desperately, scrabbling . . . fingers scraping against the concrete, rolling to my feet, dodging the whine of bullets and plasbolts. Skidding to a stop just as he rose out of the dark, the razor glinting in one hand, his claws glittering on the other.

"Game over," he giggled, and the awful tearing in my side turned to a burning numbness as he slashed, I threw myself backward, not fast enough, not fast enough—

I exhaled. My fingers were under the collar of my shirt, but instead of the mark they were playing with Jace's necklace. It thrummed reassuringly under my touch, throbbing like a bad tooth implant.

I rubbed the knobbed end of a baculum as I watched the clinic. Small movements in the shadows warned me I wasn't the only one watching the place. I settled against the brick wall, feeling the bite of hunger under my ribs. The temptation to dig in my bag and fish out the book was almost overwhelming, but strictly controlled. I had no time for research now, I was on a hunt that would only get faster.

They're not going to open for a while. Go get some breakfast, Dante.

Not while there was someone else watching. Whoever-it-was was well hidden, blending into the landscape. The brick was rough and cold against my hair as I leaned even deeper into the wall, buttoned down tightly, almost invisible.

Selene was right. There were demons in Saint City, and things were getting unpredictable. The familiar mood of the cold pulsing heart of the city's Power well had changed a bit, spiced and spiked with the musksmell of demons. I've noticed it before—when a demon or two moves in, the whole city starts to smell.

Demons are, after all, credited with teaching humanity how to build cities. Yet another thing we can thank them for.

Go over it again, Dante.

Eddie had been working on something, and a biotech company was involved. He was murdered—and Gabe either wouldn't quit digging or knew something dangerous about what he was working on. So she was executed. The little bottles of granular stuff and the papers with Skinlin notations were either a decoy—or they were what he'd been killed for. And someone who had no trouble getting inside her shields had been willing to spend the time and effort to tear apart Gabe's house and go to the trouble of cleaning up psychic traces.

That made whatever I was carrying a hot property. Not to mention the file—had Gabe lifted it from the Saint City PD before it could be copied? Or were there more copies in a police station somewhere?

I had a few contacts on the police force from the days when I would take a turn doing apparitions to assist homicide investigations. Digging in the police department seemed the next logical choice after I found out whatever was at this clinic.

A quiet place to go through Eddie's file and the book Selene had given me would help. Two mysteries: what had killed my last two friends, and where the hell was Japhrimel? He'd seemed pretty insistent on not letting me out of his sight, and if I could be used to force him into joining Eve's rebellion—and now that Lucifer had made it clear I was living on borrowed time—it made no sense for him to leave me alone with McKinley.

Not to mention the added mystery of this treasure and the Key, whatever they were.

Footsteps. Someone approaching.

I faded even deeper into shadow. Listened, taking deep

smooth breaths. Smelled a pleasant mix—the violets and white mallow of a *sedayeen* and the spiced honey of a Shaman.

My right hand closed around my swordhilt. I tensed.

They came into view, two women, neither carrying edged metal. Which usually means *helpless*. It always irks me to see a Shaman or Necromance without combat training—what good is being legally allowed and encouraged to carry weapons if you don't take advantage of it?

The irritation quickly turned to full-flowered anger as I noticed the skittering in the shadows of the alleys opposite me. I caught a glint of metal and heard the soft, definite snick of a projectile assault rifle's safety being eased off.

I was already moving.

Reverse grip on swordhilt, tear the blade up, wet gray stink of intestines slithering loose. I kicked the fifth one, a snapping side kick that smashed his ribs on one side and sent him hurtling back. The momentum of the kick brought me around in a neat half-turn, sword singing up and making a chiming noise as I blocked the downsweep of the mercenary with the machete.

They had good, corporate-laid shields. Some Magi had been paid to lay a concealment on them so their blaring normal minds wouldn't broadcast their presence to psionic victims. That alone told me they were up to no good—if they'd just been surveillance teams, they wouldn't have had both concealments *and* enough projectile-weaponry to start a new riot in the Tank District.

The fight was short, sharp, and vicious, ending with me flicking smoking human blood off my sword, Power flaring to clean the steel before it flickered back into its sheath.

I grabbed the last one left alive—the merc whose ribs I'd shattered—and hauled him up, bone grinding in the mess of his chest.

He was maybe thirty, sweating under his streaky gray camopaint, in standard merc assassin gear—a rig like mine, black microfiber jumpsuit, various clinking weaponry. His body shuddered, eyes glazing, my rings popped a shower of golden sparks as I shook him.

"Don't you dare die on me," I snarled. "*Who sent you?* Give me a name and I'll ease your passing."

I heard a low choked sound from the mouth of the alley—the *sedayeen*.

I ignored it, shook the man again as he mumbled. "So help me Anubis, if you don't tell me now I'll rip the knowledge out of your soul once you've passed the Bridge."

I couldn't, of course—I could only have someone question him as I held an apparition, as long as that person was trained in the protocol of questioning the dead. You can get misleading answers if you don't phrase the questions right.

Just like with demons.

I couldn't rip the knowledge free of his soul—but he was normal. He probably didn't know that. I felt less guilty than I should have for even threatening it.

"P-P-Po—" The man choked on blood as he tried to scream. I shook him again, his six-foot frame like a doll's in my slim golden hands. My fingers tensed, driving my claws into his shoulders.

A hand closed over my shoulder, and I almost slashed before I realized it was the *sedayeen*. A familiar deep smooth sense of restful Power slid down my skin, clearing my head and washing away some of the cold fury.

"Let him go." A clear, soft, sweet, *young* voice. "I can tell you who sent them. They're Tanner Family goons."

Blood bubbled on the man's lips. His eyes widened frantically. I saw gold-touched stubble on his cheeks, a crooked front tooth, the fine fan of his eyebrows. He'd just taken a job, after all. He was just a mercenary.

What am I doing?

I let out a short guttural sound and freed my right hand, hooking my fingers; my claws extended as I made a quick sharp almost-backhand movement. Blood gushed free, but I'd already pushed him away. The arterial spray missed me, and in any case, he was bleeding so badly internally it wasn't like he had much blood pressure left.

I tore away from under the *sedayeen's* touch. Had I not noticed her approach or had she slipped under my mag-scan because she was a healer, and harmless? *Sedayeen* are incapable of harming anyone without horrific feedback, they are the swanhilds of the psionic world, helpless pacifists without the natural advantage of poisonous flesh 'hilds have. *Sedayeen* survived by attaching themselves to the more powerful in the paranormal or psionic world, and they were valuable enough to their protectors to avoid the near-extinction sexwitches had suffered in the chaos just after the Awakening.

She was dressed in a faded *PhenFighters* T-shirt and a pair of jeans, Silmari sandals on her small feet. Short spiked brown hair stood up from her well-modeled head, and a wide pair of muddy brown eyes met mine. She had a triangular face like most healers, a sharp chin and a cupid's-bow of a mouth. Her accreditation tat was the characteristic ankh of the *sedayeen,* this one with an additional short bar through the vertical line and a small pair of wings. She wore a hemp choker with turquoise beads, and looked only about sixteen or so. But then, *sedayeen* age well. It probably meant she was around thirty.

The Shaman, a taller woman with her blonde hair braided back in rows, stood at the mouth of the alley with her oak staff raised. Yellow ribbons knotted around the top of the staff fluttered as a slight morning breeze played with them. Her eyes were a fantastic shade of amber, probably genespliced. Her tat shifted uneasily on her left cheek, the spurred and clawed triquetra of a Billebonge-trained Shaman. She stood a little too tensely to be completely untrained for combat, her hand on the staff was steady and placed just so. I wondered why she had no sword. Shamans with combat training usually like steel.

Tanner Family. Why would the Mob want to kill a healer and a Shaman now? After filling a Skinlin and a Necromance with holes. Is it a Mob war on psions? I shook my right hand out, my claws retracting slowly. My breath came in harsh gasps, not because of effort.

I was gasping because I didn't want to stop. I wanted to *kill*. The seduction of bloodlust whispered under conscious thought, tempting me. It would be so *easy*.

They were, after all, only human.

Stop it, Danny. You're human too. You're too close to the edge. This is too personal, and you're going over the line. Calm down. The cold on my left arm retreated before the heat of bloodlust as I struggled to control myself.

"Annette Cameron," I husked. "I'm looking for Annette Cameron." *Please, Anubis. Give me a little help here. I don't think I'm quite safe right now.* Rage receded slowly, leaving behind a slow smoky feeling of strain.

I'm deconstructing. This is bad. Too much stress and too little rest, my psyche was beginning to fray at the edges.

The worst thing was, I wasn't sure I cared.

The *sedayeen* nodded. Her eyes were a little wide, I think I was too much for even a *sedayeen*'s calm at the moment. "That's Cam." She pointed at the Shaman. "I'm Mercy. Come inside."

"Do you know who I am?" I managed around the lump in my throat. My shoulder was still numb, but underneath the numbness a deep broad pain began to surface.

"You're Dante Valentine." The yellow-haired Shaman's hands shook only slightly, the ribbons atop her staff fluttering. "Eddie described you. He said that if anything ever happened to him, you were someone we could trust."

I'd forgotten what it was like to be around *sedayeen*. Inside the clinic—dark because the windows were boarded up and Mercy didn't turn the lights on—the sense of peace was palpable, stroking and calming even the most jagged of auras. The smell of violets wafted through the air; one of the peculiarities of psion noses is that violet scent doesn't shut off in our nasal receptors like in everyone else's. We're maybe the only humans who can smell violets for a long time.

Call us lucky.

The waiting room had chairs and a children's corner. The sight of brightly-colored plasticine made my heart leap into my throat. I tasted bile and looked away, shoving my sword into the loop on my rig. I didn't trust myself with edged metal right now. The reception desk didn't have an AI deck, I would bet they had a psion there to get an initial read on the patients during open hours. A good idea when dealing with Chillfreaks and human refuse in a free clinic.

A maintenance 'bot retreated as we came in, its red LED blinking. The air was dyed blue with calm, freighted with the smell of flowers and mallow. Mercy led me back through a pair of swinging doors and into a maze of examining rooms, offices, and private labs.

The Shaman—Cameron—kept giving me nervous little sidelong glances. I didn't blame her. I knew what my aura looked like—the trademark glitterlamp sparkles of a Necromance threaded with black diamond demon flames, the mark on my shoulder pulsing and staining through my shifting defenses and cloaks of energy. I tore through the psychic ether like the sound of a slicboard through a Ludder convention, not as loud as Japhrimel but unable to hide with little effort like some other psions could. I looked, in short, like trouble.

It was truth in advertising. I *felt* like trouble now.

"What was Eddie working on?" I asked, as Mercy touched a scanlock to the right of a smooth plasteel door. She actually flinched. *Great, I even scare* sedayeen. "Gabe didn't tell me."

"It's not what he was working on," the healer replied. "It's what he found, what he finished." The door *fwoosh*ed aside, white full-spectrum bulbs popping into life. The light speared my eyes before they adjusted, I found myself looking into a stripped-down, empty lab. "This is where he was working."

This isn't where he died. The lab he was in had different tiles on the floor.

Then I saw the counter under growlights. Blooming under the hot radiance of the lamps, their roots safe in hydropon bubbles, were Eddie's datura plants, blossoming and healthy. Each one of them had frilly double-trumpet flowers, purple and white. Datura, used for binding spells and painblockers, if I remembered right it used to be called crazyweed or jimsweed. Poisonous, and illegal for anyone but a registered Skinlin or *sedayeen* to propagate.

"Datura," I whispered. "What the hell did Eddie find?"

The door whooshed closed behind us, and I turned to face the Shaman and the *sedayeen*. The mark on my shoulder sent a tingle down my arm, a welcome relief from numb coldness. I restrained the urge to reach under my shirt and rub the ropes of scarring that made Japhrimel's name branded into my skin.

"Cam? You want to tell her?"

The Shaman shook her head, but she answered. She stank of a raw edge of fear under her spiked scent of magick, something I understood. I'd be afraid too if I was her. "I was working with Eddie. So was Mercy. We were looking for an alkaloid-based painblocker for Pico-PhizePharm." She took a deep breath, then met my gaze squarely. She had deep dark circles under her amber eyes. "What we found was a goddamn fail-safe cure for Chill."

20

*M*y jaw didn't drop, but it was close. "There *is* no cure for Chill." I sounded like the air had been punched out of me, again. I was getting to sound like that a lot lately.

Clormen-13 was instantly addictive, it was the nastiest drug on the market. The Hegemony police were constantly fighting a losing war, not only against Chill but against the violence that flowed in its wake. Chillfreaks will do literally *anything* for another hit, and the way the drug lowers inhibitions and stirs psychoses is bad news. Chillfreaks are like dusters; they don't feel pain or exhaustion. All they feel in the last stages of Chill addiction is the *need*.

Unlike hash, Chill is addictive for psions; it supposedly gives a high greater than jacking in and riding a Greater Work of magick. The only problem is, it eats away at a psion's shields and control of Power, consuming from the inside. A psion gone Chillfreak is lethal if you aren't careful, not only for the absolute lack of any inhibition but also because they can explode on a psionic level, the magickal equivalent of walking thermonuclear bombs.

The large broad leaves of the plants stirred innocently. They looked healthy for having been dug up recently.

Eddie was—*had been*—one hell of a Skinlin. "No cure," I repeated slowly. "That's why it's so profit—oh. *Oh.*"

That's why it was so fucking *profitable,* once you got someone hooked you could take them for everything they had and all they could steal. There was no cure for Chill, the detox process killed almost as surely as addiction did. A cure for Chill would be worth a lot of money—and would cut into the Mob's profit margin worldwide.

My heart gave a gigantic slamming leap. "Who knew? *Who?*" My voice stirred the plant leaves, rattled the beakers and equipment, made the tiles groan sharply.

"Nobody from Pico-Phize knew yet. Or at least, we didn't think they did. Massadie—our contact—might have stolen a sample. Eddie had five." Mercy crossed her arms over her shallow breasts. Now that we were under full-spectrum lights, I saw the shadows of sleeplessness teasing under her eyes and at the corners of her mouth. I didn't blame her a bit. *Sedayeen* aren't frightened of much—they have a sort of genetic disposition to an almost-maniacal calm, bolstered by their training. But even a healer would lose a little sleep over this kind of thing.

And let's not forget she was faced with a patently murderous part-demon. It was probably a wonder she wasn't running screaming in the street.

"He left four at the house," I said numbly. *Sekhmet sa'es. Holy fuck. A cure for fucking Chill.* Mercy made a restless movement—maybe my voice disturbed her. I licked my dry lips. "*Sekhmet sa'es,* do you have any idea . . . a cure. A cure for *Chill.*"

"Eddie found out that when he treated the datura alkaloids with a new technique, he got something that looked a little bit like Chill. So he ran some tests, refined it; couldn't believe what he had and brought it to me. We . . . there was no shortage of volunteers. We chose three. They walked out of here free of addiction. We subjected them to every marker and psiwave test. They were *clean.*" Mercy took a deep breath. "Eddie . . . he did what he had to do. He moved out of his house and into a shitty apartment on Fiske. He came in and mainlined a packet of Clormen-13. Then we locked him in an observation room until he started to suffer withdrawal. We gave him a hypo of the datura cure."

"You did *what?*" Plasglass beakers rang softly as the words hit a shrill high. I didn't sound very much like a whispering Necromance. The daturas rustled.

"He wouldn't let us say it was a cure until he'd done it himself and knew for sure. He took a hypo of the datura solution. Sixteen hours later, he was clean. All bloodlevels normal, no aura damage—*clean.*"

"No aura damage?" The thought of a cure for Chill made me feel distinctly woozy. *I've faced down Lucifer himself, why do my knees feel weak?*

Gods above, this . . . it could topple the Mob, it could clear the streets and free millions of addicts, stop 70 percent of inner-city crime. . . . *Gods. Gods above and below, Eddie, you came up with a cure for Chill? You beautiful, dirty, shaggy bastard. Gods above and below have mercy on you, Eddie. You deserve a frocking state-sponsored sainthood and federal buildings named after you.*

"None." Mercy said it slowly, and very distinctly. She had started to look a little more relaxed. "It's a cure, Valentine. A cure that works on psions and normals, a fail-safe cure for Chill. Eddie didn't want to tell anyone yet, but I'm almost positive Massadie found out."

No wonder the Mob was out for blood. A fail-safe detox

for Chill would cut their profits by half if not more, Pico-Phize would be able to get Hegemony *and* Putchkin contracts galore as well as corner the market on other alkaloid painkillers, and other pharm companies would line up espionage agents around the block to get a sneaking peek at the technique. But if Massadie had stolen a sample, why would he be looking for me?

My brain began to work again. There was a certain ironic delight in carrying around a vial of one of the most valuable substances on earth at this point.

Then I remembered I'd given Japhrimel the other three.

Well, there was no safer place around for them. And that *still* left one vial unaccounted-for. Not to mention Gabe and Eddie's kid, in a safe place—for now.

I hoped like hell the hole Gabe had found was deep enough to hide her daughter. *One problem at a time, Danny. One goddamn problem at a time.* "Massadie. He's been leaving messages for me. Any idea why?"

The healer shrugged. "He's probably a little upset. His most profitable researcher's dead and it's appropriations time. We found a few alkaloids, but without our Skinlin and his notations it's hopeless. We'll lose funding and Jovan Massadie will slip another few steps down on the corporate ladder, losing the discovery that can pay for his retirement." Mercy's eyes lit with sudden hope. "Gabe said she was going to call you. Is she okay? And little Liana?"

Notations. The paper's notations, maybe a formula. I looked at the daturas, glowing with health. "Gabe's dead," I said harshly. "I don't know where the kid is, Gabe told me she was in a safe place. Right now I'm just concerned with icing the motherfuckers that did her parents." *Not to mention keeping the Devil off my ass and eluding my Fallen.* It was partly a lie, I did know where Gabe's daughter was, but until this was over nobody would hear it from me. *Liana. So that's her name.*

"Gabriele's *dead?*" The Shaman exchanged a long meaningful look with Mercy and made a sharp, controlled movement. It looked like pure frustration. Or was she reaching for a blade she wasn't carrying? "Son of a *bitch.*"

It jarred me then, a warning note. I stared at the healer, but she dropped her eyes. There was something going on here, something else.

Then again, I was probably only getting paranoid. This was a *sedayeen* and a fellow Shaman, Eddie's coworkers—and in just as much danger as Gabe had been.

"Do you two have anywhere you can go, get undercover?" I flipped the flap of my bag open, dug around inside. Metal clinked. I felt the hard leather edge of the book Selene had given me, the stiff but wilting paper of the murder file. I needed a quiet place to sit and do some reading. "And do you have a commnet for other Chill clinics?"

"Why?" The Shaman twirled her staff, ribbons floating on the air. Her aura, a spiked peppery glow, pulsed uneasily. Her eyebrows drew together, and she cast a meaningful look at Mercy's bowed head, as if warning me to be gentle for the healer's sake.

Irritation made my cheeks hot, made my right hand clench into a fist inside my bag. I met her amber eyes squarely. *Why? Because I fucking well said so, Shaman. If you'd taken the time to sweat a little more in combat practice, you might have been able to look after yourself and that healer. You might have even been able to give Eddie a little protection.* I swallowed, hard, burying the words. "Because I have something I want to spread around the clinic network, Shaman. Are you going to argue with me?"

The *sedayeen* stepped forward, partly to deflect me. "Let's just calm down." She spread her hands. "We can broadcast to the entire West Coast network from here, and they can send it worldwide. Is there something you want to send out?"

"You better believe it. Do you have someplace safe to go?" *Please don't tell me I'm going to have to find a safe place to stash them. I can't afford to be weighed down by a fucking healer and a Shaman too lazy to keep up on combat practice.*

The Shaman laughed. It was a bitter bark, her amber eyes hard and cool. "This *was* our safe place. What the hell *are* you?"

I'm hedaira. *That won't mean jackshit to you, though. I doubt I know half of what it means. Where are you, Japh? Hunting Eve?* My fingers drifted across the leatherbound edge again. It felt too fine-grained to be leather, really, but it didn't feel like plasilica or pleather either. *Maybe this will help—if I can translate it. Wonder what language it's in. Quit it, Danny. You have other chips to fry.* "For right now, girls, I'm your guardian angel. I'm going to keep you alive." I paused. "And out of the Tanner Family's greasy little hands."

"Why?" Cam's fingers flicked on her staff, her aura pulsing. If she was combat-trained, why didn't she have sharp steel? And why in the name of Anubis was she moving so carefully as if trying to hide it? I felt the nagging sense of some loose end, some instrument out of tune that was screwing up the whole holorchestra. Shook the feeling away.

Because you're bloody well helpless and in over your heads, that's why. I yanked the two sheets of paper with Eddie's careful handwriting out of my bag. "Because it's the honorable thing to do. Where's your commnet?"

"In the office. Cam, please, relax. Eddie said we could trust her." The *sedayeen* sounded just like Doreen used to when she thought I was being unreasonable—quiet, soothing, her tone suddenly as soft as a pampered cat's fur. But her voice shook, and fear tinted the edges of her shielding.

Gods, what a vote of nonconfidence.

Her soothing voice didn't soothe *me*. I wanted to hear someone else, a dry ironic male tone just slightly inclined toward sarcasm. It shook me to realize that the only person I felt like talking to right now was Japhrimel. I wanted to hear what he'd have to say about Eddie's jacking himself on Chill to test this cure. I wanted to lean my head on his shoulder and feel his aura wrapping around mine, that damnable sense of safety. I wanted the look that sometimes passed between us, his eyes meeting mine and the feeling of being understood, of silent agreement.

Most of all I wanted him to calm me down, because I wasn't sure I could do it myself. I was walking around with a skin full of rage and vengeance, getting twitchy and deconstructing under the pressure.

Anubis, please, help me. Stay my hand, give me strength. It wasn't my usual prayer, but it was all I could come up with.

I held up the papers. "Can you tell me if this is a complete formula?"

Cam stared. Her eyes finally widened, and she looked far more relieved.

Mercy actually choked. "Where did you—that's Eddie's mastersheet! A Skinlin would be able to decode and—"

"Great. Communit, girls. Let's go."

I didn't look while Mercy sent out the datafax to all the clinics, being busy peering out the window and scanning the street below. I *did* take the mastersheets back over her protests.

The office was cluttered with paper but otherwise neat, with the powerful smell of *sedayeen* filling the air. I was getting very tired of the smell of violets—I kept expecting to turn around and see Doreen, her eyebrows lifted just slightly and her hands clasped in front of her.

Besides, I was nervous. I felt like I was missing something crucial. The feeling irritated me—was it nerves, the result of being under stress for too long? Or was it my small precognitive talent, warning me of muddy water and danger?

The cold numbness spreading up my arm from the Gauntlet didn't help.

My bankroll was gone, and I had nobody handy to spring for a hotel room. Between them, Cam and Mercy had two hundred New Credits; it would be just barely enough. The mark on my shoulder prickled, the sensation growing to an intensity just short of pain and fading in steady waves. Was Japhrimel looking for me?

I hoped he was. He was my best bet for survival, and things were getting a little too deep for my taste.

Great, Danny. Go crying back to Japhrimel, you spineless wonder. You've got work to do and you're on your own. Even if Japh could help you, he probably wouldn't. He has

*his own problems, one of which you've got to make a whole
lot worse for him if you can.*

I hate it when that deep sarcastic voice shows up inside
my head. It's usually right. Some new faction of demons
was in the mix, and this treasure—and the Key. If Japhrimel
couldn't be sure what I'd told Eve, no wonder he wasn't
willing to give me more information. I was, at this point,
a distinct liability to him, between being hostage material
and a possible information-leak. He couldn't trust me not
to go running off to Eve as soon as I could.

*He's convinced Eve is going to lose, and he wants to be on
the winning side.* I had to shake my head, my hair tangling
forward over my shoulders. *Stop looking at things from his
side, dammit! You're furious with him, remember?*

True. But I wanted to see him just the same. Things were
getting ridiculous. And even if he did manhandle me a bit,
he'd certainly kept me alive in the face of distinct opposi-
tion from the Devil. That sort of thing will make a girl feel
charitable, even toward a lying, manhandling demon.

I got us to the Vaccavine Hotel on the edge of the Tank
District, sending the *sedayeen* in to buy the room and prodding the Shaman up the fire escape to meet her on the third
floor. Once I got them both settled, I warded the walls—
ignoring the Shaman's gasp and Mercy's open, wondering
fear. I'd gotten so used to having access to almost-demon
Power, it was a sobering experience to see even other psions
acting like wide-eyed normals.

I was fairly sure we weren't followed, but I settled myself in the window with my sword across my knees anyway.
Mercy took the bed and was blissfully asleep in moments,
a skill I envied. She didn't seem old enough to have an
accreditation tat, and I wondered about the relationship be-

tween the two women. They seemed very easy with each other.

That made me remember Doreen, and my heart twisted inside my chest.

The Shaman paced. From one end of the room to the other, she wore a line in the cheap red carpet. The ribbons on her staff made soft sweet sounds as she frowned at the floor. She didn't quite dare to scowl at me, but I got the feeling it was a close call.

I pulled Eddie's file out of my bag. It was beginning to look distinctly battered, the tough manila paper crinkling at the corners. "All right, Eustace Edward," I whispered. "Let's see what you have to tell me."

Seeing the first laserprint again was the same shock. Shattered glass and sticky-dry blood, Eddie's head smashed back too far for his neck to support. His hair was full of blood, and broken plasglass winked on his cheek. He didn't have his coat on. Jeans and the remains of a *RetroPhunk 4EVAH!* T-shirt. A winking gold chain around his neck that would probably dangle a marriage chip.

I turned the laserprint over, sourness filling my mouth. Glanced at the infosheet below, a standard Saint City cop-shop document. Name of victim, age, cause of death, scene specifics—

I read the address twice, then again. *What the hell?*

Eddie had been killed in a Pico-Phize lab downtown. And according to the file, the number-one suspect was one J. T. Massadie.

No way, Danny, I heard a familiar voice whisper in my right ear. It sounded a lot like Eddie's usual laconic growl. *If Gabe woulda had a clear lead to this guy she woulda given you his name.*

Lovely. I was dreaming about one dead man and hearing another while awake. Along with dating a demon, my life was getting too interesting even for *me,* and that was saying something. I wished I had time for some meditation, to clear out and organize my head.

I shifted on my chair, my sword singing softly inside its sheath. Massadie looked to benefit from the cure if Eddie could produce it. His position in the corporate ladder as well as his retirement account would be secure.

There's no way Massadie would have sanctioned this. Greed's a better proof of his innocence than a rock-solid alibi would be.

The investigating officer's name was Gilbert Pontside. And he was a normal. *That* was wrong—the murder of a psion was the jurisdiction of the Saint City Spook Squad. A Necromance or Shaman should have been assigned to the case, it was standard procedure. A Magi or Ceremonial might have taken the case if they had a Necromance partner.

The rules were clear. The murder of a psion had to be investigated by psions, not only because of the dangerousness of hunting psions or a normal dangerous enough to kill one, but because of the risk of Feeders—psychic vampires. Sometimes a dead psion's body, if left uncremated, could give rise to a Feeder's *ka.*

I knew enough about Feeders to shiver.

I wondered if Pontside was Gabe's friend. I wondered if he was on the Tanner Family make. And I most *especially* wondered if she'd opened her door to Pontside, or if her shields knew him and didn't react when he came to toss her house over.

It was a workable hypothesis. No wonder Massadie was

trying to track me down. Was he on the Tanner Family payroll too, or just afraid for his own miserable life?

I was thinking this over when the hair on my nape stood straight up. My left shoulder prickled urgently, I glanced at my left wrist. The cuff was quiescent, no green light.

But it was so cold, its surface dead and dark. I wished I had the time and the means to cut the damn thing off my wrist.

I jammed the folder back into my bag and made it to my feet. "Get on the bed," I told the Shaman, my right hand curling around my swordhilt. My brain began to tick over likely avenues of attack, fire angles, and what I was going to do if it came down to defending them both.

"Were we followed?" Her throat moved as she swallowed audibly, her fantastic eyes widening. I would have bet she was closer to forty than anything else, but she looked as young as Mercy at that moment. My sword whispered free, the metal ringing softly as faint blue flame slid along the keen curved edge.

"Get on the fucking *bed!*" *Goddamn civilians.* My heart began to pound. How was I going to protect two helpless humans, take down a Mob family, and keep my head down with demons in town looking to take me hostage?

I didn't get another argument from her, because three light taps resounded on the flimsy door. I ghosted toward the door and to the side, behind the wall the room shared with a small bathroom. My sword lifted just as the shields and wards I'd laid on the room turned purple.

The deadbolt and maglock both clicked open, the hinges made a rough sound, and the edge of the door rasped along the cheap carpet. I glanced back—Cam stood next to the bed, her shoulders stiff. The edges of her oak staff glowed red with a Shaman's defensive spells, and her stance was the basic stave-against-unknown-threat.

So maybe she wasn't completely helpless. Was the soft act just another defense?

"Valentine," I heard a familiar voice from the door. "Stand down. It's a friend."

My heart thudded in my throat. *I don't think you're my friend, mister.*

Footsteps, deliberately loud. The door closed behind him. He halted in the hall. "Relax, milady. You need my help. I've got some really bad news."

I stepped out, the sword held slanting up, and faced McKinley.

He looked like hell, but he'd found a new set of black clothes and his shoulder appeared to be back in its socket. He slid a familiar-looking knife—mine, was that how he'd tracked me?—into a plasticine sheath and made it disappear. His face was bruised and swollen, his nose crooked, and his right hand looked like ground beef. But his black eyes traveled down and back up again, taking in the sword and my stance. He looked almost impressed despite himself.

His left hand, with its silvery metallic coating, raised a little. "Easy there, Valentine. You don't have time to kill me."

Says who? I'm a busy girl but I could probably fit you in.

And oh how satisfying it would be to take some of my rage out on him. Dangling from his silver-coated fingers was a silver chain. Swinging on the chain was a star sapphire that cried out to me in its own tongueless voice.

I'm getting pretty used to the sensation of being hit in the gut, I thought dimly. My left shoulder woke in one vivid flare of pain that threatened to drive me to my knees. I dug in, stayed upright. I was also getting very used to the sensation of my left shoulder being run through a meat grinder. At least that drove the numbness away, down my left arm.

Gee, Dante. It's sucking to be you lately.

"The Eldest has been taken," he said. "By the Twins."

"What are you talking about?" My voice cracked uselessly. "Taken? *Japhrimel?*"

"There were too many of them, and they ran him to ground while he was out drawing them off and away from you. Their next move is going to be to try to acquire you, and they're not the only ones." He offered the necklace. The sapphire swung gently, a spark of blue light caught in its depths. "There are other demons in town, at cross-purposes to both the Prince and the rebellion. It's crawling out there, I've got to get you out. We can catch a transport—"

"I'm not going anywhere," I said flatly. "I have business here. Who's got Japh?"

He swung the sapphire again. My eyes tracked it helplessly. "You don't get it," he said quietly. "He's the Eldest, they can't hold him for long. But if anyone gets their hands on you he's *helpless*. He has to do what they want. If *any* demon takes you we're all doomed."

Helpless. Selene used that word too. "Great speech." My sword didn't dip, blueflame runes twisting and coursing along the sharp edge. The steel's heart flamed white, responding to my sudden pounding heartbeat. "Too bad I'm not convinced."

My left hand dropped the scabbard and blurred toward a projectile gun. I eased the hammer back and leveled it at him. "I'll take all the cash you have, McKinley. You're probably carrying a fair bit. Cam, wake the healer up. Get her up *now.*"

"You're an idiot." McKinley's eyes were deadly glittering black, sharp pieces of jet. "I'm on your side. We have to get you to a transport, get you to a safe place. If another faction catches you and threatens to harm you, he *has* to do as they say. With all the demons in the city, you're going to be tagged sooner rather than later." He didn't smell like fear anymore; he smelled faintly like demon and even more faintly like dust. Dry and inhuman. His shoulders hunched, he didn't shift his weight but I knew he was ready to move.

I wondered just what exactly the Hellesvront agents were—not for the last time, I might add. I wondered if I was quick enough to take him.

Let's find out, Danny. "You don't listen very well, do you. I have *business* to finish, and I'm not going anywh—" My shoulder crunched with pain again, the world went gray, and things got confused for a second as I crouched instinctively, my swordhilt jabbing forward as he came for me. A bullet whined and pinged before burying itself in the wall.

If he hadn't leapt at me I might have negotiated with him. As it was, I was sick and fucking tired of being manhandled. The difference between Japh and McKinley was that the agent, while inhumanly fast, was just a shade slower than me; he couldn't easily overmatch me the way Japh could. It was a major tactical error on the agent's part to jump me. I happened to believe him about the danger I was in, but I was fed up to the back teeth with demon-smelling men pushing me around.

I came back to myself on top of a struggling McKinley,

who was in an armlock facedown on the floor. The cuff rang with fluid green light, squeezing until I thought I heard bones grinding again. Strength poured hot up my arm from the blazing metal, the cuff that had locked itself around my wrist no longer cold. Would I have to cut my *hand* off to get rid of it?

Well, ain't that handy. Get it, Danny? Handy?

I leaned down, my hair brushing his cheek. "Don't fuck with me right now, sunshine. I'm a woman on the edge." I barely recognized my own voice. My sword lay on the carpet, but I had the gun pressed to his temple. He surged, struggling, I pushed every erg of demon strength I possessed *down*. The floor groaned under cheap harsh red carpet. "I *mean* it, you demonlicking sonofabitch. *Settle down!*"

Or I swear, by everything I hold holy, I will not be responsible for what happens.

He finally quit thrashing. I was sweating, prickles of moisture under my arms and at the small of my back. He was a handful, and if the wristcuff hadn't squeezed again I would have lost him. "Cam?"

"Here." She sounded grim but not panicked. *Thank the gods for small favors.*

"Is Mercy up?" My voice made the holovid's base chatter on the clunky half-dresser.

"I'm awake. What's going on?" The *sedayeen*, unfortunately, sounded a little less than calm. Her voice shook, and the fear mixing with the smell of violets taunted my fraying control. What was it with psions smelling of fear that pushed me over the edge so badly?

Anubis, help me. Stay my hand, keep me calm.

"Cam, get all the fiberoptic cord you can from the holovid. Slice down the goddamn curtain-strings too. Mercy, get my sword back into the sheath and come over here. I need you to pick his pocket."

This was apparently open for discussion even though she'd awakened to find me holding down a strange man in our hotel room. "You're robbing him? Who is he?"

I glanced up, my fingers digging into his flesh. "He's bad news, baby. Just trust me and do what I fucking *tell* you."

Every item of furniture in the room that wasn't bolted down rattled. *Gods help me, I sound like Japhrimel.* I took a deep breath. *Trust me, do as I say, I know best.*

Except that I *did*. These two had no idea what was going on, and the fact that I hardly knew more didn't erase the primary fact that I was in charge, goddammit. I was their best bet of getting out of this mess alive, and in order to get them out I needed them to do what I told them.

Looks different from this side of the fence, doesn't it, Danny?

I told that voice to shut up and go away again.

"You're not listening." McKinley's voice was muffled, because I had his face smashed into the carpet. "If they catch you, Japhrimel will have to do anything they demand. He can't risk any harm to you. He *won't* risk any harm to you, he—"

I felt as if a great weight had fallen away from my shoulders. Life was about to get very fucking simple. "You tell Japhrimel this. I'm through being jerked around. This little holovid script won't work. I have had enough of manipulation, enough of games, and enough of demons. Consider this a datflash breakup."

He spluttered, but Cam knelt down cautiously and gagged him with a pillowcase, tying it behind his head. His eyes rolled up and he struggled, but between my strength and the Shaman's nimble fingers we soon had him trussed nice and tight.

Poor guy, he keeps getting tied up. I didn't really feel any sympathy at all, but the merry voice of unreason just kept going inside my head.

The healer handed me my sword. "You're really going to rob him?" She sounded faintly disapproving. I guess when you didn't hunt down bounties and have demons messing with your life you could be awful moral.

What are you doing, Danny?

It was a stupid question. I knew what I was doing—the only thing I *could* do, now. I was taking off my protective gear and slicboarding through Suicide Alley.

In other words, I had officially just gone over the edge.

"I can't access any funds without getting a whole lot of heat on my tail," I said shortly. *Since I don't think any bounty hunter after me will be stupid enough not to put a tag on my datband accessing any credits.* I scooped the sapphire from McKinley's rigid fingers, found a thick roll of cash in his back pocket. Stuffed both in my bag. "And I don't have time to plan how to get in and out of a bank without being caught. We can't hide or hunt for long without money, and I've got both of you to shelter too. Come on, that's not going to hold him for more than a few minutes." *If that. It's a pity, if I could trust him not to drag me off on a hover I could definitely use him as backup. I can't wait to hook back up with Lucas.*

His eyes rolled back in his head, showing the whites, and a low steamy hissing slid out from behind the gag. I felt a trickle of cold Power along my skin, like an ice-cube trailed in a lover's hand against fevered flesh. My rings roiled and spat in the charged air. "Time to go."

Mercifully, they didn't argue after that. I had the Shaman bring up the rear, and led them out of the room. Rage boiled just under my ribs. Japhrimel hadn't wanted the necklace in the first place, he'd given it to McKinley, of all people.

Of all the things that hurt, that was the one that seemed the sharpest pain. Maybe it was only because I was numb, confused, hungry, and hurt all at once.

How many demons were looking for me? What would they do if they found me? It sounded like I wasn't just leverage to be used against Japhrimel, there was something going on with this treasure and the Key. . . .

Don't think about that. Focus on what you've got in front of you, Danny. Where can you hide these guys?

21

Jado lived on a quiet tree-lined street in the University District, in an ancient house with an equally ancient ret-rofitted hot tub on the newly renovated deck. His garden was still immaculate, but the sand-raking around the rough black rocks in his meditation garden was newly redone. It was early in the day, and he had a class in session. I could tell by the *thwock* of stave against stave and his voice, cutting through the sharp noise with a general's battlefield authority.

"No think!" I heard him yell. "No think! *Move!* One, two, *kia!*"

A ragged chorus of *kia* filled the air. *Beginners,* I thought, working my boots off. The *sedayeen* leaned against the Shaman, obviously drained and exhausted, her cheeks reactive-pale and her eyes glittering.

The sharp bite of hunger under my ribs reminded me I had to get some rest and food soon myself. "This is a safe place. You should be okay here for a couple days. By then, this will probably be over one way or another. Wait here for a couple minutes." A pause, and I heard another solid barrage of wood meeting wood. It reminded me of a Nuevo

Rio sparring-room, Eddie and Jace at staves while sunlight fell through windows onto *tatami* mats and Gabe stretched out, sweat gleaming on her pale skin.

Back when I'd been human. In my mind's eye I saw Japhrimel leaning against the wall, his hair ink-black, his coat swallowing the light.

And his eyes glowing green under straight eyebrows.

So he'd been trapped, and even McKinley admitted they couldn't hold him for very long. Talking about trapping Japhrimel was like talking about beating Vinnie Evarion at cards on the old *Vinnie, Video Sharp* holovid. It just didn't happen. He was just too old and smart. So he'd decided to go off on a solo expedition and leave me sleeping with McKinley, obviously expecting to be back before I woke up. And then what?

When we have finished with your Necromance friend, I will tell you everything you are ready to hear.

Maybe about the treasure, or would he tell me how helpless a demon felt after he Fell? That would have been nice, a little admission of need from him. A little human emotion.

For crying out loud, Dante, keep your mind on business. Japh's not your problem right now. If you don't keep moving, you'll drown. Barefoot but still wearing my coat, rig, and bag, I padded into the main space. There was a narrow strip of wood flooring before the mats started, I carefully arranged myself at the edge between "space" and "sparring space." Bowed respectfully, my sheathed sword lifted in my left hand, my right hand a fist.

Silence fell. Fifteen wide-eyed students in white *gi* and one nut-brown, leathery old man in orange robes looked up. The *ikebana* at the far end of the room under the *kanji-*

painted scroll was a different red orchid. In any case, the rest of the room looked blissfully the same.

Helps to have a friend that doesn't age, doesn't it, Danny? This time it was Lucas Villalobos's whisper, painful in my ear. I was talking to myself in some awful strange voices lately. Occupational hazard of being a psion—sometimes the voices in your head are the people who matter most to you.

Or who scare you most.

Jado barked a command and his students went back to whacking at each other with more enthusiasm than skill. All normals, all probably rich kids. The fees their parents paid made it possible for Jado to combat-train psions with potential to become canny, deadly fighters almost for free. The last time I'd been here, there had been four empty spaces in the sword-racked room above, four of Jado's true students out in the world. There might have been more, he trained a lot of psions. But the four missing swords always made me feel good in a niggling sort of way.

Four swords gone. Five, now. But still four students. I wondered who the others were. Jado had refused payment after the first few classes; the normals he taught had subsidized me. For him, that was the equivalent of adopting me. He had some funny ideas about the student-teacher relationship.

So did I, as a matter of fact. If my social worker Lewis was the father of my childhood, Jado was the father of my adulthood, the only male I always felt like trusting. I could never have said that to him, of course . . . but it was still there, unspoken between us. He was my last resort—but also my best resort.

"Danyo-chan." He stood at the edge of the *tatami*. "It must be serious, *neh?*"

I didn't have time for politeness. All the same, I bowed correctly. "You're looking well, Jado-*sensei*."

"How can you tell?" But the corners of his eyes crinkled. His ears came up to sharp points above the dome of his skull. He smelled of a dry, deep, crumbling, scaled hole; a hot exhalation of cinders and meat charred so thoroughly it smelled like woodsmoke. It was, thankfully, not a *human* smell. "Is good to see you, my student."

"And you, *sensei*." I didn't have words to express how good it felt to see him. Jado didn't play games, he simply *taught,* directly and with the smack of a fist or the deadly whistle of a swordblade. Of all the men I knew, human or not, only Jado might have truly understood me. "I have two little things I need kept safe for me. And I want to ask you something."

His nostrils flared as he sniffed. "A healer and a *kami*-talker." His tone was reflective, easy. Behind him, staves whirled; students darted curious glances at me. "There have been inquiries made of you."

"I'm sorry." I didn't want to bring trouble to his door— but my list of living friends was getting really short. I needed his help.

He waved that away, tucked his hands in his robe. "Take them into kitchen and serve them tea, student. I will make certain you are undisturbed. My house is yours." A slight bow, only the briefest suggestion of a bending in his torso.

I echoed it, my left shoulder throbbing as I moved. I realized the right leg of my jeans was still crusted and flopping from my encounter with the hellhound. I was hardly inconspicuous. "Jado-*sensei?*" There would never be a better time to ask.

"*Hai?*" He still looked amused, his dark eyes lingering on my face. His bare feet were horny and callused, and barely seemed to move when he walked.

I lifted the sword a little, watched his eyes come to rest on it. He looked pleased, and my heart swelled with probably-inappropriate pride. It *mattered,* that Jado was pleased with me. "Did you give me a blade that can kill the Devil?"

"The sword kills nothing, Danyo-chan. It is *will,* kills your enemy." He made a small clucking sound, shaking his gleaming brown head. "Young, too young. Older, you would not ask silly question." He bowed again, waited for my answering bow, then whirled and bellowed at his class. "*No!* Thousand curses on your eyes, *no!* Fight! No curiosity, fight!"

I took two careful steps back, bowed to the sparring space, and exited into the hall. The Shaman and the healer looked at me strangely, and I found I was grinning like a holovid comic.

All things considered it was the best I could do. It was already afternoon, and I had a date with Lucas at dusk. I left Cam and Mercy with Jado, and had the relieved sensation that I could just forget about them for a while. If they weren't safe there, nowhere in Saint City would shelter them. And now that the Chill cure was circulating among the West Coast clinics, the Mob interest in killing a simple Shaman and *sedayeen* would hopefully lose some plascharge.

But not the business between me and the Tanner Family. That was just starting.

I plunged back into the dense urban wilderness of the city, just one face among many. It says something for city life nowadays that even a part-demon Necromance with a holovid face can pass unremarked on the streets.

I bought two six-packs of synthprotein shakes meant to keep heavily augmented bouncers up to weight and drank them all while I sat on a park bench in the lower city. The park had a nice view of the bay, a hard glitter under the afternoon sun breaking through gray clouds. Each empty can I chucked into a nearby botbin, hearing the whoosh of the crumpler as it swallowed.

When I was finished, I shook myself, got to my feet, and headed for the streets again.

Saint City pulsed under my feet, ringing with every step. I had about four hours to twilight, so I moved a little faster than a human would, slipping between normals. I passed a Shaman at the corner of Marx and Ninth, a thin blonde woman with sodaflo can-tabs tied to her staff. They tinkled and chittered as I passed, but she merely set her back against a wall and regarded the street, wide-eyed, her feet in a stance I recognized. Another combat-trained Shaman with no sword. Who knew there were so many of them around? Her eyes, dark as her hair was golden, narrowed as she watched me go by. Maybe she would recognize me from the hunt for Lourdes, when my face had been plastered all over the holovids.

Maybe not. That had been a long time ago, and my hair was down, tangling over my eyes.

That made me think of Cam, who was a puzzle. I was almost sure I'd caught her reaching for a hilt. But why would she leave any weapon at home while she was squiring a *sedayeen* around?

I made it to the Saint City South precinct house in half
an hour. There I had my first stroke of luck in a long time.
The man I wanted stood in the usual smoking-alcove near
a botbin, curls of synth-hash smoke rising thinly around his
gleaming bald head. He hunched his turtle shoulders and
shook his head, his hands shaking a little. I judged it about
half-past a desperately needed drink. His knee-length tan
synthwool coat flapped desultorily in the faint breeze; the
clouds scudded in earnest over the sun.

Thank you, Anubis, I prayed silently. *Thank you. I'm
about due for something good.*

Detective Lew Horman worked Vice. He and I went way
back. I'd done Necromance work off and on for the Saint
City police, he'd been my liaison to the normal cops more
than once. I'd also dropped several useful pieces of information about Chill dealers to him in the past. Whenever
I'd come across any distributors in my journeys through
the shadow world of the quasi-legal, I'd turned them over
to Horman. Sometimes he couldn't do a damn thing, being
hamstrung by procedure, but more often than not he acted
on my tips. We'd had a grudging almost-partnership for a
long time, despite his disdain for psions and his general
slobbishness.

He was also one of the few cops Gabe had ever paid the
high compliment of calling "incorruptible."

I started casting around for an inconspicuous way to approach him—hugging the shadows on the opposite side of
the street and crossing in a blind spot, scanning the roofs
and alleys. No nosy little eyes that I could see. Nothing out
of the ordinary. The hair rose on the back of my neck.

*You're getting paranoid, Danny. You need a safe place
to rest for a few hours. Even if your body's demonic, your*

mind is still human and you're blurring with fatigue. This one thing, then hole up and rest so you're fresh for tonight. You've got a couple visits to make, and a few hours of rest will help you go over the file again. You can also take a look at the book Selene gave you.

I melted around the corner and found myself face-to-face with my last best chance.

"Hullo, Horman," I said pleasantly. My emerald sparked, sizzling to match my rings. "I need to talk to you."

22

"*What* the *hell?*" My voice hit a pitch just under *squeak*.

Horman flinched. He pushed me back into the alcove, stood with his three-quarters profile presented to me, watching the empty street. He smelled of synth-hash, half-metabolized Chivas Red, and the decaying of human cells. Mixed with the chemical wash of Saint City hover traffic and biolab exhalation, it was a heady brew. My own smell rose like a shield, I didn't allow my nose to wrinkle. The heaviness of incipient rain blurred on the freshening wind. I smelled electricity, suspected a storm. "But I *just* got into town!"

His hands shook, a smudge of ash drifting down from his cigarette. "You the suspect now. Half the cops in Saint City are looking to bring you in full of projectile lead as a cop-killer, deadhead. The other half won't interfere 'cause they know they'll get their own asses singed with hoverwash."

Suspecting me of killing Gabe. Why? Trying to hang it on me instead of Massadie? "Where does that leave you, Horman?"

Sweat gleamed on his bald pate. "Gabe came to me few days ago. Said she had a line on somethin' big. I told her not to get involved, told her she was retired and should stay that way. She told me you'd show up if anything happened to her. I been spending hours out here waitin' for you." Horman shivered, popping up the collar of his coat with his free hand. He flicked ash out onto the pavement.

Oh, Gabe. Looking out for me again. I swallowed, heard the dry click of my throat. "Listen, what do you know about a guy named Gilbert Pontside?"

"Homicide, Old Division. Hates psis." Horman shrugged. He was swallowing rapidly, sweating Chivas. He knew how dangerous it was to be out on the street, but nobody thought I'd be stupid or suicidal enough to try the cops. That was valuable information right there.

You hate psions too, Horman. "So why is he responsible for investigating Eddie Thornton's murder?" I dug in my bag, but he shook his head.

"If you got the original file, don't let me see it. Lots of people been looking for that, it ain't worth my career to have a peek." He hunched his shoulders even further. "I figgered Gabe lifted the original, tricky bitch." He paused. "Pontside. Investigating a dirtwitch murder? A dirtwitch married to a Spook Squadder? I din't hear that, they got a lid clapped tight on this one."

"Suspicious, isn't it?" I took a deep breath. It was time for me to go on faith. "Eddie was killed because he came up with this." I held up the vial, rescued from the depths of my bag. "It's a cure for Chill. I don't know who killed him yet, but it's beginning to look like the biotech company he was working for and the Tanner Family have something to do with this pile of crap. I'm told a bounty is out on me. Is it official?"

"'Course it ain't. Official means visible, and someone

wants this kept quiet." His eyebrows drew together. "There *ain't* no cure for Chill," Horman mumbled. He shot me a quick dark glance, his forehead wrinkling even further. But there was a ratty little gleam in his eyes I'd seen before. Horman had just made a connection.

A good connection, please. Please, Anubis. "I've got a Shaman and a *sedayeen* who worked over on Fortieth who say different; their clinic was bombed and a bunch of goons tried to off them this morning. Plus, why would a Spook Squadder and a Skinlin be killed like they were, and have it kept this quiet, unless they had something huge, huge as a fucking Chill cure?" I took a deep breath, dangerously close to pleading. "You *know* me, Lew. I'm a psion and a bounty hunter. I paid my mortgage with a little bit of illegal action like everyone else. But I don't go around killing my friends. I never went in for assassination. *Ever.*"

Gabe was about the only friend I had left. Why would I kill her? The thought that I could even be *accused* of killing her made me sick to my stomach.

And feeling just a little explosive.

He shivered. "What you want me to do, deadhead? Gabe trusted you, they say you killed her."

Score one for me. If he believed I killed Gabe, he wouldn't be out here waiting for me. He especially wouldn't ask me what I wanted him to do. *Looks like my luck's beginning to change a bit. About damn time too.*

My fingers were deft and quick. I shoved the vial of Chill cure in his coat pocket, tugging sharply on the material so he could tell what I was doing. "Figure out what this is, see if I'm telling you the truth. Visit a couple of your Vice stooges and put the word out that I'm going to erase who-ever killed Gabe. Also check the West Coast Chill clinic datanet. They should have the formula for the cure flashed worldwide by now."

"A cure's gonna put me out of a job." He didn't sound upset at this eventuality. As much as I'd lost to the ravening monster that was Chill, he'd lost more. I'd attended the funeral of his teenage son years ago, the kid had gotten hooked on Chill and died on a bad batch of contaminated drugs. He hadn't been the only casualty—the distributor cutting Clormen-13 with bad thyoline had soaked most of the city with it—but it had been the one thing that solidified Horman's innate cynicism.

And his hatred of Chill.

I made a short snorting sound. "You're a Hegemony officer, you'll get a pension. Besides, you can always chase unregistered hookers. That's a lot more fun. Or XTSee brokers, vox sniffers, bitfoxes, permaspray junkies. . . . Or corporate harassment cases." I didn't have to work to sound amused, the maniacal urge to giggle was rising again. My left shoulder throbbed with pain.

"You bitch." Horman's aura flushed brittle red with fear. His cigarette had burned down to the filter, he pitched it into the botbin with a convulsive jerk. Didn't look at me. "What you doing this to me for, Valentine? I never did nothing to you."

"And you were out here waiting. Call it a favor to Gabe. Consider me just the hand of Vengeance coming home to roost." I slid past him, out of the alcove, as light rain spattered on the sidewalk. Glanced up to check hovertraffic, the streams of cigar-shaped personal hovers and the larger whaleshapes of transports moving in their aerial ballai. "If you can, let some cops know I *didn't* kill Gabe. Let them know Pontside is the officer on record in the original file investigating Eddie's murder. But for Sekhmet's sake don't get yourself in trouble." I paused, my tone turning soft and reflective. "I'd hate to have to avenge your death too."

"Goddammit—" Horman began, but I was already gone. I knew what I needed to know.

Half the cops on the Saint City force might well think I'd killed Gabe. But the other half didn't think so, and Horman had been allowed to stand quietly out in his smoking alcove, taking nips off the bottle of Chivas brought to him by his partner. Someone else knew that a normal was the officer on record for a psion's murder, maybe someone had even figured out from the scene of Gabe's homicide that everything wasn't quite kosher. Despite Horman's shambling exterior, he was well-respected among Saint City cops—one of the good old boys. If he dropped a quiet word, it would get around.

I had just bought myself some breathing room. Or more precisely, Gabe had bought it for me, by telling a fat foulmouth cop who reeked of soy whiskey in no uncertain terms that I was to be trusted no matter what the brass said.

Still looking out for me, Gabriele. Mighty nice of you. Even my mental voice caught on a choking sob.

My chest hurt. My eyes were full of unshed tears, the pavement blurring in front of me.

I needed a place to go to ground. I didn't have one. My shoulder twinged sharply, the pain slicing through my misery. *Pay attention, Dante. Wake up. Just a little longer, then you can rest.*

Four blocks away from the precinct house, instinct poked me hard between the ribs. I stepped aside into an alley. Managed to get all the way to the dead end, brick walls rising up in three directions. I turned around, lean-

ing my back against the blind corner; even if anyone
started shooting from the roof I was sure I could make
it up the handy fire-escape and away. I braced my legs
as the freezing rain started in earnest, tapping the roofs,
mouthing the pavement. The peculiar whine of streetside
hover traffic during rainfall bounced through the alley and
rattled my teeth.

I squeezed the scabbard in my left hand, checked the
cuff. No green light, it was back to dead-cold and dull
against my golden skin. There was no way to get it off, I
couldn't even get a fingernail under its curve. It had welded
itself to my skin.

Lovely.

I slid my right hand under my shirt, touched the knobs
of the *baculum;* slid my fingertips up my collarbone. Took
a deep, slamming breath. The decision was instant, I'd just
reached the end of my tether.

*I don't care what else is going on, Japhrimel. I need you.
You lying bastard of a demon, I need to see where you are
and if you can help me.*

I touched the ropes of scarring, my fingertips delicate as
if I caressed his naked shoulder. Or his cheek. Heat jolted
up my arm, smashed through my shoulder.

I saw—

*—darkness. The single point of light was a candle, its
blood-red flame in a curious stasis. Arms stretched overhead, head hanging, hair curtaining face. The chalked
lines of the diagram writhed, fluid with demon Power, Magi
script altered subtly to make it more effective. Urgency
growing in the bones, spreading outward. The bracelet of
cold metal around his wrists softened under the lash of his
attention.*

Circle holding square holding pentacle, the diagram spun lazily against a smooth glassine floor. A hellhound paced at its periphery, red eyes glowing and massive shoulders writhing under its obsidian pelt. A laugh sharp as a razor cut the air, shivered as the candleflame bent in a nonphysical direction and returned to its stasis, standing straight up. The candle itself was a thick parchment-colored pillar set in a barbarously clawed iron stand.

Head, lifting. Eyes beginning to burn as they wrenched away from the flame.

"I will give you one chance," he said, in a chill hurtful voice.

"At last. She's calling," another replied, high and awful as tinkling bells made of frozen blood. "And he's compelled to answer."

"It was only a matter of time. I wonder who caught her, perhaps Arkhamiel?" Wait. Was this voice like the first? Identical. But the shading was a touch deeper, a slightly more masculine tone. "'Twas a fool's move to let us take you, Elder Brother. We will soon have the lai'arak *and your compliance anyway."*

"I have warned you," he said quietly. The chill had not left the words, a sharp jagged blade drawn over numb flesh. "Your time is almost done."

I tore my fingers away. Bent over, shook my head, hair swinging as I tried to clear away the sudden disorientation of seeing through his eyes as if through a sheet of wavering glass, each object freighted with different light and perspective. I choked, my stomach revolving. Black demon blood dripped from my nose and mouth, I'd driven my teeth almost clean through my lower lip.

I slid down to my knees. It was not the best place to have

a nervous breakdown, in an alley less than four blocks from the South precinct house, exposed to the stinging pellets of frozen rain and drifted with garbage. I hunched over, hugging myself, my weapons digging into various places, and started to shake.

Someone had Japhrimel in a demon-inscribed circle, with a hellhound pacing its borders. The other voices were demons—nothing human could sound that tinkling and cold. Two voices, sounding almost identical. The Twins. Eve's allies.

That answered two questions. Eve's allies had Japhrimel, and some other faction not loyal to Lucifer was in town too. That meant two groups of demons that had a vested interest in either keeping me alive or simply catching me to make Japh behave. Add that to whoever else Lucifer had sent to catch Eve if she came out of hiding, and there were at least three groups of demons double-dealing and jostling each other in Saint City. And here I was, caught in the middle. It would be a miracle if I could solve the mystery of Gabe's death without getting interrupted by whatever trouble was boiling out of Hell *now*.

I wiped tears away with the blade-edge of one hand, but more came, welling out my burning eyes and slicking my cheeks. *Japhrimel.*

Why did he have to go and get himself in trouble just as I had a Mob Family to take down? It was bad fucking timing in the worst way.

What would they do to him? If he could be caught, even if he would eventually escape—which everyone seemed to take for granted—they might be able to hurt him before he did. I didn't think Eve would hurt him willingly, but he might leave her with no choice if he tried to break free and drag her back to Hell. After all, there was Velokel, her lover, who had hunted Fallen and *hedaira* before. Even if Japh had a demon's Power he was still . . . vulnerable.

That thought sent wriggling cold panic all the way through me.

Goddammit, Danny! The voice was familiar, raising the hairs on the back of my neck. *You're goin' into shock. Get your ass movin'. Find somewhere to sit down and breathe. And for God's sake stop cryin'.*

It was Eddie's *sotto voce* growl, the one he used for sarcasm. Why was I hearing dead men? Didn't I have enough trouble? Maybe it was my subconscious interfering, dangerous for a Magi-trained psion. My control of Power depended on my having a clean psychic house, so to speak; you can't corral and contain magickal force with a scattered mind. Broken concentration sucks away the sorcerous Will.

I scrubbed at the mark on my shoulder through my shirt. *Stop it. Stop right this second. No crying, no weakness allowed!*

Bit by bit, the unsteady trembling feeling went away. I sniffed and smelled rain, garbage, and demon musk. I'd flooded the alley with my scent, glands working overtime. Had to rein it in. Would another demon be able to track me? My rings swirled with uneasy light, my shields trembling on the edge of crystallizing.

Japhrimel was taken, I was on my own. Things did not look good.

That was how they found me, crouched in the alley and sobbing. But my hand was still closed around the hilt of my sword, and I felt them coming bare seconds before they arrived—enough time for me to make it halfway up the fire escape. Plasbolts raked past me, splashing against standard-magshielded walls, plasglass shattered.

Even the toughest bounty hunter around will run when faced with four police cruisers and a cadre of what appears to be augmented Mob shocktroops. And all for one tired almost-demon.

23

I finally lost the last of the police cruisers by plunging into the old Bowery section of the Tank District. It's possible to find almost anything in the Tank, though not as much as you can find in the Great Souk or the Freetowns. The Tank population doesn't take kindly to police. It's a good place to hide, as both Abracadabra and Anwen Carlyle knew.

The Bowery is the very worst part, the cancerous heart of Chill-fed urban blight, and when I was human I hadn't braved it very often. The Tank, yes. The Bowery, no. Not unless I was desperate.

Two of the cruisers had tangled together as they pursued me through the labyrinth of what used to be the National District. I had another piece of good luck when the third misjudged a lane of slicboard traffic and a slic courier shot in front of the bristling cruiser. The cruiser's AI yanked it into a barrel roll to avoid the collision—Hegemony cop cars are all fitted with that sort of control to make high-speed chases less dangerous for civvies. The courier would get dinged with a ticket, but she was still on her board instead of spread over the pavement. And I was long gone.

The last cruiser lost me in the Hole.

Back when I'd been human, I'd had my board tuned by Konnie Bazileus at the Heaven's Arms. Occasionally I'd gone into the Hole, honing my skill on a board against the sk8s, couriers, skaheads, and flicsurfers. Jace and I had even done naked-blade slicboard duels, back in the first violent flush of our affair.

Even Hegemony federal marshals don't go into the Hole often. It isn't worth it.

The Hole itself is underground; it used to be a transport well until the last really huge earthquake. The quake ripped apart the central well and opened up a sinkhole underneath, so the walls were a collage of relays, eighty-five-year-old fiberoptic spikes and reactive strips, debris from the buildings overhead crumbling into the sinkhole. The slictribe had moved in and made it even more challenging, building ramps and jumpoffs, spikes protruding from the walls, deadzones and hoverpatches that made the air move in unsteady swirls just aching to rip a sk8 off a board.

The tangled alleys leading up to the Hole are narrow and sloping, most of them covered by cobbled-together roofs of flimsy plaswood, plasticine, and other scavenged materials. Every once in a while a few teams of Hegemony federal marshals will sweep through the Hole to pick up "criminals," but they never net much. Around the slictribes, if you don't adhere to strict codes you're out. It's all too easy to flip someone off a board and let them fall into the dark well of the Hole. The worst that comes out of here is gang warfare and XTSee for vance parties, and the authorities are more than willing to let that pass as long as the slictribes only kill each other.

I passed like a ghost through the old way into the Hole, my shoulder burning as the last bullet hole closed. The last clutch of Mob troops had actually forced me to stand and fight, peppered with projectile fire. If I'd still been human, I might be dead.

I still wasn't sure I was alive. My clothes were torn and wet with blood, my stomach burned with fierce hunger, and I still felt the last man's neck crack in my hands like pla-silica sticks. Only human.

They hadn't sent any psions after me. Only normals. Fragile, vulnerable humans, no matter if they were legally augmented with neurospeeders and muscle spanners.

Dusk was falling. I was going to miss my date with Lucas. Then again, all he would have to do is follow the sirens and listen to whatever lie the holovids were telling, and he'd know I'd had some trouble.

By the time I reached the Hole itself, I had to stop and lean against a sagging plywood shelter that smelled like humans living with chemshowers instead of regular bath-rooms. A fair number of skas lived in shacks around the Hole itself, eking out a living on their parents' credit lines while dealing XTSee and bitfox on the side, tuning boards and generally living as they always have.

That was where I saw the first sign of life. A sk8 who couldn't have been more than ten coasted up on a hum-ming, nicely-tuned Chervoyg almost as long as he was. He brought the board to a stop and hopped onto solid ground, racking the board neatly with a kick as the powercell died down. His hair stood up in gelled acid-green spikes, and his face was streaked with blue camopaint. He glanced around, not seeing me, and pulled a pack of smokes out of his breast pocket. He wore a fluttering flannel shirt and a loose pair of black pleather shorts covered in rippling silver magtape.

This was evidently a little-used part of the Hole, because

he proceeded to sit down right at the edge and smoke, looking up as the cloak of night fell across the faraway roof and tiny hole that was the main entrance to the subterranean world. Little drops of light that were antigrav and powercells began to flock through, weaving in complicated patterns.

I made a low noise, scraping against the plaswood shelter. Then I coughed, letting him know I was there.

He made no move. I stepped out cautiously.

He took one incurious glance over his shoulder, his fingers caressing his board's powercell. I stopped, the sweet scent of synth-hash filling my nostrils. He was normal, wouldn't be able to see the disturbance I created in the landscape of Power. But I still probably looked like I'd been run through a few hoverwashes.

Gabe used to smoke. Panic rose under my breastbone. I swallowed, my sword shoved into the loop on my belt. My hands were loose and raised. "Hi. I'm Dante Valentine."

He let out a chuff of smoke and a choking sound. "Fuck. Wonton w'hini."

"I know how to ride a board." I kept a firm hold on my temper. "I just don't have one right now. You can help me with that."

He had wide blue eyes, clashing with his acid-green hair. "Landerfuck," he sniffed with magnificent disdain. "Niners outa clap w'hinioo."

"Innocent until proven otherwise." I gave him a lopsided smile. Some people try to mimic slictribe lingo, I don't. It's enough that I can guess at 80 percent of what they mean. Even Konnie had been hard to understand at times.

It was a long shot, but I decided to go for it. "Konnie Bazileus. Heaven's Arms. He still around?"

I thought his eyes couldn't get any rounder. "Bazzmouth on'yo tribe?"

"I'm not tribe," I said. "I'm lander, remember?"

He shrugged. "Bingya Bazzmouth."

"Thanks." I folded myself down onto the gritty filthy floor of the ledge jutting out into the side of the hole, blood crackling as it dried on my clothes. "Bum a smoke?"

After that it was nothing but waiting. Those of the slic-tribe don't function in the same timezone as the rest of us; the less charitable say it's because of all the hash and XTSee. He smoked his way through two more cigarettes, generously sharing with me, then stood slowly, brushed his pleather shorts off, and pressed the powercell. He tossed the board and flung himself after it, his new BooPhooze sneakers thudding on the deck's surface. It used to be Re-botniks or Aeroflot were the popular brand, but no longer.

I was getting old. I even *felt* old. Creaky, my bones dry. The synth-hash didn't soothe me as much as I wished it would. As soon as he was gone I stubbed the last one out in the filthy greasy crud masquerading as dirt down here.

I put my head down on my knees and tried to breathe. The blue glow of my god's attention was comforting, hovering at the edges of my mental awareness. I'd just outrun four cruisers and what looked like Mob troops. That wasn't a new trick, cops and Mob working together; sometimes the cops needed a little help from the extralegal side. Of course, the Mob troops had only been legally-augmented, but if they were working for the cops I didn't blame them. Still, it bothered me. I assumed they were Mob, because they hadn't *behaved* like cops, cops would have shouted at me to drop my weapons.

If they weren't from the Tanner Family's war with me,

maybe they were from Lucifer pulling strings behind the scenes again, using me to trap Eve. Hellesvront had all kinds of agents on earth, it stood to reason the cops might be part of that network.

What a joy. I've got so many enemies, even I can't decide between them.

The rattling whines of slicboards began to build as the Hole woke up. Sk8s and other slictribers, like psions, generally come out and play at night.

I tilted my head up, watching the aerial ballai. It's impossible to look totally graceful while riding a board—you're always on the edge of spilling—but confidence imparts its own kind of grace. I watched the little darts of antigrav light, spinning in the figure-eight pattern slic riders use for high-traffic zones, others dipping down and peeling away to take runs around the edges. Whoops and high joyous cries echoed through the cavern. The pounding of a vance party in another part of the Hole started to throb like a heartbeat, music meant to shake dancers into a trance and keep them there for hours.

I'd thought before of using the patterns of hover traffic for divination. Now I watched the spots of firefly light that were the slicboarders, and I felt premonition flutter under my skin. Deep, unsteady panic welled up from the pit of my belly.

"Gabe," I whispered, and watched the lights tremble as my eyes filled with tears. I blinked them away.

Konnie still rode a board. And he, of all people, reminded me of just how much we'd all aged while I was letting time pass me by in Toscano. His fingernails were still clipped brutally short and painted with black molecule-drip; he probably still played in a Neoneopunk band.

Kids like Konnie rarely ever grow up. He was still riding, still part of a tribe. That meant he was still fast and mean.

He was still lean, and rode with hipshot ease. Still wearing flat golden plasmetal rings on his right hand; still the same dead flat dark eyes. His hair was different now, dyed magenta and long-braided, studded with ivory beads. He wore—since he was no longer a young punk fashion plate but an aging one—a black V-neck linen shirt, skintight purple viscose-velvet breeches, and supple black fake-shark boots. Fans of wrinkles spread at the corners of his eyes, and his mouth was bracketed with two curving lines. He still rode a Valkyrie—slictribers are nothing if not loyal to their decks.

Konnie had known my old face. My human face. I'd been taking my slicboards to him for servicing since I'd left the Academy, and we'd evolved a useful acquaintanceship over the years—an acquaintanceship I was about to use for all it was worth.

I presented my left cheek subtly as he stood with his back to the ledge, studying me. With luck he'd recognize my tat. The kid with the green hair settled down cross-legged and lit another cigarette. The sweet smoky smell of synth-hash rose and twirled around the other odors of the Hole. I was glad I'd learned to tune down some of the demon acuity in my nose.

Konnie grinned, showing strong white teeth. It was a vidflash expression, there one moment, gone the next. "Deadhead. You get augments?"

"Kind of. Against my will." I lifted a shoulder, dropped

it. Blood crackled on my clothes, almost dry now and powerfully fragrant of spice and rotting fruit. Tucked under Konnie's arm was a long slim shape in a chamois sheath. "Nice to see you too, Konnie."

"Been a long wave." He studied me carefully, scrupulously speaking my language instead of slic lingo. "You bringin' trouble. Niners all *over* all the entrances. Been a few scuffs."

"I'm sorry." My eyes burned, and my lungs. The vast dim cavern beat with the pulse of slicboard travel and more vance parties starting, the walls really beginning to bounce. Stray tufts of breeze made the beads in his hair clack together, touched my cheek and ruffled my clothes. "I'm on the warpath, Konnie. I don't want to hurt any slictribers, but my temper's real short. I want a board, and I need to get out of here unseen and send a couple messages. I can pay."

He shrugged, his lip curling. "Pay."

Oh, Sekhmet sa'es. "New Credits, you ass. Not datband dangle. You think I was born yesterday?"

His eyes were troubled as he studied me. "You look awful young."

You have no fucking idea how old I feel. "Not my fault. I lost a game with the Devil, Konnie." *There is no lie like telling the truth, is there?*

Is there, Japhrimel?

Trust me, Japhrimel's ghost replied. *Say you will not doubt me.*

I wish he hadn't left me with McKinley, I wish I'd known not to get angry at him. Maybe I could have convinced him to help Eve, maybe not. I should have tried.

"Devil?" He blew out, a long low whistle between his

strong white teeth. Business at the Arms must be good. He wore a datband plugin that registered him as constantly monitored by a security company, which meant he probably had his fingers in a few extralegal pies.

"Don't ask. Look, Kon, are you gonna help or am I going to have to figure something else out? I'm kind of in a hurry." I risked a little rudeness.

He clicked his tongue against the roof of his mouth. "Holy shit." For a moment he sounded much younger, and his dead dark eyes flared to life. The Hole pounded, confused air swirling and buffeting, making the riding even more challenging. I heard a chorus of yells—a duel, maybe. "It *is* you. Valentine."

"Don't worry," I told him. "Nobody else would recognize me either."

"Shit they won't." He weighed the chamois-sheathed package in both hands, his rings winking in the uncertain light. My own rings swirled with Power, his were merely human.

Completely human.

"You still got that look," he said finally. "We all know it, that hungry Valentine look. Who you hunting this time, baby?"

"Whoever runs the Tanner Family and killed my best friend." *And anyone else who gets in my way.* "Name a price, Konnie. If I don't have it I'll get it in an hour."

He tossed me the package. I flashed to my feet and caught it, moving too quickly to be human. He didn't flinch, I have to give him credit. But he made that little clicking sound again, tongue popping. "You always paid before. Spect you earned a little cred." He jerked his head back. "C'mon, ride wit' me. Then we figure out how get you outa here."

I need more, Konnie. "And a couple slic couriers? There's no danger in it, not for them."

"Shit," Konnie said, "this ain't nothin'. You shoulda seen the fight we had last year between the Pacers and the TankLickers. Anything a Lander comes up with we can handle."

My heart squeezed down on itself. These were no more than children, even if they were sk8 and slic couriers. *I bloody well hope you're right, Konnie. I really do.*

24

The package in chamois was a Valkyrie, sleek and black and beautiful, freshly-tuned and magclean. Good old Konnie. I wondered how much of my reputation still survived down here in the Hole.

I sent four messages by slic courier, three on paper and one on air.

The air-message was for Abracadabra, telling her I was still alive and still going after Gabe's killers. She'd make sure the information got around and caused maximum confusion. It also had a chance of reaching Lucas, who would be able to pick up my trail in the Hole if he was lucky. I'd feel a lot better about this once he managed to catch up with me.

The first paper message was to Selene. *Tell Tiens Japh's been taken and needs help*. That would also let the Hellesvront agents know I believed them without committing me to letting them "protect" me. Maybe, just maybe, they would concentrate on getting Japh out of hock or sowing some confusion to keep my trail clear of demons. I didn't hope for much—after all, they were probably more interested in finding me and spiriting me away from Saint City before another group of demons got their hands on me. Still, I could hope.

Next message, to the Tanner Family's corporate front downtown. A courier with long orange dreadlocks and the androgynous holovid figure in style now knew where it was and took a short note for me.

Hand over Spocarelli and Thornton's killers or I'll send you to Hell. Nice, sharp, direct, though I intended to pay them a visit soon after they received it. I signed it with a flourish and a certain feeling of grim enjoyment. The orange-haired courier also knew where the Tanner Family mansion was, their nerve center. It was by far the most productive half-hour I'd spent in a while, talking to her.

The very last message was to Jado. To this courier, a short, stocky mean-looking kid with a fuzz of dead black hair and a pierced lip, I gave Eddie's mastersheets, sealed in a magpouch with the homicide file and a note asking him to hide it and apologizing for the inconvenience. This about wiped out my stolen bankroll, between pressing cash on Konnie and paying the couriers hazard fees. I was a hot commodity now; it would have been cheap not to pay them for potentially running across someone who would give them plasflak intended for me.

I finally stood at the edge of another ledge, down in the well of the Hole, far enough down that I felt the dread touch of claustrophobia. This would probably be a very good place to hide if I wasn't so damn nervous in close, dark spaces. The central cavern was huge, of course, but still it was underground, and it was dark, and I could feel the pressure of the dirt overhead and to the sides bearing down on me. Konnie stood next to me, humming an old RetroPhunk groove.

A shiver touched my back. I needed food, I needed rest.

Too bad, sunshine.

A clear piercing whistle floated through the pulsing. Konnie finally tapped at his board, leaning against his leg. "Tribe's movin' to clear out an exit. Think y'can keep up?"

I shrugged. I had demon reflexes and had put in a fair amount of time on slicboards, but he was tribe. He lived on his board when he wasn't running his shop. I knew better than to show any false bravado here, especially as he was doing me a favor. "Just go slow and try not to tip me."

He sniggered. Japhrimel would have caught the sarcasm in my tone, but Konnie didn't. He simply smacked the powercell, tossed the board, and performed the same trick as the other kids, leaping out into space and letting his feet thud on the deck's surface, the antigrav giving resiliently under him. The kick of the kinetic energy meeting frictionless antigrav made the deck bounce violently, but he controlled it and whooshed away as I pressed the powercell on my own board and dropped it on the ledge, jumping and landing hard, stamping my front foot down to propel the board out over the Hole.

Space slid away under me, the board bounced, and I caught my slic legs quickly and dove after Konnie, who circled in a lazy spiral and finally nipped neatly into an archway on the west side. I followed into the choking darkness, hoping he wouldn't lead me astray.

It was a shock to go aboveground. Especially on a slicboard, bulleting past neon and keeping to streetside because the hoverlanes would bring me to the attention of the cops sooner. I hoped nobody had figured out I'd been talking to Horman—and I hoped he hadn't alerted his superiors to my presence. I was depending on him to come through for me.

I went a short way into the Tank and found a nice dark Taliano restaurant that wouldn't cavil at my appearance, got a booth, and started eating. Garlic bread first, and a bottle of chianti; calamari and bruschetta, two orders of spaghetti, and the biggest steak they had. Then another bottle of chianti—the carbs in it would help keep me fueled—and another order of spaghetti, an order of fettuccini alfredo with chicken and broccoli. Finally, comfortably full, I ordered three beers and downed them all one after another. I don't like beer, but it's a cheap source of carbs.

If I hadn't been so hungry I would have read the book Selene gave me while I ate instead of stuffing everything down as fast as I could. Long ago I stopped feeling good about the sheer amount of food I needed. I felt like a glutton, especially when I'd expended a lot of physical power. If Japhrimel had been around it would have been better, I didn't need to eat quite so much when I hung around him.

There I went thinking about Japhrimel again.

I had to pay with my datband, but that didn't matter. I didn't intend to stay in the Tank for long, and by the time any bounty hunters or police reached the restaurant, I would be long gone.

Outside it was raining again, pellets of slushy ice. Wet neon slicked the streets, painted the hovers with splashes and traceries of light. The streets hummed uncomfortably, the well of Power pulsing a little differently. I noticed less psions than usual out in the rain-washed night.

I didn't blame them. Saint City felt carnivorous tonight.

So did I.

I zipped through the streets with wet wind mouthing my hair, splashes and kisses of cold against my skin. My clothes were definitely the worse for wear, full of dried blood and artistically torn, unmarked golden skin showing through the rips and bullet holes. I had a full load of ammunition, thanks to Konnie, plus my plasguns and my sword as well as my knives.

It wasn't enough for a full-scale assault on a Mob Family.

The Tanner Family nerve center was in a rich part of town, an arc of prime bayfront property housing blueblood mansions. This wasn't the corporate front, the legal face of the Mob business. This was their home, where they would entertain and hold their most important meetings. A lone psion would be recklessly stupid to attack a nerve center.

I might be stupid, but I'm fast, I'm mean, I have a sword that can cut the Devil and the will to use it. Whoever's there will just have to die, that's all. After they answer my questions.

All my questions.

I had to approach from uphill, swinging out in a wide arc and staying below the hoverlanes likely to hold police traffic. Slicboards can't go over water, and if I'd had a hover . . . well, a hover wouldn't have changed anything. Across the water, the lights of downtown glittered like a necklace, the orange glow of antigrav and streetlights staining the rainy sky. My city throbbed and pulsed like a heart, its chambers thudding with Power—a pulse echoed by the Gauntlet, clasped to my left wrist.

There are demons in the city tonight. Something's

happened. Has Japh broken free? I don't think so, I'd probably feel it through the mark. But something's shifted.

Let's hope that's good for Eve.

The mansion was low and beautiful, a song of blue Graeco-Revival architecture, with outbuildings just as graceful and flawless. The Family had done well for itself. Good shielding wedded to the walls and property line, the kind of shielding laid for corporate clients. There would be regular security too, magscan and deepscan shields, a whole battery of defenses as well as guards roaming the grounds.

In other words, a great opportunity for me to let loose a little aggression.

I hid the slicboard under a juniper hedge, laying a small keepcharm over it. Then, my jeans and shirt flapping and crusted from my healed wounds, I walked up the broad, well-maintained sidewalk as if I belonged in the neighborhood.

The front gates were iron, stylized teeth writhing decoratively along the top curve. They reminded me of another set of gates on the East Side, gates with a gothic *R H* worked into their metal, standing slightly ajar and beckoning like every trap.

I set my shoulders, gritted my teeth.

The defenses started to quiver as soon as I got within half a block. I tasted the pulsing of the energies used to build them, could *See* the layers of Power thickening, hardening at my approach. By the time I stood in front of the gates the defenses trembled on the edge of locking down.

My sword was in my left hand, sheathed and ready. I would need it soon.

In the old days, I would have found a way to subvert

the defenses, broken in quietly and pursued what I wanted. Now I had a share of a demon's Power and no need or desire to act like this was corporate espionage. Besides, I wasn't here to steal. I was here for something else entirely.

The house at the end of its black-paved drive was lit up like a Putchkin Yuletree. I looked at it shimmering on its gentle hill and the rage rose up inside me. Whoever was in that house knew something about Gabe's murder, if they hadn't committed it. Either way, they were going to tell me what they knew. All of it. Quickly.

This time I didn't push the red, screaming fury down. I took a deep breath and jabbed my right hand forward, pushing through the layers of defenses on the property line. They went crystal, locking down—but I was already in, the stiletto of my Will driven like a physical knife between ribs.

My right-hand rings, amber and obsidian, sparked as I pumped Power into them, the mark on my shoulder blazing with soft spurred heat. I *drew* on it, drew on the brand that was Japhrimel's name, past caring that it was a demon's name I was relying on. If he had broken free and showed up here it was all to the good; if other demons came along . . . well, that was a risk I was going to have to take.

I found myself not minding as much as I should have.

The wristcuff tightened, grinding the bones underneath again too, and sent another ice-burn of welcome strength jolting through my shoulder, into my chest.

I set my feet and *pushed,* a low sound of effort jetting between my teeth. Felt a yielding like fat-rich flesh under a sharp thin blade.

I struck. A short, sharp *kia,* my eyes suddenly hot and blazing as if lasers were popping out of them. Deadly force coiling, smashing loose, I wrenched the tough fabric of the defenses apart as casually as Japhrimel might tear apart an origami animal—a crane, perhaps—in his golden fingers.

Dead silence except for my own harsh breathing. Where were the alarms, the guards? Or was this the wrong house? The orange-haired courier had said this was the place, described it to me, and a few moments at a public infoshell had confirmed that the property was legally owned by one Asa Tanner, head of the corporate identity comprising the legal front of the Tanner Family.

I stepped through the rent in the shielding, now bleeding Power into the rainy air, and pushed the gates. Metal squealed as they swung wide on well-oiled hinges. My boots crunched on the raked immaculate gravel. I drew my sword, shoving the scabbard back in its loop on my belt and taking out a plasgun.

"Hi honey," I called, my voice flashing through the rain, breaking the drops into smaller steaming tracers of mist, spraying out in concentric rings. "I'm *hooo-ome!*"

Gravel crunched like small bones underfoot. I couldn't *feel* them, the guards, hanging back out of sight. But I could imagine them just fine. *Trap.* It was a trap.

So what? Close the trap, and see what happens when Danny Valentine gets really pissed.

I walked through the rain, hair plastered against skull and nape, dripping onto ruined clothes. Steam curled up from my skin, ice melting before it could hit me. The sword sang in my hand, white flame twisting in its heart, blue runes spilling through the edges of the metal. My shields flared into the visible range, traceries of glittering light shimmering in a perfect globe around me, and Japhrimel's aura of black diamond flames had closed over mine again. As if he was behind me, walking with his soundless step, his hands clasped behind his back and his eyes burning no less than mine.

I felt other minds here, and tasted the acrid tang of fear. There was too much magshielding for it to be a plain civilian's house. I was in the right place, I *knew* I was.

So why weren't they attacking?

I got maybe halfway to the house before thunder rumbled low and ominous in the sky and the hair stood up on the back of my neck.

I swung around, sword lifting, the cuff suddenly flaming the green of Japhrimel's eyes. *"Sekhmet sa'es—"* I hissed, ready to face the trap—but what I saw froze the curse on my lips and made my heart pound thinly in my temples, throat, and wrists.

A low sinuous shadow stalked through the rip I'd made in the defenses. A flash of crimson eyes, a glossy obsidian pelt, an ungainly graceful shamble of a walk.

I dropped the plasgun and closed both hands instinctively around my katana's hilt, screaming my defiance as the hellhound—was it the same one?—finished shouldering through the rent in the Tanner house's shields and bulleted toward me.

I had time to admire each finicky-precise footfall, its head bobbing back and forth; paradoxically, I had no time at all. Gathered myself, compressing demon muscle and bone, then *threw* my body to the side, both hands on the hilt and blade blurring down as a white-fire scythe, the *kia* sharp and deadly. More steam drifted up from the hellhound's body. It turned on itself as I landed, too quick it was too quick it was *too quick,* my feet barely touched down and I flung myself in the opposite direction, gravel sprayed as it skidded and roar-hissed its frustration. Gravel also smashed up, exploding away from the sound, my cry taking on physical weight.

Black blood whipped from my blade as I shuffled back, bringing the shining length up between us. Took the high-guard, right hand over left holding the hilt almost at my right shoulder, instinct screaming under my skin.

The hellhound shook itself, snarling. I snarled back, lips skinned away from my teeth and fury scorching the inside of my throat. Then I did another thing I shouldn't have—I leapt for it, on the attack, driven past rage to fey courage. My shoulder smashed and rang, torn apart with pain as my right side tore too, the cuff singing a thin high smoking tone of cold Power. Blood burst and sprayed as thunder toppled the sky overhead and I fell, seeking vainly to get up *get up,* gravel crunching into my hair and mouth and eyes as I rammed against the hilt of my blade, driving it through smoking demon flesh.

We fell together, the hellhound and I, the bright length of my sword buried in its chest, its claws flexing and tangling with my ribs. I heard faint and faraway yells as the rain spattered on both me and the hellhound and the sky lit up with white-hot whips of lightning.

25

I sank on my back into a carpet of grass, blinking up at the endless blue depths of the sky. Sunlight touched my bare wrist with warm gold, I pushed myself up on my elbows, blinking. Each blade of grass was detailed, glowing juicy green. The field rolled, bounded only by a broken stone wall, with the purple shadows of mountains in the distance. An oak tree lifted proudly in full summer leaf. At any moment I expected to see a troop of old Christer Amish in their wide-brimmed hats on their way to one of their meetings. Or a coven of witches, carrying their baskets of food for the feast after the magick was done . . . or a group of Evangelicals of Gilead, the women veiled and the men in suits and bowties, hair parted in the center and held down with pomade under small circular embroidered skullcaps.

I like this better, he said beside me, braced on his elbows and so close I could smell him again, spiced Shaman, pepper and honey. And the clean healthy smell of male, a smell with no taint or tang of demon.

Jace lounged next to me in jeans and a white cotton button-down shirt. The sun made his hair a furnace of gold, lit his eyes with incandescence. Same expensive haircut, same Bolgari glittering on his wrist. Grass pricked at my hands as I sat up and looked down at myself—black T-shirt, jeans. Bare feet, my toes human-pale and painted wicked crimson with molecule-drip polish.

You again. *My lips shaped the dim whisper.* Jason.

One elegant golden eyebrow arched. He had a long blade of grass in his mouth, lazy, like a cigarette. I could see the smattering of freckles across his nose, ones that never showed unless he was in full sun. Even the golden tint to his shaved cheeks was there.

And oh, my heart hurt to see him in such detail.

Muscle moved under his shirt as he sat up straight, crossing his legs tailor-fashion. His knee bumped me. The strand of grass dropped from his lip, vanished into the thick mat of greenery. Absolutely, baby. Miss me?

What are you doing here? *I could do no more than whisper, the breath stolen from me by sunlight, the brush of breeze against my skin, the prickle of sweat under my arms and at the small of my back. I smelled grass, and the richness of air with no hoverwash or biolab exhalation, no sour fullness of human decay. I even smelled the faint woodsy odor of the oak tree and the rich loam of drifted leaves scattered around it.*

He shrugged. Other people get *loa.* You get me.

But you're dead! *My eyes prickled with tears. Was I having my deathdream at last? Where was the blue light and my god? Where was the hall of eternity and the well of souls?* Am I dead? *I tried not to sound pathetically hopeful, failed miserably.*

Jace's face fell slightly, turned solemn. I heard a hawk

*cry far away, saw the thin white traceries of cirrus clouds
and the haze of distance over the faraway mountains.*

Love's eternal, Danny. You mean you been dealing with
Death all this time and you don't know that? *His mouth
curled up in a half-smile, a tender expression. A butterfly
meandered past, its wings a blue reflecting the sky's wheel-
ing vault.* You always were stubborn.

*He leaned over, reaching out and bridging the gap be-
tween us. He stroked my cheek, his callused fingertips gentle. Neither of us carried a weapon here, but his hands were
still rough with practice. Then he pushed a strand of my
hair back, delicately, and I found myself leaning forward.*

*Our mouths met. Kissing him had always been like a
battle before, greedy and deliciously heated, a combus-
tion. But here it was gentle, his mouth on mine like velvet,
his hands cupping my face delicately. His thumb feathered
over my cheekbone and he made the low humming sound
he always used to after sex. My heart sped up, thundering
in my ears.*

*He kissed the corner of my mouth, kissed my temple,
closed me in his arms.* You're hurt, *he said into my hair.*
But you'll be all right.

*I buried my face in the juncture between his neck and
shoulder, smelled the human cleanness of him.* Gabe, *I
said.* Eddie.

*He stroked my back, kissed my hair. It felt so real. So
real.* Eternal, Danny. Remember? That means forever. *His
arms tightened.* You have to go back now. It's time.

I don't want to. Please. I don't want to. Let me die, let
me stay here.

I felt him shake his head, as the sunlight beat down on

us in waves. The hot simmering of a summer day, a caul-
dron of a field under the bright vault of heaven, all of it—I
wanted to stay. I didn't care where this was.

That's not the way it works, baby. Go on now. Be good.
I'm watching out for you.

A shadow drifted over the sun, and just like that I—

—snapped into full wakefulness, my hand blurring out
and sinking into vulnerable human flesh. I choked out an
obscenity I'd learned hunting down a bounty in Putchkin
territory, it died halfway and I made my fingers unloose.
Leander stumbled back, his dark eyes wide, the emerald
in his cheek flashing. My left cheek burned, I felt my tat
shifting as his did, inked lines running under the skin. My
emerald spat a single, glowing-green spark.

Now I knew who he reminded me of. The knowledge hit
me so hard I lost my breath, gasping and scrambling back,
casting around for my swordhilt.

He held his hands up. He had a fading bruise on his
cheekbone, and moved a little stiffly. "Calm down. Calm
down, Danny, goddammit!"

I gulped down air. Looked at the room. No window, one
door, a bed with a purple cotton comforter and rumpled
pale-pink sheets; a stripped-pine nightstand with a pitcher
of water. Leander was unarmed—but he held my sword.
Gingerly, as if he was afraid it might bite him. He offered it
to me as I crouched on the bed, my ribs flaring with every
heaving breath.

"What the hell are you doing here?" I rasped.

He shrugged, offered me my sword. "You're safe. I
hooked back up with Lucas. There's some news you should
hear."

"Where am I?" My throat was on fire, sore and scraped raw. The full-spectrum lights beat down, showed me my own hands reaching for my sword, slim and golden and beautifully graceful.

"In a safe place. Listen, Danny, I want your word. All right? I want you to listen to what we have to say. On your honor." His wide dark eyes met mine, I caught a faint green spark far back in his pupils. It vanished. Had I really seen it?

Honor? Do I have any honor left? "The hellhound," I croaked. "Did it—"

"You killed it. I repaired the shielding. Thought we were going to lose you, but you pulled through." He was chalky-pale under his dark hair, and his hands trembled just a little. He was afraid of me. That managed to smash the last vestiges of resemblance—Jace had never been afraid of me. Enraged at my stubbornness, driven to frustrated fury by my constant poking and prodding, gentle during my moments of weakness, and coldly lethal when we were under fire; but Jace had *never* been afraid of me.

I remembered Rio, when he had crawled into the shattered bathroom where I'd taken refuge, lit a cigarette, and simply talked to me after Japhrimel's change had worked its way through my body. It had never mattered to Jace what body I wore; he loved *me,* but by then it had been too late.

I belonged to Japhrimel. No amount of trying to regain my lost humanity would overcome that one simple fact. No matter how angry or hurt he made me, Japh was the only person who truly knew me—even if he didn't know very much about handling me. Even fighting him, being angry at him, struggling against him was better than relaxing with someone else. After all, who else did I reach for when I finally felt out of my depth, even though he'd held me up against a subway wall and bruised my arm, my heart? I hadn't thought of calling anyone else.

The demon and the fleshwife are literally one being. Whenever they're written about, it's in the singular, as if each pair is one person.

A scream rose up in me, died at the back of my throat, cascaded back down into an endless black hole of bitterness that beat like my pulse inside my chest. My left shoulder felt heavy and full, the wristcuff was dry and powdery-pale as it rested against my arm, its cold numbness temporarily gone. I still wore the blood-drenched rags of my clothes; they crackled as I moved on the bed. The spacefoam mattress whooshed a little as I eased myself down from crouching on the bed and stood, swaying and finally making my knees lock. I snatched my sword from Leander and looked him in the eye.

Nothing. Nothing but a great yawning distance between me and this human Necromance I liked. Whose company had made me feel a little better. But that was all.

"I killed it." I should have felt happy. I'd killed something even Japhrimel and McKinley had treated cautiously. My ribs ached on the right, twinging as I moved, the flesh tender as it had been after Lucifer's parting kick.

I felt like shit.

I clicked the blade free of the scabbard, examined it. Blue runes ran wetly in the steel, blazing out as soon as it left the darkness of confinement.

Still blessed. Still mine.

The sword kills nothing, Danyo-chan. It is will, *kills your enemy.*

I'd killed a fucking hellhound. Gods above and below,

I had *killed a hellhound.* "All right." I must have sounded a little more together, because Leander's shoulders eased and his hands dropped back to his sides. What sort of courage did it cost him to stand there unarmed and look at me while I had a weapon in my hands? "What is it you have to tell me?"

"Come with me," he answered. "I'll take you to Lucas."

Down a short hall with a framed Berscardi print on one side and a priceless fluid lasecarved-marble statue tucked in a niche, Leander stepped into a circular room holding two leather couches and a fireplace roaring with a real fire, the tang of woodsmoke and a low thunderous reek filling the air. My nostrils widened as soon as we reached the hall, smelling a stasis cabinet and dried blood. When we reached the room Lucas was there, dropped down on one of the couches with his arm flung over his eyes. For once he didn't look the worse for wear—I probably looked bad enough for both of us.

Standing at the only other entrance to the room was a slim tall man with a thatch of chestnut hair and bright blue eyes, his feral cleanshaven face set in an ironclad smile. He wore a shirt that looked like fur until I looked closer and realized it was *pelt;* he wore only a pair of jeans tucked into very good boots, Taliano and handmade by the look of them. The glossy, hairy shirt was flagrant advertising of his status as a werecain. And a dominant one too, he had less of the unprotected shiver around his mental walls than a more submissive 'cain's.

My right hand closed around my swordhilt. I'd already almost been trapped once by a werecain. Had Lucas and Leander betrayed me?

"Put that goddamn thing down," Lucas said, his arm unreeling away from his eyes. He glared at me, haggard and bloodshot. He looked wearier than Death after the Seventy Days War. The flat yellow color of his eyes was accentuated by red·rims. He calculated everything about me in one piercing look, and the river of scarring down the left side of his face twitched.

I dropped my right hand to my side. Tilted my head slightly, acutely aware of Leander behind me. Human, werecain, and whatever Lucas was. Add to that the decaying-fruit and spice smell of demon blood drenching my clothes and my own fragrance over the layer of woodsmoke, and it was a heady brew. "What the *mother*fucking *god*damn *shit*sucking *hell* is going *on?*" My voice stroked the bare painted walls, and the werecain made a short sharp movement. A muscle twitched in my right forearm.

"You been played like a fuckin' holoboard." Lucas didn't sugarcoat the pill. "What would you say if'n I told you we had Massadie in the next room?"

I swallowed. My voice was as raspy as his now—I was sounding less and less human all the time, even to myself. "I'd say I'd love to talk to him. Who the hell's the furboy? I haven't had a good time with 'cain lately."

"You've been hanging out with the wrong type," the 'cain said pleasantly, with only the tinge of a growl beneath his words. His fur shirt rippled, and the classic lines of his face changed, becoming more austere. His chin jutted a little further now too, and his teeth shone white and sharp. "You're Danny Valentine. I'm Asa Tanner, Head of the Tanner Family. Nice to meet you."

My sword leapt partially free of the sheath. Lucas was suddenly next to me, grabbing my hand, his breath hot and sour on my cheek. "Fuckdammittall, *listen!*" he snarled in my ear.

"I'm listening," I said calmly enough, ignoring the way my knuckles stood out white against the hilt and my entire body tensed against Lucas's hold. He was *strong*, in a wiry way, I didn't precisely strain against him but both of us were breathing hard by the time he felt safe enough to relax a little. This was the closest I'd ever been to him, his hip pressed against mine and his foot between mine, his hand locking my sword arm down and away.

I was surprised by a flare of relief. It was *Lucas*, dammit, and I was scared of him—wasn't I?

He used to scare me more than anything. Now, the strength in his skinny hands and his body pressed against mine was pleasant. Here was someone I wouldn't have to hold back with, wouldn't have to be so goddamn *careful* not to hurt.

It's Lucas, goddammit! Stop it! He scares you! You're human!

But I wasn't, was I. Not completely.

Not anymore.

Asa Tanner made a low coughing sound. It was suspiciously close to amusement. "I didn't kill Thornton or Spocarelli."

"*Liar.*" I strained forward, Lucas pressed against me as if we were lovers, twisting my right wrist until it felt almost bruised. I finally subsided, pushing away the flush rising to my cheeks. Hedaira *don't blush*, I thought. Then, *It's Lucas, Anubis et'her ka, it's* Lucas, *I don't have to hold back.*

But I did. It cost me, but I *did*.

Asa Tanner shrugged, a marvel of coordinated fluidity.

Forget my sudden acceptance of Lucas, I had a better question.

What is a werecain doing as head of a Mob Family? "What's a 'cain doing as head of a Family?"

"You think humans are the only ones who should make a little profit?" His laugh resembled a pained bark. His eyes glowed, not like a Nichtvren's but with an animal heat, like old-fashioned gas flame. "Just like a skin. You're all the same."

"You didn't show up," Lucas hissed in my ear, his dry stasis-cabinet breath brushing my cheek and sending a shiver down my spine. "Sloppy, Valentine."

"I was chased by four fucking police cruisers and . . ." I trailed off, staring at Tanner. *Hold on. Hold everything.* "So what percentage of your Family is human, furboy?"

His upper lip lifted in a snarl. "Only about thirty. Those that can keep up. We're a mongrel bunch."

But they were all human. The shock troops I'd thought were Mob were *all* human, every stinking one, and carrying very expensive gear as well as being legally augmented. I'd assumed the Tanner Family, as the dominant cartel around here, could afford that type of gear; but it hadn't made sense for them to be only *legally* augmented, especially when they were chasing a half-demon. They should have been spliced and loaded to within an inch of their mother-fucking lives.

It also made no sense for a Mob Family with a 'cain at its head to be cooperating with the police for *anything*. As dim a view as most psions take of the cops, a werecain's view is even dimmer. Back before the Parapsychic Act, some police forces had special, secret cadres to hunt 'cain. That's why werecain only work as freelancers when it comes to paranormal-species bounties; they don't cooperate with Hegemony police like kobolding or dracolt do.

It's whispered that some police stations still have hunting cadres, secret fraternities fighting a war against the furred and fanged of the Hegemony citizenry. Not to mention the feathered, winged, and clawed. I didn't know if it was true . . . but the rumor was enough.

So the shock troops weren't Tanner Family goons. But they hadn't been police troops either, had they? No badges, no insignia.

And there had been no psions among them, if they'd been Saint City PD or Hegemony marshals they'd have had psionic support teams.

Gods above, Danny, you nearly killed the wrong people. I shoved that thought down. I would examine it properly later. Later, later, later. There was a lot I was going to figure out later. If I made it to a later.

But for right now . . . maybe, just maybe, the Tanner Family wasn't the enemy.

"Fuck me." I was too tired, too hungry, and too goddamn confused. My left arm hurt, from the mark on my shoulder all the way down to the fingertips. "Okay. Let go of me, Lucas." I shook him off. "I'm halfway convinced." To prove it, I sheathed my sword.

Silence rattled through the room. The fire popped.

"You run Chill," I said finally, staring at Asa Tanner. My tone wasn't conciliatory at all, but at least I didn't want to kill him.

Yet.

Another elegant shrug, his furry shirt rippling. He could shift in less than a second and launch himself at me. I was faintly surprised I wasn't more frightened.

Danny, you're not thinking straight. You've got to get some rest, you're going to have a psych meltdown soon if you don't give yourself some slack.

But Asa Tanner was speaking. "It's going to soak the streets anyway. I make sure the distributors don't cut it with anything." He said it like it mattered if the poison was uncut when it hit the streets.

"How very *generous* of you." Contempt edged my tone.

His chin lifted half a millimeter, defiant. He was tense, his weight balanced between both feet; if he came for me I wondered if I could take him.

A shudder worked its way through me. I'd faced down a hellhound.

Again.

And lived, again.

I almost killed the wrong people. "There was a werecain. Said he was working for the Mob. . . ." I wet my lips nervously. His eyes settled on my mouth, and his smile broadened. It was a show of dominance, I realized, exposing his teeth. He was one angry werecain. The reek of 'cain vanished as my nasal receptors shut down—a stunning relief.

"I wouldn't have sent a single 'cain to eye you, Valentine. I'd've sent a full pack with a Moontalker to bring you in." He folded his arms across his broad, hair-covered chest. "Not every fucking 'cain in the city answers to me. Though they should."

Oh, I'll bet you've tried. "Okay." I tore my eyes away from him, looked at Lucas. A fine thin sheen of sweat made his pale forehead glisten, strands of his lank hair sticking to pasty skin. "What the *fuck* is going on?"

"Question Massadie," Lucas answered grimly. He

looked relieved, and for a moment I wondered about that. Lucas Villalobos wasn't scared of *me*, was he? "Then you can tell me what *you* think."

Jovan Tadeo Massadie sat in the room's single chair, staring out the window at the ripples of water on the bay. Rain lashed against the wall and the bulletproof plasglass. He was pale, and genespliced to within an inch of his life. No normal human could look that exquisitely buffed, every surface almost poreless, his face remodeled not along the lines of holovid beauty but with a strong-jawed aquiline perfection seen only in classical marbles. He wore a rumpled gray linen suit, and his pale hair was sleek and shining, a little long for a corporate clone. Almond-shaped hazel eyes completed the picture, cat's eyes in a statue's face. The eyes were an artist's choice, maybe.

He didn't glance at the door as I stepped into the room. Instead, he sat, for all the world as if he was meditating. Faroff thunder muttered over the city.

Silence crackled. This room was painted white too. I got the feeling this mansion was more of a stage set than a Family nerve center. Asa Tanner looked like he'd be more at home in a Tank bordello; I wondered where he *really* slept. Probably in a heap of other furry dozing beasts, 'cain are pack animals.

I wondered what it was like to have a pack, to be sure of absolute loyalty from those who shared your blood and fur. Every single person whose loyalty I never doubted was dead: Lewis, Doreen, Gabe, Eddie. Jace I'd mistrusted, but he'd proved to be just as loyal as Gabe in his own way.

Japhrimel? Loyal to me in his own way, too. And not dead yet. But still.

I folded my arms, my clothing shifting and rustling. I was just glad it covered the decency bits—if this kept up I would soon be dressed in nothing but bloody rags like a zombi in the old *Father Egyptos* holovid.

Massadie still said nothing. He probably wanted me to sweat a little—pure corpclone strategy.

He was practicing hard-line corp psych crap on the wrong person.

My thumb caressed the katana's guard. I'd let out a little of the fury boiling under my breastbone, but there was plenty more. I could easily—oh, so easily—slip the blade free of the sheath. Press it against his throat, watch a bright line of blood well against pale human skin, hear a corporate monster begging for his life.

It would feel good to kill him. It would be wonderful to smell his fear, even if he's only human.

I realized I was smiling. The smile cracked on my face, made a thin rill of fiery Power scream through the air, touching each wall and tearing along every surface. My thumb pressed against the guard.

Such a small movement would click it free.

Massadie bolted to his feet, his almond-shaped eyes wide as he scrambled, overturning the chair. He stared at me, blinking furiously, and I now saw he had been crying. Tear-tracks glittered on his planed cheeks, his mouth trembled but firmed as he faced me, drawing up his shoulders as if preparing for a fight.

The fury leaked away. Mostly. It settled back into a granite egg of coldness in my chest. I shoved my sword into the loop on my belt, shook my hands out, and looked at him.

"You're *her*." His voice was a pleasant baritone, now a little squeaky with fear. "Valentine."

I nodded. Found I was capable of speaking. "That's what they call me." It was a flip answer, but better than what I *wanted* to say. "You have—" I checked my datband, a little bit of theater to drive the point home. "Exactly two standard minutes to convince me not to kill you. Start talking."

"Eddie's dead. I suspect his wife's dead too, or you wouldn't be here." His throat worked as he swallowed dryly. "I know who killed him, and I can guess who killed her."

I folded my arms, sank my fingernails with their chipped black polish into my arms. Japhrimel's mark was warm, pulsing Power down my skin. What if he'd escaped, if he was tracking me? What if he came into the room and found me facing down this human? What would he do?

What would *I* do? "I'm waiting," I reminded him, my voice full of sharp edges. I saw him wince and took another look at him.

Anubis et'her ka. He's a psion.

Not enough for schooling or accreditation, but he had a little shine to his aura, and the clear edges of his personal Power field told me he meditated regularly. Whatever small psionic potential he had, he took good care of it. "That's why Eddie would work with you," I realized out loud. "You're a psion."

"A little bit. Four point three on the Revised Matheson, not even worth teaching."

I nodded. He'd just missed being taken into the Hegemony schools for training; a five on the scale gets you into the program. It wasn't quite legal to think maybe he'd been lucky. "Must be a real asset when dealing with us freakheads." My tone was still sharp and cool. I didn't sound human at all.

His cheeks flushed, a faint blush high on the arc of the bones just like a girl. "Not really."

I guess not. Normals might not trust you if they knew, and we don't trust you either since you're not trained. You're not in either world, are you?

The chilling thought that I wasn't in either world too—not a demon, not truly human, in-between, stuck—made the last few flickering vestiges of killing rage die back. They went hard, tearing at my throat and eyes, but finally left only a black aching hole in my chest. I leaned against the door and met his eyes, the tattoo on my cheek burning.

"Dante Valentine." He lingered over my last name. "Named for a saint whose day became a celebration of fertility and romantic love. Born in a Hegemony hospital, father unknown, mother's name erased under the Falrile Privacy Act. Rated thirty-eight on the Revised Matheson scale, attended primary schooling at Rigger Hall. Attended the Amadeus Academy, graduated with honors and went straight into apparitions. Made your reputation while still in school by raising Saint Crowley the Magi from dust. Also made another type of reputation when you entered the mercenary field under the direction of a Mob Shaman turned freelancer—"

"Stop it." If he said Jace's name I was going to draw my sword. Not because I was angry, but because I didn't think I could stand to hear this polished little god of a man use his mouth on Jason Monroe's name. *"Stop."*

He stared at me. We were even, I suppose. Maybe he wanted to kill me too, his almond-shaped eyes narrowing and burning with something too complex to be hatred and too frightened to be loathing.

"I've done my research," he said. "Eddie mentioned your

name when things started to get too deep. Then I found myself with a mystery in front of me, a dead fucking Skinlin,
and my name on a hit list."

I folded my arms again, dug my fingernails in. "Eddie
found a cure for Chill. And the shock troops chasing me
with the cops were corporate crack-squadders." I drew in a
slow, soft breath, my hands squeezing. Warm blood trickled down my arms, dropped off my elbows, and plinked on
the floor. "Pico-Phize troops."

"No." He shook his head. His eyes locked with mine,
maybe pleading with me to believe him. "Probably Herborne Corp. They work with alkaloids, they're one of our
biggest competitors in the painblocker field. We were infiltrated. I believe it was routine corporate espionage, but one
of the agents happened to . . . find out. But there's something else. The Pico lab security was taken out by a focused
EMP pulse—"

"So was Gabe," I said, but he overrode me, shouting
because my voice had risen too. The room groaned under
the rough lash of Power in my tone, but his next words cut
through mine.

"It was *Saint City Police Department tech!*" he yelled,
and I slumped back against the door. I don't think I've
ever been reduced to speechlessness from rage so quickly
before.

Say what? I replayed mental footage, decided that he
had said what I thought I'd heard. *Saint City Police Department tech. What the fucking hell?*

Massadie knew he had my attention now. "There is a
fuck of a lot of Chill money that goes to the cops, Miss
Valentine." His tone was soft, reasonable, and utterly
truthful. "Not just from routine payoffs but in other ways.

Herborne found out what we had and leveraged every contact it had inside the police force, I'd guess. They're scrambling to keep this quiet. You're creating a lot of trouble for them, and they need to shut you *up* just like they needed to shut Eddie's wife up. She made it god-damn hard for them, yapping at the heels of the IA division about where the Skinlin was getting all the trouble from. It wasn't the first time they tried to kill him."

Not the first time? Oh, Gabe. Eddie. Gods forgive me.
"How many?" I whispered. "How many times?"

"Six or seven." He shrugged. "He said it was no big deal. Then I came home to find my house tossed—"

"All fun and games until you get your own fucking hands dirty, right?" The contempt in my tone could have drawn blood. The picture-window shivered, and thunder tore the clouds overhead like wet paper. *Six or seven times and Gabe didn't call me?* The knowledge hit home. She hadn't thought I would show up. She'd known Japhrimel was alive, had she thought I wasn't interested in my *human* friends anymore?

What had I done? I would have dropped everything and come running for her marriage, for the birth of their daughter, for the first attempt on Eddie's life. Hadn't she *known* that?

Had she? Or had she not been sure I would show up, even when she sent me the datpilot message? Had she held off contacting me because she wasn't sure? How could she have *doubted* me? Was I her last hope, because she wasn't sure I'd respond?

How could she have doubted even for a *moment?*

I lied to her about Japhrimel. She probably felt betrayed. Guilt crawled into my stomach. I tasted bile.

"That same night, Eddie's wife was attacked. She had the kid with her. It was them getting attacked that did it, Valentine. Eddie told me they were safe, but . . ."

"Did Eddie tell you where?" Tension spilled down my back, brought me back to myself. "Where he'd put the kid?"

"He said you'd know. She's safe." He blinked at me. "You mean you—"

You mean you didn't know? If there was one phrase I was beginning to hate, that was it. This time, however, I just wanted to be sure this greasy genespliced son of a bitch didn't know where Gabe's daughter was. "Who?" I interrupted. "Who is it?"

Who betrayed them?

He folded his arms in a copy of my pose. He was sweating, his crumpled suit beginning to wilt. "Are you going to kill me, Valentine? Where's the cure?"

"In a safe place." *Three vials held by a demon in hock and the recipe and the murder file with Jado.* A very nasty thought hit me after I finished the sentence—I'd given one vial to Horman.

I'd been so sure he could be trusted. But right after that four police cruisers had descended on me. And one vial was gone—maybe stolen by whoever Gabe had trusted, whoever had gone in her house and searched it as she lay bleeding and dying in her own backyard, stunned with a focused EMP pulse maybe triggered by a member of her own police force.

Sekhmet sa'es, I'm even suspecting Horman. He wouldn't be mixed up in this; he doesn't play like that. But the suspicion had taken root, and bloomed in my chest with a feeling uncomfortably close to panic.

I was well on my way to being paranoid. Rain slapped the window with rattling spatters of ice. Blood dripped off my elbows, I felt the blades of my claws slide out of my flesh. My eyes dropped to Massadie's chest. "Who?" My voice had dropped a whole octave, it worked its way free of my throat and I tasted the copper fruit-spice of demon blood. *I am not in the mood to fuck around. Don't push me. For the love of every god there ever was, don't push me, you fucking little pile of corporate shit.*

He gasped in a short choppy breath. I twitched, and he yelled the name as he went backward, his shoulders pressed against bare white-painted wall as I found myself halfway across the room, my boots suddenly skidding on the plush blue carpet and my right hand raised, claws springing free. My hand no longer resembled anything human, graceful and golden-skinned, the black-tipped claws glassy and glinting dully as they extended. Black-tipped because I painted the ends just like they were fingernails—or I had, before. The molecule-drip polish was chipped and cracked now.

I stopped. We stared at each other. I blinked. "But . . . ." I trailed off.

"It's true," he squealed, his face no longer the polished perfection of a statue but distorted into a tragedy-mask of fear. "I swear it, I *swear on my mother's grave it's true!*"

I believed him. As fantastic as it was, I *believed* him. It made sense now. Everything about the puzzle clicked into place—everything except who in the Saint City PD had murdered Gabe.

I'd find that out soon enough, though. I was sure of that.

My hair fell in my eyes, but if I moved to swipe it back

I wasn't sure I could stop myself from drawing my sword. I swallowed, heard the click in my dry throat. The pattern completed itself, everything in its proper place. "You're a loose end too. So you came running to find me."

"I knew Asa. His . . . he . . . Pico, we sell Chill through him." Massadie shook like a junkie in withdrawal. The rich gassy scent of his fear filled the room, went to my head like wine. In that single moment I understood far more about demons than I ever wanted to. It would be so fucking *easy* to kill him, and nobody would blame me. The fear was good. It was *power*, it was warm and heady and I could have gorged myself on it.

The cuff chilled against my wrist. Numbness spread up my left arm, but the heat pulsing from Japhrimel's mark drove it back.

You and your damn sense of honor, Gabe's voice echoed. Had she been surprised that I still kept some shards and slices of that honor? Would she be proud of how I was refraining from killing this polished genespliced leech?

Of course the pharm companies sold Chill. It was highprofit, easy for a fully equipped lab to make, and they could test other acid-based addictives and narcotics with it. So the pharm companies were in bed with the Mob, and the cops were in bed with the pharm companies, everyone got along well and made a tidy bundle. Until, of course, a Skinlin doing routine research came up with a cure and everyone started scrambling to own it and shut him up, not necessarily in that order.

"*Sekhmet sa'es.*" Japhrimel's mark grew steadily warmer, a lasecutter-spot of heat against my skin. I caught a glimmer of green, the cuff reacting. Why? I didn't care just at the moment; I *needed* whatever this corpclone could tell me. "Who's her contact on the police force, Massadie? You give me that and you can walk away, I won't kill you."

"M-my career's r-r-ruined anyway," he stammered, sweat rolling off his perfect skin. How much genesplicing had Pico paid for, to make sure it had a beautiful face to present to the world? A pretty face on top and a mountain of bodies of dead Chill junkies on the bottom—and all the other victims too. Like Lewis, the closest thing to a father I'd had, choking on his own blood because a junkie needed a fix.

"Isn't that a fucking shame." I was having trouble caring. "Who?"

His voice broke. "Some fucker named Pontside. Her stepbrother."

I nodded. Everything came together in a tidy little package. *Her.* The traitor.

I turned on my heel and stalked for the door. The aroma of fear and shed demon blood turned the air velvet-soft, a red-painted scent like the inside of a sexwitch House.

The thought hit me with almost physical force, I almost staggered with a sudden panicked burst of fear. But nobody knew where Gabe's daughter was, nobody but me and maybe the Prime's Consort.

If anything happens to that kid not even a Nichtvren will be able to stop me from killing everyone who might have had a hand in this. Not even Japhrimel.

And that was why, even though I loved him, I could not let him hurt Eve. The fierce feeling under my breastbone was instinctive. Even though I'd never even contemplated having children I still would not let either Doreen's daughter or Gabe's be harmed if I could stop it.

Mine. Both of them are mine now.

I halted near the door, my hand on the knob. "If I see you again, I'll kill you." I didn't bother looking back. *He should be glad he's still alive,* I thought coldly. If he'd been less frightened of being found out as a psion, maybe Eddie would still be alive. Or if he'd just been a little more decent as a human being, he might have warned Eddie they'd been infiltrated instead of just trying to save his own miserable skin.

Why hadn't Gabe called me when the trouble started? I twisted the knob and stepped out into the hall.

I knew why. She probably felt guilty, since she'd asked me to take the Lourdes case and I'd ended up mind-raped and unable to think about the Hall without shuddering like a Chill junkie. Jace had died; how my own grief must have tortured her. She'd probably felt accountable since she'd called me in. When I disappeared without saying anything about Japhrimel she probably thought I couldn't stand to see her again; all the things we couldn't say to each other on the phone convincing her that somehow she was culpable. That she was to be blamed, or that I blamed her in some way for the whole rotten, ugly fiasco. As honorable as I tried to be, Gabe was intrinsically. How it must have hurt her to think she'd been responsible for my pain.

Oh, Gabe. Gabriele. I should have told you. I should have known.

I'd have taken the Lourdes case anyway. Some circles had to be closed; some debts had to be paid, willing or not. I had been chosen to close the murderous circle of Rigger Hall, whether by the gods or the ghosts of murdered and mind-battered children or by Fate itself. It had been my duty.

More than that, though, I would have done it because

she'd needed me; she was my friend. My family. My *kin,* though we shared no blood. It had never occurred to me before that she could blame herself. That there was *anything* to blame her for.

Oh, Gabriele. I'm so sorry.

I paced down the hall and stopped, my nostrils flaring. Spice and heat filled my nose. The cuff squeezed, running with cold green light. I felt the bones in my wrist grind together.

Not another hellhound, please. Please, Anubis, not another hellhound.

Something didn't smell right. There was no sound other than the soft slap of rain and the rolling iron balls of thunder. I took the last step, around the bend in the hallway, and saw the room was empty. No Lucas, no Leander, and no Asa Tanner. The drapes moved near the window, wet wind pouring in through the broken window. I hadn't heard the glass shattering. My nostrils flared. The reek of demon was thick and overwhelming.

I heard faint sounds, as if there was a fight outside. Clashing steel, and the roar of a werecain in a rage, and Lucas rasping a crescendo of obscenities.

What the hell—My hand closed around the swordhilt, too late.

The skinny, red-skinned demon slapped my blade aside and backhanded me, the force of the blow like worlds colliding. His eyes glowed yellow, cat-slit, and he exhaled foulness in my face as darker lines of red like tribal tattoos writhed over his skin. The thin, high, chilling giggle raised the hairs on my nape. It was oddly familiar, had I heard that voice before?

Then he was on me, knee in my back, and something

that *burned* clapped around my wrists. A noxious cloth pressed against my face, a whispered word in my ear, and darkness took me struggling down into a whirlpool. The last thing I saw was the edge of the drapes, slapping wetly at the wall below the window, and the green glow painting the walls as the wristcuff flared with icy vicious light before guttering out.

26

I remember only flashes. A face over mine, a face I'd seen in DMZ Sarajevo while a nightclub full of Nichtvren and other paranormals danced to the throbbing beat below and a hellhound dozed at his side. Round and heavy, square teeth that still looked sharp, cat-slit glowing eyes. The face wasn't human, for all that a human Magi's hand had once drawn it in a charcoal sketch. The eyes were too big, the teeth too square, and the expression was . . . inhuman.

Velokel? The Hunter. Allied to Eve. Anubis, help me.

"She was *not* to be harmed." A harsh unlovely voice, but with its own compelling undertone. A voice that demanded obedience, burrowed along the nerve endings and *hurt* as it yanked at my bones, ran hot lead into my marrow. I moaned softly, half-swallowed the sound. I could barely even *think,* the disorientation was so intense.

"She'll live." Someone else, clear and chill as a bell. I recognized it, didn't I? I'd heard it taunting Japhrimel, when my fingers were glued to the ropy scar of his name against my shoulder.

"Here is your payment." Clink of something light and

metallic, a short chuffing inhale of breath. "Consider our alliance renewed."

Darkness took me again as I strained to open my eyes, to see, to *fight*.

The next flash—a candleflame. Red flame, crimson as blood. Standing up straight, then wavering in a nonphysical direction, not guttering but seeming to shudder anyway. I struck out with fists and feet, dimly aware I was in danger. I heard shouts, and someone caught my wrist, a touch that sent fire through me and made my left shoulder crunch with vivid pain.

"Be still," he said, the voice that demanded I *obey*. I struggled against it, against him, felt the python squeeze of another mind close around mine, Power crushing down until my strangled scream choked the air. He *squeezed,* almost as I would with a werecain, but harder, determined— this was no warning, this was a prelude to brutal mental rape.

No. The core of stubbornness in me rose, something hard and ugly as biting on magtape. It was the strengthless endurance that had kept me alive and conscious during some of the worst parts of my life.

What you cannot escape you must fight. What you cannot fight, you must endure.

Scars in the fabric of my mind tore open, bled afresh. Tearing, ripping, my defenses resisted, denying him entrance to my mind, to the innermost core of me. For a dizzying eternity I was back in the shattered cafeteria in Rigger Hall, choking on ectoplasm as a Feeder ripped and stabbed through my psyche—

—shoving against the back of my throat, against my nose and eyes and ears, fingering at the zipper of my jeans,

another tide of slime as Mirovitch's ka *tried to force its way in—*

A breathless scream spiraled up out of me. *No.* I would fight, I would *die* before enduring another vicious mental assault. I could not be violated that way again and remain sane.

"Stop." Female, young, and edged with steel, a smell like baking bread and heavy musk, a smell I recognized. The smell of Androgyne.

Eve, Doreen's daughter. Lucifer's child. And maybe mine too.

"*Stop* it. Didn't I tell you not to hurt her?" The sharp guncrack of a slap, and I fell into darkness again, the mental pressure falling away and my slight helpless moaning spiraling into silence.

Next came the gutwrench of hover transport, my stomach turning over in purely psychosomatic reaction to the rattling hum of antigrav. My cheek against freezing-cold metal, the Gauntlet on my left wrist propping my head up. I moaned, soundlessly, my mouth hung slack. Something was very wrong. I felt too weak, too fevered. What was happening to me?

Burning fingers stroked my forehead. "Hush," Eve said, gently. "It's all right, Dante. I'm here now."

I don't want you, I thought hazily. *I want Japhrimel. It should be him saying those words to me. Where is he? Japh?*

Power jolted down my spine, spread through nerve channels still screaming-raw with pain, detonated agony in my belly and my side, as if all the old wounds, from Lucifer's kick to the hellhound tearing into me, were slashing back open. I screamed, more and more Power forced into me, with no regard for pain or humanity.

"There," she whispered, stroking my forehead again. "Better?"

It *wasn't* better. Japhrimel wouldn't have hurt me like that, he had *never* hurt me like that. Childish faith rose up in me, I was too exhausted to fight it. Darkness, since I couldn't open my eyes, the crackling breathlessness of a small space full of demons, a heavy spice in the air that closed around me and soothed even as my nervous system jolted with more electric pain, raw acid tracing through my bones.

"Japhrimel," I heard myself whisper, cracked lips shaping the word.

"Soon enough," she said, and I heard cloth moving. She walked away, but the aura of her scent lingered, sinking into my head, confusing me until I passed out again.

When I woke next, my fingers slid against my breastbone. I lay on my back, on something soft. I felt the arc of my collarbone, the calluses on my fingertips scraping as I reached instinctively for my left shoulder. Then, *contact,* Japhrimel's mark writhing and hot, bumps and ropes of scarring moving under my skin like the inked lines of my tat.

I don't care, I thought hazily. *I need you. Please.*

The vision swallowed me whole, I sank into seeing out through his eyes as if I had never stopped. Had I always resisted before?

—spine straight, sitting in the middle of the circle holding square holding pentacle, the diagram spinning lazily against the glassy floor. Wrists braceleted with ignored

agony, shoulders afire, staring straight ahead with dry burning eyes. The candleflame was low and guttering, now and then stretching. A few more hours, and he would be free.

The door opened, slowly, and she had come. As he had suspected, she could not ignore the chance to taunt him. Tall demon, the mark of the Androgyne on her forehead, a sleek cap of pale hair and a half-smile that tore at him, reminding. She was not the woman he wanted to see.

She wore simple blue, the marriage-color, a sweater and loose breeches hiding none of her slender grace. The aura of an Androgyne—spice, the potent smell of possible breeding, the attraction of fertility—teased at him.

It was not the scent he wanted.

"A spider emerges." Forcing the words out between his teeth, no politeness, no petty games of silence. "The trap was baited well."

She shrugged, pushing her sweater-sleeves up. "Sometimes the clumsiest tools are the most effective. You could be free in a single moment, Eldest. All that is necessary is to say the word." Her voice stroked the air, the weapon of an Androgyne, meant to seduce, cajole, entice.

His right hand became a fist, and the flexing of muscle pushed at his wrist, a red tide of pain sweeping up his arm.

She laughed, a low sarcastic bark of merriment. Perhaps he truly did amuse her. "Then I will be forced to treat with your companion, Fallen. She, at least, will listen to reason."

Both wrists burned now as his fists knotted. The candle guttered, recovered itself slowly. "If she is harmed—"

"Why would I harm her? She is so amenable, so willing to please."

It was his turn to laugh, sweeping his eyes across the room at the windows. No sunlight. Another day gone while he worried at the walls of his prison, tearing apart the demonic magick that held him bit by bit, thread by thread. Inhuman patience, a single-pointed will, spurred by the need burning in his veins. Need, like addiction. He wanted to see her again, he needed to see her again, to reassure himself she was alive, unharmed.

He needed to touch her.

"You have not found her so?" Eve continued, patent surprise in her tone. "But of course not. And now all her frustrated passion for you will fall upon me. I am, at least, willing to simply ask her. She does not trust you."

"She will know better in time." The words scraped his throat raw, he forced down rage. It would blind him, and he needed clear vision now.

"She escaped and killed a hellhound, Eldest. Even now she cries out your name as she lies wounded—no, not by my hand, I assure you. Such a thing has never been seen before, a Fallen's concubine overmatching a Hound."

He shrugged, the movement spilling pain into his shoulders. The heavy liquid of his armored wings slid against his skin. "You do not deceive me."

It was not an answer.

Her tone was gentle. Of course, she did not need to shout. "You are Fallen, yet with a demon's Power. She is hedaira, bound to you and sharing in your newfound status. Such a pair could help me topple him, Eldest. Such a pair could name their price for support or service."

He closed his eyes. "You bore me."

"What side will you choose if she ties herself to me? Answer me that, Deathbringer. Should I add any of your other titles, Right Hand? Kinslayer?"

He said nothing.

"She had this," the Androgyne continued, and he opened his eyes again. Saw, with no real surprise, the book. How had she found it? How had she had time to find it? Or was it another lie? "I think perhaps I should read it to her, I may even teach her the language it is written in. It will make a wonderful bedtime story."

His legs twitched, ready to bring him to his feet. But it was still not yet time. He closed his eyes again, did his best to close his ears.

The silvery laugh taunted him. "Pleasant thoughts, Eldest." The door scraped along the floor as she closed it, and the sound-not-sound of another hellhound appearing, its padded obsidian feet striking against the floor like fingers caressing a drumhead, scored his ears. His—

—fingertips fell away from the mark, and I blinked up at a ceiling made of blue. Deep dark blue velvet hung in waves, stitched with tiny little things that glittered in the low clear light pouring in through a gray, rain-speckled window.

The bed was fit for a princess, four-postered and choked in dark blue silk and velvet. I pushed myself up on my elbows, flinched as my tender head reminded me someone had been messing with my psychic shields. Silk sheets slid cold against my naked skin. There was a nivron fireplace spitting blue flame, and the decor ran to heavy faux-Renascence. A slice of white tiled bathroom gleamed through an open door. Two chairs, both of blue watered silk, and something incongruous—a steam-driven radiator, painted white, set under the window.

I thought there weren't any of those left. If I hadn't been so research-oriented, I might not have recognized it. As it was, I'd swallowed history books whole all my life. A printed page was a psion's best friend—books didn't point, or mock, or beat, or manipulate. They simply told the story.

My eyes closed, slowly, as if my eyelids were falling curtains. The moments seen through Japhrimel's eyes had taken on the quality of a dream, fuzzy and fading. I sighed.

What dream is this, before my eyes? I heard Lewis's voice, even and deep. *Dreams, the children of an idle brain . . . I dreamed a dream, and lo my dream was taken from me. . . .*

My head echoed with jabs of pain, poking into my temples. My mental shields had held up, demon-strong—but old scars had ripped apart again, as if my psyche was part of my flesh and torn open. A nervous trembling like voltage through a faulty AI relay quaked up from my bones. I shivered, cold and feverish at the same time.

After life's fitful fever he sleeps well, Lewis's ghost whispered. I could almost smell the coffee he used to drink, thick espresso cut with cream. Could feel my child-self's cheek resting on my small hand as I listened to his flexible voice slide through the ancient words, strangely accented. *Lord, what fools these mortals be. Night and day the gates of dark Death stand open. . . .*

Another voice cut across the recitation. *I will always come for you.*

Japhrimel. My eyes flew open. My sword lay sheathed

next to me. My right hand curled loose around the hilt. My bag, a dimple of darkness, lay against the bottom of the bed. I heard stealthy creaks, little tiny sounds, telling me others moved in this place. But the sounds were . . . different. Too light and quick, or too groaningly heavy. They were not the human sounds of an inhabited house. The air was thick and heavy with crackling Power, the walls vibrating with demon shielding. I recognized it as the type of shields Japhrimel had laid in every room we'd shared. Shielding to keep a room invisible, to keep everything inside safe.

My bedroom in Toscano had been blue, too. But the light in that bedroom had been warm, southern sun flooding every surface. This light was cold, gray, and wet. Saint City light.

I reached for my bag, making a small noise as my abdomen protested. The sight of the Gauntlet, no longer dull silver but turned dark as if corroded, barely stopped me. I couldn't tell if the cold clasping my flesh was from the cuff or not.

I didn't care, either.

I dragged my bag across velvet, flipped it open, and found it unransacked. Even Selene's book was still there. It was small, the size of a holovid still romance, and in the light I saw the cover, too fine-grained to be leather.

Had I really seen the book in Eve's hands, through Japhrimel's eyes? Had Eve slipped it back into my bag? Or was Japhrimel even able to lie to me while I looked through his eyes, since he was no longer a familiar but Fallen?

I wouldn't put it past him. But there would be no way for him to know when I was going to touch the mark. Eve wants my help, she wants his help too; If she can't have both of us she'll take me. I don't blame her at all. I didn't even mind her telling him about my "frustrated passion" for him.

Hey, you can't argue with the truth.

My fingers trembled, the chipped black polish on my nails glowing mellow. My cuff ran and rang with green light, the fluid lines carved in it twisting and straining. Sheets and blankets pooled in my lap, my golden skin unmarked but feeling stretched-thin, too strained.

Hedaraie Occasus Demonae, stamped into the cover with gilt. It looked old, and the faint spice of demons clung to every closely-written page. It was written in a spidery alien hand, the ink deep maroon on vellum pages. It was in a language I had no hope of reading, vaguely Erabic but with plenty of spiked diacritical marks I couldn't decipher. Useless unless I did some more research, found someone who knew what language it was and had time to teach me or translate it. I glanced at a few pages without truly seeing them, examined the binding, and dropped it in my bag as if it had burned me.

It was skin, but not animal skin. Bile whipped the back of my throat. I yanked my bag closed and tightened my grip on my sword.

I sensed her before the door opened, the black diamond fire of a demon's aura. When the door opened—I heard no click of a lock—and Eve stepped in, I sucked in my breath and pulled the sheet up with my right hand, covering my chest and wadding the silk against the mark on my shoulder. My left hand closed around my sword so tightly the knuckles turned white.

She was slim, with sleek pale hair and flashing darkblue eyes. Today she wore white, a pristine crisp buttondown shirt with the tapered sleeves that were fashionable

now, a pair of bleached jeans, good boots. Doreen had always worn sandals.

Doreen. The cuff squeezed my wrist again, so hard the
bones creaked.

She *looked* like Doreen, the same triangular face and
wide eyes, the same way of tilting her head. She folded her
arms, a fall of material caught in them, and I breathed in the
smell of Androgyne, the Power flooding from her sparking
along my nerve endings.

"Dante," she said quietly. "I've brought you clothes.
And explanations."

"The h-hellhounds." I sounded like a little girl. The
wristcuff above my datband glowed green. "Velokel?"

"Only one was ours, and only supposed to *find* you
so I could speak with you. The other, I do not know. Kel
would not harm you, Dante. He knows how much you
mean to me."

*Is that why he tried to tear my head open like a sodaflo
can?* My throat was dry. "You have Japh."

She nodded. "It was a stroke of luck, capturing instead
of killing him." Her pale hair didn't ruffle, it was as sleek as
a silken cap. Her skin glowed, burnished gold. "I'd hoped
you would be able to distract him."

Me too. "He's persistent." The thin trickle of heat in my
belly made my stomach turn. *I am not a sexwitch. I do not
respond this way to Power.*

But I did, didn't I? After all, I was staring at her, at the
shape of her lips, filling my lungs with the scent of her.
Fresh bread, musk, and demon, a smell that whipsawed me
between terror and desire, a smell that made it difficult to
think straight. Pheromones like a sexwitch, drenching the

air. She smelled like Lucifer, but she didn't scare me the way he did.

She sighed. "We've had a difficult time evading the Eldest."

"You and me both. He kept putting me to sleep without my realizing it. I asked him not to hunt you, Eve. I *begged* him not to hunt you, and not to lie to me." *I sound like a whiny three-year-old.* But it was suddenly very important for Doreen's daughter to understand I'd tried my best to keep him away from her.

She made an expressive gesture with one hand, brushing away the need to explain. "Demons lie, Dante. It's in the nature of the thing." Her lips quirked up into a half-smile, my own expression, familiar. Was it true? Was she also my daughter, the sample Santino took from Doreen contaminated with my blood as well?

Doreen's daughter, Gabe's daughter. Both mothers dead and depending on me.

How am I going to pull this one off? My mouth was dry, my lips cracked. "You too?"

"Maybe. I suppose you'll have to figure out if you can trust me. There are no guarantees." She held up the handful of material, jeans and something else. "I brought you fresh clothes. Then I'll take you to see the Eldest."

My throat closed up. *He's here. In the same building, maybe? The mark was numb, maybe because whatever they have him trapped in cuts him off from me?* "What if I don't want to see him?" It was a rusty croak. The light caressed her face, ran its fingers over her hair, touched the arc of her golden neck where the pulse beat.

She shrugged. "How else are you going to know if I'm lying?"

I tore my eyes away from her face, away from the slope of her breasts under the crisp white cotton. My eyes fell on my sword's curved length, resting against the velvet in the glowing indigo sheath Japhrimel had given me. "I have a revenge to do." I still sounded like a little girl; high and squeaky, and breathless.

"I won't force you, Dante. I'll ask for your support, but I won't force you." She approached quietly, cloth whispering as she laid the clothes on the end of the bed. "Your weapons are there, on the floor. Whenever you're ready, you may go on your way or see the Eldest, as you wish. If you decide to . . . to throw your lot in with us, we'll welcome you. You killed a hellhound; there's not many that could have done so."

It almost killed me too, it was trying to take my heart out through my ribs the hard way. "The h-hellhound was t-trying t-t-to—"

"The one we sent was supposed to find you and bring you to us, not harm you. I'm sorry, Dante. Events have become . . . complex."

Complex. I was getting to hate that word. When someone said *it's getting complex,* the translation usually was *Danny Valentine's about to get screwed.*

My head hurt. I had revenge to accomplish and Gabe's daughter to collect; I didn't have time for demon games.

My heart thudded behind my breastbone. "Leander. And Lucas. The demon—"

"The demon who brought you to us was uninterested in the others, Dante. Or so he told us. I believe he was led to you in a manner I would not quite agree with." I felt more than heard her back away, toward the door. "Kel mistreated you, and for that I am sorry. I will punish him, if you like."

Oh, gods. I shook my head, speechless. *Leave me the hell out of this. I don't need another demon mad at me.*

"If you like," she repeated, patiently.

"No," I whispered. *Where did they go? Did they sense the demon coming? Gods grant they got out of there in time.* I shuddered again, ice water creeping through my veins. I wasn't thinking straight. "No," I repeated, louder.

The gods knew I didn't want to make another demon enemy. *Just add it to my laundry list,* the merry voice of unreason chirped brightly inside my skull. I choked down a maniacal giggle.

"As you like." She paused. "If you change your mind, all you have to do is tell me."

I shook my head again, and she retreated.

When she closed the door with a quiet click, I scrambled up out of the bed to get dressed. My legs were a little shaky but still solid, and once I had clothes on I felt a lot better. If I kept moving, the vision of Eddie's shattered body—and the vision of Gabe's broken, battered, bloody one—wouldn't torture me so much. If I could just keep *moving* I might be able to get through this.

The clothes were . . . well, they were almost certainly Eve's. The sweater was too big for me, as was the silk T-shirt. But they were clean, and the jeans fit, and the boots were my size even if they were too new. They would need hard use before they were good.

My head gave an amazing flare of pain, so did my left shoulder. I crouched at the foot of the bed for a little while with my sword in my hands and my forehead pressed into the velvet of the coverlet. The shivers and hyperventilating finally stilled. Even my god was silent. There was no blue glow, no comforting sense of being held in Death's hands. There was only the breathless sense of waiting. For what?

True to Eve's word, my weapons rig was tangled on the floor by the bed. Everything was undisturbed, I buckled myself in and wished for a microfiber shirt and a coat. Jace's necklace still rested against my throat, pulsing reassuringly as my fingers touched the knobs of the baculum. The mark on my shoulder had turned warm but quiescent, feeling like normal skin for the first time since it had been pressed into my flesh.

The cold retreated bit by bit, and the sense of being watched returned, but oddly distant. As if something was trying to see me, through layers of interference. Something deadly and inimical.

The Gauntlet was still dead-dark against golden skin, its surface swallowing instead of reflecting light.

I don't think I'm thinking clearly.

My right hand shook when I held it out in front of me. I tried to stop it, but the harder I tried the harder it vibrated. My fingers jittered like a slicboard needing tuning.

That reminded me of the Valkyrie, under a hedge in the rich bayfront part of town. I wanted the slicboard. It was a ridiculous thing to focus on, but it seemed the only thing that mattered was the sleek black deck, gleaming as I pressed its powercell and flung myself into open air, going fast enough to outrun . . . what?

First things first, Dante. Get this the fuck over with so you can kill the fucking traitors. Then you can go on living. Everything else—demons, Hell, Lucifer, even Eve—can wait.

I stopped the trembling in my hands by simply clamping them around the sword's slenderness. Once I got right down to it, the world was really simple. All I had to do was just cut out the bullshit and decide who to kill first.

I found Eve waiting for me in the hall, leaning against the wall and looking out a long window while gray light washed her face. She had tucked her pale hair behind her ears and stood slumped, as if tired. But she turned to me with a smile, as Doreen always had, and my heart thudded in my throat. "It's so nice to see the sun," she said, a little wistfully. Her smell mixed with mine, a fleshy ripe combination of musk and cinnamon, demon and female. "I missed that, in Hell."

A year in Hell is not the same as a year here, they all told me. I hoped I'd never find out. I glanced out the window, saw a slice of green and a high concrete wall. The hall was long, with high narrow windows. Blank doors stood at even intervals.

"You weren't ever allowed to come out?" Miraculously, my voice didn't shake. I clenched the sword in my hands, the hilt bobbing a little as my arms jerked.

She shook her head slightly, her eyes dropping. "Coming to your world, is a privilege for us. One earned only by obedience." Eve peeled herself away from the wall, pushing her sweater-sleeves up. "I have not been obedient in the slightest."

The hall was painted white too, with a hardwood floor. It looked like an institutional hall, and the skin on my back roughened to phantom gooseflesh at the thought that it might be a school. Or any old abandoned government building, maybe. Who knew? About all I could tell was that I was still in Saint City.

My arms jerked again.

Eve's fingers closed around mine. She was too close; I flinched. Demons had a spooky habit of getting too damn close to me; maybe they liked to move in on humans and see them flinch.

Only I wasn't quite human, was I?

The Androgyne's hand was warm, her skin impossibly soft. "*Avayin, hedaira,*" she murmured. "Peace, Dante. Breathe."

I did. It was what Japhrimel always told me—*Breathe, Dante. Simply breathe.* It was enough like him that I felt my shoulders unloose, I closed my eyes. The iron bands squeezed around my lungs loosened a little, I dragged air down into the very bottom of my belly, and blessedly saw the blue glow of Death rise behind my eyelids. It wasn't much—just subtle traceries of blue fire—but it made the shakes settle down.

My god, at least, had never betrayed me.

When I opened my eyes, I found Eve's face inches from my own, her nose almost touching mine. Her eyes were like Doreen's, dark blue, and except for the gold of her skin and the green gem glittering above and between her eyes, it was like looking at Doreen again. The crucial millimeters of difference weren't so visible close up, the overlay of demon that made her so exotic. Was there a similarity to my own face lurking in her bones?

My daughter. All I had left of my *sedayeen* lover.

"Better?" she asked again.

I nodded, just a slight dip of my chin. "I've got to go," I managed through the lump in my throat. "I've got a revenge to finish before I'm free to handle the rest of this." Now my knees were shaking for a different reason. She was so close I drowned in her smell, fire rising through my bones and blood and flesh, a heat I recognized pounding in my wrists and throat—and low in my belly.

I stepped back, breaking her hold on my hands. She let me go. There was a faint smile playing on her lips—an expression that was neither Doreen's nor mine, or even her own.

It reminded me of Lucifer. A slight, cruel lift of the corners of the lips, the eyes lit from within, the entire shape of the face changing from sweet or tired to predatory.

Desire turned to ice, crackling through me. Gray light bleached her platinum hair even further, made her eyes lighter than their usual dark blue. With the emerald glowing in her forehead, her eyes took on a slightly green cast.

Gods—My heart hammered. "Eve?" The word shattered on my lips, fell to the floor.

She shook her hair back and was again familiar. Or if not familiar, then at least more like what I thought I recognized.

Demons lie, Dante. Demons lie.

But Eve hadn't done anything to make me distrust her. As a matter of fact, she was the only demon I seemed able to believe at this point.

"See him," she said. "Please. If you would, Dante."

Weariness swept over me, sucked at my legs. What did it matter? I knew what I needed to know, knew where my revenge lay. Five minutes facing down Japhrimel wouldn't matter one way or another. Would it? "Can he get out?"

Her shrug was a marvel of even fluidity. "He's the Eldest. Even an Androgyne can't hold him for long, even in a circle made harder to break by the use of his *hedaira*'s name. No one except the Prince could hold him, and perhaps not even that." She studied me for a moment, her hands dropping graceful and loose to her sides. "Of course, if you broke even a single line of the circles around him . . . that would set him completely free. I only ask for a little warning, enough to get my people out of here. We fear him."

The set level look in her blue eyes convinced me. *You used my name in a circle to trap him? No wonder he's pissed.* I swallowed, tasted copper. "There's a bunch of demons running around loose. What's going on?"

Her eyebrows lifted slightly. "My rebellion, it seems, has spread. I suspect that isn't what worries *him* the most, though." As usual, when she mentioned Lucifer her lip curled and her expressive eyes filled with disdain and loathing, not to mention a healthy dose of fear.

I stared at her face. "The treasure." A thin croak, the words turned to dust. "The Key."

"So he's told you?" She looked puzzled.

I shook my head. I felt gawky next to her sleek beauty. She was so comfortable inside her golden skin, and I felt like an imposter every time I saw my face in the mirror. "He wouldn't tell me. We saw the Anhelikos in Sarajevo, though. I didn't have time to tell you."

Eve nodded. "We're searching for something, Dante. A weapon that can change our fortunes and turn our rebellion into a successful coup. It will take time to track it down, but there have been *most* encouraging signs." Her mouth tilted up in a smile, so much like Doreen's gentle, forgiving expression I almost choked. "And once we have that weapon, *he* is welcome to find us."

A weapon. So the treasure is a weapon. "What's the Key?" I asked, my heart sinking.

"Not what, Dante. *Who.* We don't know who the Key is yet, but I have a good idea. I think I'm the only one who does." She was looking brighter and happier all the time. "When the time comes, the Key will be revealed. I think that's what the Eldest is afraid of. If he finds the weapon first, he will be in a position to dictate to the Prince. If I find it . . . he may find himself on the losing side. If that happens, you may well be the only person who can save him. He's too dangerous to be allowed to live."

She sounded as calm as if she was discussing dinner plans. "You mean you'd. . . ."

"For your sake, I want to give him every chance. You are, after all, the only mother I have left." Now her eyes were large and dark. The rainy sunlight fell over the curves and planes of her face, so like Doreen's. "Will you help me, Dante?"

Gods above and below, you don't even have to ask. I'm already in up to my neck because I'm helping you, I might as well drown.

"Okay." My throat was dry, my heart pounding in my wrists and temples. I could even feel the pulsing of my femoral arteries, my heart thundered so hard. "Fine. Lead the way, let's get this over with."

27

I was right, this had been a school. I knew because they had him in the gymnasia, a huge wood-floored expanse pierced with shafts of cool light from the high-up windows. Bleachers had been pulled away from the walls and taken out so nothing remained but bare stained expanses of painted wall and gravball hoops bolted to either end of the long room. He was in the south end.

It was just as I'd seen it, and I had to shake away the persistent doubled feeling of living out a premonition. Eve had paused near the door and asked if I wanted to be alone, I shook my head and motioned her inside. She closed the door with a precise little click—the maghinge had been taken off—and leaned against it, waiting. Her eyes were dark again, blue and lit from below like a swimtank with cloned koi flicking through its depths.

I squared my shoulders and walked across the wooden floor, the heels of my new boots tapping on the wood. Halfway there, the mellow shine turned to glass underfoot. Seamlessly, a glossy black obsidian sheet rose up and supplanted the flooring.

Demons are such snazzy interior decorators. I grabbed

at the darkly humorous thought as if it was floating debris and I was drowning. If I was still cracking jokes, I was okay. Maybe. Kind of.

Not really.

The Key isn't a what, it's a who. And if I can't convince Japh to back off . . . a weapon that could kill the Devil. My fingers tightened on the hilt, the Gauntlet's heavy cold weight a reminder of the promise I'd made—the one I was about to break. *It could just as easily kill Japh. Then I'd have to resurrect him. I never want to do that again, I don't even know for sure what will bring him back, other than fire. Lots of fire. And maybe blood. He says enough blood would do the trick, but how do I know for sure?*

The air in here was thick and still, curdled with magick. It raised the fine hairs on my nape, coated the back of my throat, almost made my eyes water.

He sat cross-legged in the middle of the circles, his back straight and his long black coat lying wetly against the floor behind him. In front of him, the candle with the blood-red flame now flickered and guttered, the streak of red light a good four inches high. There was about three inches left of wax for it to burn through.

When the candle was snuffed, what would happen? But he'd probably be loose by then.

I could See the layers of magick, woven too tightly and skillfully to be human, glowing with the icy tang of demon Power. I could also See his careful patient unraveling, working at the threads that held the borders of the circles—my eye traveled over them, marking each symbol in a Magi-trained memory. This was demon magick, a kind Japhrimel would never share with me. If it could trap him here like a silkworm in a kerri jar, I could almost understand why.

And if Eve had used my name in the binding, and it held him here this long . . . I didn't want to think about that. I didn't want to think about how furious he was going to be once I finished what I was about to say.

My hands were shaking again. I clasped them around the sword. Then I remembered something.

I freed my right hand for long enough to dig in my bag, eyeing him nervously the whole time. Japhrimel said nothing, merely sat, his head dropped. Ink-black hair fell down, hiding his eyes. His shoulders were military-straight under the liquid blackness of his coat. His golden hands lay loosely in his lap, I could see no mark on his wrists. His sleeves covered them.

The chain twisted, dangling the sapphire from my fingers. I held it out, swallowed harshly, then forced my shaking hand open and let it drop.

It hit the glassy floor with a tinkling sound, four feet from the border of the outside circle, the one holding the pentacle that nested the square and inmost circle in its heart. I could see the shimmering brittle veils of energy, focused and curved so any direct attack from Japhrimel's side would shunt the force directly back at him. Eve wasn't lying—all I had to do was *touch,* and the outer layers of the magick would crack and fall away. You could not make a shield like this impervious on both sides, even with all a demon's Power.

At the small chiming of the necklace meeting the floor, he slowly raised his head and looked at me, his eyes halting for just the barest moment at my left wrist and the dead black weight of the Gauntlet.

I would have backed up, lifted the sword between me and his laser-green gaze again, but the granite egg inside my chest cracked. Rage boiled up, hot and satisfying, I returned to myself with an incendiary jolt. It felt good to let the anger out, as if a valve had been opened, some of the awful pressure bleeding away.

I narrowed my eyes and stared back, hoping it was just as uncomfortable for him. It wasn't bloody likely, but a girl could hope, couldn't she?

His lips moved. "Dante," he said, quietly. Evenly. With no particular weight of emotion.

Hey, sunshine. Glad to see me? I clamped down on the shudders jolting through me. "Japhrimel."

His eyes bored into mine. The command was immediate, peremptory. "Release me."

Not even a "Hi, how are you?" The fury mounted another pitch. Giving me orders, again. Well, now that he couldn't manipulate me and lull me to sleep while he ran around doing gods-knew-what, I suppose it was about all he had left. It shouldn't have made me angry—but it did.

"What the hell *for?*" I shook my head, my hair brushing my shoulders and spilling into my face. I needed to find something to tie it back with. "I told you, I warned you. I *begged* you not to hunt her, didn't I? I begged you not to lie to me, not to keep things from me. But I suppose that's all a human's good for. *Begging.*"

He shrugged. He *shrugged* at me.

It was a good thing my hands were shaking so badly, I decided. Otherwise I might have done something completely idiotic, like draw my sword and charge through the circles. As it was, I stared at him, my eyes moving over the face I'd thought was familiar. Why was I always so surprised to find him so attractive? His nose was a little too long, his lips too thin, the planes of his cheeks too harsh, his eyebrows too straight. But I liked it better than Lucifer's golden beauty or Massadie's genespliced perfection.

Japh was beautiful like a blade was beautiful, anything well-oiled and deadly dedicated to a single purpose.

Hate surged inside me, all the more intense for the spoiled affection and broken trust underneath it. It wasn't fair to blame him for everything, but it was so easy. So convenient. He was here, and so was my daughter, and I might be the only thing standing between them.

I would have to be enough.

"You *bastard*," I whispered. "You motherfucking *demon*."

"I am," he returned calmly, "what you make of me." His right hand curled into a fist. His eyes flicked away to the red candleflame, which began to smoke and splutter. "I warned you not to make me savage, Dante."

My voice hit a pitch just under "shriek." "Me? This is *my* fault? You're the one who deceives, and manipulates, and—"

The candleflame guttered under the weight of his gaze, recovered with a sound like air sliding past a hover's hull. "You are the Prince's Right Hand, and you are implicitly aiding his enemies. Against your own *A'nankhimel*, I might add, the demon who Fell through love of you. Where is your precious honor in *that?*"

I don't think either of us believed he'd said that. The glassy floor creaked and shifted as the circles fought to contain him—and won, but just barely. They were right, he was going to get out soon.

And all the gods help us when he did.

"So it's war," I said. "Me and Eve on one side, you and the Devil on the other."

"Do not be so sure." But his tone was now colored faintly with sarcasm. "I will have your compliance, Dante, one way or another. Free me now, and I can promise I will deal gently with the Androgyne and her rebellion. I can perhaps even save some of them."

Well, at least he's being honest about not being on my side, for once. A jittering, thready laugh burst out of me. The gravball hoop nearest us shivered, the bolts holding it to the wall squeaking a thin song of agonized metal. The air sparked and danced like carbolic tossed across reactive paint, glittering and smoking.

"There's not a single thing you could swear on now that I would believe, Eldest." I backed up one step, two, unwilling to turn my back on him. My traitorous eyes still drank in his face. I wished he would look at me, buried the wish as soon as it appeared.

"I could swear on my *hedaira*." He even managed to say it with a straight face.

"Save it for someone who gives a fuck." Each word was bitterness itself, almost bitter as the taste of Death in my mouth as I brought a soul back. "We're *over*, Japhrimel. It's war."

His eyes left the candleflame, traveled slow and scorching across the floor. Met my boots, slid gelid and heavy up my legs, caressed my torso, and finally found my face. The mark on my shoulder crunched with fresh sensation, steel fire braiding into my skin and turning to velvet, driving a fresh wave of numbness back down my arm and almost to the cuff.

I ignored it. I was getting very good at ignoring that feeling. Just like I was getting very good at jamming down the squealing wall of rage. What would happen when I couldn't push it away anymore?

He drew in a sharp breath, two spots of color flaming high on his cheekbones. His eyes were incandescent, and he had never looked so much like Lucifer. "There is *nothing,* on this earth or in Hell, that will keep me from you. *I am your Fallen.*"

I lifted the sword slightly, the hilt mercifully deflecting his eyes from mine. "Whatever weapon Eve's looking for, I hope she finds it. The next time I see you, I'm going to fight you with everything I have." My throat closed on the words, bit each off sharply. Made them a husky promise. Here among demons, I didn't have to worry about the invitation in my voice, the Power that coated my words, my own unwanted ability to seduce. "I *trusted* you, Japhrimel. You betrayed me first."

He said nothing. There didn't seem to be much else to say.

I turned my back on him. I walked away, each footstep echoing. His eyes were on me the whole time, a weight against my shoulders.

It took an eternity to reach the door. Eve slid her arm over my shoulders, and I was glad because I didn't think I could stay upright much longer. She glanced back over her shoulder at Japhrimel and ushered me out into the hall. When the door closed with a quiet click I felt something inside my chest snap like a bone breaking.

I ducked away from under her arm as soon as I could stand. "I need a slicboard and I need to get going. I've got business to finish."

She nodded, sleek hair swinging. "Whatever it is, be quick about it. That won't hold him for long." She looked like she wanted to say something else—maybe something ridiculously human like *are you okay?*

But I knew the answer to that. I was *not* okay.

I was not ever going to be anything close to "okay" ever again. I'd just thrown down the gauntlet, ha ha, and when he got out of there he was going to come looking for me. It was all out in the open now—his lies, and my refusal to live up to my end of the bargain we'd made with Lucifer.

Now it was war. I didn't think he'd fight fair.

I didn't think *I* would fight fair either. Not with Eve depending on me. I squared my shoulders, willed my legs to stop trembling. "I've got some business to finish. Where are we going to hook up?"

She nodded slightly. It was an implicit agreement. I was breaking my word to Lucifer, I had betrayed Japhrimel. It was all over but the screaming, as they used to say.

Now I just need to get this wristcuff off, and we'll be ready to tango.

Her dark-blue eyes held mine, a velvet cage. "If you can, meet me in Paradisse. If not, I'll find you."

Paradisse, in Hegemony Franje, the glittering suspended city of a thousand lights and the Darkside underneath. A great place to hide, especially for a demon. I nodded. My eyes were suspiciously full and hot.

Eve leaned forward. Her breath brushed my cheek, and then her cool scented mouth met my skin.

It was a gentle chaste kiss on my cheek, and very short, but it scorched all the way through me. When she backed away, I found I could stand up straight. I could even unlock my hands from my sword and push back a few strands of my rebellious hair. The hallway quivered, the dust in the air holding its breath.

Does that mean the bargain's struck? Sealed with a kiss. The kiss of betrayal. I can't win against Japhrimel, but I can't betray Eve either. I'm fucking doomed.

"Thank you," she said gravely. "I won't forget this."

I have a sneaking suspicion I won't either. I just did the one thing a Necromance should never do—I've broken my word. "I know," I whispered. "Do me a favor and get out of here fast. He's closer to breaking out than you think."

I called Jado from a public callbox in the University District, leaning against the side of the booth and watching the crowd of late-afternoon shoppers contending with the steady persistent drizzle. Another storm was moving in, I could tell from the way the rain smelled and the air was full of uneasy crackles. Whether that storm was weather or trouble, I couldn't tell. I suspected it was both.

Jado could tell me nothing except that Cam and Mercy were gone. Not particularly surprising; I'd expected it. He still had the sealed pouch with the mastersheets and file—it would take more than either of them had to steal from *him*.

He asked if I had found what I was looking for.

"After a fashion, *sensei*." I hardly trembled at all, though I did sound husky and ruined. For once, I felt just as tired as I sounded. "Thank you. I'll keep in touch."

That done, I hailed a hovercab at the corner of University and Thirteenth. The driver, a fat pasty normal in a blue felt hat, for once didn't mutter or turn pale when he saw my tat. He seemed blissfully unaware that I was a psion.

Well, little miracles do happen.

"Trivisidiro, North End. Get me there fifteen minutes ago."

I only hoped I wasn't too late.

28

Jace taught me more about bounty hunting in a single year than all the law-enforcement supplements at the Academy had in five. The first rule, he always said, was to *understand* your prey. When you comprehend the nature of what you hunt, you understand what it is capable of—and can anticipate its next move.

I watched as dusk fell over Trivisidiro, chill purple shadows gathering in rain-drenched corners. The high walls of Gabe's property line stood mute under a lash of rainy just-above-freezing wind; the shields were still viable, the work I'd done binding them together holding steady. I leaned against the wall of my hiding spot, tucked between another house's high walls and a dripping holly hedge prickling against my hand and shoulder and hip, poking through wet fabric. My skin steamed where the rain hit it, but the steam shredded before it could rise above the hedge and give away my position. I waited still and quiet, counting on the instability of the storm and the flux of Power to keep me hidden—since I was having a hard time keeping myself buttoned down anymore. I needed rest, I needed food, I needed sleep.

I wasn't going to get any of what I needed. Best just to deal with it.

There's a mind-numbing brand of circular mental motion that takes place while you're on stakeout. I thought about Japhrimel, would remind myself not to think about him and wrench my mind into remembering Gabe, lying tangled in a young hemlock. I would think of Gabe's daughter and a holostill smile. Would she have the dimple in her left cheek, like Gabe? Would she have a hoarse little braying laugh like Eddie? Would I be able to protect her while I was running from both Japhrimel and Lucifer, trying to keep Eve alive long enough to make a difference?

Though Eve didn't seem to be doing too badly. What the hell did she need *me* for? What was it with demons being so interested in me?

Which would lead me right back to thinking about Japhrimel. I'd begged him not to hunt her. Yet he'd refused to tell me what was going on, left me with McKinley while he went out looking for her. If he *had* managed to catch her and return her to Lucifer, what would have happened? Would he even have told me?

I shouldn't have been, but I was still surprised. Wearily, heart-wrenchingly surprised, each time I thought of it. He was a demon. His idea of truth wasn't necessarily mine. To him, I might be no more than a valued possession; a pet, even. You love your cat or your cloned koi, but you don't treat it like a human. No, you pet it, feed it, take it to the Animone for its shots and checkups. You don't treat it like a partner, or an equal.

Even if it's referred to in the singular, with you.

Had he thought that it would push me back on Lucifer's side if he appeared to be in danger? Or had he miscalculated, not thinking Eve was strong or smart enough to catch him *or* hold him this long?

Why? If I could have asked him anything, that little word would be it. It would cover so much, if I could trust his answer.

But he had held me while I cried, hadn't he? And no matter what kind of trouble I was in, I usually could count on him to bail me out. That was worth something, wasn't it?

I cherish my time with you. His voice, smoky-dark and smooth.

I tore my thoughts away from him again with an almost-physical effort, wondering about Lucas and Leander. Where were they? Were they even now frantically looking for me? Or had they been killed?

There was no more time for thinking. My prey came down the sidewalk in the early-morning dark, walking arm-in-arm as if they hadn't a care in the world. They might even have believed themselves safe.

After all, what did a *sedayeen* and a Saint City cop have to fear?

Only me, I thought, silent and deadly in the shadow of a holly hedge.

Only me.

I let them get through the shields. The layers of energy flushed a deep blue-green, settled as the healer stroked them. Bile rose in my throat. Gabe would not have denied a *sedayeen* entrance into her house, especially one working with Eddie. So she would have been already *inside* when something alerted Gabe to a possible attack on her property and the defenseless healer inside. Gabe, sword in hand, went out alone to defend her home and got shot. Then it was child's play for the healer to "clean" the psychic traces inside Gabe's house after she and the normals she'd let in through Gabe's shields searched for the vials.

Just like now it was child's play for the healer to slip in through the defenses with her normal in tow.

I let them get inside the dark, silent house, then drifted across the street and touched the shields. Softly, a kitten's brush of a touch, warning them not to react to me. Gabe's work recognized me—how could it not?

Oh, Gabriele. I failed you. I should have stayed. Even though it was hard, I should have stayed. Why didn't you tell me you were getting married, you had a kid, you were afraid for your life? Why? Didn't you trust me to come if you needed me?

No, she hadn't, because I'd lied to her about Japhrimel. With the best of intentions, because it would only raise more questions, because I couldn't stand to admit to her that I loved a demon and I was no longer fully human. Each phone call, with its long silences and the things neither of us could say, was another failure on my part. I should have told her.

It was my fault. I hadn't been here to protect her.

I slid through the layers of energy slowly, so slowly. Gabe's front gate squeaked as I pushed through it, but they wouldn't hear. Even if there had been Saint City PD mag-shielding or a lock on the place as the site of a homicide, a cop would have no trouble getting clearance, especially a normal homicide deet flush with dirty Chill money.

Everything so neatly arranged. Everything so perfectly planned. Down to the fact that I'd bet hard credit the cop had the missing fifth vial to sell to the highest bidder—the

sample the healer had probably talked Gabe into produc-
ing after Eddie's death. I didn't know for sure, but that *felt*
right.

The front door was open, the shields on the house quivering with the presence of intruders, even acceptable ones.
The windows, blank empty darkened eyes, watched as I
approached carefully, cautiously, and closed my right hand
around my swordhilt. Up the stairs to the massive double
door, not the side door that any friend of Gabe and Eddie's
knew to go to. I slid through the front door, my new boots
soft and soundless.

Just like a thief.

I found the trigger by the front door, my fingers sliding
over the base of a bronze statue. The statue was Eros in
Psyche's embrace, his wings pulled close around the half-
nude female. Eddie had called it Classic Porn, sniggering
every time he passed it. Gabe would icily remind him that
it was an *antique,* and that it had been in her family for *gen-
erations,* and that the artist had been a *close family friend.*
I could just see her immaculate eyebrow lifting as she repeated this patiently, as if Eddie was a primary-school kid
with a dirty mind.

Of course, Eddie did have a primary-school kid's dirty
mind. It was one of his greatest personality traits.

It was dark, but demon sight pierced the darkness easily, showed me the coats and boots from Gabe's hall closet
scattered in careless lumps, each pocket sliced. They were
coming back for another search, looking for the four vials
I had given away.

I smelled *kyphii* and Gabe's particular scent, the tang
of Eddie's dirt-drenched aura. Then I felt the other psion's

shock as I dropped the outer layer of my shielding and blazed through the Power-soaked house like a star.

I pressed down on the trigger, and had the satisfying experience of hearing the locks on each window and door click shut. Maglocks, to turn the house into a fortress. The front door whooshed on automatic hinges, thudding closed and locking too.

I'm sorry, Gabe. I walked through the foyer, my boots absolutely silent. I could *feel* them both, the sloppy wash of the normal man tainted with fear and thudding heart, copper adrenaline. And the healer's deep well of violet-scented calm, underlain with a slight nasty wet-fur smell of panic fighting with her training and genetic disposition to tranquility.

The kitchen. I gave them plenty of time, walking slowly, the rage rising until my aura flushed red, almost in the visible range. A low punky crimson stain spread through the trademark swirling glitter of a Necromance's aura, mixing with the black diamond flames of an almost-demon. Strength flowed hot down my left arm, poured through the mark on my shoulder. I wondered if Japhrimel could feel me drawing on the mark, could feel my anger.

I didn't care.

The sword whispered out of its sheath as I stepped into the hall. Nothing had changed—the place still looked like a tornado had hit it. It hadn't even been dusted or scanned for prints; it hadn't even been touched by a Reader or another Necromance.

I would have thought they would go through the motions of investigating, for a cop as good as Gabe. Or had this case been given to Pontside too? Of course, if the Chill cure was still here, they couldn't run the risk of anyone else finding it. Not after they tossed the house with a psion to clean up the traces of normals trooping through.

If the cops didn't care or were unable to investigate, Gabe would never be avenged, and her daughter would remain in danger.

Not while I'm alive. Not while I have a single breath in me.

Tension, screaming in my shoulders; the cuff blazed with dappled, fluid green light. Light like Japhrimel's eyes, blazing while he looked up from the floor. I drew in a long sweet breath scented with *kyphii* and the old delicious smell of Gabe's house, the scent-landscape of a place lived in and loved by generation after generation of Necromances.

I stepped around the corner and into the kitchen.

A ricocheting blaze of loud pops, pain tearing into my chest. Black blood rose to seal the bullet wounds away even as I blurred, moving with inhuman speed. The bullets from a Glockstryke 983 projectile repeater would have killed a human psion—but I was no longer human. My sword was a solid arc of silver, white flame singing in its heart, as I carved Pontside's hand off at the wrist.

He was blond, but his muddy hazel eyes were the same as hers. He wore a crumpled gray suit and a damp tan trenchcoat, a gleaming badge clipped to the front pocket of his blue cotton button-down shirt. I could see the resemblance—they shared a parent, at least. Did Pontside hate psions because his half-sister was one and he wasn't, or did he simply hate all of us except her because he was a cop? Did he even hate his sister? Or was the rumor about him hating us just coffee-break fodder?

Blood sprayed. He howled and I kicked him, heard ribs snap under the force of the blow. He fell backward, grinding into broken dishes, before Mercy even had time to scream. The gun, with his hand still clutching it, thumped wetly on Gabe's kitchen floor.

Revenge filled my mouth, sweet and hot. I let out a chilling little giggle that shivered glass from the cabinet doors and made the windows squeal as they bowed out in their frames. Then I stamped down hard into his fair blond face.

It was like kicking a watermelon with fragile glass bones. Mercy let out a short, violent cry, I looked up as Pontside's body jerked and twitched, flopping. I saw the light as the soul fled, one sharp burst of brilliance fading into the foxfire glow of false life, the nerves beginning to die in increments.

I wanted to stuff his soul back into his body and kill him again. But I'd settle for *her,* the bigger traitor.

Mercy's eyes were wide and dark. Sweat stood out on her pale skin, darkening her plain blue T-shirt. The smile stretched my lips, a grimace that made her flinch and cower against the kitchen island, her hip smacking a piece of broken plate and pushing it down to shatter on the floor.

I studied her for a long moment, my sword flicking. Blood smoked off the blade. The smell of violets and white mallow mixed with the reek of blood and stink of released bowels.

I lifted the blade. "Why?" Again the windows squealed, as my voice throbbed at the lowest registers of what could be defined as "human." "You're a psion! A *healer! Why?*"

Her hands curled into fists as she stared at me, her proud spiked hair beginning to droop. Spots of fevered color blossomed on her cheeks and her lower lip trembled.

I can kill her. I can kill her right now. Right fucking now.

I shook with the urge to do just that.

But I wanted to make it *last*. And I wanted to know *why*.

"We were poor," she choked out, her eyes falling past me to linger on the mess of meat that was her brother. "Herborne paid for my Academy schooling, I was in debt up to my eyeballs and Gil . . . he never made enough." Her chin quivered. "Eddie was going to *give it away*, Valentine! Give away the cure! The stupid motherfucking Skinlin was going to ruin everything." She sucked in a deep painful breath. "You don't know," she whispered. "He was *rich*, he had his little rich-girl Necromance and—"

So she had hatched this plan, bombed her own clinic, arranged Eddie's death, arranged Gabe's death, collaborated in the murder of how many? "For *money*." My contempt smoked, shattered more glass, made the walls tremble. "How many have you killed? And how many have fucking *died* of Chill while you tried to cover everything up?"

Noise, cutting through the syrupy tension and crackling static of my fury. Sirens in the distance. I heard them, and maybe she did too. Pontside probably had time to trigger a call for help on his HDOC. The Saint City PD was on their way.

Doesn't matter. If they had a hand in this I'll kill them too. The ease and naturalness of the thought should have disturbed me.

My hand twitched, the tip of my blade making a precise little circle, painting blue flame on the air from the runes running along the keen edge. The steel's heart flamed white, and the sword sang to itself, a low echoing song of bloodlust and chill certainty.

"You've never been poor," she whispered. "You don't—"

What the fuck? "I've been *poor.*" My voice sliced through hers. "I've eaten heatseal—and sometimes not even that. I was poor and hungry for *years,* you stupid bitch. I did espionage and bounty hunting. But I never assassinated anyone." It wasn't strictly true—I'd killed in self-defense, and I'd killed Santino.

But that was different. Wasn't it?

I don't kill without cause. My own words rose up to taunt me. But by the gods, this was cause.

This was vengeance.

"Congratulations." She jerked her chin in the direction of the still-twitching body. "That makes him your first."

How dare you, you piece of shit? The fury rose in me again and blue fire answered, crawling up my sword to caress my hand. I stopped, my jaw dropping as I stared at the shivering *sedayeen.* The sirens whooped and brayed, getting closer.

No. It *couldn't* be.

The world slowed down. Time stopped. Blue fire closed over my vision, and I felt the touch of my god, slipping through the stubborn, torn-raw layers of my mind. The feeling was weightless, like leaving the meat of the body behind and rising into the clear rational light of What Comes Next, the great secret Death whispers into the ears of the departing. My left shoulder squeezed with sudden pain so sharp and fierce I gasped, falling back into the low guard, the blade slanting up and singing a high thin keening note as my steel recognized the presence of the only Power I bowed my head to, Death Himself.

This? This little bitch, this *traitor,* was who Death

wanted me to spare? This was the geas laid on me by my god, who I had always trusted with everything, my life, my fears, my vulnerability itself?

The choice is yours, He said, His deep infinity-starred eyes resting against mine. *It is always yours.*

"No," I whispered. *"No."*

I wanted to kill her. I ached, I *hungered* to strike, to carve, to watch the blood flow, to end her miserable life. I'd *sworn*. Was I required to break the oath I had sworn to my best friend, my only friend?

The sirens dipped closer, and I heard the whine of police hovers. I heard my voice, shaking, freighted with a fury so intense it shivered more glass into breaking. *"Anubis et'her ka. . . ."*

The prayer died on my lips. My vision cleared. I saw her teeth pulled back in a grimace of effort as she cowered against the counter. She was *sedayeen,* a healer, incapable of defending herself.

But she was perfectly fucking capable of betraying Eddie, of tossing Gabe's house while looking for the cure, capable of lying to me. Lying like Japhrimel, lying like a stone-faced demon. Lying worse than a demon, even; Japh hid things from me for a reason!

"Cameron," I croaked. "Your bodyguard. Pico-Phize."

Mercy shook her head, sadly. "She suspected. We were going to eliminate her at the clinic, but. . . . She was Pico-Phize corporate too, she was going to meet Massadie yesterday, when he called from Tanner's, gabbling something about seeing you. It was . . . we had to . . . well." Her eyes flicked down to Pontside's body again. "He did it."

Realization, detonating like a reaction fire in my head. The team waiting to assassinate near the clinic hadn't been

Tanner Family troops. They'd been off-duty Saint City police normals, crooked cops, to get rid of an inconvenient bodyguard who had maybe started to ask too many questions. Then I'd shown up, and Mercy had lied with a cool ease that would have put even Lucifer to shame.

Cam had been going to meet her death yesterday, while I'd been in a demon house. If they hadn't taken me I might have saved her too. "Herborne supplied the staff for the hit on Eddie, it was routine given the amount of profit you were talking about. But for Gabe, you needed more. You needed crooked cops with your *brother* in the lead."

Her teeth chattered. She said nothing. There was nothing she could say. I was right.

"I should kill you." A strained, unhealthy whisper. She shivered and cowered even more, sliding down the side of the island until she crouched, making a small screaming sound like a rabbit caught in a trap. "I should kill you slowly. I should send you to Hell in the flesh. *I should kill you.*"

"Go ahead!" she screamed, lifting her contorted face. She didn't look young now. *"Go ahead, you goddamn fucking freak!"*

The next few seconds are hazy. My sword chimed as I dropped it, my boots ground in shattered dishes and broken glass, and I had her by the throat, lifted up so her feet dangled, my fingers iron in her soft, fragile human flesh. The cuff pulsed coldly; green light painted the inside of the kitchen in a flash of aqueous light. She choked, a large dark stain spreading at the crotch of her jeans. Pissed herself with fear.

My lips pulled back. Rage, boiling in every single blood vessel. Heat poured from me, the air groaning and steaming, glass fogging, the wood cabinet-facings popping and pinging as they expanded with the sudden temperature shift, the floor shaking and juddering. The entire house trembled on its foundations, more tinkling crashes as whatever Pontside and Mercy and their merry crew of dirty fucking Saint City cops hadn't broken as they searched the house shattered.

It is your choice. It is always your choice. Death's voice was kind, the infinite kindness of the god I had sworn my life to. If I denied Him, He would still accept me, still love me.

But He should not have asked this of me.

She was helpless and unarmed, incapable of fighting back. But she was guilty, and she had lied and murdered as surely as any bounty I'd ever chased.

Anubis et'her ka . . . Kill. Kill her kill her KILL HER!

I could not tell if the reply was Anubis, or some deep voice from the heart of me. *But she can't fight back. This is murder, Dante.*

There was only one prayer I could utter as I shook, trembling, on the verge of grateful insanity.

"Japhrimel," I breathed, and the mark on my shoulder twisted again. I *reached* for him, for help, for strength, for anything. "*Japhrimel* . . . oh gods help me. . . ."

Strength flooded through the demon mark on my left shoulder. No answer, except the soft velvet heat of Power sliding through his name scarred into my skin, dappling my entire body with heat.

A piece of his power, given without reserve or hesitation. Did he feel it when I drew on the mark? Did he care?

Did it matter?

I dropped her. She thudded onto the floor and lay there moaning. My hands shook. Hot tears splashed onto the sweater Eve had given me. The house groaned again, complaining, and settled on its foundations.

The god waited, his presence filling the room, invisible but heavy. I smelled *kyphii* and the odor of stone, felt the invisible wind of the blue-crystal hall of Death touch my cheeks, ruffle my hair. My god waited to see what I would do, if I would spare this traitor at his request . . . or if I would *strike*.

If I killed her, like this, would I be any better than her and her brother? Was I any better right now?

Oh, gods. Who am I?

I no longer knew.

"Thy will be done," I grated out, and backed away. She groaned again, scrabbling against the floor as terror robbed her of everything but the urge to get *away*. I sobbed, once, hoarsely. Sirens rattled the air, and I heard shouts. Someone was pounding on the magsealed front doors.

My sword made a low metallic sound as I picked it up from the debris-littered floor. Mercy gurgled. I slid the blade home in its sheath slowly, every muscle in my body protesting. My hands and legs shook with the urge to rip the metal free, pace back to the helpless cringing animal on the floor, and finish her off as bloodily and painfully as I could.

The sense of the god's presence faded, bit by bit. I felt it go, swirling away from me.

Kill her. Rage swirled through my skull, tender bruised places on my psyche cracking under the strain. *She betrayed Gabe. Kill her.*

I walked heavily out of the kitchen. Paused for a moment in the middle of the dark hallway, my head down, hair curtaining my face. I heard the whine of lasecutters at the front door.

Blood slicked down my skin, warm and wet. My feet moved, carrying me into the front hall. I lowered myself down on the steps, watching the bright points of light as the lasecutters began slicing through the magshielded door to let the Saint City PD back into Gabe's house.

As I sat there, I rocked back and forth, both hands wrapped around my sword, softly repeating in the deepest recesses of my brain the only prayer I had left since my god had betrayed me too.

Japhrimel. Japhrimel, I need you. Japhrimel.

29

*H*orman hunched his shoulders like a turtle, pulling his bald head down and back. "Asa Tanner's confirmed everything. The lab's sent out the formula to the West Coast Chill clinics, for real this time." Fog crept up to the sides of the house, moisture breathed in the air, the storm had moved inland and left a foggy dark five A.M. in its wake. Gabe's house rose above us, lights blazing. Finally, her death was being investigated by the cops for real.

"I should have checked," I said dully. "All Mercy had to do was send it to a dropfax number." My throat ached. I'd been hoodwinked by a *sedayeen*. If I'd been able to care, I might have blushed with embarrassment. "I never guessed you were Internal Affairs, Lew." *I wonder if that was what Gabe meant when she called you incorruptible.*

"I never guessed you was a fucking moron." His beady eyes sparked for a moment. The shoulders of his tan trench were damp, his breath plumed in the air. "You didn't even check for a tran number on a fucking datafax."

I shrugged. Dried blood crackled on my clothes—Pontside had shot me six times, probably counting on volume of lead to kill me as it had killed Eddie and Gabe. Most of the bullets had gone right through me, black demon blood closing the holes and inhuman flesh twitching to expel any chunks that hadn't escaped. The twitches were only now fading as demon adrenaline leached out of my tissues. My heart beat thin and sour in my throat.

We watched, the night exhaling fog between streetlamps, as the lights went out and the last of the techs filed out of Gabe's house. The entire place had been dusted and scanned finally, and a Reader would be sent in tomorrow morning. Not that it was necessary—there was more than enough proof to indict Mercy, and she was so terrified she would probably testify against both Herborne and the circle of dirty cops—whoever was left after I'd attacked them at the clinic and escaped them in the Rathole. There were going to be a lot of empty desks in the Saint City South Precinct house. And a lot of freelance bounty hunters would be very busy tracking down whoever fled from justice. It would take a long time to get it all sorted out.

I was no longer suspected of killing my best friend. The police hovers I'd destroyed and cops I'd killed in self-defense wouldn't be mentioned—after all, the department wouldn't like to admit to a conspiracy this big, funded by Chill money, in its own hallowed halls. It was bad for their image.

Horman, leaning against a police hover, shifted his bulk from one foot to the other. The hover's landing-springs sighed as he settled his ample ass more firmly against the plasteel hull. "The kid," he said finally.

"She's safe. I know where she is." *I can't believe I was so stupid as to miss that even for a moment. I'm slipping in my old age.* Guilt pinched me. I should have been planning to hunt down the rest of them. I should personally dispatch everyone who had *anything* to do with the whole sordid plot. I owed it to Gabe.

It was a debt I wasn't going to be able to pay. I had broken my word twice now, once to Lucifer and once to my best and only friend.

"Don't suppose you're gonna tell." Horman sighed.

"Not with half the precinct implicated in a murder plot against her mother, no." My tone was just as flat and ironic. The simmering smell of decaying fruit and spice from my blood was damped by the fog, beginning to thicken in earnest, wrapping the world in cotton wool.

"It ain't half the precinct, deadhead. Just some dirty-ass cops." His neck flushed beet-red, he reeked of Chivas soy whiskey. His tie was askew, and there was a stain on his shirt that looked suspiciously like mustard.

I'm still alive. I let out a long soft breath. Herborne Corp was already disassociating itself, claiming Mercy hadn't been acting under its directives. That told both Horman and me that they had supplied the team for Eddie's death. It would come out in court and the corporation would be dissolved. The publicity was going to be *hell.*

Gil Pontside's pockets held, among other things, a hand-held EMP pulse generator that should have been sitting in a techlocker at the precinct house. Annette Cameron had been found in the Tank, her body riddled with bullets and her datband blinking, flushed red. I wondered if the bullets would match up to the ones used to kill Eddie or Gabe, and if her death was to have been blamed on me or the Tanner Family as well.

I wondered how Asa Tanner had survived the demon attack on his house to capture me and bring me to Eve.

Wondered if we were even now, the werecain Mob boss and me. Wondered where Lucas and Leander were.

I wondered if Japhrimel was free yet.

Time to get back to work. My shoulders ached with tension. I rolled them back in their sockets, my sword thrust through the loop on my rig. I still didn't trust myself. "I've got other business to handle," I said finally, when the silence had grown too uncomfortable even for me. "I trust I won't have any more problems with you brave boys and girls in blue?"

"Go fuck yourself." Horman looked miserable. I didn't blame him.

"Thanks to you too." I turned, ice on the slick pavement crunching underfoot as my new boots scraped. Night air was chill through the bullet holes in my clothes. Eve's clothes. I was getting hard on my laundry.

Three long strides later, Horman spoke again. "Hey, Valentine."

I stopped but didn't turn, my neck steel-taut, my shoulders as hard as hover mooring cables. The sensation of being watched returned, stronger than ever, scraping against my nerves. The Gauntlet was silver again, and so very cold.

As cold as the inside of my chest, perhaps. "What?" *Be careful what you say to me right now, sunshine. I'm in a very bad mood.*

It was the goddamn understatement of the year. I was ready to explode, and I wasn't sure anyone in my path would be safe once I did—guilty *or* innocent.

"You a good friend." For once he wasn't sneering. I suppose he had to wait until my back was turned to say it. "Gabe'd be proud."

I didn't do what I promised. I left her killer—Eddie's

killer—alive. I turned my back on the man I love and I'm about to break my word once more and turn against the Devil, who is going to be very unhappy with me if he isn't already. "Thanks." My voice cracked.

He said nothing else as I walked away, heading for Gabe's front gate and the rest of all my problems.

Coda

In the depths of the Tank, I found a callbox that hadn't been gutted. Picked up the phone and dialed a number still scored into my Magi-trained memory. It rang seven times—it was dark, and everyone there was likely to be busy with the night's games.

Finally, the phone picked up. "House of Love," a honey-scented voice purred in my ear, strangely androgynous for a sexwitch's soft submissive tone.

I cleared my throat, staring out through the plasglass of the booth's sides, scanning the street. *I look like hell. Can I please go for a few days without getting shot, or blown up, or having my goddamn clothes shredded?* "Dante Valentine, for Polyamour."

There was an undignified squeak at the other end, a gabbled apology, and I was put on hold. No music, just a crackling silence.

I watched a hooker pace her piece of cracked concrete across the street. She wore blue pleather pants and a white synthfur coat, her clear plasilica platform heels twinkling in the foggy light from the streetlamp. The faint clacks of her heels hitting the pavement beat slower than my heart,

she cocked a hip as a hover drifted by. Her shoulders slumped as it passed out of sight. She went back to pacing. Dried blood made little sounds, crackling on my clothes and skin as I breathed.

"Dante?" Polyamour's voice, even caramel. My shoulders tightened a little more.

"Poly." The words cracked yet again. I said her other name, the name she'd been born with. "Steve."

She sucked in a breath. "It's all over the news. Don't worry, everything's taken care of."

"I've got some business," I whispered. Why was my throat so full? "Will you take care of . . ."

"I said it's taken care of. Dante, you sound . . ." Her voice deepened, a young boy's instead of a woman's. I could almost see her, leaning against a chair with a sleek white ceramo phone pressed to her ear, her exquisite transvestite face ever-so-slightly creased with worry.

The effort to speak louder almost tore my throat in half. "I'll be back, but I don't know when." *I'm lying. I'm sorry, Poly. I don't think I'm coming back. I promised Gabe I'd look after her daughter, but if I've got demons after me, what else can I do? She's safer with you.*

"It's in good hands, Dante. Come back soon." She paused. "If you wanted to come tonight, I would be happy to see you."

"I can't." *It's too dangerous, especially with demons in town.* "But I'll be back as soon as I can. I p-promised." *I promised Gabe, and I'm about to break that promise. Break my word. Again.*

"Be careful." Her voice changed again. "Dante, we had a . . . a visitor. A green-eyed thing, he said he was from you. I didn't give him anything."

My heart froze in my chest. "Blond?" If Lucifer knew about Gabe's daughter. . . .

"What?"

"Was. He. Blond?"

"Nope. Tall, dark and grim. Long black coat, nice boots."

"When?"

"Three hours ago."

I closed my eyes. Japhrimel was out, and probably looking for me. "I'll be back when I can. Do you need—" *What? Money? An armed guard? What can I possibly give her now that I'm about to be hunted by something more than a few dirty cops?*

"It's taken care of." Her tone became again the even restful purr of a sexwitch. "When you come back, you're free to stay here. I haven't forgotten."

"Neither have I." One of the curses of a Magi-trained memory: I couldn't forget even if I wanted to. I didn't bother saying good-bye, just hung up and rested my forehead against the plasglass. One problem temporarily shelved.

The cold crept up my arm and finally slid past Japhrimel's mark on my shoulder. A fishhook, settling into flesh and twitching. After a few moments of tranced, exhausted wondering, I finally placed the sensation.

It wasn't a sense of being watched, now. It was the knowledge that I was being *pulled.*

The premonition rose in front of me. Now that I was too exhausted to move, it had a chance to rise through dark water and unreel in front of me, the inner eye blind except for the vision of my boot-toes moving against cracked pavement.

I lifted my head, shaking free of the vision with an effort.

When I could look out at the world again, everything had changed. Not much, just . . . a little of the color had gone, my demon-sharp sight blurring. A layer of gray covered every surface, from the cracked street to the uneven paving and the tired skin of the hooker still pacing across the street. The old wounds—Lucifer's kick, hellhound claws, and now bullet holes—all twitched as if they were about to reopen. I'd wondered what the limit was to my body's regeneration. Maybe I would find out now.

Dante, that's a spectacularly pessimistic thought even for you.

There was a faint green gleam at the edges of my eyesight, reflected off the plasglass of the booth's walls. The cuff glowed, and as my eyes locked onto it I suddenly *knew,* with an instinctive jolt, what I had to do next. The compulsion settled home, humming in the metal of the demon artifact, and the sensation of numb cold Japhrimel's mark had been fighting off closed around me like walls of diamond ice.

Time to throw all the dice down and see where it lands, Danny. If you can't do something right, do what you have to.

I sucked in my cheeks, biting gently. Trailed my fingers over my swordhilt.

What I was contemplating was madness. It was sheer *suicide.* The compulsion tapped at my brain, whispered in my ears, pulled at my fingers and toes.

Come on, it cajoled. *Come with me. Someone wants to see you, Dante.*

I lowered my head and banged out of the callbox, my

bootheels clicking against the pavement. I knew where I needed to go. Compulsion married to premonition—instinct and logic rising and twining together—spoke in an undeniable whisper, like the voice of a star sapphire on its platinum chain.

Like the chill lipless voice of the wristcuff, glowing on my wrist and finally tugging me in the right direction. Gently, but with increasing urgency.

I caught a cab on the corner of Fiske and Averly, tapping my swordhilt as the driver kept up a steady string of invective at other hoverpilots. A cab can run on an AI deck for everything other than takeoff and landing. But the hovercab drivers won exemption status under the AI Job Loss Prevention Act and so were mostly fanatically determined to prove that a human was better than an AI for the cab-riding experience. I suppose it was nostalgia or nervousness that made my driver keep cursing.

When he let me out, I smelled the heavy wet blind scent of the sea. Fog was rolling in. I could catch a transport out to Paradisse or hovertrain to North New York Jersey or another hub. Would Japhrimel and Hellesvront be watching the transports for me? I would have to figure something out, I didn't want to lead him to Eve.

Dante, you know it doesn't matter.

When I got to the low slumped building, I found the demonic shields on the dilapidated place that had once been a school were now earthed. There was no sign of anyone—demon, human, or other—as I pushed through the broken-down fencing and paced over the cracked concrete of the outside gravball court.

I shivered, right hand clamped around my swordhilt. The place was silent. Too silent, and it reeked of spice and

Power, the smell of demon. Gravel crunched underneath me, the sounds of tiny breaking bones. I flinched as soon as I thought that, drew my sword. Blue flame dripped along its keen edge, glad to be free. The cuff on my wrist thrummed, pulling me forward as if a fine chain was attached to it, pulling me along. Just like a leash bringing a bloodhound in.

If I couldn't spill the traitor's blood I would settle for trying to kill a demon. I would die, of course—I couldn't kill a demon, no matter how minor.

Could I? I'd killed a hellhound. The memory of claws tangled in my ribs made a small sound escape my lips. I'd also killed an imp, with the help of a lot of reactive paint.

A hellhound's not the same thing, Dante. Neither is an imp. What you're about to try is suicide.

It was. What else did I have left? Even the most faithless of traitors could redeem themselves by choosing the moment of their death.

"Just going to have a chat with an old friend," I whispered. The chilling little giggle that rose in my throat didn't comfort me. There was no amusement in it.

I let myself into the building I'd left just this afternoon. It felt like a lifetime ago. Eve wasn't here, and Japhrimel in all likelihood wasn't here . . . but I thought someone might be here. Someone I'd met before. Premonition blurred under my skin, pushed me forward, impelled as surely by my own minor talent for seeing the future as by the cold glow of the Gauntlet leading me on.

The mark on my shoulder was a glove of soft heat, curiously distant, trying to reach through the shell of ice. The wristcuff dulled. Green light stretched forward, easing me along. Seducing me through the labyrinth, luring me just as my own voice could lure a human.

Gods help me. Head held high, sword ready, I walked into the open jaws of the building.

The school resembled a stage set now, its walls bare and white, no furniture left. Everything was gone except the faint echo of musk and thrumming in the air, the sound of cackling, little whispers just out of human auditory range. Nasty little voices that jeered and whimpered even as they screamed and begged for release.

I *extended* a little past the borders of my shields. Power swirled, uneasy, my own fragrance of spice and musk rising to twine with a darker scent. I knew that smell. Phantom goosebumps crawled up my spine, ruffled my upper arms, and spilled down my forearms. My teeth chattered until I clenched my jaw, pain blooming down my neck. But my stance was good, and I checked the halls and empty rooms, working closer to an almost-familiar part of the building.

The gymnasia.

The layout of the school was clear in my mind. In the end, I simply stopped checking the rooms and walked slowly through the halls. Fog creeping up from the bay wrapped the entire building in a cotton blanket of silence. It might have been the last night of the world.

For all I know, it might be. The cuff on my wrist pulled me on, I didn't resist. It was useless to resist.

The voice of self-preservation shrieked at me. I paid it no mind. There was only one thing I could do now, one action that was mine alone.

Lucifer wanted to kill me.

Fine. But *I'd* choose the place and the time.

The door to the gymnasia reared up in front of me. I didn't even have to touch it, because it opened at my approach. A slice of ruddy light showed, and I could see leatherbound books, a rich patterned-red rug. I smelled woodsmoke, heard the crackle of flames.

The door was wrong. It pulsed, its lintels swaying like seaweed. I blinked, hoping my eyes were deceiving me for the first time in my long angry life. Power fumed in the air.

There were no books here before. Goosebumps—*real* goosebumps—turned hard and prickling on my arms, little fingertips trying to claw free of my skin. I had never had goosebumps before, not in this demon's body.

My blade began to sing, blue flame dripping wetly from its point to smoke on the floor, scorching the hardwood. My shields shivered, on the verge of locking down to protect me. The blood cracking and simmering on my clothes heated up, rough dried edges brushing my shivering, shrinking skin.

There was only one demon who would go to these absurd lengths of theater.

The door swung open all the way, its hinges uttering a small protesting squeak. I peered through a door torn in the fabric of the world and into a room I was unhappily almost-familiar with. A neoVictorian study done in crimson and heavy wood, carpeted in plush crimson. Leather-clad books lined up on bookcases against the dark-paneled wooden walls, three red velvet chairs in front of a roaring fireplace, red tasseled drapes drawn over what might have been a window. A large mahogany desk sat obediently to one side. Next to one red velvet chair by the fireplace stood a slim figure clad in black. His mane of golden hair blazed in the firelit richness of the room, a second sun.

The cuff on my wrist glowed, frosty green light swirling around me like colored oil on water. The Gauntlet was from Lucifer; I'd been warned several times not to take anything from the Prince. Yet Japhrimel had put it back on my wrist again while I slept, hadn't he?

Hadn't he? *I* hadn't done it. Then again, if I'd been asleep so deeply I didn't know Japhrimel was leaving me during the day to hunt down Eve, would I know Lucifer was sneaking into the room? McKinley was a Hellesvront agent—and anyway, would he be able to stop the Prince of Hell from opening up reality and walking right into a room?

The thought of lying asleep, dead to the world while the Devil was in the room, sent a sharp spike of terror through me.

Everything else was gray, covered with a leaden film. But through that door, in Hell, color sprang to life, sparked by his hair. The shadows of bullet holes, twinging fiercely, melded shut in the warm bath of Power that curled along my skin and stifled the sob trying to escape my throat. My left wrist yanked forward, the Gauntlet thrumming, pulling me behind it. Japhrimel's mark on my shoulder was warm and forgiving, humming with taut alertness.

Lucifer looked back over his silk-clad shoulder, presenting me with a quarter profile of a face more sheerly beautiful than any demon's. The emerald glowed mellow in his forehead, and the wristcuff sparked with light. *His eyes.* The thought was almost delirious in its fevered panic. *It echoes his eyes, it's exactly the same color as—*

It was a door into Hell, and the Devil had his back to me.

"Come in, Dante," Lucifer said. "Sit down. Let us better understand each other."

to be continued . . .

Glossary

A'nankhimel: (_demon term_) 1. A Fallen demon. 2. A demon who has tied himself to a human mate. _Note: As with all demon words, there are several layers of meaning to this term, depending on context and pronunciation. The meanings, from most common to least, are as follows: descent from a great height, chained, shield, a guttering flame, a fallen statue._

Androgyne: 1. A transsexual, cross-dressing, or androgynous human. 2. (_demon term_) A Greater Flight demon capable of reproduction.

Animone: An accredited psion with the ability to telepathically connect with and heal animals, generally employed as veterinarians.

Anubis et'her ka: Egyptianica term, sometimes used as an expletive; loosely translated, "Anubis protect me/us."

Awakening, the: The exponential increase in psionic and sorcerous ability, academically defined as from just before the fall of the Republic of Gilead to the culmination of the Parapsychic and Paranormal Species Acts proposed and brokered by the alternately vilified and worshipped Senator Adrien Ferrimen. _Note: After the_ *culmination of the Parapsychic Act, the Awakening was said to have finished and the proportion of psionics to normals in the human population stabilized, though fluctuations occur in seventy-year cycles to this day.*

Ceremonial: 1. An accredited psion whose talent lies in working with traditional sorcery, accumulating Power and "spending" it in controlled bursts. 2. Ceremonial magick, otherwise known as sorcery instead of the more organic witchery. 3. (*slang*) Any Greater Work of magick.

Clormen-13: (*Slang: Chill, ice, rock, smack, dust*) Addictive alkaloid drug. *Note: Chill is high-profit for the big pharmaceutical companies as well as the Mob, being instantly addictive. There is no cure for Chill addiction.*

Deadhead: 1. Necromance. 2. Normal human without psionic abilities.

Demon: 1. Any sentient, alien intelligence, either corporeal or noncorporeal, that interacts with humans. 2. Denizen of Hell, of a type often mistaken for gods or Novo Christer evil spirits, actually a sentient nonhuman species with technology and psionic and magical ability much exceeding humanity's. 3. (*slang*) A particularly bad physiological addiction.

Evangelicals of Gilead: 1. Messianic Old Christer and Judic cult started by Kochba bar Gilead and led by him until the signing of the Gilead Charter, when power was seized by a cabal of military brass just prior to bar Gilead's assassination. 2. Members of said cult. 3. (*academic*) The followers of bar Gilead before the signing of the Gilead Charter. *See Republic of Gilead.*

Feeder: 1. A psion who has lost the ability to process ambient Power and depends on "jolts" of vital energy

stolen from other human beings, psions, or normals.
2. (*psion slang*) A fair-weather friend.

Flight: A class or social rank of demons. *Note: There are, strictly speaking, three classes of demons: the Low, Lesser, and Greater. Magi most often deal with the higher echelons of the Low Flight and the lower echelons of the Lesser Flight. Greater Flight demons are almost impossible to control and very dangerous.*

Freetown: An autonomous enclave under a charter, neither Hegemony nor Putchkin but often allied to one or the other for economic reasons.

Hedaira: (*demon term*) 1. An endearment. 2. A human woman tied to a Fallen (*A'nankhimel*) demon. *Note: There are several layers of meaning, depending on context and pronunciation. The meanings, from most common to least, are as follows: beloved, companion, vessel, starlight, sweet fruit, small precious trinket, an easily crushed bauble. The most uncommon and complex meaning can be roughly translated as "slave (thing of pleasure) who rules the master."*

Hegemony: One of the two world superpowers, comprising North and South America, Australia and New Zealand, most of Western Europe, Japan, some of Central Asia, and scattered diplomatic enclaves in China. *Note: After the Seventy Days War, the two superpowers settled into peace and are often said to be one world government with two divisions. Afrike is technically a Hegemony protectorate, but that seems mostly diplomatic convention more than anything else.*

Ka: 1. (*archaic*) Soul or mirrorspirit, separate from the *ba* and the physical soul in Egyptianica. 2. Fate, especially tragic fate that cannot be avoided, destiny. 3. A link between two souls, where each feeds the other's destiny. 4. (*technical*) Terminus stage for Feeder pathology, an externalized hungry consciousness capable of draining vital energy from a normal human in seconds and a psion in less than two minutes.

Kobolding: (*also:* kobold) 1. Paranormal species characterized by a troll-like appearance, thick skin, and an affinity to elemental earth magick. 2. A member of the kobolding species.

Left-Hand: Sorcerous discipline utilizing Power derived from "sinister" means, as in bloodletting, animal or human sacrifice, or certain types of drug use (*Left-Hander:* a follower of a Left-Hand path).

Ludder: 1. Member of the conservative Ludder Party. 2. A person opposed to genetic manipulation or the use of psionic talent, or both. 3. (*slang*) Technophobe. 4. (*slang*) hypocrite.

Magi: 1. A psion who has undergone basic training. 2. The class of occult practitioners before the Awakening who held and transmitted basic knowledge about psionic abilities and training techniques. 3. An accredited psion with the training to call demons or harness etheric force from the disturbance created by the magickal methods used to call demons; usually working in Circles or loose affiliations. *Note: The term "Magus" is archaic and hardly ever used. "Magi" has become singular or plural, and neuter gender.*

Master Nichtvren: 1. A Nichtvren who is free of obligation to his or her Maker. 2. A Nichtvren who holds territory.

Merican: 1. The trade lingua of the globe and official language of the Hegemony, though other dialects are in common use. 2. (*archaic*) A Hegemony citizen. 3. (*archaic*) A citizen of the Old Merican region before the Seventy Days War.

Necromance: (*slang:* deadhead) An accredited psion with the ability to bring a soul back from Death to answer questions. *Note: Can also, in certain instances, heal mortal wounds and keep a soul from escaping into Death.*

Nichtvren: (*slang:* suckhead) Altered human dependent on human blood for nourishment. *Note: Older Nichtvren may possibly live off strong emotions, especially those produced by psions. Since they are altered humans, Nichtvren occupy a space between humanity and "other species"; they are defined as members of a Paranormal Species and given citizen's rights under Adrien Ferrimen's groundbreaking legislation after the Awakening.*

Nine Canons: A nine-part alphabet of runes drawn from around the globe and codified during the Awakening to manage psionic and sorcerous power, often used as shortcuts in magickal circles or as quick charms. *Note: The Canons are separate from other branches of magick in that they are accessible sometimes even to normal humans, by virtue of their long use and highly charged nature.*

Novo Christianity: An outgrowth of a Religion of Submission popular from the twelfth century to the latter half of the twenty-first century, before the meteoric rise of the Republic of Gilead and the Seventy Days War. *Note: The death knell of Old Christianity is thought to have been the great Vatican Bank scandal that touched off the revolt leading to the meteoric rise of Kochba bar*

Gilead, the charismatic leader of the Republic before the Charter. Note: The state religion of the Republic was technically fundamentalist Old Christianity with Judic messianic overtones. Nowadays, NC is declining in popularity and mostly fashionable among a small slice of the Putchkin middle-upper class.

Power: 1. Vital energy produced by living things: prana, mana, orgone, etc. 2. Sorcerous power accumulated by celibacy, bloodletting, fasting, pain, or meditation. 3. Ambient energy produced by ley lines and geo-currents, a field of energy surrounding the planet. 4. The discipline of raising and channeling vital energy, sorcerous power, or ambient energy. 5. Any form of energy that fuels sorcerous or psionic ability. 6. A paranormal community or paranormal individual who holds territory.

Prime Power: 1. The highest-ranked paranormal Power in a city or territory, capable of negotiating treaties and enforcing order. *Note: usually Nichtvren in most cities and werecain in rural areas.* 2. (*technical*) The source from which all Power derives. 3. (*archaic*) Any nonhuman paranormal being with more than two vassals in the feudal structure of pre-Awakening paranormal society.

Psion: 1. An accredited, trained, or apprentice human with psionic abilities. 2. Any human with psionic abilities.

Putchkin: 1. The official language of the Putchkin Alliance, though other dialects are in common use. 2. A Putchkin Alliance citizen.

Putchkin Alliance: One of the two world superpowers, comprising Russia, most of Territorial China (except Freetown Tibet and Singapore), some of Central Asia, Eastern Europe, and the Middle East. *Note: After the*

Seventy Days War, the two superpowers settled into peace and are often said to be one world government with two divisions.

Republic of Gilead: Theocratic Old Merican empire based on fundamentalist Novo Christer and Judic messianic principles, lasting from the latter half of the twenty-first century (after the Vatican Bank scandal) to the end of the Seventy Days War. *Note: In the early days, before Kochba bar Gilead's practical assumption of power in the Western Hemisphere, the Evangelicals of Gilead were defined as a cult, not as a Republic. Political infighting in the Republic—and the signing of the Charter with its implicit acceptance of the High Council's sovereignty—brought about both the War and the only tactical nuclear strike of the War (in the Vegas Waste).*

Revised Matheson Score: The index for quantifying an individual's level of psionic ability. *Note: Like the Richter scale, it is exponential; five is the lowest score necessary for a psionic child to receive Hegemony funding and schooling. Forty is the terminus of the scale; anything above forty is defined as "superlative" and the psion is tipped into special Hegemony secret-services training.*

Runewitch: A psion whose secondary or primary talent includes the ability to handle the runes of the Nine Canons with special ease.

Sedayeen: 1. An accredited psion whose talent is healing. 2. (*archaic*) An old Nichtvren word meaning "blue hand." *Note: Sedayeen are incapable of aggression even in self-defense, being allergic to violence and prone to feeling the pain they inflict. This makes them incredible healers, but also incredibly vulnerable.*

Sekhmet sa'es: Egyptianica term, often used as profanity; translated: "Sekhmet stamp it," a request for the Egyptos goddess of destruction to strike some object or thing, much like the antique *"God damn it."*

Seventy Days War: The conflict that brought about the end of the Republic of Gilead and the rise of the Hegemony and Putchkin Alliance.

Sexwitch: (*archaic: tantraiiken*) An accredited psion who works with Power raised from the act of sex; pain also produces an endorphin and energy rush for sexwitches.

Shaman: 1. The most common and catch-all term for a psion who has psionic ability but does not fall into any other specialty, ranging from vaudun Shamans (who traffic with *loa* or *etrigandi*) to generic psions. 2. (*archaic*) A normal human with borderline psionic ability.

Sk8: Member of a slicboard tribe.

Skinlin: (*slang:* dirtwitch) An accredited psion whose talent has to do with plants and plant DNA. *Note: Skinlin use their voices, holding sustained tones, wedded to Power to alter plant DNA and structure. Their training makes them susceptible to berserker rages.*

Slagfever: Sickness caused by exposure to chemical-waste cocktails commonly occurring near hover transport depots in less urban areas.

Swanhild: Paranormal species characterized by hollow bones, feathery body hair, poisonous flesh, and passive and pacifistic behavior.

Synth-hash: Legal nonaddictive stimulant and relaxant synthesized from real hash (derivative of opium) and kennabis. *Note: Synth-hash replaced nicotiana leaves (beloved of the Evangelicals of Gilead for the profits* *reaped by tax on its use) as the smoke of choice in the late twenty-second century.*

Talent: 1. Psionic ability. 2. Magickal ability.

Werecain: (*slang:* 'cain, furboy) Altered human capable of changing to a furred animal form at will. *Note: There are several different subsets, including Lupercal and magewolfen. Normal humans and even psionic outsiders are generally incapable of distinguishing between different subsets of 'cain.*

EXTRAS

www.orbitbooks.net

About the Author

Lilith Saintcrow was born in New Mexico and bounced around the world as an Air Force brat. She currently lives in Vancouver, Washington, with her husband, two children, and a houseful of cats. Visit the official Lilith Saintcrow website at www.lilithsaintcrow.com

Find out more about Lilith and other Orbit authors by registering for the free monthly newslettter at www.orbitbooks.net

Introducing

TO HELL AND BACK

The fifth Dante Valentine novel

by

Lilith Saintcrow

1

Darkness closed velvet over me, broken only by the flame of a scar burning, burning, against my shoulder. I do not know how I wrenched myself free, I only know that I *did*, before the last and worst could be done to me.

But not soon enough.

I heard myself scream, one last cry that shattered into pieces before I escaped to the only place left to me, welcome unconsciousness.

As I *fell*.

Cold. Wherever I was, it was *cold*. Hardness underneath me. I heard a low buzzing sound and passed out again, sliding away from consciousness like a marble on a reactive-greased slope. The buzzing followed, rattled around me, became a horde of angry bees inside my head, a deep and awful rattling whirr shaking my teeth loose, splitting my bones with hot lead.

I moaned.

The buzzing faded, receding bit by bit like waves sliding away from a rocky shore. I moaned again, rolled over. My cheek pressed chill hardness. Tears trickled hot out of my eyes. My shields shivered, rent and useless, a flooding tide of sensation and thought from the outside world roaring through my brain as I convulsed, instinct pulling my shields together, tissue-thin, drowning in the current. Where was I?

I had no prayers left.

Even if I'd had one, there would be no answer. The ultimate lesson of a life spent on the edge of Power and violence—*when the chips are down, sunshine, you're on your own.*

Slowly, so slowly, I regained my balance. A flood of human thought smashed rank and foul against my broken shields, roaring through my head, and I pushed it away with a supreme effort, trying to *think*. I made my eyes open. Dark shapes swirled, coalesced. I heard more, a low noise of crowds and hovertraffic, formless, splashing like the sea. Felt a tingle and trickle of Power against my skin.

Oh, gods. Remind me not to do that again. Whatever it was. The thought sounded like me, the tough, rational, practical me, over a deep screaming well of panic. *What happened to me?*

Am I hungover?

That made me laugh. It was unsteady, hitching, tired hilarity edged with broken glass, but I welcomed it. If I was laughing, I was okay.

Not really. I would never be *okay* again. My mind shuddered, flinching away from . . . something. Something terrible. Something I could not think about if I wanted to keep the fragile barrier between myself and a screaming tide of insanity.

I pushed it away. Wrestled it into a dark corner and closed the door.

That made it possible to think a little more clearly.

I blinked. Shapes became recognizable, the stink of dying human cells filling my nose again. Wet warmth trickled down my cheeks, painted my upper lip. I tasted spoiled fruit and sweetness when I licked my lips.

Blood. I had a face covered in blood, and my clothes were no better than rags, if I retained them at all. My bag clinked as I shifted, its broken strap reknotted and rasping between my breasts. I blinked more blood out of my eyes, stared up at a brick wall. It was night, and the wall loomed at a crazy angle because I lay twisted like a rag doll, pretty-much naked against the floor of an alley.

Alley. I'm in an alley. From the way it smells, it's not a nice one either. Trust me to end up like this.

It was a sane thought, one I clung to even as I shivered and jolted, my entire body rebelling against the psychic assault of so many minds shoving against me, a surfroar of screaming voices. Not just my body but my mind mutinied, bucking like a runaway horse as the something returned, huge and foul, boiling up through layers of shock. Beating at the door I had locked against it.

Oh gods, please. Someone please. Anyone. Help me.

I moaned, the sound bouncing off bricks, and the mark on my shoulder suddenly blazed with soft heat, welling out through my aching body. I hurt everywhere, as if I'd been torn apart and put back together wrong. The worst hurt was a deep drilling ache low in the bowl of my pelvis, like the world's worst menstrual cramp.

I could not think about that. My entire soul rose in rebellion. I could not *remember* what had been done to me.

The rips in my shields bound themselves together, tissue-thin, but still able to keep me sane. The scar pulsed, crying out like a beacon, a flaming black-diamond fountain tearing into the ambient Power of the city-scape. The first flare knocked me flat against the ground again, stunned and dazed. Successive pulses arrived, each working in a little deeper than the last, but not so jolting.

Breathe. Just breathe. I clung to the thought, shutting my eyes as the world reeled under me. I made it up to hands and knees, my palms against slick greasy concrete as I retched. I don't usually throw up unless poisoned, but I felt awful close.

Too bad there was nothing in my stomach. I curled over on myself, retched some more, and decided I felt better.

The mark kept pulsing, like a slow heartbeat. Japhrimel's pulse is slower than mine, one beat to every three my own heart performs, like a strong silt-laden river through a broad channel. It felt uncomfortably like his heartbeat had settled in the scar on my shoulder, as if I was resting my head on his chest and hearing his old, slow, strong heart against my cheek and fingertips.

Japhrimel. I remembered him, at least. Even if I couldn't remember myself.

I cursed myself then, in my head and aloud as I found the other brick wall confining this alley. Drove my claws into the wall, my arm quivering under the strain as I hauled myself to my feet. I couldn't afford to call on him. He was an enemy.

They were all my enemies. Everyone. Every single fucking thing that breathed, or walked, or even touched me. Even the air.

Even my own mind.

Safe place. Got to find a safe place. I could have laughed at the thought. I didn't even know where I was.

Not only that, but where on earth was safe for me now? I could barely even remember who I was.

Valentine.

A name returned to me. My name. My fingers crept up and touched a familiar wire of heat at my collarbone—the necklace, silver-dipped raccoon bacula and blood-marked bloodstones, its potent force spent and at low ebb. I knew who wore this necklace.

I am Valentine. Danny Valentine. I'm me. I am Dante Valentine.

Relief scalded me all over, gushed in hot streams from my eyes. I knew who I was now: I could remember my name.

Everything else would follow.

I hauled myself up to my feet. My legs shook and I stumbled, and I was for once in no condition to fight. I hoped I wasn't in a bad part of town.

Whatever town this is. What happened? I staggered, ripped my claws free of the brick wall, and leaned against its cold, rough surface, for once blessing the stink of humanity. It meant I was safe.

Safe from what? I had no answer for that question, either. A hideous thing beat like a diseased heart behind the door I'd slammed to keep it away. I didn't want to know right now.

Safe place, Danny girl. I flinched, but the words were familiar, whispered into my right ear. A man's voice, pitched low and tender, with an undertone of urgency. Just the way he used to wake me up, back in the old days.

Back when I was human and Jace Monroe was alive, and Hell was only a place I read about in classic literature and required History of Magi classes.

That thought sent a scree of panic through me. I almost buckled under the lash of fear, my knees softening.

Get up, clear your head, and move. There's a temple down the street, and nobody's around to see you. You've got to move now. Jace's voice whispered, cajoled.

I did not stop to question it. Whether my dead lover or my own small precognitive talent was speaking didn't matter.

The only thing that mattered was if it was right. I was naked and covered in blood, with only my bag. I had to find somewhere to hide.

I stumbled to the mouth of the alley, peering out on a dim-lit city street, the undersides of hovers glittering like fireflies above. The ambient Power tasted of synth-hash smoke, wet mold, and old silty spilled blood, with a spiked dash of Chill-laced bile over the top.

Smells like North New York Jersey. I shook my head, blood dripping from my nose in a fresh trickle of heat, and staggered out into the night.

2

The street was indeed deserted, mostly warehouses and hoverfreight transport stations that don't see a lot of human traffic at night. There *was* a temple, and its doors creaked as I made it up the shallow steps. It could have been any temple in any city in the world, but I was rapidly becoming convinced it *was* North New York Jersey. It smelled like it.

Not that it mattered right at the moment.

The doors, heavy black-painted iron worked with the Hegemony sundisc, groaned as I leaned on one of them, shoving it open. My right leg dragged as I hauled myself inside, the shielding on the temple's walls snapping closed behind me like an airlock, pushing away the noise of the city outside. The damage to my leg was an old injury from the hunt for Kellerman Lourdes; I wondered if all the old scars were going to open up—the whip scars on my back and the brand along the crease of my lower left buttock.

If they did open up, would I bleed? Would the bleeding ever stop?

Take out all the old wounds, see which one's deepest. The voice of panic inside my head let out a terrified giggle my chattering teeth chopped into bits. The door in my head stayed strong, stayed closed. It took most of my failing energy to keep that memory—whatever it was—wrestled down.

Every Hegemony temple is built on a node of intersecting ley lines, the shields humming, fed by the bulge of Power underneath. This temple, like most Hegemony places of worship, had two wings leading from the narrow central chamber—one for the gods of Old Graecia, and one for Egyptianica. There were other gods, but these were the two most common pantheons, and it was a stroke of luck.

If I still believed in luck.

Jace's voice in my ear had gone silent. I still could not remember what had been done to me.

Whatever it was, it was bad. I'm in bad shape.

I almost laughed at the absurdity of thinking it. As if that wasn't self-evident.

The main chamber was dedicated to a standard Hegemony sundisc, rocking a little on the altar. It was as tall as two of me, and I breathed out through my mouth because my nose was full of blood. I worried vaguely about that—usually the black blood rose and sealed away any wound, healing my perfect poreless golden skin without a trace. But here I was, bleeding. I could barely tell if the rest of me was bleeding too, especially the deep well of pain at the juncture of my legs, hot blood slicking the insides of my thighs.

I tried not to think about it. My right hand kept making little grasping motions, searching for a sword hilt.

Where's my sword? More panic drifted through me. I set my jaw and lowered my head, stubbornly. It didn't matter. I'd figure it out soon enough.

When I held my blade again, it would be time to kill. I just couldn't think of who to kill first.

My bag shifted and clinked as I wove up the middle of the great hall, aiming for the left-hand wing, where the arch was decorated with dancing hieroglyphs carved into old dark wood. This entire place was dark, candles lit before the sundisc reflecting in its mellow depths. The flickering light made it even harder to walk.

My shoulder pulsed. Every throb was met with a fresh flood of Power along my battered shields, sealing me away but also causing a hot new trickle of blood from my nose. My cheeks were wet and slick too, because my eyes were bleeding—either that, or I had some kind of scalp wound. Thin hot little fingers of blood patted the inside of my knees, tickled down to my ankles.

I'm dripping like a public faucet. Gods. I made it to the door and clung to one side, blinking away salt wetness.

There they sat in the dusk, the air alive with whispers and mutters. Power sparked, swirling in dust-laden air. The gods regarded me, each in their own way.

Isis stood behind Her throned son, Horus's hawk-head and cruel curved beak shifting under Her spread hand of blessing. Thoth stood to one side, His long ibis head held still but His hands—holding book and pen—looking startled, as if He had been writing and now froze, looking down at me. The statues were of polished basalt, carved in post-Awakening neoclassic; Nuit stretched above on the vault of the roof, painted instead of sculpted.

There, next to Ptah the Worker, was Anubis. The strength threatened to leave my legs again. I let out a sob that fractured against the temple's surfaces, its echoes coming back to eat me.

The statue of the god of Death regarded me, candles

on the altar before Him blazing with sudden light. My eyes met His, and more flames bloomed on dark spent wicks, our gazes flint and steel sparking to light them.

I let out another painful sob, agony twisting fresh inside my heart. Blood spattered the floor, steaming against chill stone. This might be a new building, but they had scoured the floor down to rock, and it showed. My ribs ached as if I'd just taken a hard shot with a *jo* staff. Everywhere on me ached, especially—

I shut that thought away. Let go of the edge of the doorway and tacked out like a ship, zigzagging because my right leg wouldn't work quite properly. I veered away into the gloom, bypassing Anubis though every cell in my body cried out for me to sink to the floor before His altar and let Him take me, if He would.

I had given my life to Him and been glad to do it— but He had betrayed me twice, once in taking Jason Monroe from me and again in asking me to spare the killer of my best and only friend.

I could not lie down before Him now. Not like this.

There was something I had to do first.

I kept going, each step a scream. Past Ptah, and Thoth, and Isis and Horus, to where no candles danced on the altars. The dark pressed close, still whispering. It took forever, but I finally reached them, and looked up. My right hand had clamped itself against my other arm, just under the scar on my left shoulder, each beat of Power thudding against my palm as my arm dangled.

Nepthys's eyes were sad, arms crossed over Her midriff. Beside Her Set glowered, the jackal head twitching in quick little jerks as candlelight failed to reach it completely. The powers of Destruction, at the left hand of Creation. Propitiated, because there is no creation without the clearing-away of the old. Propitiated as well in the hope that they will avoid your life, pass you by.

What had been done to me? I barely even remembered my own name. *Something* had happened.

Someone had done this to me.

Someone I had to kill.

Burn it all down, a new voice whispered in my head. ***Come to Me, and let it burn away. Make something new, if you like—but first, there is the burning.***

There is vengeance.